OCT 2 9 2009

S0-BAW-867

PATTERNS IN THE SAND

Stains 6/19

Water damage 6/26 (SG)

DATE DUE

FEB 05 2010			
MAR 01 2010			
MAR 12 2010			
JUN 29 2010			
OCT 05 2012			
JUL 05 2013			
JUL 05 2013			
SEP 10 2014			
DEC 27 2016			

Demco, Inc. 38-293

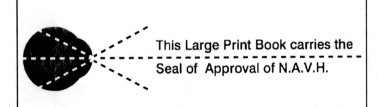

This Large Print Book carries the
Seal of Approval of N.A.V.H.

A SEASIDE KNITTERS MYSTERY

PATTERNS IN THE SAND

SALLY GOLDENBAUM

KENNEBEC LARGE PRINT
A part of Gale, Cengage Learning

GALE
CENGAGE Learning

Detroit • New York • San Francisco • New Haven, Conn • Waterville, Maine • London

GALE
CENGAGE Learning

Copyright © Sally Goldenbaum, 2009.
Kennebec Large Print, a part of Gale, Cengage Learning.

LIBRARY OF CONGRESS CATALOGING-IN-PUBLICATION DATA

Goldenbaum, Sally.
   Patterns in the sand : a seaside knitters mystery / by Sally Goldenbaum.
      p. cm. — (Kennebec Large Print superior collection)
      ISBN-13: 978-1-59722-949-4 (pbk. : alk. paper)
      ISBN-10: 1-59722-949-0 (pbk. : alk. paper)
      1. Knitters (Persons)—Fiction. I. Title.
   PS3557.O35937P37 2009b
   813'.54—dc22   2009016508

Published in 2009 by arrangement with NAL Signet, a member of Penguin Group (USA) Inc.

Printed in the United States of America
1 2 3 4 5 6 7 13 12 11 10 09

For Luke Robert McElhenny,
Atticus Sage Goldenbaum,
and Ruby Jane McElhenny

ACKNOWLEDGMENTS

Many thanks to my family, my sisters, friends, and readers — who have offered support, knitting patterns, ideas, and most of all, have invited the Seaside Knitters into their homes. A thank you to my brother Bob, whose art inspired Aidan Peabody's. And a special thanks to Polly Arango and Mary Bednarowski, who are always there at the end of an e-mail with a welcome supply of sleuthing support.

PROLOGUE

Sunday

The fireworks that exploded in the midsummer sky were a surprise. None of the Art at Night flyers pasted on store windows along Harbor Road mentioned that the ocean sky would light up like the Fourth of July.

But Nell Endicott suspected that few people in the packed crowds that milled about the narrow streets — moving in and out of art galleries and studios, greeting friends, nodding to strangers, enjoying a beer or iced tea — would focus first on the extravagant display when thinking back to that sultry Sunday night.

What they would think of first was not dazzling colors against a black sky, but a death that would change the course of their summer days in a heartbeat — adding suspicion and gossip to long days at the beach and fishing off Pelican Pier.

CHAPTER 1

The Friday before . . .

It was Purl, curled up in the center of a cushy pile of organic cotton yarn in the deep bay display window of Izzy's shop, who first took notice of the stranger — a small young woman with a magnetic gaze matched only by that of the cat's own green stare.

It seemed to be love at first sight. Or at least an understanding between souls who may have shared a similar past.

The Seaside Knitting Studio's window display was more than a changing smorgasbord of rich, soft yarn. It had also become the calico cat's favorite place to watch the people of Sea Harbor go about their lives. The task brought purpose to Purl's day.

In winter she'd find a circle of sun in the window and settle in its center, watching figures wrapped in downy jackets scurry up and down Harbor Road, to the bookstore next door or the dentist above Harry's deli.

11

To Jake's Gull Tavern on the corner or the county offices just off the main street. People walked fast on those snowy days, with direction, shoulders rigid, bracing themselves against the freezing ocean air that brought color to their cheeks.

In the summer, Sea Harbor slowed to a languid pace, and through the glass Purl watched tan, half-bare bodies stroll down the road, wandering in and out of shops, sitting on wooden benches with strawberry ice-cream cones or Coffee's famous frozen mochas.

And in summer, Izzy's window boasted bright cotton and silk yarn for airy sweaters or lacy stoles. This night, Purl had found a wicker basket piled high with spun balls of pink and celery green organic cotton that could be knit up into the perfect light sweater for ocean-chilled evenings. Purl curled up cozily in the center, her white paws resting on the basket's edge. A sliver of moonlight touched the white V on her forehead. Life was good.

Beyond the window, gaslights blinked on, allowing Purl a cat's-eye view of the village's nighttime activity. Though many of the boutiques and shops were closed for the evening, music poured from Jake's tavern on the corner, Harry Garozzo's deli still served some lingering customers, and restaurant doors were held open to the soft summer breezes, welcoming summer people to a Friday night fish fry or lobster feast. Not many people paused at Izzy's window at this time of night, though the security lights were on, offering a glimpse of lovely yarn if anyone cared to stop.

But this Friday night — a treat for the sociable Purl — someone did.

When Purl looked up into the striking black eyes of the young woman, she welcomed the attention and purred in delight.

The visitor placed one hand flat on the cool plate glass that separated them — woman from beast. Her eyes locked onto Purl's. For a long time the two looked at each other, steady and unwavering. Then she smiled as if finding a friend, stepped back, and looked up at the weathered Seaside Knitting Studio sign above the door.

The name of the store seemed to register on her face and she smiled again at the cat, then slipped a thick handful of dark hair behind her ear. She shifted the heavy backpack between her shoulder blades and walked over to the front door, a weathered door with an awning above it. The knob refused to turn. She rapped lightly, peering through the glass on the door.

From her perch inside the bay window, Purl followed the movements of the young woman with interest. The store was locked, of course — a routine even shopkeepers in this sleepy ocean town practiced.

When no one answered, the young woman walked back to the window and stood there for a few minutes, looking at Purl as if the kitten would know the next step. Her brows lifted and her dark eyes grew round as the moon above. She had come a long way and was bone-tired. She needed to rest. A locked door was a minor inconvenience — and the kitten was welcoming.

With a nod and a smile to the cat, she lifted up a battered duffel bag, shifted the backpack once more, and walked around to the side of the store.

A narrow alley ran between Izzy Chambers' knitting shop and Archie and Harriet Brandley's Sea Harbor Bookstore. At the end of the alley, beyond the granite rocks that kept the tide at bay, was the ocean. The young woman stopped short, as if paralyzed for a moment, her steps frozen. She stood still, listening to the sound of the night waves lapping against the seawall. Slowly, she breathed in the salty air, closing her eyes against the magnificent emotion. Her heart soared. And for reasons beyond her understanding, she felt that she was home at last.

When she opened her eyes, the feeling was muted, nearly gone. And for that, the woman said a silent thank-you. She had a task, a purpose. Emotion couldn't play a useful part in why she had come to this small town, thousands of miles from home.

She turned her attention back to the shop. In addition to a flight of stairs leading to the second story, there were several windows on the first floor, too high off the alley to reach, and a side door.

The security lights on the side of the shop lit the alley, and she spotted her access easily. Climbing up several steps, she leaned over and examined a window.

This was too simple, or maybe one of those moments her mother used to call serendipity. The latch at the top of the window was jammed and didn't close completely. She wouldn't even have to break anything. With a few tugs, the latch shifted and the window opened a crack, then wider as Willow's strong arms pried it up. She picked up the duffel bag from the step and pushed it through the open window, then listened as it hit the floor. The drop wasn't much, a few feet at most. The backpack was next. With one smooth movement, she swung a jeans-clad leg over the sill, then the other, and slipped easily into the shadowy room.

The lights from the alley and along the back of the shop outlined a long table, bookcases, chairs, and at one end, a sitting area with a couch and fireplace. She frowned. The sign had said this was the Seaside Knitting Studio. But even in the shadowy light, this room looked more like a cozy family room, a place to kick off shoes and settle in. Settle in and knit, maybe that was it. But she couldn't settle in. Not yet.

Faint light coming from the front of the store lit an archway. She picked up her backpack and duffel and walked through it, her Birkenstocks flopping softly on the wooden floor. She saw shadowy racks and cubbyholes filled with yarn and the outline of a checkout desk, then the window beside it, where streetlight poured in and cast long shadows on the wood floor.

She dropped her belongings to the floor and with a twist of narrow hips, wedged herself behind a display of soft baby hats and into the raised display window. Pushing aside a sign announcing a new shipment of organic cotton, she slid her whole body in beside the piles of yarn. Folding her legs beneath her, she settled in and smiled at the cat. Her heartbeat slowed.

It was nice not to be alone.

Purl came into her arms in an instant, as if they were coated with sweet cream. She curled up against the young woman's worn yellow T-shirt, her purrs loud enough to bring in a security guard, had the shop owners taken the time to hire a new one. But they hadn't, and Purl shared the warmth of the newcomer's body in private.

The woman's tired body relaxed beneath the comfort of the furry kitten, and in a short while, with Purl still purring against her chest, she curled up in a ball herself, and fell soundly asleep in the shadows of Izzy Chambers' yarn-filled display window.

CHAPTER 2

Friday nights at 22 Sandswept Lane were predictable. Deliciously predictable.

The only true surprise, Birdie Favazza liked to say, was the kind of fish that Ben Endicott sizzled on his oversized grill. And that was just jim-dandy with her. Although the silver-haired octogenarian usually loved change, the comfort of Ben's martinis, a blanket of stars overhead, and the warm company of friends on the Endicott deck were constants she cherished.

And this Friday night had been no exception.

"This is my new favorite," Izzy Chambers declared. She rested her head back against the Adirondack chair and looked up at the dusting of stars across the black sky. Then she closed her eyes and with deep satisfaction sighed into the soft breeze.

"You say that every week, Iz," Ben said.

"And I mean it every week," Izzy murmured. "Scallops and cucumber sauce — who would have thought? I didn't even know I liked scallops."

"Of course you did, sweetie." Nell Endicott reached over and patted her niece's tan knee. "Everyone likes scallops. At least the way we fix them here."

"It's great, Mr. and Mrs. Endicott," Brendan Slattery agreed. After three helpings, Brendan had finally settled into the chaise with a contented smile on his angular face.

Nell smiled at the high school art teacher. He was still quiet in their company — a trait that wouldn't last more than another time or two on the Endicott deck. Although he'd taught for years in Maine, Brendan had just finished his first year teaching in Sea Harbor and didn't know many people in town. Friday night suppers were the perfect remedy for that, Nell had decided when she insisted he join them.

Ben picked up a bottle of wine from the makeshift deck bar. "If you're going to hang around here, Brendan, you'll have to get used to first names. It's Ben."

"Sure. Ben it will be." Brendan nodded. "A leftover trait from very old-fashioned parents."

"And Nell," Ben added.

"And Cass," Cass said, piping up from

the other side of the deck.

The group laughed. No one ever called Catherine Mary Theresa Halloran anything but Cass, no one except Mary Halloran, of course, who prayed daily that her daughter Catherine would meet a nice young man and have a houseful of babies. And occasionally Birdie Favazza used the baptismal name when admonishing Cass about such things as refusing to rip out a lumpy row on a scarf or not washing her lobster gear thoroughly. But calling her "Ms. Halloran" wouldn't even get a turn of Cass' head.

"Well, no matter what you call Cass, we're glad you're here," Birdie said. "Jane tells me that you're spending your summer break helping out in some of the galleries."

Brendan nodded. "Mostly Billy Sobel's. But I help the Brewsters and Aidan when they need it."

"And he's invaluable," Jane said. "Brendan knows a lot about art. We're happy to have him."

"Looks like you're strategically placed to give us the scoop on those new paintings Billy just acquired."

"The James paintings?"

Nell joined in. "Imagine, finding those paintings all these years after Robert James' death."

"Billy was fortunate to get them," Rachel Wooten said. "That man has more connections than anyone I know." An attorney in the county office building, Rachel was an infinite source of information, though she was always discreet in her conversation about things going on in the granite building. Rachel and her husband, Don, were among the handful of lingerers reluctant to leave the comfort of the Endicotts' deck after enjoying platters of grilled scallops, Nell's vegetable pasta, and icy martinis made with Ben Endicott's secret touch.

"It came at the perfect time for Billy," Jane Brewster said. "The Sobel Gallery needs a boost. It seems Billy is either riding high and leading the good life or desperately coming up with ways to bolster his bottom line, and right now he'd like to see a little more profit."

"I think this new wife of Billy's might need bigger coffers," Ham suggested. He stroked his graying beard. "Natalie Sobel likes nice things."

The others laughed. Billy Sobel was a colorful character in Canary Cove, the small artists' community in Sea Harbor. He'd had a number of wives and lady friends, and as Ben, Nell, and their artist friends knew, his financial situation was often directly related

21

to his love life. Or how well he had done in Atlantic City. Or at Foxwoods. His new wife was a powerhouse, and they had all noticed that Billy was marching to a different drummer since Natalie Sobel had entered his life.

And that wasn't all bad, Ben had confided to Nell. Natalie liked to spend money, but she kept track of it, too — something Billy wasn't always so good at.

"Billy always lands on his feet, though," Ham Brewster continued. "He'll be fine."

As founders of the Canary Cove art colony, Jane and Ham Brewster were like parents to the artists and gallery owners who called the Sea Harbor neighborhood home, and though the Brewster gallery always did fine, Nell knew that "fine" for Jane and Ham happened only when the entire colony of artists was thriving.

"What about the Fishtail Gallery, Aidan? Anything new with you?" Nell looked over at Aidan Peabody, his long, lean body stretched out on a deck chair. "If Ben is a barometer, you're doing fine. He's brought home three of your carvings this summer."

"Ben has excellent taste." Aidan's slow smile softened the lines of his face.

"I find that I can communicate with your art, Peabody," Ben said. "It speaks to me."

The group laughed. Aidan's imaginative

22

woodcarvings of everything from craggy-faced, life-sized fishermen to sea urchin mirrors always drew a crowd of visitors.

"He won't sell me the mermaid, though," Ben said. "And I have fallen head over heels in love with her." The small wooden carving of a mermaid sat next to a vase of flowers on the desk in Aidan's studio. And no matter how many times Ben suggested he take her home to live a lifestyle more suitable to her charm and beauty, Aidan refused to part with her.

Nell looked over at Ben. When she smiled, the deck lights reflected off her cheekbones and the lines in her face disappeared. She was twenty-five again, and in love with her college suitor all over again. "I'm only a bit jealous, Aidan," she said, her eyes on Ben.

Aidan rested his head back against the chair and tilted it toward Nell. "And you've no need to be, lovely Nell. I have my mermaid . . . and Ben has his." Aidan took a drink of wine and his eyes half closed. He breathed deeply, his chest rising and falling. "I don't quite know what I'd do without this Friday time on your deck. There's magic in whatever you two do for us."

"The magic is probably in Ben's martinis. But you do look like you need a break tonight." Nell pulled her chair closer to

Aidan's chaise while others moved off to refresh drinks and reload the CD player. She'd noticed how quiet Aidan had been for most of the evening. He'd arrived late, and then had spent most of the evening nursing a martini or talking quietly with Ben.

Jane caught the end of the conversation and turned her chair toward Nell and Aidan. "I've noticed the same thing. What's up?" She looked over at her husband and motioned him over. "Ham mentioned it, too. Not that we want to butt in, but if we can help . . ."

Aidan took another drink of wine and set the glass down on the table beside the chaise. "Don't worry about me, my friends. Life is good."

"I hear you and Billy Sobel seem to be at each other's throats," Ham said. "What's that about? He claims you're interfering just a tad too much in his business — that being chair of the arts council has gone to your head. Any truth to that?"

"Nah. Billy will be fine. We're working something out between us. He'll see it my way soon." Aidan looked up at Ham with a crooked smile. "You know I'm always right, don't you?"

"You're being cryptic, not right. And

you're usually more outspoken when it comes to colony affairs. . . ." Jane swirled the wine around in her glass, her eyes on Aidan.

Aidan rolled his head on the pillow and looked over at Nell. "What our good friend Jane is really saying is that I am way too outspoken concerning Canary Cove affairs."

"I wouldn't say outspoken —" Jane began.

"Oh, sure she would," Ham interrupted. "You can be a real SOB, Aidan. But you keep people on their toes. And that's not all bad. Those art council meetings were mighty dull until you took your turn as chair. Watching you and Billy go at each other is almost as exciting as a Patriots playoff game."

"Thanks, buddy," Aidan said, sitting up in the chaise and swinging his long legs to the side. "SOB may be the nicest thing I've heard all week. But, hey, it is what it is. We all have our opinions on the best way to take care of our little neighborhood of shops." He forced a laugh. "Let's just hope Billy doesn't bring his buddies from Jersey to lean on me."

They all laughed. Billy Sobel owned a gallery in New Jersey as well as one in Sea Harbor, and he represented dozens of artists' work. Rumors were always spinning

25

around the cove about some of the more colorful — and shady — aspects of his life. Nell remembered when he first came to Canary Cove and the joke around town was that a *Soprano* had settled in *Canary* Cove — and could the two fly together? But Nell knew Billy to be generous — and even gentle under the tough exterior and gravelly voice.

"Speaking of opinions," Jane said, "D. J. Delaney seems to have taken quite an interest in our artists' neighborhood of late."

Nell saw the expression on Aidan's face turn sour at the mention of the Sea Harbor developer's name.

"D.J. is . . . how shall I say it . . . ambitious?" Ham said. "He is determined that his construction and development company own the Cape, I think." Ham looked over at Aidan. "Rumor has it that he plans to get his sticky hands on your extra land and turn it into a nice, fancy, moneymaking inn for art collectors and tourists."

"And he talks like he's almost there," Rachel added, walking back over to the group and joining into the conversation. "He's been doing some title searches over at the county offices. Are you making a deal with D.J. that you haven't told us about, Aidan?" She lifted her brows in a teasing fashion, knowing, as they all did, that selling the lovely treed acreage behind his studio and home would be the last thing Aidan Peabody would do.

"Over my dead body. He came to the council meeting this month and threw that plan on the table as if he had sense. Can't you see his marketing plan? 'Come see the artists at work.' Monkeys in a zoo." Aidan shook his head in disgust. "He's a damn fool, and I told him as much."

"As you said, Aidan, each to his own opinion." Nell picked up a plate of truffles and passed it around, trying to soften the conversation. Nell didn't mind conflict, but not around good food.

"What exactly does that arts council do?" Brendan spoke up from the side of the deck.

"Jane and Ham are really the experts," Aidan said, nodding to his friends. "They set it up some years back as a way to keep the colony strong. All the artists contribute some of their earnings to the council treasury — and we do repairs, make sure the city keeps our streets clean, help out new shops, that sort of thing."

"We have something to say about new shops coming in, too, and what kind of improvements are made to galleries, how exhibits are handled. It's a little like a

27

homeowners' association," Jane added. "It helps all of us in the long run, though there are some mighty heated conversations in the process."

"Of which Billy is a fine example," Ham added. "And D.J. Everyone gets their say. And we take turns as chair. This happens to be Aidan's year."

"And the council is responsible for starting the Arts Foundation, too," Nell said, pointing out a wonderful entity begun a couple years back. In addition to scholarships and grants, a summer arts academy for kids had been started the year before, thanks to Foundation money. Nell herself spent time writing grants for it and sitting on the board.

"But . . . ," Aidan started to add a comment, then stopped abruptly and sat back in the chair, holding his silence.

"Tony Framingham has contributed heavily to the Foundation," Ham said.

Nell nodded. The young businessman, wealthy by default — because of the dishonest dealings of his family — had tried to make up for some of his family's devious and tragic past by contributing to Sea Harbor causes, especially the Arts Foundation. "And that money will be put to good use, as Tony intended."

Izzy spotted a lull in the conversation and walked over to the group, carrying a stack of flyers. "Did everyone see the posters Brendan brought?" She spread them out on a low table near the chairs, then smoothed one of the pieces and held it up. The poster read:

Art at Night
Join us one and all.
Sunday at dusk . . . and beyond.
Canary Cove

In broad colorful strokes the poster announced the next open-studio night of the summer, inviting the whole town to gather in the Canary Cove neighborhood to support the artists' work, to experience art beneath the stars, and to eat, dance, drink, and be merry. Beneath the words was a soft watercolor of the quaint old galleries and shops clustered together along the windy lanes at the edge of the sea. It was a night scene, and tiny lights — like the smallest Christmas tree lights — twinkled out from the print.

"This is beautiful, Brendan," Jane said, rising out of her chair and moving to Izzy's side. She picked up another poster. "Just lovely. I'm tempted to frame one. We will ask storekeepers to keep them, and put them up each month."

"We can plaster the town with them," Cass said, looking over Jane's shoulder. "My fishing buds will hang them in every tavern in town."

The others laughed and passed the posters around the admiring group.

Aidan pushed himself off the chaise and walked over to look at the poster. "Good job, Slattery," he said. "These should help get the good word out. Thanks."

Brendan shrugged, seemingly embarrassed at the attention. "Opening the studios and shops to everyone is a good idea."

"It most certainly is," Birdie said. "The whole town loves it." Birdie picked up one of the posters and looked down her nose, through her glasses, at the painting at the bottom of the poster. "And you, young man, have done a lovely job of portraying the evening with your lovely brushstrokes. So you paint?" Birdie asked.

Brendan nodded. "Watercolors," he said. "Plein air."

Birdie's white brows lifted again. "Oh? That impresses me. Painting from photographs and imagination is lovely, but I am most admiring of artists who get out there in nature and paint what is right in front of them. I'd like to see your work sometime. I'm always interested in promoting local artists."

"You should take her up on that," Jane said. "Birdie Favazza is the best friend an artist could have. She's kind of an arbiter of taste. If she likes something, she tells her legion of friends about it — and they usually like it, too."

"Kind of like Oprah," Ben teased.

"Do you have favorite places to paint?" Birdie said, glaring at Ben to hush.

"Well, I'm a mountain biker — I take my paints with me and paint what I see up in the mountains."

"There aren't too many of those in Sea Harbor," Izzy said.

Brendan laughed. "I'll adapt. I'm not here forever."

"Well, even though we are down here at sea level, your painting of Canary Cove is lovely," Birdie said. "And a wonderful depiction of our festive Art at Night gathering."

Opening the studios, galleries, and small restaurants to the whole town one Sunday night a month was Aidan, Jane, and Ham's brainchild. Festive and upbeat, townspeople and vacationers alike packed the narrow streets and shops on the open-studio night — a perfect summer pastime — and a boon

31

to the artists in the neighborhood.

"You're all coming, right?"

"Are you kidding, Jane? We wouldn't miss it," Izzy said. "Not to slight the rest of you, but I've become addicted to Rebecca Marks' handblown beads. They're amazing . . . and Ellen Marks tells me they're having a special sale every Art at Night."

"Rebecca is terrific," Cass said. "Or at least her art is. She can be kind of a pill. But I must admit I've bought more than my share of her beads — they're miniature works of art."

The magical glass beads had received several awards recently, and Nell found herself nodding in agreement. In just one year, the Lampworks Gallery had become a favorite Canary Cove studio. Rebecca was the artist and Ellen managed the shop, handling the business end. Nell sometimes felt sorry for Ellen for having to deal with the flamboyant, temperamental Rebecca, but she seemed to have infinite patience when it came to her younger sister.

"Seems they're doing some remodeling over there, too," Ham said. "Ellen tells me that Rebecca wants skylights. They pass your code, Peabody?"

Aidan passed up the truffles Nell passed around a second time and he sat back down at the edge of the deck chair. "It's ridiculous," he muttered, looking down at the floor.

The sharpness in Aidan's voice went unchallenged, and Nell suggested a final call for seconds on dessert. She didn't want the conversation to hover around Rebecca and Ellen Marks. Aidan had dated Rebecca for a short while, recently calling it quits. The fact that the Lampworks artist hadn't come with him tonight added near certainty to the rumors. It was a short-lived romance, Nell thought, and perhaps explained Aidan's sharp tone. But whatever the reason, though an evening on the Endicotts' deck often stirred spirited conversation, Nell insisted it end peacefully.

Reading his wife's thoughts, Ben walked through the group with two brandy snifters balanced between his fingers and a carafe in the other hand. "And on a more pleasant topic, brandy, anyone?"

Aidan rested his elbows on his knees, a crooked smile on his face, and reached out for a glass. "A half inch, perhaps. You know my weakness, Ben."

"Well, one of them, anyway." He smiled at his friend and poured the amber liquid into the snifter bowl.

"Speaking of weakness," Ham said, blunt

fingers smoothing his beard, "I've got to find me a bed. Saturdays are busy days in the cove." He pulled himself out of his chair and reached a hand down to his wife. "Come, Janie, dear. Your chariot awaits. And Brendan, you, too. You're on early duty at Sobel's tomorrow — want a lift?"

Brendan stood and yawned. "Sounds like a plan."

Aidan began unfolding his lanky body from the chair. "It's contagious. I guess I ought to move along, too."

Nell watched her old friends with affection. Ham and Jane had been fixtures in Sea Harbor since a rock concert drew them to Boston from Berkeley in the early seventies. A side visit to Sea Harbor changed their lives. They fell in love with the winding coast, the sleepy village, and the rock formations, and they never left.

Aidan Peabody came along a while later, a decade after the Brewsters. He bought up some prime real estate on the shore, right in the heart of the artists' development, and became another rock in the community by the sea.

Good friends, all of them.

"I've wrapped up key lime pie for each of you," Nell said, following Aidan across the deck. "Ben and I don't want it around."

"Meaning Nell doesn't want me to eat it," Ben said. He reached over and patted Nell's arm as she walked by. "She likes me lean and rock-solid."

Nell's soft laugh trailed behind her as she headed through the French doors to the open kitchen. She liked Ben healthy, was what she liked. And a heart attack scare a few years earlier had changed their eating and living patterns, though a little bit of key lime pie on a moonlit Friday night could be easily walked off along the beach in the morning.

A muffled ring broke into strains of soft jazz coming from the speakers. Nell glanced at the clock above the stove, then down at a lumpy knit bag near the kitchen counter. Her heart skipped a beat. A sliver of worry cut into the evening's peace. *Silly,* she scolded herself.

Just because she and Ben would turn out the lights and head upstairs as soon as the last car rolled down their driveway didn't mean other people's night ended. Cass and Izzy's evening might be just starting — Brendan Slattery, too — and it was Izzy's phone, after all. It was probably friends inviting her to meet them at the Gull. Or maybe the Edge over near Pelican Pier, where the thirties crowd often gathered to bring their busy week to a relaxing end.

"Probably Sam," Izzy said, coming up behind Nell and bending low to dig through her purse for her phone. She looked up at Nell while her finger tips rummaged through the cavernous bag. "He's coming back into town for a few weeks and usually calls when he gets in so I don't worry if there are lights on above the shop."

Of course, Nell thought. Sam Perry, who had come to Sea Harbor the summer before and never left, at least not completely. Between tours for his book of photographs and simply doing his job as a photojournalist, Sam always managed to find his way back to the tiny apartment above Izzy's knitting studio, where he was welcomed by Purl — and Izzy, too. He was the ideal tenant, she said. He was never there long enough to mess it up or have crazy parties, and he always paid his rent on time. Good reasons to welcome him back — but not the whole picture, Nell suspected, especially when she saw the light in Izzy's eyes at mention of Sam's return.

Izzy stepped out of the kitchen light and spoke into the sliver of her cell phone, her voice low.

But Nell caught the cadence, caught the fear in her niece's voice. It sliced through

36

the evening air like an ice skate on a frozen Pelican Pond.

"What did you say?" Izzy's voice rose on the single question. And then it flattened into a tone that matched the next word out of her mouth.

"Dead?" she repeated after the caller.

And then, "No."

Izzy's tone was declarative and louder than before. "You're absolutely, positively wrong."

She snapped the phone shut.

"People don't die in my knitting shop," she said firmly to Nell. "They simply don't."

CHAPTER 3

The call had come from Esther Gibson, a dispatcher at the Sea Harbor police station.

For her sixty-fifth birthday five years earlier, Esther had treated herself to knitting lessons at the Seaside Studio, and she was now one of the most prolific knitters in town. Esther had single-handedly filled the children's wing of the Beverly hospital with knit bears and bunnies, knit up sweet little hats for the hospital nursery, and donated hand-knit blankets to the homeless shelter and the four-cell Sea Harbor jail. "Those men deserve some trace of human kindness, too," she scolded the chief of police when he expressed reluctance to support her latest project.

And in the process, Esther became one of Izzy Chambers' biggest fans.

"Izzy, dear," Esther had said, her voice a hiss into the phone. "You need to run like a jackrabbit down to Harbor Road. There's a dead body in the window of your shop, right next to that sumptuous pile of lovely organic cotton. Harry Garozzo saw it with his own eyes. Dead as a doornail, Isabel. Go now, before those clumsy police get in there and mess up your yarn. Go, Izzy."

Izzy went, but not alone.

In a flash, Ben had his car keys out and ushered Nell and Izzy to his car and the four-minute drive down the hill to the Seaside Knitting Studio. The others stayed behind to clean the dishes, douse the remaining coals, and wait for news.

The police arrived at number 7 Harbor Road at the same time Ben's CRV pulled up to the curb. The two young officers tumbled out of the car, hands on their pistol handles. Harry Garozzo stood near the curb, scratching his bald head with his thick baker's fingers.

On the other side of the window, Purl, awakened by the racket, stood on all fours, staring at the scene unfolding on the sidewalk. She mewed loudly and arched her back.

Nell's gaze immediately shifted to movement next to Purl. A young woman, small in stature, lifted her head, then tugged herself up to a seated position. The woman squinted against the bold glare of the flashlight, her hand shielding her eyes, and from the expression on her face, Nell suspected she had no idea where she was.

But the important thing, Nell thought, was that she was most definitely not dead — and surely incapable of extreme violence.

"Izzy, do you have your keys?" Nell asked, hurrying toward the door. The police, she knew, had faster ways of getting inside if they thought a robbery was in progress. There was no reason to damage the door.

"We'll take care of it, Miz Endicott," Tommy Porter said. "You just stand back — we have it under control."

Izzy slipped a ring of keys from her bag and followed Nell to the door as Ben blocked the pathway.

"It's all right, Tommy," Ben said. "The gal doesn't look dangerous. Let Izzy unlock the door, and we'll see what's up."

"Is she a . . . a friend of Izzy's?" Tommy asked. A lifelong crush on the shop owner made helping Izzy Chambers a priority in the young policeman's life. A friend of Izzy's would be a friend of his as well, burglar or not.

Ben shrugged. "We'll find out, Tommy. But at least she's not dead. That's a good thing, eh?"

"Sure looked dead to me," Harry Garozzo

said from his stand at the curb. He clasped his hands in front of his ample belly, his legs spread apart. "I'd just closed up the deli and was on the way home when I spotted her. I knocked on the window once or twice but the body didn't move. Looked dead, Ben. Sure did."

Ben nodded. "Good of you to check, Harry. I appreciate you keeping an eye on Izzy's shop."

"Well, you can't be too careful — that's what I say. Summer folks can do crazy things." Harry scratched his head again and yawned. "Looks like you have things under control. I'll be getting myself home now. Saturday mornings start at four." The deli owner gave a small nod to Ben and shuffled on down the street toward his home, a short walk away.

From the doorway, Nell motioned Ben inside. "I'm surprised we haven't frightened this poor girl half to death," she whispered.

Ben nodded. "Why don't you help Izzy handle things here? I'll call home and let them know the body is up and yawning."

Behind Nell, Izzy had switched on a light and walked over to the window, moving the display stand to the side. Purl jumped out of the bay window and rubbed against Izzy's bare legs, her summery skirt swirling around the cat's head.

Following close behind the kitten, Willow slowly swung her legs to the floor and sat on the edge of the bay window, her eyes adjusting slowly to the light. A well-worn Birkenstock dangled from one toe.

"Hi," she said. Her eyes went from Izzy down to Purl, then traveled to Nell and Ben. She shivered and wrapped her arms around her body. "I . . . I was asleep."

Just outside the door, Tommy and his partner waited patiently.

Nell wasn't sure what she expected the young woman's voice to reveal — fear? Embarrassment? But neither fit the low and slightly husky voice. It was soft but held an odd determination. And not what one would expect from a trespasser who had just broken into a shop and could be spending the rest of the night in a jail cell.

"Who are you?" Izzy asked.

"I'm Willow. Willow Adams." She looked at Izzy as if her name somehow explained why she was sitting in her window.

Nell watched the young woman with curiosity. She was taller than Birdie, but not long and bending in the breeze as her name would suggest. She looked to be in her early twenties, ten years or so younger than Izzy. Worn jeans and a long-sleeved yellow T-shirt covered her slight frame, unusual attire for the warm summer night. A thick mass of dark brown — almost black — hair was tangled from sleep and partially covered by a floppy hat that reminded Nell of the sixties and a few pieces of clothing she herself had worn, much to her mother's chagrin. A smattering of freckles brought color to Willow's cheeks and nose and made her seem even younger than Nell suspected she was. She had a look in her eyes that tempted Nell to wrap an arm around her shoulders and take her home to a bowl of chicken soup. "Waif" was the word she would use later with Birdie and Cass.

"Sorry about the police," Willow said. She looked over toward the door.

"How did you get in?" Ben asked.

And why? Nell wondered. She watched Purl leave Izzy's side and jump back into the bay window, curling up familiarly on Willow's lap. The knitting shop's resident kitten seemed to have accepted this stranger in their midst easily.

"I found a window that wasn't locked. You should probably watch that. I think your latch is broken." She smiled at Ben, as if she'd help him fix it if he wanted her to, and then she looked back at Izzy and Nell. "I didn't mean to cause trouble, honest. I

43

wanted to get here before the shop closed, but it took a while to hitch a ride up from Boston —"

"You hitchhiked here?" Nell's voice rose. What was this young woman thinking of? Thumbing a ride on the highway in the middle of the summer season. She remembered once when Izzy and two college friends had done the same thing after their car broke down on the way up to the Endicotts' for a weekend break from studies. They'd arrived in Sea Harbor late at night. After feeding them, Nell refused to let them go to bed until she extracted firm promises that they'd never, ever do that again. Although she and Ben didn't have children of their own, Izzy was as close as any daughter could be — and Nell had the furrows in her forehead to prove it. That night she'd added a few more.

"I don't understand," Izzy said. She raked a hand through her hair and stared at the young woman sitting in her window, looking, somehow, as if she belonged there. "You hitchhiked from Boston to come to my store?"

Willow's heart-shaped face softened with a smile, and she looked at Izzy intently. "So *you* are Izzy. I wasn't sure which of you was, though I supposed it had to be one of you.

But you can't tell from e-mails if someone is young or old, right?"

Nell frowned, not sure how to accept the "old" designation.

Beside her, Izzy said, "Yes, I'm Izzy Chambers, and this is my store that you've broken into."

"Oh, no." Willow said. "No, no." She shook her head to emphasize the point and her hands flew in different directions, her eyes round and begging Izzy to understand. "Sure, it might look that way. But you invited me to talk to your customers. So I didn't exactly break in. Not really."

A confused look passed between Izzy and Nell. They looked back at Willow.

"Talk to my customers?"

"Or teach a class, whatever. You know, on fiber art." Willow motioned to her battered duffel bag sitting on the floor beside the checkout counter as if it explained everything. "Remember? You saw some of my work in a coffee shop in Cambridge. And you e-mailed me that if ever I was in this part of the world, I should come by your shop. I was. So I did."

Recognition registered with Nell and Izzy at the same time. A small coffee shop in Harvard Square. They'd stopped in after shopping for a birthday present for Ben and

45

admired a piece of fiber art that hung on one wall.

"Sure. Of course. I remember now," Nell said. "W. Adams, the flyer said. Your pieces were beautiful. It was a year or so ago, right?"

Willow nodded. "Yes. I don't live around here. I'm not from here, so it took a while, you know?"

Nell didn't know, and neither did Izzy. The young woman wasn't making a whole lot of sense, and Nell wondered for a moment if she was on something. But she remembered the young woman's work. Bright, bold yarn, woven into interesting shapes and patterns and textures. The Harvard Square coffee shop owner had said that the artist didn't live in the East, but she gave them each a flyer with her name, e-mail address, and some interesting information about her creative process.

"I shouldn't have shown up on your doorstep like this, but, well, here I am." She offered another small smile and looked down at Purl, purring contentedly on her lap. "I guess I should say window, not doorstep."

Willow seemed totally focused on the kitten, her fingers rubbing Purl's back and neck. Finally she looked up again. "But you invited me to come. Right?"

Izzy nodded. "I guess I did."

Nell found herself smiling kindly at the young woman. There was something guileless about her — yet beneath the surface, Nell suspected Willow Adams bore the weight of a life that hadn't been totally carefree.

"Will you be in Sea Harbor for a while?" Izzy asked. "I think we could plan something. When would you like to come in?"

"I could do it now. Well not *now*. But soon?" Willow's brows lifted again and her eyes opened wide.

A hopeful look. "So you're staying in Sea Harbor for a while?" Nell asked.

Willow shook her head yes. "Well, a short while. Just a few days."

"We might be able to do something next week," Izzy said, walking over to the checkout counter. She picked up the shop calendar. "I'd need time to send out an e-mail to our customers. We'd need to put up some posters along Harbor Road, get it in the paper."

"I think that means Ben can send the police away?" Nell asked Izzy. The young woman seemed harmless enough, though the fact that she had somehow broken into Izzy's shop wasn't totally overlooked.

Izzy looked at Ben, who was now standing in the doorway, holding Tommy and his partner at bay. "I guess that's fine, Uncle Ben. Please tell Tommy we're okay. I don't think there's any damage."

"Oh, no. There's no damage," Willow said, holding one hand out in front of her. Her voice rose slightly. "I don't steal. Honest, I don't. It's just that it was so late, I'd been on the road awhile, and I didn't know where else to go." She scratched Purl behind the ears while she talked, and Nell knew that if for no other reason, Izzy would accommodate Willow because she liked Purl. And the feeling was clearly mutual.

"Where are you staying?" Nell asked. She was beginning to feel the late hour, her back giving notice that it had been a long day. It was time for bed. "We'll give you a lift."

Willow set Purl down beside her in the bay window and stood up on the shop floor. She forced a smile. "I guess the window's not an option? If it hadn't been for kitty here, I probably would have settled on the couch in that back room. But the two of us were getting acquainted, and the next thing I knew, her purring put me to sleep."

Ben had returned from convincing Tommy and his partner to go on back to the station. There would be no charges pressed, he'd told them, much to Tommy's dismay. Ben stood just inside the door, listening to the conversation. Finally he stepped forward, into a circle of light next to Nell.

Nell looked up at her husband, and she knew what he would say before the words formed. Thirty years of marriage did that.

"You can't stay here, Willow," Ben said. "This is Izzy's shop. And someone else rents the apartment above. Come home with Nell and me. We've a guesthouse that happens to be empty right now. It has a bed that beats Izzy's window — even with that ocean of yarn in it. It's yours for tonight."

Before Willow had a chance to respond, Ben had lifted the lumpy duffel from the floor with one hand and threw Willow's backpack over his shoulder.

"But it's now or never, ladies. This body needs a bed."

CHAPTER 4

"Izzy, is Willow at your shop?" Nell walked out onto the deck, the phone pressed to her ear. She looked down toward the guesthouse, shielding her eyes against the early-afternoon sun. The gray, shuttered cottage was partially screened from view by sheltering hawthorn and pine trees and a giant oak that still held a children's rope swing. The cottage nested cozily at the east end of the property, tucked up against a thick wooded area that was striped with paths worn smooth from years of Endicotts traipsing down to the ocean beach beyond.

"Nope," Izzy said. "But she was waiting on the front steps when I opened the store. She must be an early riser. She only stayed a half second and didn't seem at all interested in talking about her art to me or anyone else. She just wanted to thank me for not turning her in to the police last night, she said, and then she was off again, balancing a cup of coffee in one hand and that lopsided old bike that I totaled more times than I care to remember. Where'd she get that?"

"That old bike? Willow was riding it?" The bike had been hanging on a hook in the garage. Willow must have seen it when they drove in the night before. It was surprising that she had taken . . . well, had used it. It was fine, of course. But . . .

Nell leaned against the railing. "I got up early for a run today and it was quiet down at the cottage. I assumed she was still asleep. The poor thing looked like she needed a few days of it. Ben went down later to invite her up for breakfast on the deck, but she was gone."

"The whole situation is a little freaky, Aunt Nell. Willow showing up like that. She seems sweet — and maybe just a little bit sad. But on the other hand, it's all a little strange. It was nice of you and Ben to offer her a place to spend the night."

"The guesthouse wasn't being used. It made sense."

"But we don't even know her. She could be another Lizzy Borden."

Nell laughed and took a sip of her coffee. "No one who creates such lovely pieces of fiber art can be an ax murderer. I dug up

51

that old poster before I went to bed last night and was reminded how beautiful her pieces are. She has a unique design sense. Quirky, kind of unexpected."

"Quirky. Unexpected. That fits, doesn't it?" Izzy's full laugh traveled over the line. "Do you suppose that she has some of her creations in that duffel bag? She was wearing the same jeans and T-shirt today, so I don't think it held clothes."

"She looks like she needs someone to care for her. But I agree. The situation is a little strange. Ben says to remember that she's an artist and lots of our artist friends have idiosyncrasies."

"I asked her how she wanted me to advertise her talk, but she was in a hurry and didn't want to talk about it much."

In a hurry? Nell wondered where she'd be hurrying to. Willow knew no one in Sea Harbor, or so she had insinuated last night. Nell's gaze settled again on the quiet cottage in the distance. She wondered if Willow had enjoyed her night in the wide, high bed — so high that Ben had made a little foot stool for visitors to help them climb up beneath the cotton sheets. It had been Ben's parents' bed and Nell loved it. When Izzy was little and would visit her aunt and uncle each summer — a much-anticipated break

52

from her rambunctious brothers back in Kansas — she'd always ask for a night in the stepping bed, as she called it. A night stretched out on the high mattress, with Aunt Nell beside her and the windows open to the cool, salty air.

And Nell, herself, often slipped down to the small cottage porch to write or think or do yoga, the pounding of the ocean waves a lovely mantra in the near distance.

Did Willow find that kind of peace last night in the cottage? Nell wondered. The little thing looked like she could use a dose of the guesthouse's magic. Did she sleep soundly and feel safe from whatever had pushed her to hitchhike to Sea Harbor?

"Aunt Nell?"

Izzy's voice drew Nell back from her scattered thoughts.

"Yes, sweetie, I'm here."

"I have to run — the shop is crazy today. Knitters by the thousands, and Mae is urging me to pay attention to them. I received a gorgeous supply of Mongolian wool and it's like a stampede. I'll save you some. Mae is about to take my phone away."

Click.

Izzy was gone, rushing to help her shop manager satisfy a customer's needs. Mae Anderson had been an amazing find for Izzy

53

— she loved the shop and knitting nearly as much as its owner did. And with decades of retail experience supporting her no-nonsense style, Nell knew Mae was as integral to the Seaside Knitting Studio's success as its smart and talented owner was.

"Nell, where are you?" The front screen door banged shut and the light sound of Birdie's tennis shoes pattered on the hardwood floor and out the open door to the deck. "So what's this I hear about you taking in a sweet little hippie who broke into Izzy's shop?"

Birdie dropped her backpack to the deck floor and sat down on a reclining deck chair. She stretched her legs out in front of her. Her silver hair was damp, her cheeks flushed, and her forehead glistened with beads of perspiration. She took a few steadying breaths and pressed one hand against her bright orange T-shirt.

"Birdie, are you all right?"

"I rode my bike over, and I swear on my sweet Sonny's grave that this hill outside your door is growing. Can't you have dear Ben flatten it out a bit?" Birdie pulled a water bottle from the backpack and took a long drink, her gray eyes sparkling above the rim of the bottle. She wiped her forehead with the edge of a cotton scarf tied loosely around her neck.

"There. I'm fine now, love. Come. Sit." She patted the chair next to her. "Tell me about last night's adventure."

Nell looked at Birdie carefully, making sure her breathing normalized. It was Ben's encouragement that got Birdie to purchase the flaming red road bike. Before the bike, even teenagers had scattered when Birdie drove her 1981 Lincoln Town Car down Harbor Road. Ben had strongly suggested that it'd be better for everyone if the Town Car stayed in the garage more often than not. Good for the environment, he'd added with a convincing smile.

Birdie had complied under protest, but soon discovered the bike could get her places the car could not. Soon she was a familiar figure tooling down the winding roads of Sea Harbor, her lined face tilted to the wind. Nell marveled at her friend's stamina. If twenty years hence she had half the energy that was bottled up in Birdie's small frame, she'd consider herself blessed. But even so, her friend was at an age when most people slowed down considerably, and moving from a gallop to a trot might be something Birdie should consider. "Birdie, can I get you anything?"

"Oh, pshaw. I'm fit as a fiddle. All I need

is a little gossip. Do tell me about the young girl. I stopped at the deli to get a loaf of rye, and Harry filled me in on some of it — how he'd spotted her curled up in Izzy's shop window and thought she was dead. Lordy, as if our Izzy needs a dead body in her store window."

"She was asleep, poor thing. She's like a waif."

"The Saturday crowd at Coffee's had several versions of your waif. Jake Risso thought she'd probably escaped from the women's prison up in Goffstown. Gracie Santos suggested she was a starlet hoping to get in a movie filmed on our Cape. And Laura Danvers was sure that she was smoking something or another. A runaway, Laura said, though she couldn't quite pinpoint what she'd run away from."

"I suspect the truth is a little less dramatic." Nell looked down toward the cottage again. The thought that perhaps Willow had disappeared just as she had arrived — without announcement or notice — hovered like an irritating fly, but Nell brushed the thought away with a shake of her head. She had a feeling about Willow. She didn't fit any of the roles Coffee's customers suggested, and she surely wouldn't run off again without saying thank you or at least good-bye. Nell felt sure of that.

Birdie was intrigued to learn that Willow was a fiber artist, but horrified at the hitch-hiking story. "Though I must confess," she said, "I hitchhiked a time or two in my day. But things were quite different back then."

"Willow was determined to get to Sea Harbor, it seems."

"That's a tad odd, isn't it?" Birdie said. "Not that seeing Izzy's lovely shop isn't worth the trip from wherever on earth she came. But breaking into it? That shows a rather surprising determination. What do you suppose she was thinking?"

"That there might be a place inside to sleep, I suspect. And maybe that someone who was nice enough to send her a compli-mentary e-mail about her art — and some-one who loved yarn on top of that — would surely understand."

"And of course she was right. Though it must have scared everyone half to death to find her in the window like that."

"Except Purl. Purl seemed to accept it all in good spirits. She seemed quite fond of Willow and happy to have the company."

"That's definitely in Willow's favor. Our Purl is a fine judge of character."

"The true mystery to me is where Willow is right now. You'd think she'd be at the

57

Seaside Knitting Studio — or here in the cottage sleeping. Or at the least, that she'd have stopped in to say good morning or ask directions or something."

"I suspect she's out exploring Sea Harbor. If I were Willow and had dropped into this amazing village unexpectedly, I would be out soaking in every minute of it." Birdie leaned forward and patted Nell on the knee. "You don't know her well enough to worry about her yet. Give it a day or two."

Nell's husky laugh floated across the deck. Her penchant for taking on the problems of people's lives was the object of continuous teasing among the Seaside knitters, and Nell was quite adept at brushing it off. It was genetic, she would tell her friends, and there simply wasn't anything she could do about it.

"Since we've determined Willow is alive and well, how about you give me a ride to the farmers' market?" Birdie said. She checked the large round watch that dwarfed her wrist. "It's already midday and I've a list a mile long. My bike basket isn't nearly big enough to carry it all."

The summer market at the pier was one of Nell's and Birdie's favorite Saturday things to do. It wasn't just the smell of the fruits and vegetables piled high on the farmers' stands. It was the people watching, greeting neighbors, the music and kites flying and icy containers of clams, lobsters, and oysters being sold by local fishermen. It was Peggy Garner's stand, filled with freshly baked blueberry, rhubarb, and cherry pies, and Frank and Lucy Staff's Mason jars of fresh homemade salsa — pineapple and raspberry and spicy tomato. And it was even the incongruous appearance of Joe Quigley, who appeared every summer in the seaside town and hawked his Chicago dogs, piled high with onions and mustard and pickles, from a tiny booth right beside the pier.

Birdie's sack was nearly full by the time she and Nell had walked halfway through the maze of stands.

"Birdie, how will you eat all that in a week?" Nell asked, eyeing the array of vegetables and fruits.

But Nell knew how she'd do it. By handing it over to Ella Sampson, who worked for Birdie and lived with her husband, Harold, in Birdie's carriage house. Ella would do magical things with whatever Birdie brought home. At Birdie's suggestion, she'd make large quantities, enough for a crowd, and after dinner each night, Harold would quietly drive over to the homeless shelter near the highway and leave healthy dinners in the back kitchen.

"There's Cass," Nell said, waving above the heads of a clump of teenagers.

Cass wove her way to their side. "I finally met her."

"Who?" Nell asked.

"Willow, that's who. The star of the night. The window dressing."

"She's here at the market?"

"No. I went over to the cove to deliver some lobsters to Jane and Ham — my traps were overloaded and I owe them lobsters for life for that painting Ham gave me of my boat." Cass slipped a band from her wrist and twisted it around a thick handful of hair.

"So Willow was with Jane and Ham?"

"No. She was sitting on a little bench in that grassy area near Aidan Peabody's Fishtail Gallery. She had on huge sunglasses — like a movie star or something — but Tommy Porter pointed her out to me. He said he was sure that's who it was behind the shades — the gal who broke into Izzy's shop — but the one whom Izzy didn't press charges against. Typical Izzy. No wonder she quit her law practice. She's way too soft for a lawyer.

"When you called last night to say things

60

were okay, you didn't say you'd be bringing her home. We'd have stuck around longer, if we knew there was going to be drama."

"No drama, except what the police provided. Willow was exhausted, poor thing, and we sent her to bed as soon as we got home."

"What was she doing in Canary Cove?" Birdie asked.

Cass shrugged. "Things were bustling around the colony because of the Art at Night tomorrow night. Jane said she'd seen Willow peering in open doors, looking into the studios and galleries, but no one paid much attention to her because they were busy. She seemed intent on a brochure of the area, almost like she was looking for something to buy or find. She had a notebook and was taking notes, maybe names of the shops she liked?"

"I guess it makes sense she'd head toward Canary Cove. She's an artist, after all, and in addition to the lovely posters Brendan put up on his way home last night, Harbor Road was full of makeshift notices about tomorrow's open studios. I should have thought of that myself when I started worrying about her disappearing."

"Did you talk to her?" Birdie asked.

"Yep. I introduced myself, told her we

were all friends. She was a little uncomfortable, fidgety, as if she shouldn't be there. Or at least didn't want anyone to know she was there."

"You didn't ask her why she was there?"

"No. And I got the feeling it would be better if I didn't. I figured she had as much right to be there as anyone else. Ellen Marks walked by and stopped to thank me for some lobsters I dropped off for her and Rebecca, so I introduced them. Willow perked up when Ellen invited her to stop by the Lampworks Gallery and see Rebecca's new glass bead collection. She told Ellen about her own fiber art, and Ellen grooved on it, asked lots of questions. Willow seemed to come alive when she talked about her art, just like Jane and Ham and Aidan do when they talk about theirs."

"And then what happened?"

"Well, that was curious. While they were talking, I ran over to the tea shop to get a couple cold drinks — I was sweating up a storm. I told Willow I'd be right back with one for her. But when I came back out, she was gone." Cass snapped her fingers. "Just like that. Disappeared into thin air. I spotted Ellen through the window of Lampworks, talking to a customer, so I knew she wasn't there. She had simply disappeared."

"Strange," Birdie said.

"She seemed comfortable talking to Ellen, but even with her sunglasses on, I could tell she was checking things out while they talked, looking at people walking by, checking traffic in and out of the galleries — Aidan's and others down the road."

"As if she were looking for someone?" Birdie wondered.

"Could be. As I walked back to my truck, I thought I caught a glimpse of her yellow T-shirt walking back up that alley next to Aidan's. But I had more lobsters to deliver, so I moved on — I had promised Joe the hot dog guy I'd bring him some before the market closed — the thought of the Chicago hot dog king craving lobsters was just goofy enough for me to promise him a couple."

"Catherine, you have a heart of gold," Birdie said.

"Don't tell anyone. It'll be our secret."

A vibration in the pocket of Nell's slacks pulled her attention away, and she pulled the cell phone from her pocket. She stepped away, leaving Cass and Birdie admiring a pile of melons, and snapped the phone open, frowning at the unfamiliar number.

It wasn't what Nell had supposed. Not Polly's Salon reminding her of a hair appointment next week, or Nancy Hughes with a question about the historical society's last board meeting, or Ben calling from a friend's sailboat just to check in.

It was Willow, her voice so soft Nell could barely hear what she was saying. She was crying.

At first, Nell wondered how Willow got her cell phone number. Perhaps Izzy had passed both their numbers along, wanting to be sure Willow had someone to call if she needed anything. And then she remembered the little card she kept near the guesthouse phone. Her number was on it — a way for guests to reach her if they had a question, needed an extra blanket, or just wanted to know if the coffee was on yet. Just like the finest B and B, Ben had teased her. She was glad Willow had seen it. And used it.

"Nell," Willow began, "I didn't steal your bike."

"No, of course you didn't."

"I shouldn't have just taken it without asking."

"It's fine, Willow."

The silence that followed was so long that Nell thought Willow had hung up.

And then she heard her blow her nose.

"It's been a long day, is all," she said softly. Then added. "I'll be leaving in a couple days, but . . ."

"Of course. The guesthouse is all yours."

She heard Willow breathe again, sucking in air, as if steadying herself.

"For just a few more days?"

"Of course. And the bicycle, too."

"Thank you."

The last two words were so soft that Nell wasn't sure what she'd heard.

And then the line went dead.

CHAPTER 5

"It was odd, Ben. I'd swear she'd been crying. And the abrupt way she hung up was almost to cut me off so I wouldn't ask any more questions."

After receiving Willow's call, Nell was hopeful that when she got home, she'd find Willow on the deck with Ben, drinking a cold beer and filling him in on her life, her home, her art. *Or who she was,* Nell thought.

A name. An artist. That was absolutely all they knew so far of this enigmatic wisp who had fallen into their lives.

But there was no bike in the drive or on the guesthouse porch, and a knock on the door went unanswered.

"Maybe it's not so strange." Ben sipped a small glass of brandy and slipped his other arm around Nell's shoulder. They sat together on the deck, the black sky above and their feet lifted onto the stool Ben had pulled over. "The fact that she found her way to Canary Cove, for example — that makes sense to me. Artists find one another. And I'm sure she was intrigued with the colony, more intrigued than she'd be sticking around here to have breakfast with two people twice her age whom she doesn't know from Adam."

Nell leaned back into the curve of Ben's arm and looked up at the sky. A late-night breeze was gently sweeping away the heat of the day, and in the distance, just beyond the thick wooded area that ran down to the edge of the Endicott land, the sound of the waves against the shore soothed the day's jumble of events.

"And she broke into Izzy's shop and fell asleep in the window because —"

"Because she was tired. Which is exactly what I am, love." Ben rolled his head sideways on the back of the double chaise and kissed Nell on the forehead, then pulled himself from the chair. He looked down at Nell. "Are you coming?"

"In a minute. I'll get the lights."

Nell watched Ben walk back into the house.

Nightly rituals. And with them came a rush of comfort that Nell couldn't begin to explain. She pushed herself up from the

67

chair and walked over to the edge of the deck, the wind flapping her loose cotton blouse around her body. She looked down again at the guest cottage nestled at the edge of the woods.

Where could Willow have gone tonight? Maybe she'd finally connected with Izzy to plan the presentation she'd offered to give. Or maybe they were looking over Willow's pieces of art, which Nell herself was anxious to see.

But as Nell's gaze strayed across the deep yard, a cloud shifted overhead and a sliver of moonlight highlighted the cottage. Then Nell heard the sound. An animal? There were reports of coyotes on Cape Ann — Ben had seen one following their neighbor down the street last winter. She listened carefully. The sound carried on the breeze — a soft howling sound.

Nell walked down the deck steps and toward the flagstone path leading to the back of the yard. A sliver of fear shot through her. She wondered if Ben had heard the sound through the open upstairs windows.

But as she walked farther down toward the guesthouse, she spotted a slight figure, dressed in a familiar yellow T-shirt and jeans and hunched down on the floor of the narrow porch. Her knees were bent, and she hugged them tightly to her chest — and from beneath the thick tangle of hair that fell across her arms and legs came a mournful, muffled keening of grief.

Willow seemed to feel Nell's presence before Nell said a word. She lifted her head slowly and looked up at Nell, tears running down her cheeks and her hair tangled and unbrushed.

"Willow, can I help?"

But before Nell had a chance to act on instinct and gather the young woman up in her arms, Willow uncurled herself, wiped the tears away with the back of her hand, and stood up.

"It's silly to cry, isn't it? I don't do it often. I'm through crying, Nell. I've cried so much."

Willow forced a smile to her face. And with a slight gesture toward Nell, a touch to her arm, and a nod, she turned and walked through the door of the guest cottage, disappearing into the darkness within.

CHAPTER 6

Later, Nell would remember that it was an unusual night, that Sunday. The crowds were the same — a jolly mix of summer folks, Sea Harbor residents, and others from the Cape who drove in or motored their boats over to Sea Harbor because they enjoyed the festive atmosphere that Art at Night created.

There was music, as usual, from the deck of the Artist's Palate, as Pete Halloran's band filled the air with old Beatles music. "When I'm Sixty-four" and "Come Together" rolled down the winding street like a red carpet, welcoming people and fashioning the evening's mood.

But the air was sultry, with little breeze. Only a few stars dotted the sky, and a strange current — "anxious" was the word that stayed with Nell — ran beneath the light banter of friends and neighbors or the more serious discussions that the gallery owners and artists engaged in with customers.

But that was only in memory, only after the evening had played its course. A memory colored by what happened that Sunday night. And how valid such memory was, Nell had no way of being sure.

Join us tonight, Nell's note to Willow had read. She taped it to the door of the guest cottage early Sunday, not wanting to disturb Willow if she were sleeping. *I think you'll love the art, the people, and the night air. It's a good time.*

To her surprise, Willow stopped by the house on her way to Izzy's knitting shop a few hours later, and they settled on a time. Willow's face was scrubbed, and she wore a clean white T-shirt and denim shorts. A thick braid down the center of her back took more years off her face, and if Nell didn't know better, she'd wonder if she should car-pool Willow to soccer practice or the swim team.

The familiar Birkenstocks looked a little too big for her narrow feet, Nell thought, as Willow took the cup of coffee Ben offered her and slid up on a kitchen island stool, her feet pigeon-toed on the rung. Her mood was pleasant, if not upbeat — and she never mentioned the night before, when Nell had found her huddled beneath the stars, her

71

young body seeped in sadness.

Nell didn't mention it either, relieved that what had bothered the young woman seemed to have lessened. Homesickness, perhaps? Or a relationship problem. They knew next to nothing about Willow, after all, and, admittedly, she'd lived nearly two dozen years before stepping into their lives so recently.

"You two are great," Willow said. "Thanks for letting me stay here. As great as Izzy's window was with all that scrumptious yarn, your big high bed in the cottage can't be beat. I fell asleep before I hit the pillow."

She looked over Nell's shoulder at a contemporary print of a brilliant red sailboat flat against an azure ocean and pointed at it. "That's a nice print. And your guest cottage has such great art, too."

"Most of what we have is from artists right here on the Cape," Ben said.

"So do you all know one another?" Willow tugged on a strand of hair that had escaped her braid and shifted her gaze to an abstract sunset, a canvas washed with pinks and greens and yellows hung near a bookcase in the sitting area.

"Most of us do. Our Cape is small. And Canary Cove is an intimate place."

"I met Cass this afternoon. Everyone

seems to know everyone."

"It's usually a good thing," Nell said with a smile.

Willow's smile slipped from her face, and she seemed to give Nell's comment undo attention. Finally, she pushed away whatever thought had furrowed her brow. She stood and picked up her bag.

"You're right. I lived in a small town, too. And it's mostly good." And then the smile came back, but slightly guarded this time.

"So tonight," she said, heading for the door. "I'll be here at eight. You can count on me."

True to her word, Willow showed up on time, her hair washed and brushed and restrained again by a thick dark braid that trailed down the center of her back.

The three parked on a side street, and made their way together along an already crowded Canary Road. Even in the unusual heat of the night, Willow seemed bright and interested, her eyes taking in the sights around her.

Nell imagined Willow growing up in a small town, and wondered how she had fared in that environment. She was like a flower child, a free spirit. Had she fit in — or had she grown up waiting to leave?

They passed by Ellen and Rebecca Marks' Lampworks gallery, crowded as always with people admiring Rebecca's glass. Through the window, her platinum head moved in slow motion as she greeted customers graciously and explained the art of hand-blown glass. When talking about her art, Rebecca was charming.

Down the street, the small tea shop had a line of people winding out onto the street as they waited for a cold glass of tea or soft drink.

The road was blocked off for the evening and the threesome wove their way through pockets of people spanning the area between the shops on either side. The door to Ham and Jane's gallery was held open by a large brass frog, its head shiny from the many hands that had rubbed it smooth for good luck. Nell reached down and touched it out of habit, then spotted Jane standing inside, talking to customers.

Jane stepped aside from the small group and greeted them, shaking Willow's hand. "I noticed you around here yesterday, Willow, and have been wanting to meet you."

Willow looked slightly embarrassed, as if she'd been caught with a hand in the cookie jar. "I was just walking around the neighborhood for a little while. Exploring, I guess. It's a . . . a nice place."

Sensing the slight awkwardness, Nell pointed to a tall narrow pot standing near the wall. "That's Jane's work. Beautiful, isn't it?"

Willow's attention turned immediately to the piece of pottery and she walked over and touched the irregular ripples along the side. "This is beautiful," she said in a hushed tone. "This whole shop is."

"Some of the work is ours but we also exhibit others' works. Ham and I get tired of looking at our own things all the time. Nell tells me you're a fiber artist, Willow. I'd like to see your work sometime. Do you have any with you?"

"Just a couple pieces. But Izzy is giving me her customers' scrap yarn — silk, wool, organic cotton. It's amazing what people left behind. I feel like I'm in heaven in her knitting studio."

Nell saw the excitement light up Willow's face as she talked about the yarn. Her cheeks pinked and her dark eyes flashed in a pleasing way, pushing away the tension of minutes before. Jane had seen the discomfort, too, Nell could tell, but the look on her friend's face indicated she might understand the reason for Willow's earlier discomfort. She made a mental note to ask Jane about it later.

Nell turned away from the conversation briefly, pulling a tissue from her bag to blot the dampness collecting on the back of her neck from the night's heat. The usual ocean breeze was absent tonight, and in its place a heavy blanket of still air pressed down on the crowds that worked their way in and out of Jane's shop. In the distance, music filled the streets and Nell knew that even the sultry air wouldn't suppress the spirit of the evening.

She waved at Ben across the room, then turned back toward Jane and Willow, but Willow was gone. Jane stood near an exhibit of ceramic vases, talking to a customer.

"Where's Willow?"

"Beats me, Nell. She hurried out and asked me to tell you she'd meet up with you at the restaurant later." Jane wiped her forehead with the back of her hand. "It's hot, Nell. Where did this come from?"

Nell nodded. "It's oppressive."

A question from the customer drew Jane away and Nell gave a small wave, then slipped out the door to wait for Ben, hoping the air outdoors was less stagnant, with maybe a slight sea breeze to cool the back of her neck.

Izzy and Sam Perry were sitting on a small bench just outside the Brewster Gallery. "Nell, your face is as red as a lobster," Izzy said, patting the open seat next to her on the bench.

Sam stood and kissed her on the cheek. "Hi, Nell. We spotted you deep in conversation and didn't want to interrupt."

Nell hugged Sam. "You can interrupt me anytime. It's good to have you back. Are you here for a while this time?"

"Probably most of the summer. I'll be teaching another photography class at the kids' art academy like I did last summer — the funds for the summer academy are a little low this summer and Aidan knew I was cheap." Sam laughed. "Besides, Izzy missed me more than a lost shipment of organic cotton — or whatever it is she sells in that little shop."

"In your dreams, Perry," Izzy said, standing up and nudging Sam gently in the small of his back. "Believe it or not, Nell, Sam is looking for a place of his own in Sea Harbor." She looked up into the face of the sandy-haired man who had been her renter for more than a year now — and a friend for nearly her whole life.

"You're buying a house here?"

Sam nodded. "I've soaked up Izzy's hospitality long enough. She needs to rent that apartment out permanently and not worry about me coming and going. I think that spot could use someone a little more dependable to keep an eye on things."

"So you heard about Izzy's late-night visitor."

Sam nodded. "Sounds innocent enough, I guess," he said. "But it could have just as easily been otherwise."

"And what would you have done, had you been here?" Izzy asked, her brows lifting up into a mass of highlighted hair, damp with perspiration.

"You doubt that I could be your hero, Iz? Save the lady's shop from looters and pillagers."

"Like I have so many of those. Willow Adams couldn't hurt a fly. She was just tired, that's all."

Nell could read Sam's thoughts easily, and they weren't that far from her own. Willow might be harmless — that was probably true enough. But just a year before someone had broken into the apartment above the shop and caused considerable damage. And what happened once could happen again — even in a peaceful town like Sea Harbor. Having someone in the shop apartment who actually lived and worked in the town might be a very good thing, indeed.

Ben walked out, then, a wrapped painting beneath his arm. He greeted Sam warmly. "I'm on my way to Peabody's. He's hanging on to a piece for me, and I want to make sure no one talks him out of it. Anyone want to come along?"

"His place is packed," Izzy said. "Between the Fishtail and Rebecca Marks' new collection of beads, the cove is rocking."

"And hotter than hell," Sam added. "Way too many bodies for me. Birdie's holding down the fort at the Artist's Palate. I think I'll join the lady."

"Keep an eye out for Willow," Nell called after them as they disappeared into the crowd.

The black sky felt heavy to Nell as she and Ben wove their way through the crowds of people staving off heat with cold beers and icy fruit drinks. But Canary Cove was still a magical place, even with the humid salt air blanketing the shops and studios. People were everywhere, talking and laughing, energized by the art that surrounded them. Tiny white lights outlined trees along the road and the narrow lanes that wound back behind galleries to studios and small cottages. And beyond them, a perfect backdrop for the sea of art, was the real sea, its waves slapping against the shore.

As predicted, Aidan's Fishtail Gallery was packed. Like most of the galleries along Canary Road, Aidan's shop was small, but his property stretched back up beyond the studio and his small home, into a wooded area that filled the side of a steep hill. The extra land was the envy of the crowded colony. Aidan let it grow as it willed, with sea grass and wild roses surrounding his house and a thick copse of trees beyond. The only tended part was a small plot between the studio and the house, where Aidan had carved out a garden — a quiet, almost hidden retreat.

"Aidan needs more room in here," Ben said. "This place is jammed."

Nell nodded in agreement. She looked around at the jostling crowd and focused on a small group that surrounded a life-sized mermaid. She was carved from a single piece of pine and stood tall on her flayed fins. Her shape was exaggerated and fanciful, her full lips in a wide smile, and her wavy locks a brilliant cascade down over her breasts. A small discreet knob on the front opened the wooden sculpture to reveal a bookshelf and several small drawers — a perfect place for hidden treasures.

Nell felt the vibe of the admiring crowd

and moved over to the side of the room, where Aidan stood, watching people's reactions.

"Aidan, you've outdone yourself with the mermaid — they seem to be a specialty of yours. She's gorgeous. But please, do not let Ben buy her. We're going to have to build an addition to satisfy his addiction."

Aidan looped an arm around Nell, his weight heavy on her shoulders and his voice deeper than usual. "She's a pretty one, isn't she?"

Nell noticed the slight slur in Aidan's voice. She looked into his face, wondering if perhaps he'd been drinking. The glass in his hand was nondescript, but nearly empty. "Are you all right, Aidan?"

"Damn heat, that's all. Where did it come from?" He wiped his forehead and upper lip on the rolled-up sleeve of his shirt. "But it isn't keeping folks away. It's a good night, Nell." Aidan reached out and touched Nell's arm, as if to steady himself. "This is what we need, these kinds of things. Not Sobel's exhibit."

He stopped talking then, as if he wasn't sure of what he had said. His brows pulled together in an attempt to focus. Then he looked at Nell again. "Billy isn't a bad guy. He'll be okay."

Nell touched Aidan's arm and looked into his eyes. They seemed cloudy, unfocused. "Let's go outside, Aidan. Get some air."

"There you two are," said Ben, walking up behind them. "Nell is probably paying you not to sell me anything."

"Ben," Aidan said, hanging on to Ben's hand, "I need to talk to you. Tomorrow?" With his other hand, Aidan wiped the moisture from his forehead.

"Sure, Aidan. Name the time."

"Put some things in order."

Ben nodded, and Nell listened, concerned about the unsteadiness of her friend.

It didn't surprise her that Aidan was asking for Ben's help — that happened frequently, and Ben was always there to help. Ben's business law degree and experience — not to mention his big heart — pulled him into more family affairs than Father Northcutt's confessional.

But what surprised her was the urgency in Aidan's voice, and the fact that his face had lost most of its color in the short time they had been standing together.

A discussion at the counter over the cost of a carved box forced Aidan's attention away, and Nell watched him weave unsteadily through the crowds.

"I think he's coming down with something," she said half to herself, but Ben was already on the other side of the room, checking out a tall, wooden fisherman with a marlin standing beside him.

Nell shook her head. Where in heaven's name would she fit a fisherman in their home? Probably beside the mermaid.

She wandered around the shop for a while, admiring a wall of intricately carved mirrors that Aidan had assembled. She often wondered if an imagination like his ever ran dry — or if there was always another sea urchin, another mermaid or fisherman waiting to be born of his knife and spirit.

The dampness on Nell's neck was becoming uncomfortable, and beads of perspiration covered her upper lip. It was time for air.

She looked around the gallery for Ben. Because he was well over six feet, his slightly graying head was easy to spot in a crowd. He was standing in the far corner, his head bent low as he listened attentively to Annabelle Palazola. Annabelle was probably seeking advice on some paperwork for her restaurant — a conversation Nell knew would go longer than she could bear to be in the overheated gallery.

An open doorway near the back of the gallery offered Nell a getaway and she quickly slipped into the warm night and away from the press of people. A slight breeze lifted the hair from the back of her neck as she walked along the flagstone pathway into Aidan's secluded garden.

"Ah," she murmured into the breeze, enjoying the reprieve and the instant peace Aidan's garden provided.

Low garden lights lit her path and cast shadows from pieces of art nearly hidden in the tall grasses or hanging from a small magnolia tree or Japanese maple — a playful ceramic owl, an old clay frog, a string of colorful elves. The cooler air was a welcome relief, and Nell stood still for a moment, adjusting to the darkness and fanning the air with her hand.

It was when Nell sat down on a teak chair near a small fountain that she realized she wasn't alone. Stretched out on the stone bench opposite her, resting in the night's solitude, was a long figure of a man, looking up at the black night.

It was Aidan — he'd escaped the crowd and the heat. A necessary reprieve.

Thank heavens, Nell thought. He had looked like he was going to collapse inside. She opened her mouth to speak, to greet her friend and apologize for invading his private moment, probably the only one he had had in hours.

And then, just as quickly, Nell's mouth snapped closed. She was across the garden in an instant and slipped to her knees beside the still figure. With two fingers pressed against Aidan's neck, she lowered her ear to his mouth.

But Nell knew before she ever touched him that his eyes weren't seeing the night sky . . . nor was his skin cooled by the slight breeze.

Aidan Peabody was dead.

CHAPTER 7

It took less than two days for the autopsy results to be splashed across the front page of the *Sea Harbor Gazette.*

ARTIST'S DEATH RULED A HOMICIDE

A heart attack had been Nell's first thought as she'd looked down on Aidan's still body the night he died. And he'd been perspiring and unfocused when they had talked a short time before.

But it didn't take Doc Russo long to discover a stomach filled with pentobarbital mixed with chloral hydrate. Something no sane person would have ingested intentionally. "Someone slipped him a Mickey Finn," Doc said sadly. "Just like in the movies."

"I can't believe Aidan is dead," Cass murmured, her eyes reflecting the group's sadness.

Nell, Izzy, Birdie, and Cass sat together on Coffee's patio, leaning over the paper as if the words would suddenly focus into copy that made sense. Not an awful, illogical tale of a friend's murder.

"We went out a couple times," Cass went on. "It didn't sit well with my mom — she thought Aidan was too old for me. I think she worried about the number of progeny such a match would bear."

The group mustered smiles at Mary Halloran's continuous attempts to have grandchildren.

"There weren't any fireworks between us, but we sure liked each other as friends," Cass said. "He was a good guy. I just can't get my arms around this."

"I can't either." A shiver passed through Nell, and she pulled a half-finished scarf from her bag. Touching the deep blue cashmere yarn and slipping it onto her needle, one stitch after another, somehow brought comfort to Nell, just as the cabled scarf would bring comfort to Ben on a cold Sea Harbor morning.

Even though Aidan didn't let anyone get too close to him, he and Ben had sailed together and Nell was always pleased when he showed up for Friday suppers. His

87

knowledge of art was extraordinary, and Nell loved talking to him. He was a friend, plain and simple — and his loss was keenly felt.

She and Ben had relived Sunday night in their minds and conversation over and over. But it had happened so fast that Nell could barely remember the order of events. They had talked to Aidan not a half hour before she found his body in the garden.

And in that short span of time, a man's life had ended.

Immediately after she discovered Aidan's body, Ben had appeared in the garden, looking for her. He made a call and in minutes the emergency ambulance drove into the narrow alley beside the gallery. Together Ben and Nell filled in the necessary information, and the ambulance, slipping in and out of Canary Cove as surreptitiously as possible, took Aidan away.

Outside the Fishtail Gallery, Pete Halloran's band had switched to hard rock and filled the night air with a pulsing beat. Art was admired and sold, and when the shop doors closed, fireworks exploded off Canary Cove and filled the simmering black sky. People danced and drank frosty beers. Gossip was shared. Lovers wandered down to the ocean's rocky edge, bodies entwined.

Life went on.

And in a hospital morgue just a few miles away, quietly, without fireworks or fanfare, Aidan Peabody was pronounced dead.

"Aidan has no family we know of," Nell said. "In the years I've known him, he's never spoken of anyone."

The sadness blanketed them, and around Coffee's patio, hushed voices said that others were experiencing Aidan's loss as well.

"So what will happen to his wonderful gallery and studio? That land that Aidan loved and protected," Birdie said. "There'll be more than a vulture or two picking away at it, I suspect."

"Ben says there's a will. They're checking."

"Sam talked to Aidan briefly Sunday afternoon," Izzy said. "He stopped in to say hello since he hadn't seen him for a while and knew he'd be too busy to talk that night. Aidan was in the back, going over a bunch of paperwork and seemed really distracted, but happy in an odd way, Sam thought."

"Did Sam know why?"

Izzy shook her head. "He said something kind of cryptic — though at the time Sam just thought he was distracted because of the evening affair. But when Sam asked him

89

how things were going in his life, he said they'd never been better. And he smiled at Sam in a way that made him think maybe there was someone new in his life — someone special. So Sam said, 'What's her name?' Aidan just laughed and said Sam'd find out soon enough. Odd, huh?"

"Well, maybe not so odd," Birdie said. "Women have always gravitated to Aidan, and once Rebecca Marks disappeared from the picture, I'm sure there were others waiting in line."

"But Aidan wasn't like that," Nell said. "He seemed to move slowly when it came to allowing women into his life. Oh, sure, he'd talk to them, but he certainly didn't jump into relationships. I think the only reason he paired up with Rebecca was because Rebecca insisted."

Cass laughed. "And what Rebecca Marks wants, she usually gets."

"Well, at least for a while," Nell said. "But I wonder if Aidan could have meant something else when he talked to Sam." But even Nell was at a loss as to what that something else could be.

A flash of red distracted Nell, and she looked over Izzy's shoulder, toward the patio entrance.

"Look — there's Willow. Poor thing, we've

nearly abandoned her with all the happenings." Nell stood and waved for her to join them.

At first Willow didn't see them. She stood in the entrance of the coffee shop's patio, nearly lost in the movement of people balancing trays of takeout coffee cups and pastries on both sides of her. She wore a pair of cutoff jeans, a red tank top, and her dark hair puffed out beneath a flowered headband that ran across her forehead and around her head like a crown. Her feet were slightly apart, her stance strong, as if to ward off any danger. But when Nell looked up into her eyes, she saw little bravado.

Willow finally spotted Nell's waving hand and wound her way to their table, one hand gripping the familiar backpack and the other a cup of coffee.

"I saw Sam outside your shop, Izzy. He said you'd all probably be here."

"And Sam was right. He knows all our bad habits."

"Come, sit." Cass patted a chair that she'd pulled over from another table.

"Things have been a little nuts, Willow. I'm sorry I haven't scheduled something at the knitting shop for you. Does later this week sound good?"

Willow hesitated. She looked down into

91

her coffee cup, then finally met Izzy's eyes. "I don't know, Izzy. I think all of you are great — I really do. You've been terrific to me — but this just doesn't seem like a good time around here. I'm thinking of moving on, maybe heading back to Wisconsin."

"No, Willow, you're wrong about it not being a good time. You've come all this way, and my customers will love learning about your art. It's the *best* time."

"Izzy's absolutely right," Nell agreed. "This is a sad time because the artist who died was our friend. But having something beautiful to look forward to is a good thing at times like this."

"And besides, dear, we simply won't let you leave Sea Harbor on the cusp of such sadness. Our town is really a lovely place."

The others reinforced Birdie's sentiment, and Willow finally shrugged, but the shift of her narrow shoulders didn't indicate a promise either way.

"I came down to the guesthouse yesterday," Nell said. "You'd already gone out. I wanted to explain what was going on, though you can't help but be aware of it."

"I went running on the beach."

Willow looked at Nell and smiled. "I really love it down there. I walk through your little bit of woods, smelling those giant pine trees, and then it all opens up and there's the sea, right smack in front of me. It's like everything I imagined it would be. And running on the sand like that clears my head."

"Of course it does. It must be a bit disconcerting to have a murder occur almost before your eyes," Birdie said.

"My eyes?" Willow looked at Birdie in surprise.

"Figuratively speaking. We were all right there, milling around Canary Cove and having a grand time. And at the same time, Aidan Peabody was dying. It's quite awful." Birdie pulled a section off her cinnamon roll and began to chew it slowly.

"I know people are sad about his death."

"He was a lovely, talented man. His art is enchanting," Nell said. "Did you meet him Saturday when you were wandering around the studios?"

"Meet him?" Willow seemed startled by the question. She took a drink of coffee, her eyes seeming to focus on Birdie's cinnamon roll.

"Well, if you didn't, it's a shame. You would have liked him. Aidan was as unexpected and irreverent as his art," Birdie said. "He made me laugh, a wonderful trait to have. I will miss him."

"We'll miss him. And his huge art following will miss him. But, unfortunately, there are some people who won't," Cass said. "Word on the water yesterday was that D. J. Delaney is moving ahead full force to get Aidan's land."

"You gossip while you're pulling traps, Catherine?" Birdie looked up from her coffee.

"Old Finnegan's traps were empty so he served up some gossip instead. Slow mornings seem to bring that out of him. Besides, the guys were all bummed. They liked Pea-*buddy,* as they called him. He was definitely the fishermen's artist, with all those sea-related things he carved. We all have at least one small carving — a mirror with an octopus' arms around it or some fishy thing."

"So what did Finnegan say?" Izzy prompted.

"He was over at the Gull last night and D.J. was practically salivating at the thought of getting his hands on this land. Aidan had three times as much land as he needed, he claimed, and it could serve others well. Like himself, for example."

"He wants to build a set of condos or an inn or something that would put money in his pocket. That's what he's done with the old fish hatchery south of town," Nell said.

"Rachel Wooten told us he looked up deeds and city restrictions weeks ago."

"He'd better be careful what he says," Izzy said. "It sounds like a motive for murder, if you ask me."

"Some of the gallery owners saw better uses for that land, too," Birdie said. She pulled a pair of double-pointed needles from her backpack. A strand of bright pink yarn dangled from the cast-on row. "But Aidan liked having some green space and that lovely woods. Elbow room, as my sweet Sonny used to say. And that was certainly his choice. It's his land."

Birdie's needles began clicking as she started to turn the heel on a half-finished pink-and-green-striped sock, deftly decreasing the stitches in the short row. Birdie's portable knitting projects were predictable — socks for cafés like Coffee's, sweaters for sitting in a friend's home, scarves and mittens for the beach, a long walk, or a car trip. If a knitting project could not travel, she told her friends, the project would have to find other fingers to work it up.

Nell watched as Birdie purled two stitches together and turned the sock in the middle of the row. It was the part of knitting socks that initially scared some of them away, until Birdie made it look so easy that even Cass was thinking about trying a pair.

"Was," Izzy said. The sadness in her voice reminded them all that beneath the gossip of neighbors, they had lost a good friend.

"The police chief thinks they'll wind this up quickly," Nell said. She wondered how many similar conversations were going on at other tables around the patio. Plenty, she guessed, from the hushed voices and coffee-stained newspapers sitting on tables.

"Ben talked to Jerry Thompson early this morning, and he seems confident that the town isn't in any danger. The murder had the MO of a personal act — someone who clearly had an ax to grind with Aidan Peabody."

Cass pushed a thick strand of hair behind her ears. "It seems that way, I guess. But I'm sure the Canary Cove artists will sleep better at night once the person is caught."

A shadow fell across the table, blocking the sunlight, and Nell looked up into Brendan Slattery's smile. "You're up and about early this morning. Would you like to join us?"

Brendan raked one hand through his smooth, slightly long brown hair. "Thanks, Nell, but I'm headed over to the Sobel Gallery. Billy needs some help with the James paintings. I just wanted to ask Willow if

96

she's going running tomorrow."

Nell looked from one to the other. "Do you two know each other?" She'd noticed the smile on Willow's face when Brendan walked up.

"We met on the beach," Willow said. "Brendan runs, too. And he's an outsider like me."

"Well, sort of," Brendan said, looking apologetically at Nell as if the comment might offend her. "One year here doesn't exactly make one a native."

"No, I suppose not," Birdie said, "though Sea Harbor is an open-arms kind of place, I've always thought."

"I think it's the circumstances," Willow said. "It's what's happened this week that makes us not fit in. It's a time for friends to be together, not strangers."

Nell listened to the conversation and heard the uncomfortable edge to Willow's voice. *But she was right.* She and Brendan didn't fit in — but especially Willow. She was a young woman passing through town who had fallen into a town's personal tragedy, without understanding or intent. And if she wanted to pack up her few belongings and leave that very day, Nell would completely understand.

But instinct told her that was not going to

97

happen. Willow Adams was not going to leave Sea Harbor soon.

Even if she wanted to.

CHAPTER 8

Aidan Peabody's funeral lived up to his wishes. It was a festive, lively affair.

"So like Aidan," Nell said, walking up the wooden steps to the outdoor restaurant where tables were ready, a microphone set up, and baskets of peanuts and chips set out. Strings of tiny lights outlined the perimeter of the deck.

Hank and Merry Jackson's Artist's Palate, located just off the main road of Canary Cove, down a small side street that ran right into the Palate's parking lot, was the perfect place for a gathering. The small bar and grill was known for its deck, which hung over the edge of the water and hosted local bands in the evening hours — reggae, rock, or soft jazz — whatever seemed to suit the night and the crowd. Hank's food was plain but delicious — hamburgers, brats, and lobster rolls. And few left without at least a taste of Hank's beer-batter calamari heaped high in wicker baskets.

" 'A wild celebration of life,' were Aidan's exact words." Jane Brewster climbed the steps to the Artist's Palate's deck just behind Nell. "He felt strongly about it, not that planning funerals was a daily conversation in Canary Cove. But you know how you do, sometimes sitting in a bar or at the end of the old dock, just hashing out the mysteries of life. Ham, Aidan, and I used to do that a lot, hanging out at the end of the old dock."

"And always with a Sam Adams in hand, I'd guess," Birdie said.

"You've got that right." Ham helped Birdie up the last step.

"I wonder if Father Northcutt is offended that the funeral isn't in the church."

Jane chuckled. "Aidan might have been able to use those special blessings. But I don't remember him ever setting foot in Our Lady of Safe Seas, though he liked Father Northcutt well enough. He was the first to donate his art to the church auctions and made sure everyone else around here did the same. And I think he gave chunks of money to any cause Father Larry set down in front of him. But a noisy affair for his final good-bye seems far more to Aidan's taste."

Ham scanned the room, looking for a place to sit. A waving arm drew their attention to a large round table in the corner of the deck. Over the tops of heads, Izzy mouthed that she'd grabbed chairs for all.

Cass and her brother Pete were already at the table, frosty mugs lined up in front of them and a basket of calamari rapidly disappearing. Sam appeared, balancing a tray filled with platters of shrimp and a full pitcher of beer.

"Where's Willow?" Izzy asked as she kissed Nell on the cheek. "And Uncle Ben?"

"Well, not together," Nell said. "Ben got called into a last-minute meeting downtown but promised that he'd be here. It was important, he said. And Willow was meeting Brendan for a run or a bite to eat. A festive celebration for someone who died didn't sit comfortably with her."

"Especially someone she didn't know," Cass added. "I can't say I blame her."

Jane slipped down next to Cass and poured herself a glass of beer from the pitcher. She gathered up her long, flowing cotton skirt and tucked it beneath her. "Willow didn't know Aidan?" She frowned.

"She didn't know anyone here until she landed in my window last Friday night," Izzy said.

"Hmm," Jane said. "You're sure?"

"That's my understanding," Nell said. She paused, puzzled by Jane's look. Clearly her friend had information that said otherwise. But before Nell could pursue it, the echoing screech of a microphone hushed the crowd into silence.

Father Northcutt stood at the mic, looking more priestly than usual in his pressed black suit and stiff Roman collar.

"Good evening, everyone." Chairs shifted at the echoing words and faces turned to face the familiar voice.

"Our thanks to Hank and Merry Jackson for letting us all gather here at their restaurant tonight." The microphone screeched and Father Lawrence Northcutt frowned at it, then backed up a step.

"Well, I'll be damned," Ham said quietly. "Good old Father Larry. If the funeral won't come to you, then you go to the funeral. Good man."

The gray-haired pastor, a fixture in Sea Harbor for decades, waved his hand over the crowd as if bestowing a blessing or sprinkling holy water. Nell suspected the black suit wouldn't be intact for long. As soon as his blessing was finished, the jacket would be hung over the back of his chair and the collar would come off while the night was still young.

"We're not here to mourn a tragic death. Aidan would come down and curse us all if we did that," the amiable priest continued. "We're here tonight to celebrate a colorful, rich life."

"He's right about that," Ham murmured and the group smiled.

"Our friend Aidan Peabody was a champion of the arts and I'm sure you all have stories to share." Father Larry went on to invite the crowd to pick up the microphone when the spirit moved them, to toast their friend, to share a story or two. And above all, he urged them to follow their dear departed friend's wish that they eat, drink, and be ever so merry.

Nell looked out over the crowd as the priest talked on about his relationship with Aidan and the generous donations the artist had made to the Our Lady of Safe Seas children's center and food pantry. The deck was packed with artists, gallery owners, townspeople, many friends of Aidan's, some associates, and a handful of people who were curious and enjoyed a festive gathering, whatever the reason for it.

Billy Sobel was there with his new wife, Natalie, and a large table filled with Canary Cove artists and shop owners. Billy was a stolid sort, with thinning hair and strong limbs. Nell liked him, though she'd never experienced firsthand his reported temper. Keep him calm and happy, was Ham's advice when dealing with Billy. He seemed calmer, though, with this new wife. She was a carefully made-up woman, years younger than Billy, with a show business background, some said. A dancer in a New Jersey casino, Birdie had heard. That was where they'd met.

Her husband's gallery on Canary Road represented many New England artists. His recent acquisition of the lost James paintings, for all of Aidan's protests, would benefit the whole art colony. Nell suspected that by summer's end the paintings would be sold and Bill Sobel and his wife wouldn't have to worry about money for a long time to come.

Across the table from Billy, Rebecca Marks sat in a flowing dress hand-dyed in oranges, reds, and saffron, the neckline low and accentuating her enviable figure. Rebecca was a work of art herself, Nell thought, her beautiful features and fiery temper somehow befitting an artist. She wondered what Rebecca was thinking tonight, sitting at a memorial service for a man she seemed to have developed a recent, intense dislike for.

And a man whose bed she had shared.

Nell felt sure Rebecca would soon stand up at the microphone and talk about Aidan in glowing, respectful terms, the way one did when someone died. She'd charm the group with stories about Aidan's work in the colony, his colorful wooden carvings, his immense knowledge of all kinds of art. And she'd tastefully hide her contentious relationship with the artist behind a perfect smile and magnetic green eyes.

Ellen Marks sat next to her sister, quiet as always. Ellen was the more stable of the sisters, or so it always seemed to Nell. They were an odd pair, but no matter, their partnership was certainly successful. The Marks women ran Lampworks, an acclaimed handblown glass gallery that had been on the cove for less than a couple years, but in that time it had established a robust reputation. The two women were day and night, yin and yang — the colorful, gorgeous artist, Rebecca, and introspective, smart, and financially savvy Ellen, preferring to be in the shadows but, Nell suspected, one to be reckoned with if push came to shove. In recent months their success had become obvious by an addition to the gallery and the purchase of a lovely home in Sea Harbor. Some called it showy, but as Jane and Ham Brewster told Nell, they didn't care who called it showy — the shop was successful — and that meant success for the whole of the art community. And though Rebecca might be a tad arrogant at times, Ellen's allegiance to the Canary Cove effort made up for it. She spent long hours helping Aidan and all of them on the arts council, building monthly reports and balancing the Foundation books, a thankless volunteer job that Jane said no one else wanted to do — but Ellen took it on.

The toasts continued as the evening sky turned dark. Glasses were raised again and again, and Nell listened with half an ear, observing the crowd as people came and went.

Billy was quiet tonight, Nell noticed, but his bride, Natalie, dressed in a short fitted skirt and a gauzy blouse with a scalloped collar that curled around her neck, stood at the microphone and gushed about their friend Aidan — a surprising toast since Natalie had been in Sea Harbor less than a year. Nell watched Billy as Billy watched his wife. But his thoughts seemed elsewhere and his round face was a blend of emotions Nell couldn't quite read. She hoped whatever bone he and Aidan had picked recently was forgotten now. He kept his eyes focused on his wife, his head inclined slightly, and his fingers fiddling with a thick gold chain around his neck.

"Did you get enough to eat?" Hank Jackson asked the group a while later, pulling a chair up to the table and squeezing in between Birdie and Nell. "Y'know even this menu has Aidan written all over it. Fresh shrimp. Calamari and oysters, brats and beer. Aidan could never decide if he was a New Englander or a cheesehead."

"Cheesehead?"

"Yeah — remember? He went to Madison, studied all that history stuff about art. He used to show off, sitting here with a beer, challenging the other guys on all the fine points, like who painted what, and what style, and when and all that crap. Guy was brilliant."

Ham laughed at the memories. "You're right. He was a bit of a show-off, but he knew his art."

"But old mother ocean lured him back here as soon as he had that degree in hand. He had sea fever, he used to say. Born of the sea."

Birdie put her napkin on the table. "We are all stuffed to the gills, Hank. You throw

107

a very nice funeral." She patted his hand. "Aidan would have loved this party."

Hank nodded in agreement. "Say, where's the 'willow-the-wisp' who landed in your window, Iz? I haven't met her yet, though Merry pointed her out to me yesterday when we were over at the beach. She was running as fast as a deer, her little legs pumping like I don't know what. Made you wonder what she was running from." He looked over at Nell. "My fleeting glimpse made me think she had spirit."

"I think she probably does. She's an artist. Fiber art," Nell said.

"So why isn't she here with all the artists? She hung around the cove this past weekend, Merry said, poring over that little tourist map we have, asking people questions, wandering all over the place. If she's an artist, maybe she was looking for a gallery?"

"You mean to exhibit her work?"

Hank shrugged. "What do I know? I'm not an artist. I just keep them fat and happy." He laughed at himself and then looked out over the crowd to make sure no one was waving down a waiter or had an empty pitcher on his table. "But Merry says she checked out every nook and cranny in the cove."

"Well, I don't know about that, but who

knows? I'll ask her. I'm sure we could find someone interested in showing her work in the cove."

Izzy leaned into the conversation, propping an elbow on the table. "It's a good idea, but I don't think it'll happen. Willow made it pretty clear she wasn't going to hang around long. It's funny, though, because I think she loves the ocean. She talks about it as if . . . I don't know, as if this is what she's been looking for." She shook her head and frowned. "I'm not making much sense, am I? She told us why she came, and that was just to visit the shop. And then move on."

"She came all this way just to talk at the Seaside Studio?" Cass asked. "Weird. Not that the Studio isn't worth it —" She lifted one dark brow until she drew a smile from Izzy.

"She's just young and carefree," Birdie said. "She wants to see the world. A free spirit, like our Sam here." Birdie patted Sam's tan arm. Sam's camera and photo shoots took him across the globe, but in recent months he'd come back to Sea Harbor more and more frequently. "He's become a homing pigeon," Birdie had suggested to Nell. "And maybe home means being where Izzy is?" The thought was not an unfavorable one, not to Ben or Nell or the knitting group who worked diligently at planning one another's lives.

"Young and carefree?" Sam laughed. "Not so much, Birdie. And I'm actually about to become a homeowner for the first time in my forty years. How's that for trashing your young and fly-by-night theory?"

"You found a place?" Nell said. "Wonderful, Sam."

"Yes, it's that," Sam said, wrapping an arm around Izzy's shoulders. "Izzy here helped me. She found it entertaining to find a place I couldn't resist or afford."

"Just like my Merry over there," Hank said, inclining his head toward his young wife. Merry stood near the outside bar, her blond ponytail waving as she greeted guests and bid others good night. Merry was a lovable live wire who loved the good life — and was determined to make Hank provide it for her.

"A Realtor friend found the place," Izzy said. "You'll love it. It's set back a little from the beach, but not much, and it's perfect for Sam. Airy, open, simple."

"I won't even touch why open, airy, and simple are perfect for me," Sam said. "But in spite of Izzy's description, it's nice. Spacious, a room I can use for a studio. Skylights. And a deck big enough for all of us to watch the sunset with a Ben Endicott martini in hand. I'll let you know when Izzy says I'm settled. Right now a couple of Adirondack chairs and a mattress mark the spot."

"There's Ben," Birdie said, breaking in. She pointed toward the staircase and frowned. "And he's not alone."

Nell peered over the tops of heads to the deck steps. "Who's with him?"

"The world. He's carrying it on his shoulders."

Nell stood and saw then what Birdie saw: the lean to Ben's broad shoulders, the slow stride, and the incline of his head. He looked weary. Shopworn, as Birdie would say.

Over here, Nell said silently.

And as if she'd shouted the words across the sea, Ben spotted her and made his way around a milling group of people, thinning now as some folks headed to their cars or bicycles, making their way back home.

Ben still wore a jacket and tie, signs of his late-afternoon meeting. He sat down and shrugged out of the jacket, slipping it over the back of the chair. He tugged on his tie until the knot loosened, then looked around the table, offering a tired smile. "It's been a day," he said.

Sam pushed a scotch and water in front of him. "Looks like this might suit you better. You okay, Ben?"

Ben nodded. "Sure, Sam, thanks. Life is never simple, you know? Even in death."

"Your meeting was about Aidan?"

"Yes. I had asked the police about a will because Aidan had asked me the other night to meet him to go over it. They found one at his place, and the chief wanted to talk to me about it. It's a murder case, even though we don't want to think about that part of it. But wills are important in investigations."

"And?" Nell searched Ben's still-handsome face. The shadow of a day-old beard darkened his chin and his chestnut brown eyes held concern, though Nell couldn't intuit the source, not like she sometimes could.

"It's not a secret," Ben said. "A reporter got ahold of it, too. You'll read about it in the paper soon, I'm sure."

Sam leaned forward, his arms resting on the table. "Aidan owned the gallery," Sam said. "But I never got the feeling there was much more."

"The land is worth a lot, Sam, as well as the two buildings. And Aidan was frugal. I don't think he ever spent a dime except on his beloved Hinckley. He was a smart investor, too. There's a sizable estate."

"But that isn't what's causing the furrow in your forehead." Nell looked at Ben in a way she had that prevented him from looking away.

He wrapped an arm around the back of her chair, his hand dropping to her shoulder and his thumb gently rubbing the back of her neck. "No," he said. "Frankly, I'm not sure how worried to be."

"Whom did Aidan leave it to?" Izzy asked. "He's had lots of relationships, so I don't think there'd be an inheritance heading in that direction."

"Maybe the Arts Foundation?" Cass wrapped her hands around a frosty mug of beer. "I could see him doing that. He loved this place and the Foundation does good things."

"Or Father Northcutt's causes," Birdie suggested.

Ben shook his head. "No, none of the above."

He shifted in his chair and took a long swallow of scotch, then set the squat glass down in front of him and stared at it as if it were a crystal ball.

"Here's the scoop," he said, lifting his eyes to his circle of friends. "Aidan Peabody left every last dime — his studio, his gallery, his sailboat, his art collection. The cove land, and that noisy old Jeep he drove around town. He left every inch of it to Izzy's trespasser, to our houseguest. He left it all to Willow Adams."

CHAPTER 9

"Willow!"

The single word rose up into the warm evening sky, propelled by an orchestra of voices. It was followed almost immediately by a barrage of questions, most of which Ben had no answer for, especially the biggest question of all — *Why Willow?*

"We aren't sure why, and we called around, but didn't find Willow, so we couldn't get any clarification from her. She told someone she was going running with Brendan, so I drove along the beach, but it's pitch-black tonight, and I couldn't see much of anything. It's hot enough to fry eggs on the sand, so I presumed they gave up and went off to drink beer or something."

"Did you check the guesthouse?" Nell asked quietly. Willow surely wouldn't leave, not without a good-bye. But suddenly the ominous thought caused Nell's heart to skip a beat.

"We think alike, m'love. Her things are still here."

Nell breathed normally again. "There is probably an easy explanation for this, a mistake, most likely. Willow didn't even know Aidan. She said as much when I suggested she come with us tonight. 'Why should I celebrate the life of a stranger?' were her words. I'm sure it's a mistake."

"Maybe." Ben swallowed the rest of the scotch and water in a single gulp and set the glass down on the table. The ice clanked against the sides. "Maybe not."

They all knew that Ben's friend Chief Jerry Thompson was anxious to put an end to this investigation. And the whole force was hungry for a solid lead. They would jump on this, surely.

"Well, there's an explanation," Birdie said. "There always is. Willow will fill us in, I'm sure."

"When we find her," Ben said.

"She isn't lost, Ben. She went running, that's all. And then, just as you said, they probably got a drink or a sandwich."

Nell's words were slightly clipped. The tone in Ben's voice bothered her, as if Willow had done something wrong by being the recipient of someone's will. "Why is there any concern, supposing this inheritance is legitimate? Aidan always has supported new artists, just like you two do." She looked over at Jane and Ham. "Maybe he saw Willow's work and liked it — Aidan did random things all the time."

"You're right," Ham said. "Aidan has helped other young people. But . . ."

Izzy jumped in. "This could be a wonderful thing for Willow."

"Yes, one could think that," Ben said.

"But," Izzy said. "Uncle Ben, I can read you like a book. There's a huge *but* at the end of that sentence. And I don't like it a single bit."

"I want to talk to her, that's all. Before . . . well, soon."

"Before what, Ben?"

"Before the police do. I'm all for Willow inheriting money. She looks like she doesn't have much. But when an unexpected person inherits this much money, people wonder. Especially the police. We all have to face it. Someone killed Aidan Peabody."

Ben paused and looked around the table at each of them, and then he went on. "The suspicion and rumors percolating over this murder are bad for every aspect of life in Sea Harbor — business and beach living, and most certainly selling art in Canary Cove. This all means the police are very anxious to find out who killed Aidan so the town can be relieved of this burden and move on. And whether you like it or not, whether you agree with the police or not, inheriting every last dime Aidan Peabody had is certainly a motive for murder that they can't ignore."

The group fell silent. From the corners of the deck, large industrial fans hummed into the silence and pushed warm air across the grim faces. In the distance, waves lapped languorously against the rocks and the sound of late-night vessels pierced through the hot, muggy air.

Nell peeled her knit top from her damp skin. "So the police think Willow killed Aidan Peabody?" Nell said. Her voice was flat. "That's what you're saying."

"They think it's a possibility, and they're anxious to talk to her," Ben said.

"Well, good. Hopefully they'll talk to Willow, realize she had no earthly reason for killing a man she didn't know, that the will was some kind of a mistake, and that she's here to talk about yarn art. And that will be that."

Jane started to speak up. "I think Willow knew him," she began.

But the blinking of lights brought their attention away from the conversation, and they looked up to see Hank waving at them from behind the deck bar, a dishrag in his hands. "Sorry, folks. Time for this body to close up shop and hit the hay."

"Thanks, Hank." Ben, Ham, and Sam pulled bills from their pockets and stuck them under the salt and pepper shakers as the others pushed out chairs and picked up purses. Sam gathered the remaining glasses and carried them over to the bar.

"No problem," Hank said. "You folks are my favorites, and I'd let the whole bunch of you stay till breakfast if you were enjoying yourselves. But Merry is nudging me from inside. And when the wife is anxious to head home, well, you know how it is."

Nell laughed. "You go on home, Hank. We're as good as gone. We didn't realize we were closing the place down."

"Sounds like you were having a heated discussion?"

"Anything would seem heated tonight," Nell said, sidestepping Hank's question.

But as they said their good-byes in the parking lot and went off into the night, it wasn't the heat that pressed down on the group of friends. It was the plethora of questions about a young woman barely large enough to shoulder them.

CHAPTER 10

Nell found sleep difficult.

Beside her, Ben tossed and turned until the white sheets became tangled around both their limbs and the night air dampened their bodies and bedsheets. Finally, when Ben's breathing slowed, Nell slipped out of bed and down the back stairs to the kitchen.

Warm milk never soothed her during restless nights like this, but a cup of lemon balm tea and a few minutes on the deck often brought the sleep that was just beyond her grasp.

An unexpected northern breeze whistled softly through the pine trees and Nell looked up, watching the slow-motion movement of the heavy branches. Thursday would not be so hot, Nell thought. And that was a good thing. But the day was sure to bring things more difficult to deal with than weather. She slipped down onto a chaise and sipped the tea, willing her mind to settle down.

There was nothing more to say or do tonight, as Birdie had wisely reminded them. It was late, tomorrow was another day, and by the time the morrow ended, Willow might have straightened out the whole thing.

Or not.

The disjointed thoughts — none of which had resolution — became jumbled in Nell's mind and she willed them to stop. She wanted to sleep. After all, she barely knew this young woman. But they had all somehow *connected* to Willow in a visceral kind of way. Birdie, Izzy, and Cass had felt it, too. And with a certainty that defied reason, Nell knew that Willow had not murdered their friend.

She looked down through the trees at the quiet cottage. The lights were out, the blinds pulled. Willow was probably asleep. Nell hoped she had known to push the windows up to cool the small bedroom.

It was odd. She didn't know where Willow came from or even why she had hitchhiked to Cape Ann, other than to visit the Seaside Knitting Studio to talk about her art. And now that seemed a frivolous reason — one that wouldn't bear the weight of what had happened since she arrived.

All she knew was that Willow was an artist — a talented one — and that she had enormous eyes that looked carefully into your own when you talked to her. That was it. And yet the protective instinct had grabbed all four knitters, and Nell suspected Willow would not walk out of their lives quite as quietly as she had come in — asleep in a storefront window.

The lemon tea slid down her throat easily, and the stillness of the night seeped into her body, easing away the turmoil of the day. In the near distance, waves lapped against the smooth shore of Sandpiper Beach. *Night sounds run deepest,* she thought, sinking into the blackness around her.

A sudden sound startled Nell from her musings, and she pressed against the back of the chair, peering into the darkness. A twig, probably, broken by the breeze. Or, more likely, some broken branches that she and Ben had yet to clean out had fallen from the giant pines.

Nell took a sip of tea and settled back into the chair. One thing Nell rarely felt in Sea Harbor was fear. She might be anxious if Izzy had a problem with the store, or worried before Ben went in for a doctor's appointment. She'd be concerned if a neighbor or friend was having personal problems, and she experienced joy and delight and happiness of some sort most of the time. But she was almost never afraid.

Again, the crackling of branches stirred the night air, cutting through the silence. And then the murmur of a voice, and Nell realized that a figure was walking slowly down the flagstone pathway to the guest cottage at the back of the Endicott backyard.

Willow, she thought, and instinct drew her forward in the chair, ready to call out to be sure the young woman was all right, to offer her some nighttime tea. Or to talk.

But the deeper tone of a second voice stopped her.

Nell watched as the dark figures, arms wrapped around each other, passed in front of the low solar lamps lighting the pathway. They walked on down to the cottage, talking to each other in soft, muted voices.

Nell hesitated, not wanting to get up and go inside for fear of frightening them and creating an awkward moment. But sitting in the darkness, a ghost in the night, was also uncomfortable and a seeming invasion of their privacy.

Before Nell had a chance to make a choice, the couple paused at the edge of the cottage, just beneath the low security lamp attached beneath the eaves. And before Nell could turn away, Brendan Slattery's tall figure bent low over Willow's diminutive form and wrapped her closely in a hug that spoke of a familiarity Nell knew she had no right viewing. They embraced for a long moment, and then the two figures slipped noiselessly through the door and were lost to sight. Only the sudden soft yellow haze of a light beyond the window convinced Nell that Willow had, indeed, come home for the night.

CHAPTER 11

Nell was still in the sleeveless tank top and light knit pants she had worn to bed when Izzy appeared at 22 Sandswept Lane.

Birdie had arrived minutes earlier and was sitting with Nell at the kitchen table, a mug of coffee in front of her. Her short white hair was mussed from riding up the hill on her bike, and she raked her small hands through it, seeking some order.

"Birdie, what are you doing here?" Izzy breezed in without announcement. "It's not even eight o'clock." Izzy poured herself a glass of water from the sink. Her sun-streaked hair was pulled back in a ponytail and looped carelessly through the band of a Red Sox cap. Her tank top and bare tan shoulders were damp and shiny.

"Is Willow up yet? Did you see her last night? She's here, isn't she?"

"Good morning to you, too, Izzy," Birdie said.

Izzy laughed and Nell shook her head. "Not up — as far as I know."

Nell had told Ben that Willow had come in last night — early morning, really — with Brendan, but there was no reason to spread the details around. Nell had gone to bed herself, immediately after Willow and Brendan went into the cottage, and she had no idea when — or if — Brendan left. But, as Ben had said earlier that morning, Willow was going to need friends — and Brendan Slattery was a decent choice.

"Don't you work today, sweetie?" Nell asked.

"Mae opens the shop on Thursday so I can run." Izzy leaned over Nell's shoulder and peered through the kitchen window, looking beyond the deck and down the sloping lawn toward the cottage. "You can't see anything from here, can you?"

Nell reached up to touch Izzy's arm with her fingertips. "Izzy, Izzy."

"Well, I hope she's okay, that's all. I feel responsible in a way. After all, Willow showed up here because I invited her."

"Maybe," Nell said.

"What do you mean, *maybe?*" Izzy straightened up and pulled out a chair. Her nylon running shorts slipped across the wooden surface.

126

"She might have had other reasons, too." It was Ben, walking down the back stairs and across the kitchen, fresh from a shower and dressed in his summer uniform of khaki shorts and a knit shirt. "But whatever the reason, we'll get it straightened out today. Sleep has a way of leveling concerns, and I think once we talk to Willow, we'll have some answers."

"You never told me where the will was found, Ben," Nell said.

"That's interesting," Ben said, "but not unlike Aidan. The police found it in one of his sculptures — that carved figure of the old fisherman that stood by his desk in the studio. You've seen it, Nell."

"I have," Nell said. "I believe you tried to buy it."

Ben laughed. "It's a great old guy. Aidan captured the fisherman stance perfectly. He has this wise, knowing, longing-for-the-sea look. If you pull on the fellow's gnarled hand the front of the wooden sculpture opens up, and Aidan kept papers and things on the shelves inside. There was an envelope with my name on it. Inside it was the will. He'd even gotten a couple of fishermen over in Gloucester to witness it."

"So that's what Aidan wanted to talk to you about," Nell said.

Ben nodded. "I've talked to Aidan a few times about financial things and this was an update, I guess."

"There is no rest for the kindhearted, Ben Endicott," Birdie joked.

"I believe the word is 'wicked,' Birdie," Ben said.

"No matter." Birdie's fingers waved the air. "But it is a good thing you do, my dear friend."

Nell smiled at Birdie, knowing she had sought Ben's advice on an occasion or two. And the Canary Cove artists, especially, seemed to prefer Ben's advice to a lawyer with LTD behind his name and an office with a polished lobby.

"What does the paper say, Nell?" Ben asked.

"Not much. It must have been too late last night when news of Aidan's heir leaked out. There's talk about other things, though — the problems with the art council, Aidan's many romances, that sort of thing. I am sure the news will be leaking out in dribs and drabs. Mary Pisano seems to be devoting her chatty little column entirely to solving the murder."

"Suspects," Birdie said. "Everyone wants suspects."

In the distance, Nell heard the sound of a

128

bike crunching on gravel. She looked up and saw Willow pedaling down the side pathway toward the front of the house. She was alone and looked determined to get somewhere quickly.

"Ben, it's Willow. Let's not let her find out about her inheritance from some rumor making its way around Coffee's or wherever she's headed in such a hurry."

Ben moved quickly toward the front door, opened it, and called to her. Minutes later, Willow appeared in the family room, her backpack hanging from one shoulder. She lowered it to a lump on the ground and cast a puzzled look at Nell. "What's up?"

"First, have some coffee," Nell said.

Izzy beat her to the counter and filled a mug halfway, then poured in half-and-half until the coffee turned a rich mocha color. "You seem like a cream kind of person."

Willow smiled, her eyes still holding questions. "I was on my way to the knitting studio, Izzy. I thought I could help you so we can get this over with, like maybe Saturday. Then I need to leave. I'm moving on."

"You may need to stick around for a bit, Willow," Ben said. "There's something we need to talk about."

"I knew there was something going on, with all of you sitting here like this, like a jury or something. What happened? Did the police decide to press charges because I slept in your window, Izzy? That was so dumb of me. Could Purl be my defense? She lured me in." She attempted a smile. "If I go to jail, Purl goes with me."

"No, of course not. No charges."

Ben cleared his throat. "Willow, we found out last night that Aidan Peabody — the man who died last Saturday —"

"The man who was killed," Willow said.

Nell looked over at Willow, surprised at her tone. It was more curious than the expected low, sad tone people used with deaths — planned or otherwise. But then, she reminded herself, Willow was a stranger in this town.

Ben nodded. "Aidan left a will."

Willow leaned her back against the center island, her sandals planted firmly on the floor. She looked at Ben and held her coffee mug up to her lips so the steam rose in front of her face. "Is that unusual? People do that, right?" she said. "Most artists are starving though, I guess. His place was an awful mess. He probably didn't have much."

"Actually, he had plenty," Ben said.

Willow's expression didn't change. She leveled a look at Ben and said, "Oh?"

"And he left it all to you, Willow. Every

130

last penny."

Willow's mouth fell open but no words came out. The only sound was the coffee cup that slipped from her fingers and shattered across the hardwood kitchen floor. Nell, standing near the island, was the closest to Willow. She reached out instinctively and, in one swift movement, was able to cushion her fall as Willow's body slid down the side of the island and onto the floor in a silent, graceful faint.

CHAPTER 12

Nell's first thought was to call the Endicott family physician, Doc Hamilton.

But in the next minute, Ben scooped Willow's limp body from the floor without a puff of exertion and settled her on the couch in his den. Almost immediately her eyelids began to flutter, then pulled open to look blankly into the four faces staring down at her.

And then her eyes closed again, by design this time, Nell could see. She was blocking them all out briefly — a temptation Nell could completely understand.

"Willow, honey, I'm leaving a glass of water on the table," she whispered. "And we're in the next room if you need us."

A slight nod indicated consciousness, and the group moved into the kitchen.

Minutes later Chief Jerry Thompson showed up in a police car, but without the circling lights that brought neighbors onto their porches.

"He did it as a favor to us," Ben told Nell a short while later.

Izzy had left before the chief arrived, sprinting the few short blocks to her own home to shower and dress for work, and Birdie had climbed onto her bike and headed to the retirement home where she taught tap dancing on Thursdays. In the den, Chief Jerry Thompson sat with Willow behind closed doors.

"A favor, Ben?" Nell frowned. After fainting the way she had, Willow needed some orange juice, a spinach omelet, and some toast with jam, not the chief of police.

"He could have sent Tommy Porter or some other rookie to ask her to come to the station to talk. But he didn't."

"But why does he need to talk to her at all? Being in someone's will is not a murderous offense."

But Nell wasn't asking a real question, and after more than a quarter century of being married, Ben knew that, too, and held his silence. She was protesting a situation she found awful, whether valid or not — that was all.

Willow was clearly surprised to be Aidan's heir. Nell was surprised — they all were. In fact, it made no sense, and Nell would have

133

preferred being the one to talk with Willow first about why a stranger would leave her all his earthly belongings, not the chief of the Sea Harbor police, as nice a man as Jerry Thompson was.

Ben said he'd handle the situation in the den and show the chief out when he was finished, and Nell gratefully escaped upstairs to finally take her morning shower. The clean spray refreshed her body and her spirit, and after rubbing her hair briskly, she felt far more ready to face the day. She glanced in the bedroom mirror and pushed her shoulder-length hair into some sort of order. Gray flecks melted into the warm honey brown waves like cinnamon and powdered sugar. Every once in a while Nell considered asking Mary Jane at the salon to put some college brown — as her friends called it — into her hair. But she never quite went through with it, deciding she was more comfortable letting come what might. Ben liked it — and they matched better, he said, his own flecked sideburns warmed with white highlights. But most likely it was avoiding the fuss of having to do one more maintenance task as she aged. And Nell liked keeping those at a minimum.

She pulled on a slim pair of tan cropped pants and a cornflower blue cotton sweater that Izzy had knit for her, and headed down the back stairs. She'd insist on making the spinach-and-feta omelet for Willow. They'd sit on the deck and talk. And things would fall in place.

But when Nell walked into the kitchen and family area, the house was eerily quiet.

The chief was gone, and a glance out the window told her his police car was blessedly absent from the driveway as well.

But Willow was gone, too — and the old bike she was borrowing no longer lay on the lawn where she'd dropped it when Ben called her in.

And Ben — much to Nell's chagrin — Ben was gone, too.

Sometimes men have no sense, she thought. *He should never have allowed Willow to get back on that bike without eating some breakfast.*

But Ben had saved himself somewhat from Nell's displeasure by leaving a sticky note on the kitchen island, right next to the portable phone. He had a meeting over at the yacht club, it read. And Willow had gone out to Brendan's cottage to have breakfast with him. She had assured Ben before she left that she was fine, after drinking a full glass of orange juice to satisfy him.

A follow-up phone call, pulling Ben briefly

from his meeting, gave Nell the details he had neglected to address. Willow had told the chief she had absolutely no idea why Aidan Peabody left her anything in his will. She had never met the man, she'd said. And, frankly, she didn't really want any of his things — they could auction them off and give the money to a children's foundation or something, she told Jerry.

Nor, Willow said, did she murder the man. A ridiculous suggestion, she had told the chief in very clear, somewhat colorful terms.

But in spite of her bluster, Ben thought he saw a dampness in the corner of her eyes. And he had no idea what that was about.

The interview, Ben said, had left Jerry Thompson frustrated. But it had brought color back to Willow's cheeks, lit her eyes with fire, and by the time she set off on the bike, she had enough energy in her small body to ride from Massachusetts to Michigan or Wisconsin or wherever the hell she was from.

Grilled shrimp satay with a light, tangy peanut sauce, toasted pearl couscous with lemon basil, tomatoes, and chunks of fresh mozzarella cheese from Harry Garozzo's deli. That should do it, Nell thought. Birdie would arrive with chilled wine, and Cass had already put the pistachio ice cream from Scoopers into the freezer.

The food wouldn't lessen the drama of the day, Nell knew, but it would definitely help. And Thursday night knitting without food and drink simply wasn't Thursday night knitting.

Nell walked over to the wall of windows at the back end of the studio's knitting room and looked out over the harbor and the sea beyond. This view from Izzy's shop usually brought her peace on hectic days. From here she could see all the way to the breakwater and protected beach of the yacht club at the northern edge of the town. A tentacle of land below it jutted out into the sea and held a park that was special to the whole town, Anja Angelina Park — or Angus' Place, as the locals called it.

And a little closer in, the shore swung around like a jump rope and embraced Canary Cove, its narrow roads dotted with the studios and galleries. She could see the old rickety dock below the Artist's Palate. It looked empty today, though from this distance, Nell couldn't really tell. Several small motorboats, probably belonging to artists from the cove, were moored to the side of the dock closest to her and bobbed in the water. For a minute, she imagined

Aidan sitting at the end of it with Jane and Ham, their legs hanging over the edge, cold beers in hand as they mused about life, art, and love — and funerals.

Had Aidan thought of his will while sitting out there with his good friends? Had he entertained the thought of leaving everything he owned and had worked a lifetime for to a strange young woman named Willow? Maybe she had come into his studio that day as she wandered around Canary Cove. Maybe he'd looked at her with those deep, penetrating eyes — and he saw in the young woman the seeds of a talented artist, one without obvious means — and on a whim, he wrote her into his will. It was not a gesture most people she knew would make — but Aidan marched to a different drummer. There was no telling what Aidan Peabody would do.

Nell sat down next to Purl on the padded seat below two open windows. The cat was curled up tight and looked like a ball of calico yarn. Absently, she scratched Purl behind her ears, thinking about Willow and half listening to Izzy and Cass in the next room — the cotton room, Izzy called it, because three walls were filled from floor to ceiling with white cubbies crammed full of soft and nubby, bright and muted skeins of cotton yarn. A new shipment of a cotton-silk blend had arrived today — an event not unlike Christmas morning for Izzy — and the two women were emptying the packing crates and filling the cubes, but not without touching and smelling and rubbing the fibers against their cheeks.

It was an addiction, Nell thought with some pleasure. There was far more to knitting and purling than making a sweater or scarf or pair of socks. Far more.

"There you are." Izzy came into the room, taking the three steps beneath the archway as one. Her arms were filled with twisted skeins of yarn, rich blends of cotton and silk in shades of peridot, cornflower, and all the colors of a summer rose garden. Cass followed close behind and immediately headed over to the table, where Nell had set out a basket of pita chips and a round of creamy Camembert.

"Oh, my," Nell breathed, taking in the beautiful colors of the yarn. She got up and walked over to touch the vibrant yarn.

"I know, Aunt Nell. Aren't they beautiful?" Izzy dropped the yarn on the coffee table, then sat down onto the couch and began lining up the skeins. "They're all hand-dyed. It's so scrumptious you won't be able to keep your hands off it. The colors are unbelievable. I brought an assortment for you to see, but it's the peridot-and-cobalt blend that I think you should use for your next project."

"Use?" Nell had more unfinished projects than she could count — a knitter's badge of honor, Izzy told her — but she was trying very hard to finish the blue cashmere scarf for Ben and a wool shawl for Birdie's birthday. The shawl would give Birdie some warmth during the long Sea Harbor winter — something to wrap around her shoulders as she curled up in Sonny Favazza's den, Birdie's favorite room in the seaside estate Sonny left her. And then there was the sweater she wanted to make for Izzy. "What am I going to use it for?" She braced herself for Izzy's answer, suspecting strongly another project was less than a few inches away from her.

"I think it'll be perfect to use for Willow's sweater. It will be all the colors of the sea blended together. This will be perfect, and I know she will love it."

"Willow?"

"Don't you think so? We can take turns working on it if you're too busy — our stitch tension is about the same. It'll be a nice reminder of Sea Harbor — and a thank-you for sharing her art with us."

"She's still willing to talk to your customers?"

"Well, I'm not sure, actually. We were going to meet today, but she never showed up. I guess maybe she won't want to, with all this craziness going on in her life. But Sam saw her today — she was over at Brendan Slattery's house. It's right near Sam's new place — he was having it inspected and ran into her and Brendan bringing in some groceries. Anyway, she told Sam she might join us tonight."

"So she stayed with Brendan all day," Nell mused, half to herself. She had walked down to the guesthouse several times, worried about Willow after the morning's trauma, though Ben had assured her that the Willow who drove off on the bike looked like she could handle just about anything that came her way. A beach house was probably a good place for her, Nell thought, away from the speculations that had already begun to spread around the town.

Cass looked over from the table, where she was cutting a fat wedge of Camembert. "So another mouth for our knitting feast?" She raised a questioning brow.

"Nell always brings too much food — you know that, Cass. Name the Thursday we didn't have leftovers."

141

"But the leftovers are the best part of it," Cass grumped. "They're my Friday lunch and dinner."

Nell laughed at Cass' feeble protest. For all her complaints, she'd be the first to invite someone to join them if there was a need. Though Izzy, Cass, Birdie, and Nell had met in the back room of Izzy's studio almost from the shop's beginning and *were* the Thursday Night Knitting Club, they never turned anyone away who needed company or a brief hiatus from their life. And they hadn't yet been short on food, even when Cass went back for her usual seconds and sometimes thirds.

The group itself had formed by serendipity — a chance meeting on a lovely summer night of four women who shared a passion for knitting.

Well, that wasn't exactly true, Nell thought. Cass had clearly come in that night because she smelled the lemon seafood pasta. Nell had brought it in for Izzy, who was working late. Cass' own cupboard held a scanty collection of canned soup and ramen noodles, and the Thursday night feast had changed her life forever, she claimed. And even her knitting had changed — after a few seasons of knitting scarves and hats for nearly every fisherman in Sea Harbor and one wrap for her mother, Cass was hooked — and maybe ready to move on to socks, though the thought of turning heels still caused a slight tremor in the lobster-woman's hands.

Cass carried the plate of cheese over to the table and sat down in one of the leather chairs — one of Ben Endicott's contributions to the back room after Nell redid his den. "Actually, I hope she comes. We need to get the scoop on what's going on."

"Scoop?" Birdie Favazza walked down the three steps into the knitting room. "You must be talking about dear little Willow. Even the retirement home folks are talking about Aidan's will. Goodness." Birdie shook her head sadly. "It certainly gives Willow a motive for his murder, though I don't think that little thing could hurt a fly."

Birdie moved over to the fireplace and set her knitting bag in front of it. She pulled two bottles of chilled pinot grigio out of her backpack and displayed them on the square table in the middle of the sitting area.

"Light lemony-citrus flavor. Refreshing," she said, giving her weekly wine review. "My Sonny used to order this from Italy by the case." Though Sonny Favazza had died years before, he had been — and would always be — the light of Birdie's life. Her true and forever love, she said. All subsequent husbands knew the rules of courtship and marriage early on — they could live in the three-story Favazza home — a grand stone structure that commanded a sweeping view of the sea and town of Sea Harbor. And Birdie would keep the name Favazza. All or nothing was Birdie's credo.

"When is Willow coming?" Birdie continued. "I see our Cass is on her way to devouring the Camembert." She leaned down and pulled a half-finished cap from her knitting bag.

"There's another in the fridge," Cass said, glowering at Birdie.

"I'm just teasing you. A sign of great affection." Birdie held the soft cap up. It was a grassy green head-hugging hat, worked in soft cashmere with accents of fleecy eyelash yarn. It was bright and eye-catching, and as silky as a newly sprouted lawn.

"Birdie, that's just wonderful." Izzy leaned over and touched the soft fly-away yarn. "It will be our demo for my next cap class. You're the best."

"It's cheery," Nell said. "It's perfect."

"I already have a dozen people signed up for the next head-hugging class. I think we'll have enough caps to fill the whole oncology center by summer's end."

Nell fingered the cap and thought about the good things Izzy's shop had provided for Sea Harbor residents in the scant year and a half it'd been open. A place to be together and share one another's burdens, to exercise that instinctive need to help someone else.

When Harriet Brandley, wife of the bookstore owner next door to Izzy's shop, was being treated for breast cancer and lost her hair in the dead of a Sea Harbor winter, the Seaside knitters kept her comfortable and her head warm with a collection of brightly colored knit hats — some for bedtime, others for home wear and about town, and even a fancy golden cap for the annual Christmas party.

Seeing the caps lying around the back room, customers signed up by the dozens to help. And the cap class became a regular event in the Seaside Studio back room. They'd explored other groups online, collected patterns, and instantly felt connected to women all over the country keeping bare heads warm.

"So you'll do the sweater?" Izzy asked, her non sequitur going unchallenged. "Here's a pattern I thought that would be perfect. It's a fisherman knit — kind of — but more delicate and slouchy because of the fleecy blend. I think it will be absolutely perfect. And maybe you can do a hat if there's any left over."

Izzy handed it all over to Nell — needles and all — ready to go.

Nell looked at the picture and read through the pattern. She looked up. "It's wonderful. You're absolutely right. It will be the perfect gift to remind her of the good parts of her stay in Sea Harbor." The sweater was a little longer than usual, and would be soft and comfortable to wrap up in on cold winter days. The broad waistband was worked up in a rickrack pattern for definition, and the main body design was a combination of cables — sand pattern, horseshoe, and shadow — with stockinette stitch in between. But it was the yarn itself that sold Nell. It would not only look amazing on Willow with her dark, thick hair and eyes; it would be a joy to knit. She let it slip through her fingers, the silky soft blend bringing with it a kind of comfort. This yarn and the lovely pattern it would grow into were about as far away from thoughts of murder as Nell could possibly imagine. Izzy was right. It was the perfect project — and Ben's scarf and Birdie's shawl would get done, too — all in good time. Nell measured out a stretch of yarn and began casting on for her gauge.

Voices in the outer room and the sound of Birkenstocks on the wooden floor signaled Willow's arrival. Nell smiled to herself, strangely comforted by the fact that Willow had, in fact, come.

Willow walked down the steps and looked around the room. Her dark hair flew in wild tangles around flushed cheeks. Her voice was tentative. "Mae said I should just come on back."

"That's exactly what you should do. Welcome, Willow." Nell put her knitting down and walked across the room to give her a quick hug. She wasn't quite sure yet if Willow was a hugging kind of person, but no matter. Living in the Endicott guesthouse for almost a week and fainting on Nell's kitchen floor surely granted Nell some kind of hugging rights.

Willow allowed the embrace, but Nell could feel the tension in her small frame. She was tight as the spring on Pete and Cass' lobster traps. Nell held her apart and looked into deep black eyes.

"You've had quite a day, sweetie. Come, sit, and have a glass of Birdie's pinot grigio. It will cure all what ails you."

Willow's brows lifted into an impromptu line of bangs. "I think it might take a whole case to do that, Nell." She sat down beside Izzy and dropped her backpack to the floor. She looked around the room again.

"This is the first time I've seen this room without a crowd of Izzy's customers milling around." She took in the windows opening to the sea, the clean white walls and bookcases filled with books, magazines, an iPod playing soft strains of an old Melissa Etheridge song. The heavy wooden table, pocked from needles and scissors and the press of pencils on patterns, stood in the middle and Willow walked over to it, running her fingers along the surface.

"What a friendly place. It makes me want to curl up and never leave. I know why Purl loves it here." She looked over at the sleeping cat on the window seat. "I think I want her life."

"The Seaside Knitting Studio is a welcoming refuge for Sea Harbor knitters," Nell said.

"Even the UPS guy likes coming back here and having a cup of coffee," Cass added. "Though making coffee isn't exactly Izzy's forte, but the man in brown doesn't seem to mind."

"Quiet, Cass," Izzy said. "Mae has pretty much taken that over. Our coffee has vastly improved."

"Well, this whole place is cool," Willow said.

As if on cue, Purl, having bided her time on the window seat, moved across the room and leapt up into Willow's lap.

They all laughed. Purl to the rescue, breaking the awkward tension of a room filled with questions but dealing with pleasantries to cover it up. "Well, it looks like our Purl wouldn't mind a roommate," Birdie said. She leaned over and poured Willow a glass of golden pinot. "And here you are, my dear. We don't have a case at the ready, but one glass is a fine start."

"So . . . you want to come in on Saturday and talk to folks?" Izzy asked, pulling out a pair of buttery yellow socks that she was knitting up as a demo for the next Sumptuous Socks class. "We get so many people in here on Saturday that we wouldn't need to advertise." Tentacles of soft yarn trailed across her lap.

Purl looked over with interest, then settled her head back on Willow's lap.

"I dunno, Iz. I don't know if that's a good idea."

Nell watched as Willow reached over, as knitters do, and touched the squishy cashmere socks. Her face registered the pleasure of fingers on exquisite yarn.

149

"Willow, we're friends here," Nell said. "You're safe." The words came out without thought.

But the effect on the young woman — curled up like Purl, her Birks abandoned on the floor and her T-shirt sporting a faded image of the Beatles — was unexpected.

Willow's forehead wrinkled first, and in the next instant, huge tears filled her black eyes and began to roll down her cheeks in rivers, dripping from her chin and dampening the worn shirt.

The four women leaned slightly forward, each ready to take away the sorrow that filled the young woman's eyes.

"Dear," Nell said.

Izzy's arm instinctively wrapped around her shoulders.

Willow looked at the four women surrounding her like a fortress. "I didn't kill him," she said.

"Of *course* you didn't," Birdie answered in a tone that would have melted a prosecutor in one robust swoop. She handed Willow a tissue and repeated her words like a mantra, impressing it on each of them. "Of course you didn't kill him."

Willow took the tissue and shook her head. "I couldn't have killed him. I wouldn't have done that."

She brushed the tears from her cheeks with the tissue, her head shaking from side to side to emphasize the truth to her words. And then she looked up, a calmness slowly returning to her body. "I wanted to kill him. I've wanted to kill him my whole, entire life."

The women stared at her: Izzy from behind her cranberry cashmere sock and Birdie from the cast-on row of another soft cap — this one a bright canary color designed for a child. Nell set her finished gauge in her lap next to the balls of yarn that she could already picture Willow wearing.

No one said a word. They waited silently for Willow to continue.

Purl looked up into the tearstained face of the woman whose lap she had claimed and purred loudly.

Go on, it's okay, she seemed to say.

Willow looked down at Purl and her voice grew strong again.

"I couldn't have killed him. He was my father."

CHAPTER 13

The dam had burst, right there in the middle of Izzy's back room. Once Willow began talking, the words poured out.

"My mom met him in college. At least he was in college. And that's where he left her, too — in Madison, Wisconsin, in a walk-up apartment, a crummy studio that didn't even have a window. It was the only place my mom could afford. He just walked off into the night. Wham, bam, thank you, ma'am. At first my mom told me she was in college, too. But later, one of my friends told me that she heard my mom never went to college. She got mad at my grandma one day and she and a friend ran away to Madison. She was still in high school. When she got pregnant, her friend called my grandparents and told them where they were. They showed up in the middle of the night and took her back to their farm near Green Bay."

For a moment there wasn't any sound except Purl's purring. Finally Nell leaned forward, her thoughts jumbled as she tried to fit this new version of Aidan Peabody into the man she knew.

"So . . . did he . . . Aidan . . . know where she'd gone?"

Willow's narrow shoulders lifted, then dropped. "I don't know."

"Did you know your father's name?" Izzy asked.

"No, not until a couple months ago, after my grandmother died. For my whole life I heard about the man out there somewhere who had ruined my mom's life. That's what my grandparents said over and over and over. And when my mom died, Grams said that he had killed her."

It was Izzy's turn. "Killed her? Aidan Peabody killed your mom?"

Willow hesitated a minute before answering, as if she were choosing her words with care. She shifted on the couch and looked at Izzy. "Not like that. He didn't use a gun or a knife or poison. But he destroyed her life, Grams said. He took her soul."

"How old were you when your mom died, Willow?" Birdie tucked her glasses up into her hair and set the cap down on the table.

"I was six, but I remember it. It was cold

153

out, and I remember the wind blowing through the cracks and making the shutters creak. I was scared that night. Then my mom came into my room and kissed me good night. She said she loved me. And I never saw her again. My grandparents didn't think I knew what happened that night. They told me it was time for the angels to take my mom to heaven.

"But everyone knew what happened — you know how small towns are. I heard neighbors and kids on the school bus talking. I knew. My mom went out that night and she got drunk, and her car crashed into a tree. My grandparents never got over it."

Nell resisted the temptation to wrap the young woman in her arms. At that moment, Willow's pain seemed as acute as if she had lost her mother that very day.

Willow looked at the cap Birdie was knitting and touched the edging. "It's so pretty, Birdie. I'd like to make one, too. Grams had cancer."

"Well, my dear, of course you will make a cap with me," Birdie assured her.

"It looks like I'll have time." A flash of anger lit Willow's eyes, fighting against the sadness. "I wanted to leave. I don't even know why I came. I guess . . . I guess to see this . . . person. To tell him how awful he was. How he killed my mom. He needed to know what he did. He just needed to know that. And then I was going to get as far away as I could and put my life in order. But then . . ." Willow paused.

"But then he died," Nell finished.

Willow swallowed around the lump in her throat and looked up. "He's still ruining my life — isn't that the best part? The police said I can't leave, not for a while. They don't believe me, of course. They think I killed him."

"Do they know Aidan Peabody is your father, Willow?"

Willow shook her head again. "I didn't tell them. I was so mad that they would think I could kill someone that I didn't tell them anything."

"Sometimes the police have a problem sorting through things — that's true enough," Cass said. She'd been plenty annoyed with the Sea Harbor force when they took weeks to find the man pilfering her lobster traps the summer before. She leaned forward, her elbows resting on her knees and her eyes, nearly as dark as Willow's, looking at the other woman. "But they're not bad guys, Willow. We don't have a lot of murders around here. They try their best."

"And, sweetie," Birdie added, her voice

laced with common sense, "Aidan's death made you a relatively well-off young woman. In the law's eyes, that's a pretty strong motive for murdering the man. You need to face the facts that they are looking at. And then we need to show them that they are wrong."

"I didn't know he had a penny. And I don't much care. I told the police that. In a way it makes it worse that he had money."

It *did* make it worse, Nell thought, a lot worse. Though not in the way Willow meant. She was probably imagining how helpful that money would have been growing up — to her mother and to herself. To her, it was just another black mark on her father's soul. "You'll have to tell them that Aidan is your father, Willow. If you're sure about that?"

"I'm sure. I wasn't at first, not until I saw him. When I was closing up Grams' house I found some things — newspaper clippings, pictures, things that my mom had hidden away in the attic because my grandmother would probably have burned them. Grams hated this man so much, it just ate her up inside.

"I knew my father probably had some artistic ability — my mom couldn't draw a stick figure, but I doodled and painted from the time I could hold a crayon. Anyway, the clippings were about a show a while back, and there were several people on it. I don't know how my mom got it. But I did some snooping, went through every scrap of paper. I found some notes with the name 'Peab' in them. I guess they called him that in school. Peab." Willow said the name as if she were holding it, examining it, then throwing it away. "For some reason, Mom saved them."

And hid them from her mother, who would have burned them. Nell wondered about the origin of the anger in Willow's small frame against a man she never met. Was it from her mother . . . or perhaps from a grandmother — an angry bear revenging her wayward young?

"So the paper trail finally brought me here. The fact that I had a loose connection here —" Willow nodded slightly at Izzy. Her hint of a smile was warm. "That would be you, Izzy — that e-mail you sent me a while ago, though I never thought I'd be using it this way. When I got it, I was so happy — thinking someone who lived on the ocean liked my art — or even just knew about it. It was like a ticket to the world. I'd never been out of Wisconsin — but my art had. And someone had seen it. And liked it."

"Liked it a lot. Nell and I both did. That's why I e-mailed you."

"I could tell you liked it by what you said. I don't know why exactly — but that note was the best thing. I kept it. Read it when things got bad with Grams. I thought maybe, just maybe, I'd someday get out there and get to see the ocean. Maybe meet the two nice ladies who took time to look at my art. And then write me about it."

Willow paused and picked up a ball of Izzy's cashmere yarn. She touched it carefully, like a delicate flower.

Birdie and Nell continued the click of their needles, Birdie's hat narrowing as she neared the top. Nell's sweater now had a first row and soon the moss stitch would appear, lovely ribs on the wide band. The only noise in the room was the click of their needles and Purl's soft purr.

Willow went on.

"Knowing about your store somehow made it easier to show up here. I know small towns. Everyone knows everything. If I had a reason for being here, maybe people wouldn't wonder about why I'd come or notice me. It would be easier."

Easier to do what? Nell wondered. In one short week of knowing Willow, she felt sure the woman couldn't kill anyone. But growing up beneath that cloud of hatred that her grandparents had nurtured in her could certainly do awful things to one's mind.

"Do you need a lawyer, Willow?"

Willow shook her head vehemently. "No. I talked to Ben today. He was helping someone move into a house near Brendan's and we talked a bit. He told me he'd find me a lawyer if I needed one."

"Ben was helping our friend Sam," Nell said. "So Ben knows what you've told us?"

"Yes. He said I should tell the police about the relationship thing, too, that it'd be better if I told them Aidan was my father rather than them finding out on their own. He said he'd help me deal with it."

"Well, then, you're in good hands," Birdie said. Her needles were moving more slowly as the weight of Willow's story settled in. She put her knitting down, sensing the end of the story. At least for now.

"And speaking of hands, I suggest we help ourselves to Nell's feast. I, for one, am starving." She reached for her wineglass.

Cass stood up, the mention of food a reprieve from the weight of the evening.

"You'll think you've died and gone to heaven." Cass moved toward the food with a speed far greater than the lobsters that crawled into her traps.

Willow managed a small laugh at Cass' quick rush toward food. "Heaven? I'll race you, Cass."

The shrimp satay lightened the mood considerably, and though Nell was swallowing at least a dozen questions along with the couscous and shrimp, she suspected the answers would come out in their own good time. Willow seemed to trust them now. Too many questions might disturb that trust.

Izzy settled herself back on the couch, a full plate in her lap, and looked down at Willow's backpack. "You've been here a week, and I have yet to see any of your work." She picked up a wooden stick holding a marinated shrimp and dipped it into the sauce that Nell had set on the coffee table.

"I have one piece here, almost finished." Willow took a forkful of Nell's couscous and bit into a creamy chunk of fresh mozzarella, flavored with the lemon, dill, and olive oil. She wiped a small grain from the edge of her mouth. Her eyes closed and she smiled contentedly. "Amazing," she murmured. "Cass is right. Heaven. Grams was pretty much a potatoes and pressure-cooker pork cook. I never imagined food could be so tasty and light."

"The backpack," Izzy said, nudging Willow in the side.

Willow leaned over and unzipped the battered canvas bag and pulled out a mass of startling color. Brilliant blues, greens, and deep red yarn spilled from her fingers. And at the bottom, she pulled out the piece she was working on: handspun yarn fashioned into a work of art, not yet finished, but its shape already showing definition.

Nell reached over and touched a twisted row of kettle-dyed wool in as many thicknesses as shades of blue. The colors ranged from the deep blue, nearly black of ocean water at its purest, to the startling blue-green when sunlight and the ocean's microscopic plants turn the water into a turquoise blanket. Willow had used sensuous silk threads — reds, corals, and shimmering gold — to bind the yarn together into a blend that resembled, in its flowing curves and hanging strands, an octopus or jellyfish, or strands of algae or plankton.

"It's lovely, Willow." Nell traced the graceful curve of the bound yarn. Some of the strands were knit together and others, chunky and sinewy, draped from the piece gracefully.

"It's beautiful," Izzy said.

Birdie and Cass chimed in, amazed at the wondrous art coming from the beat-up backpack lying on the floor.

"Do you have other pieces?" Nell asked.

"I thought about doing a series about sand and sea. Weird, huh? I've never seen the sea. But it was in me somehow. Something trying to get out."

"You don't need to be giving a talk to my customers." Izzy rose from the couch and took her empty plate over to the coffee table. "Lots of people need to see these."

Cass got up to help, dropping a half-finished bouclé hat on the chair behind her. Once Cass discovered that the handwoven yarn hid her mistakes like a bleach pen on coffee spills, she never went back to fine wool for the hats and scarves she doled out to her fishermen friends — and an equal number for the chemo caps. Even her mother was amazed at the chunky wear that came from Cass' fingers.

"Your art has an ocean feel to it," Cass said, talking around the last piece of shrimp. "It seems perfect for people who come to Canary Cove looking for regional art. Sam's photos of my *Lady Lobster* have sold like crazy — and he took those shots as a favor to me. But people love that kind of thing. Canary Cove would love this." She scooped up the napkins, wiped a few crumbs off the table, and took them into the galley kitchen off the knitting room, retrieving a cold bottle of Birdie's wine on her way back.

162

"As long as you have to sit around here for a while, we might as well make it productive." Birdie sat back in her chair and began to work on her cap, a satisfied smile on her face. "Who knows? Maybe we should plan a show."

Nell looked up from retrieving a dropped stitch on Willow's sweater. "Willow, sweetie, you haven't said a word. Here we are, planning your future and not letting you get a word in edgewise."

Willow folded her legs up beneath her, the pair of shorts looking slightly too long on her legs. She looked down at her lap and fingered her work-in-progress. And then she looked back at the women who had taken her into their lives without question or judgment.

"You are kind of amazing. I don't think I've met people like you, even in our little Wisconsin town — and people were pretty nice there. But think about it — I break into your store, Izzy, and take over Nell's guesthouse. And Birdie and Cass treat me like family. And here you are, all of you, sticking your necks out for someone you don't know at all. And what you *do* know isn't all that wonderful." Willow stopped and looked around the room, as if committing it to memory.

"But I can't let you do that," she said.

"And why not?" asked Birdie, her words carrying a touch of indignation. Her back straightened and she slipped her glasses into her smooth nest egg of gray hair.

Telling Birdie what she could or couldn't do wasn't a habit of people who knew her.

"Well, here's why. Do you honestly think anyone — even in this nice town — is going to spend time looking at the art work of a suspected murderer? A . . . a . . . a Lizzie Borden? Think about it now."

She looked intently into each one of their faces, her black eyes flashing. "Well, do you?"

The irony of it was, Nell told Ben as they sat down to coffee the next day, that Willow Adams' words matched — if not exactly, very closely — a headline in Mary Pisano's "About Town" column in the *Sea Harbor Gazette* the next morning:

Is there a Lizzie Borden in our midst? Mary asked her readers.

CHAPTER 14

"So, Nell, whattaya think?"

Harry Garozzo leaned over the small deli table, his square hands pressed flat on the surface and his nose hovering perilously close to Nell's.

Nell pushed back in her chair, not wanting to offend Harry but requiring a slight distance. "About what, Harry?"

One blunt finger pointed to the newspaper lying next to Nell's mug of coffee. *Wisconsin woman a suspect in artist's murder,* the headline read.

"They're talking about our little friend. One week ago I find this flower child asleep in Izzy's window. Today she's maybe a murderer? What gives, Nell? What gives?" The furrows in his brow deepened in concern.

A breeze blew in the open deli window behind Nell, carrying the sounds of a Sea Harbor day — charter boats carrying tourists over to Tillie's Ledge or Wildcat Knoll to snag a striped bass or bluefish for dinner. Captain Jeremiah's whale-watching boat chugging out to the open sea, filled to the brim with tourists hoping for a humpback sighting. Cass and Pete would have left the harbor hours ago, taking the *Lady Lobster* out to check and bait their traps.

A normal day.

But it didn't seem normal at all.

Willow's demeanor the night before hadn't fooled any of the knitters. Beneath the bravado hovered a vulnerable woman who had stumbled into a most unfortunate situation.

"She's not a murderer, Harry. She's a frightened young woman who came to Sea Harbor looking for her father."

"And found him dead? What. A coincidence?" Harry's thick brows lifted up into his receding hairline. "A coincidence, Nell?"

Nell looked out the window. A coincidence. Yes. That was exactly what it was, Nell felt sure. And a deadly one.

"I've heard talk, Nell —" Harry went on.

"Of course you have, Harry. There will always be talk."

"Harry Garozzo, what are you stirring up here?" Birdie Favazza walked up behind him

166

and placed her small hand on his wide back. "Gossip? Shame on you, Harry."

Birdie pulled out a chair and sat opposite Nell, a sweet smile followed her chiding to the deli owner.

"Birdie, my love, the only thing I'll be stirring up today is my cold strawberry soup. You come back in an hour and I'll have you some." He grinned at Birdie, then dropped the smile to accommodate more serious conversation. "As I was just saying to Nell, people talk in my place. And Willow Adams' name is being bandied about between bites of my Italian egg sandwich like I dunna know what." He looked at Birdie and touched his lips with two fingers. "Your Sonny, he woulda loved them, Birdie Favazza: thick rustic bread, my marinara sauce —"

"I'm sure he would have, Harry. And I will indulge at a later date. Now you were saying?"

Harry dropped his hands back to the table and looked from one woman to the other, his thick brows pulling close together until they formed a single line across his face. "Rebecca Marks was in this morning to pick up a box of my taralli, and her pink tongue was wagging like the flag at Pelican Pier." Harry looked around at the tables on either side to be sure no one was listening, but most of his midmorning customers were summer people more interested in Harry's chocolate chip cannoli than in town gossip. He turned back to Birdie and Nell.

"Rebecca says that we all shoulda known Aidan had a secret life. He was the kind who'd have a kid hidden somewhere. A love child, she called it."

"*Her,* Harry. Willow is a person."

"Sure. Her. Of course she's a person. I even kind of like the little thing. But people are pulling out facts, not letting their hearts rule them like you sometimes do."

Nell frowned at him.

"That's a *good* thing, Nell. You care about people. But no matter — rumor has it that the young girl was probably driven to her crime by her own father's misdeeds."

"Now that's downright foolish." It was Birdie, speaking in the voice that sank ships, as her Sonny used to say.

Harry shrugged. "I'm just the messenger, ladies. But Rebecca was pretty convincing that once we all faced facts about Willow Adams, and cleaned up and sold Aidan's messy gallery to some respectable artist, we could get on with our lives. That's what she said in a nutshell. And she herself would promote doing that soon."

"And just how is she going to do that? It's not hers to sell."

"You know Rebecca. She could move the Rockies to Cape Ann if she set her mind to it. And for all their nice gestures at Aidan's funeral, Rebecca says there were lots of Canary Cove artists who share her suspicions and feelings. Even Jane."

"Jane Brewster?"

Harry nodded, his lips pressed together as if guarding a secret, not something Harry did easily.

The sounds of the bell above the door and the bright chatter of customers brought Harry's attention back to more immediate things. He straightened his stance and looked from Nell to Birdie.

"Now, ladies, for more pleasant concerns, what are you two wanting this fine Friday morning?"

"I'm waiting on a sack of sourdough rolls for dinner tonight. Margaret is getting them for me — they weren't quite ready when I came in.

"And don't worry your head, Harry," Birdie added. "We'll not hang on to a valuable table once your lunch crowd starts coming in. Nell and I are not for loafing today — we're squeezing in a brisk walk."

A brisk walk and time to collect their

thoughts, but Nell wasn't about to share that with Harry. Things weren't moving fast enough to clear Willow's name, and if the police weren't going to do it, then Cass, Birdie, Izzy, and Nell were not above snooping around themselves.

Harry laughed and wiped his palms on the smudged white apron that covered his ample girth. "Well, you two girls be about your business then and have a nice day. Looks to me like the lunch crowd is early and Margaret will have my hide if anyone has to wait longer than a heartbeat." Harry turned and walked over to greet a crowd of tourists, who were eyeing the meats and cheeses behind the glass of the deli case.

"Jane Brewster?" Birdie whispered when he was out of earshot. "Jane and Aidan were good friends. What do you suppose Harry was talking about?"

"There's one sure way to find out," Nell said. "Seems like Canary Cove might be a good destination for us. Who knows what rumors are starting — and once things percolate too long, they become truth in some people's minds. We can't let that happen to Willow."

The narrow road that ran through the center of Canary Cove was alive with people moving in and out of the small galleries and boutiques. The first building along the stretch was a small cottage that housed the artists' association office and two small, one-room galleries. The association was manned mostly by volunteers, who handed out brochures, planned special art events, and gave the council a place to meet. Nell waved to Mary Pisano, who was walking inside to put in her volunteer hours.

Nell and Birdie walked briskly toward the heart of Canary Cove, down past the tea shop and a small pottery shop, heading toward the Brewsters' gallery.

Ellen Marks and Billy stood together in front of the Sobel Gallery, and Nell waved across the street. The two were so deep in conversation that the wave went unnoticed. Billy's brows were drawn together, his head lowered, and his hands on his hips. In front of him, Ellen spoke earnestly, her long hands gesturing as she talked. Finally Billy spread his hands wide, his palms up, and shrugged. He touched Ellen lightly on the shoulder, a gentle gesture that seemed to indicate regret, then turned and walked back inside his gallery.

Ellen looked after him, then turned and walked slowly back to the Lampworks Gallery.

"An odd couple," Birdie murmured beside Nell.

"They're longtime friends, I think. Ellen says Billy has a huge heart."

"The big heart seems to be delivering unwanted news to Ellen. She looks disappointed."

Ellen was walking slowly back to the Lampworks Gallery. Her head was lowered but her body language indicated Birdie might be right.

"And if Billy was so bighearted, what was the beef he had with Aidan? Bighearted fellows shouldn't have beefs."

"Good point." But Nell supposed the disagreement between the two men was something they would have worked out, just as Aidan had indicated at dinner. It seemed more of a disagreement about how to exhibit Billy's paintings — nothing too serious, Nell supposed.

They crossed over to Jane and Ham's gallery — right in the center of the row of artists' shops. The location was second only to Aidan Peabody's prime acreage. Behind the gallery, Jane and Ham had turned a cozy cabin into a clean white space, a lovely home, filled with paintings and prints collected from fellow artists. It hosted many dinner parties and late-night discussions.

The door to the shop was open today and several children played on the wooden bench in front. Nell tousled the hair of a redheaded boy and peered into the cool interior.

Ham stood in front of a display of Jane's large pots, talking to a customer and absently fingering his bushy beard. Brendan was helping out and stood on the other side of the room, talking to another group of visitors and drawing their attention to a large watercolor painting of Ham's that Nell knew would grace their own home if they had a wall big enough to hold it. It was a beach area north of town, craggy and dramatic, with enormous granite boulders reaching directly out to the sea. Ham had captured light on water and granite with an agility that reminded Nell of some of Fritz Lane's paintings.

Ham looked up and spotted Nell. "Looking for Janie, Nell? She had some association business but will be back shortly."

"We'll circle around and be back," Nell called and stepped back onto the road. Birdie stood straight, shielding her eyes against the glare of the noontime sun, and peering down the street.

"Looks like there's activity at the Fishtail Gallery."

Nell followed the point of Birdie's finger and spotted the Delaney Construction truck sticking out of the small alley beside Aidan Peabody's closed-up gallery. She fell in step as Birdie headed down the street.

"It makes my stomach lurch to see police tape circling Aidan's lovely shop this way," Birdie said.

"Ben said the police are about finished and will take the tape down today. They've scoured the place looking for clues but haven't had much luck. With the number of people in and out of Aidan's gallery — and his sculptures begging to be touched the way they do — I'd guess nearly half of Cape Ann has left fingerprints in that place."

"So no fingerprints. What are they thinking?" Birdie paused, then said, "Don't answer that. I know what they are thinking. For a minute I was able to forget."

"Ben said they had hoped to find some note, someone who had heard something, seen something, that would put Willow in the right place at the right time."

"Or wrong is more like it."

Nell nodded. "She needs us. Right now we're the only ones convinced she's innocent. We need to prove our case."

As they neared the Fishtail's front door, Nell heard voices coming from the small dirt alley next to the studio. The alley was more of a driveway that dead-ended beside Aidan's lovely shade garden and the hilly, wooded land beyond.

"D.J., what's going on?" Nell asked. She pushed her sunglasses up into her salt-and-pepper hair.

D. J. Delaney stood in front of his truck, dark sunglasses shielding his eyes and a yellow pad in his hands. Two men in muscle shirts and deep tans stood on opposite sides of the drive, extending a tape measure between them.

"Hey, Nell, how ya doing?" D.J. said. Building condos and renovating Sea Harbor property had turned D.J.'s body into a solid mass of muscle. Today a knit shirt covered his chest and his thinning hair was hidden beneath a baseball cap. "We're getting some stats on this place. I'm thinking the whole damn thing should maybe be torn down."

Nell's hands knotted into balls and pressed into her hips. "And why are you thinking that, D.J.?"

"See those woods, Nell? It'd be a perfect outdoor area for guests of the inn. Scoop out a clearing and lay flagstone, maybe a little pond. Make it completely private. Beautiful plantings, a place to have morning coffee or lunch. Art lovers from Boston would pay big bucks to have that kind of pampering in the fine little inn."

"Inn?" Birdie said. Her eyebrows lifted with her voice.

"It's just what Canary Cove needs, Miss Birdie. A sweet elegant inn, right smack in the middle of the artists' colony. It will help everyone — the artists, the town —"

"Not to mention your pocketbook." Birdie frowned at him.

D.J.'s laugh was deep and gravelly. "Have ta feed the wife and get the kids through college."

"How do you propose to get your hands on this property?" Nell asked. "It's not yours."

"Not yet," D.J. answered with a wry smile. "You wait and see. The girl is guilty as sin. She won't be needing this land where she's going, but she'll sure need the money for lawyers. Now excuse me, ladies. I've some numbers to write down." He tipped his head, dismissing Nell and Birdie, and strode up the alley to his crew, listening and jotting down figures on the yellow pad.

"Well, I'll be," Birdie said. "Okay, let's get out our own yellow pad. And if we want suspects to deflect attention from Willow, D. J. Delaney is now at the top of my list."

Jane had just returned when Nell and

Birdie walked back in the front door of the Brewster Gallery.

"Ham said you stopped by," Jane said, smiling a welcome. "I was over at the Association office."

"We walked right by there but didn't spot you. Is everything okay? You look worried."

Jane waved off Nell's remark. "I'm sure it'll be fine. I've been trying to stay on top of things that Aidan used to take care of for the art association, and am having a hard time. Just little things, a couple of overdue bills . . . and some numbers that don't match up. I should probably mind my own business. The reports aren't due for another month, but I want to be sure the summer arts program is okay and all the bills get paid on time."

"You mentioned the other day that the funds were low. Maybe we need another benefit."

"Maybe." Jane leaned back against the glass counter. "Now what brings you two over here on a Friday? You look like you have more on your mind than strolling in and out of galleries."

"It's about Willow," Nell began.

Jane's smile disappeared. She nodded, pushing a lock of slightly graying hair back behind one ear.

Jane looked the quintessential artist today, Nell thought, dressed in jeans and a colorful Art at Night T-shirt. Her voice, too, was flowing and clear, matching the lines of the smooth, unique pots she displayed in her gallery. She was aging with elegance.

"That poor young woman. What a tragedy," Jane said. "As close as I was to Aidan, I never imagined that he had a daughter. There was one night — he'd had a little too much to drink, and we were sitting out on the dock underneath that old roof. We were talking about the insane things Ham and I did when we were at Berkeley, and Aidan matched them with his antics at Wisconsin. He started talking about this thing that had happened to him there — that last semester of school when things get crazy, things happen."

"Like what?"

"Some young gal came on to him, he said. She was everywhere he was, following him around campus, making him dinner, showing up at his house. She was very pretty, he said. Flirty. She told him she was a coed at Wisconsin. Then the night before he was to leave town — he was skipping the graduation ceremony because he couldn't wait to get back to the coast — she showed up at his apartment. They'd not seen each other for a while because he thought there was something dishonest about her, something not quite right. And he suspected from the way she talked that she might be lying about her age and he didn't want to have anything to do with it.

"So that last night she showed up at his apartment and told him she was pregnant, that she was sixteen and had run away from home. But she loved him, she said, and she wanted to run away with him."

Two sides to every story, Nell thought, thinking of Willow's grandmother, determined to save her daughter's image.

"Good grief," Birdie said.

"Aidan was flabbergasted, as you can imagine. They'd been together once, maybe twice. He didn't say much that night because he was so stunned, just that he needed a few hours and a little space to collect his thoughts. He'd talk to her the next day."

"He must have been scared silly he'd be accused of rape."

Jane nodded. "There was that, yes. But you know Aidan. He'd do the right thing, whatever that was. So he spent the whole night thinking about it. And the next day he went to the place where she worked, but they said she'd left suddenly. He went to her apartment, but she was gone — lock, stock, and barrel. She disappeared off the face of the earth.

"Aidan said he's thought about her over the years, tried to find her. Wondered what happened . . . if there really was a baby. And that was the last time he talked about it to us. He never mentioned it again after that night. Sometimes Ham and I wondered if we'd really heard the story right or if we'd imagined it. But that night, at least, Aidan had been haunted by the thought that he might have a child out there, someone he never had a chance to know or to hold or to love."

"Aidan rarely talked about himself."

"No, hardly ever. It was a rare night. Mostly, Aidan was all about his art. Even the women in his life never seemed to dominate his attention — they were more like peripheral distractions. At first Rebecca made an impression, I think. But that's because everything Rebecca does makes an impression."

"Apparently Willow didn't think she made an impression, either," Nell said. "She never knew who her father was until recently. It must have been difficult, growing up like that."

"And living with a mother and relatives who colored her version of the kind of man

180

he was," Birdie added.

"I'm not so sure it was her mother's doing," Nell said. "The grandparents seemed to be a strong force in her life, from the little she's said."

"Jane, there's a lot of talk around town. People seem to be targeting Willow, convinced that she is guilty of murdering her father," Birdie said.

"Almost wanting her to be guilty," Nell added. "She's a stranger here. If Willow did this awful thing, it could be tied up neatly and we could go on with our lives. But I don't think Willow is guilty. Rebecca Marks is in the camp that thinks she did it, and according to Harry, she's using you as an ally in convicting Willow. Do you know something that we don't?"

Jane turned to see who else was in the shop. A few customers, Ham, and Brendan. All involved in asking questions about art or listening to informed explanations of the intricacies of watercolor and pottery, plein air art or bronze sculpture. Jane moved a little closer to Birdie and Nell.

"Once Aidan moved on, Rebecca turned on him. Being dropped was bad for her ego, I guess. But anyway, she happened to be in our shop when I was talking to the police — they questioned all of us, of course. We were talking quietly in the back room, but Rebecca must have overheard the conversation."

"I don't want to put you on the spot. But if Rebecca is spreading rumors, I want to stop them. Would you mind telling us what you said?"

Jane looked down at the floor for a minute, as if collecting her thoughts. Then she looked back at Nell. "I would trust you and Birdie with my life. I'm not sure what Rebecca is throwing out there, but here's what happened. And what I reluctantly told the police.

"I went into the Fishtail Gallery the day before Aidan died — last Saturday, I guess, though it seems a lifetime ago. I was borrowing some display fixtures from him for Sunday's Art at Night. People were hovering around Aidan's wooden pieces, like they always do, opening them up, looking for the secret drawers and compartments. But I didn't see Aidan, so I headed for the back door, thinking maybe he'd taken a break in the garden. He did that sometimes — he loved that garden. He told me once it was his meditation spot.

"So I walked out the door and discovered I was right — I heard Aidan's voice right away. It was . . . I don't know . . . kind of emotional. Stirring, almost. And then I heard another voice and glimpsed the back of a young woman with dark hair. Her voice was loud — angry and emotional, all at the same time."

"And you think it was Willow?"

"At that moment I didn't know who it was — I hadn't met Willow yet. But I recognized her later and the backpack she carries around was distinctive. I started to back away because it was clearly a personal conversation. I turned back into the shadows of the shop, but I was an instant too late."

"Too late for what?" Birdie asked.

"To avoid hearing the woman yell at Aidan. But even then, I thought it was just a disagreement. Maybe an old girlfriend, someone with a bone to pick. Even what she said didn't seem that awful. Although once Aidan was murdered, the words took on new meaning."

"What did she say?" Nell ran her fingers through her hair, lifting it from her neck, an unconscious gesture when she needed to know something — but didn't want to hear it. She looked at Jane and felt suddenly sad about what her friend would say.

Jane paused for just a moment, then looked at Nell and Birdie. Her face mirrored Nell's sadness. "Her voice was choked but her words were crystal clear. She said, 'I wish you were dead.'"

CHAPTER 15

Nell was hoping that Willow would show up for Friday night supper. She'd left a note taped to the guesthouse door, assuring Willow that the gathering was casual and relaxing. Brendan could attest to that, too, Nell said in her note — an unspoken invitation to bring him along.

Nell was sure that if Jane spent more time with Willow, she'd see immediately what she herself knew to be true — that Willow's remarks to Aidan Peabody were uttered out of twenty-two years of pent-up emotion and were certainly not a murderous threat. She was a hurt young woman whose life had been shaped somehow by an absent father. And she needed to vent those feelings to plan the rest of her life. That was what this was all about. It was certainly not about murder.

"Nell, don't worry about what I think," Jane

said later that evening. She stood at Nell's wide butcher-block island, rinsing a handful of lettuce in the island sink. The kitchen windows were wide-open, the white shutters folded back, and the fading light of day filled the airy space.

Nell pulled a knife from the drawer and put it on a chopping block. Overhead, a round rack anchored to the ceiling held copper and stainless-steel pots and pans in every shape and size, and glass cupboard doors displayed Nell's collection of plates and glasses. It was her dream kitchen: a wide-open space where friends gathered and chopped and diced — and drank in the pleasure of being together. At the other end of the room, a smooth stone fireplace rose from floor to ceiling. The cherry floors were covered with sisal rugs and the light neutral palette of the sofas and chairs — soft greens and tans and whites — gave full play to the sky and pine trees, the sloping green lawn, and the ocean beyond, a piece of it visible from every window along the back of the house. It was a lived-in room, a room that welcomed people, invited them to sit down, to be safe and comfortable — exactly what Nell had envisioned when she and Ben added it onto his family's vacation home and made the house their own.

"I know you had to tell the police about the conversation, Jane. I would have done the same thing." Nell washed off a bunch of green onions and began chopping them into tiny pieces. "I was asking how *you* feel about Willow."

"The bigger concern is what the police think," Ben interjected. He stood with Ham and Sam Perry at a built-in bar in the living area, pulling bottles from beneath the cabinet and placing them on the polished top. "They aren't going to care who likes or doesn't like Willow. They want a strong motive and a way to wrap this up as quickly as possible. And unfortunately Willow is falling right into that category."

Nell scooped up a handful of the onions and tossed them into a wooden bowl. She had rubbed the inside of the bowl with garlic, mint, and lemon juice, and the pleasant combination of odors circulated around the cooking area. "But the police have absolutely nothing to connect her to Aidan's murder. It's all circumstantial."

"Sometimes circumstantial can be a powerful thing," Sam said.

"Especially when the police don't have anywhere else to turn." Birdie walked over to the bar and set down a bowl of stuffed martini olives.

187

"I didn't tell the police about Willow and Aidan's conversation to hurt Willow or to add to any kind of evidence." Jane chopped a fresh tomato from Nell's garden as she talked. The knife clicked rhythmically against the bamboo cutting board. She pulled her brows together and her fine-boned face registered distress. "Nor do I think that poor little thing killed her father. But I had to answer their questions. Besides, there were others around that day and I know they heard some of it — or at least they knew that someone was arguing with Aidan. But they were farther away than I was, and who knows how they would have repeated the conversation? Rebecca's dramatic flair could have blown the story clear across the Cape. It could have been even worse for Willow — distorted and incriminating."

Nell held her silence, not mentioning that it was, indeed, Rebecca Marks who had passed the story along and embellished it here and there.

"What it really comes down to," Ben said from across the room, "is that wishing someone was dead is not the same thing as murdering him. And that's all that Willow's words really indicate."

"Darn right," Cass said, coming in from

the pantry and handing Nell a fresh bottle of sesame oil. Cass never pretended to be a cook, but she had finessed the role of chef's helper, and could sometimes anticipate Nell's needs before Nell herself did.

"Is Willow coming tonight?" Birdie asked. She held the deck door open for Ben as he carried a platter of tuna out to the grill. Sam and Ham followed, carrying spices and grilling tools.

"She knows she's welcome. I haven't seen her all day."

"She was in the shop for a while," Izzy said. "She keeps the conversation neutral — doesn't really tell me what's going on inside her head. I think she thinks she poured out too much to us the other night and has pulled all of us into this awful web. She doesn't want to make it worse for us." Izzy plucked a bread stick from the basket and broke off a piece.

"She's sad. This whole thing about finding her father, then the murder — her emotions must be tangled and frayed. She doesn't want me to set anything up with my customers. Not now, she said. I think she's afraid people would come to stare at her, and I can't say I blame her. But she's been told she can't leave town. The days must be horribly long for her. We're encouraging her to concentrate on her art — I'm collecting all the leftover yarn people leave around the shop and passing it along. . . ."

"Of course," Jane broke in. She brightened up considerably. "That's the perfect medicine for an artist — to create beauty. And after all this is over, we'll have an exhibit of her work."

Nell smiled. Jane had jumped right on their idea, just as she knew she would.

"Ham and I will host it at our place," Jane went on. "We will make it wonderful, I promise."

"That's a generous offer, Jane. We'll put a positive spin on all this. It will remind Willow of who she truly is: an artist, not someone under house arrest."

Underneath it all, Nell knew Jane's offer was a way to make up for what she had had to tell the police — something beyond her control, but contributing, nevertheless, to Willow's situation. But it didn't matter. It was what it was — a gift to Willow. The Brewster Gallery hosted lovely exhibits and would draw a crowd. And by the time the exhibit was ready, Willow's name would be cleared, and it would be a positive beginning to the next chapter in her life, whatever that might be.

"Are things clearing up with the paperwork, Jane? If the foundation needs donations, be sure to let me know. I can write a grant or two."

"I think we'll figure it out. I asked Ellen to dig a little, and she's been great. She said she'd take care of it. Her head for numbers is as great as her sister's art talent. But on to more pleasant things. Do you think Willow could have enough pieces by the next Art at Night?"

The planning for Willow's art exhibit would have continued — well into the mushroom appetizers, beyond the juicy grilled tuna coated with pecans, even to the cranberry pie that Birdie had brought from her housekeeper Ella's oven. It certainly would have gone longer than the firing of the coals on Ben's grill.

Except that at that exact moment — the same moment the inviting, sizzling sound of the match hitting the coals rose up on the deck — the Endicott doorbell rang, an unfamiliar sound.

People usually opened the front door and called out their arrival, or just walked in, as was Izzy, Birdie, and Cass' custom. But rarely, other than when someone was soliciting donations for the firemen's picnic or selling Girl Scout cookies did anyone actually ring Ben and Nell's doorbell.

Ben looked back into the house from the darkening deck. "You want me to get it, Nell?"

"I've got it." Nell frowned, then wiped her hands on a dish towel and walked toward the front door.

Tommy Porter stood on the wide step. His powder blue police shirt was buttoned from top to bottom and the creases ironed in crisp, straight lines.

Beside him, on either side, silent and displeased, stood Brendan Slattery and Willow Adams.

CHAPTER 16

The odd threesome was silent for one moment. And then they all spoke at once.

"I d-don't know what's going on, Ms. Endicott, but —"

"It wasn't Willow's idea," Brendan interrupted.

"I'm so sorry about this, Nell." Willow's tone was earnest, but with an edge of irritation. "But this fellow is way too diligent."

The mix of voices brought Izzy, Birdie, and Cass to the door.

"What's going on?" they asked in a jumble of words.

The light outside the front door shined down on the group like a spotlight, encircling them.

"Come inside," Nell said. "All of you. I don't want the neighbors talking. And, Tommy, I hope for heaven's sake you didn't have your light circling when you drove up. People will think someone died."

"No one did, right?" Cass asked. "Die, I mean. We've had enough of that."

"No, no, no, ma'am." Tommy looked down at his shiny black shoes. "No spinning light. No one died."

Cass, Izzy, and Birdie stepped aside as Nell led the three visitors into the family room.

"What gives?" Ben asked, coming in from the deck. "Ah, more diners. That's great. Welcome. We always have plenty."

"No, s-sir, Mr. Endicott," said Tommy.

Nell felt sudden pity for the young man. She'd watched Tommy Porter grow up, knew how hard he had worked in school and how diligently he tried to control his stammering as he trained at the police academy. Tommy was the only member of the Porter family not in the fishing business, and Nell knew it had taken a very supportive mother and father to allow him this shift. It had been Tommy's dream to be a policeman — and he'd accomplished it.

"So, Tommy, what happened?" The look Nell passed to Willow and Brendan strongly suggested they let Tommy have his say.

"I was . . . over there at Canary Cove, checking out the activity at the Artist's Palate. It gets . . . it gets wicked wild sometimes on Fridays. And I saw the light in

Aidan's place."

"The Fishtail Gallery?" Ham came up behind Ben, a martini in hand.

Tommy nodded. "So, well, it's not open, y'know, because of, well, Aidan."

Because Aidan is dead, Nell finished silently. She wondered briefly if being a policeman was the best career for Tommy after all.

"So you investigated, Tommy. Good for you," Birdie encouraged.

Tommy smiled at Birdie. She seemed to bring him focus, and he went on more robustly. "And I found these two in there, going through things. Shuffling things around. Doing things they shouldn't have been doing. The Fishtail is off-limits. Everybody knows that."

"You were good to check," Nell said.

"The police tape was down," Willow said. "They're through with that part of things." She held up a set of keys and dangled them in the air. "And I have keys."

Tommy frowned. "Where did you get those?"

Izzy stepped forward, touching Tommy lightly on the arm.

He smiled at her.

"Tommy, Willow owns the Fishtail Gallery."

Tommy was silent, trying to process Izzy's words.

Nell was glad Izzy had spoken up. Tommy would listen to her carefully. But she also realized he was in a terribly awkward position, surrounded by all of them. A deer in the headlights.

"Ben," she said out loud, "how about tea or martinis or Diet Cokes for all? Whatever's your pleasure. Tommy. You will love these crab-stuffed mushrooms I made. We got the fresh crab today from your uncle Duane's market."

Immediately bodies moved, some to the deck, Jane to the kitchen to retrieve a platter of stuffed mushrooms, Sam to help Ben rekindle the coals, and Ham on a convenience store run for more ice.

"It's okay," Nell said gently, "you were doing your job. That's an admirable thing."

Tommy looked at Willow and Brendan. "I'm . . . I'm sorry. He was killed, and then you were in there."

Brendan spoke for the first time. "Hey, it's okay, Tom. You did as we asked and you brought us here, not to the station, so we could clear it up. That was cool."

Willow sat on the edge of a wide chair arm, listening to the conversation going on around her.

Nell sensed the unrest in her — Willow was not the most patient of people. But she also sensed a sadness in her — that enormous mix of emotions they had talked about earlier. When she looked into her dark eyes, she saw the puffiness of tears shed, then wiped away.

Tommy accepted the Diet Coke but only in a can so he could take it with him — he was still on duty, he said, and you just never knew what kind of ruckus might erupt on a Friday night in Sea Harbor. He'd heard rumors of some young kids having a bonfire out near the breakwater, and it just might need his attention. And then he'd be off duty and would meet some friends for a beer.

Nell waved him off, and Tommy drove out of the driveway and down the street with a speed that would garner him a ticket were he not the only policeman in sight.

She turned back to Willow and Brendan, now sitting next to each other on the couch, drinking cold beers that Cass had slipped into their hands.

"So," Nell began.

"It was a bad idea." Brendan spoke first. "And it was my fault. I'm ten years older than Willow — been around the block a few times. I should have known better."

Willow looked at Brendan. Nell saw the softness in her eyes.

"It's okay," Willow said. "And no one has to accept fault because we didn't do anything wrong." She looked over at Nell and Birdie, sitting next to each other on the opposite couch. Izzy and Cass hovered nearby. "I told you I didn't want anything that was his. And I meant it. But when Brendan suggested we go over there — that he'd be right there with me — it seemed like a good idea, like something I had to do. We just went into the studio, not the house or anything. I . . . I wanted to see it, you know?"

The tears that Nell had seen earlier started to return but Willow held them at bay. "I have his genes. There's . . . that biological connection. And my mother loved him, at least for a while. Somehow I just wanted to see a part of his life, to maybe understand."

"Did the police give you the keys?"

Willow shook her head no.

Brendan looked uncomfortable. Finally he met Nell's eyes. "I gave her the keys. I closed up for Aidan sometimes, just like I do for the Brewsters. And Billy Sobel. They all gave me keys."

Nell frowned. Brendan had clearly overstepped his bounds. He should have turned the keys over to the police last week. But she could certainly understand Willow's need to see her father's art. And she could even understand why someone who cared about her, as Brendan seemed to, would want to help. And then there was that ambiguous line they were all walking — it was, after all, Willow's property, or at least it would be, once the estate was settled. The will, Ben had said, was indisputable. Simple. And would take care of Willow the rest of her life.

"I know, Nell. A stupid thing to do," Brendan went on. "But it hasn't been the easiest week for Willow."

"Nor any of us," Birdie said.

The group fell still, the only sound coming from sizzling tuna on the grill and John Mayer in the background, singing about being a bad boy. *Appropriate,* Nell thought.

"You two are staying for dinner," she said then, feeling the need for a change in topic. "Ben has already added the extra steaks. And Jane has something she needs to talk to you about, Willow."

"Thanks. That'd be great." Brendan stood and made his way to the deck, his offer to help Ben with the grilling traveling ahead of him.

Cass and Birdie followed, lured by the gentle sounds of Ben's martini shaker.

Willow looked from Izzy to Nell. And then the held-back tears surfaced. "He was my father, you know?"

"And you have every right to look at his things. They're *your* things now, or at least will be soon. But . . ."

"But you need to be smart about it," Izzy said abruptly.

"The thing is," Nell said, "though it may go against your grain, you need to be aware that people are watching you. And the way they interpret your actions matters — whether it should or not. It simply does. Especially now . . ."

"Especially now that people think I killed my father."

"I don't know who thinks what. But the police need to look into anyone with a motive. So they'll be looking at you. And others, too."

"It's just the way people are, Willow. We know you didn't kill your father. And Ben and Nell — all of us — are going to do everything we can to help you." Izzy leaned forward, balancing her chin on her hands. Her brown tank top matched the deep chocolate of her eyes, and she looked at Willow with a look that refused to release its target.

"Does that make sense, sweetie?" Nell

asked. "People — even good people — will talk and interpret things you might say or do. Like going into Aidan's place so soon after the police took the tape down. They may think you were looking for something —"

"I was," Willow said softly, and a lone tear rolled down her cheek until it dropped from the tip of her chin. "I was looking for my father."

CHAPTER 17

Saturday mornings at Coffee's was a favorite destination for Nell when Ben was off for an early-morning fishing expedition or sail with a friend. She always had a knitting project tucked into the outer pocket of her large bag, and sometimes she'd bring her laptop, too, and work on a talk or a grant she was writing for an arts group or children's center. Ben teased her that morning that she'd be perfectly entertained for at least a month, should she and her bag ever get marooned on a desert island.

And he was right, Nell thought as she walked down her shady street toward Coffee's. She didn't have her computer today, but she'd tucked a skein of baby-soft cotton yarn in her bag, along with circular bamboo needles, to work up another cap for Izzy's project. This one would be for a little girl — a bright blend of pink and green, yellow and purple, with tiny soft white roses, curled from tightly knit yarn, placed around the cap like a crown. It would be soft and warm and beautiful, a soft touch of comfort for a sweet young child who had lost her hair.

Even at this early hour, several outdoor tables on Coffee's patio were already occupied. Nell looked around and spotted a familiar face immediately, partially hidden behind the morning *Sea Harbor Gazette.*

Cass was camped out at a round table, her feet propped up on an adjacent chair. Her head was buried in the newspaper held up in front of her.

"Cass, I think you might need glasses. You're holding that paper way too close to your eyes." Nell pulled out the opposite chair and sat down.

Cass looked up and smiled. "I was thinking you might pop on down here. Ben mentioned he had a predawn fishing date with Don Wooten and Sam." She slipped her feet off the chair and put the newspaper down on the table.

"You're looking nice today. Special occasion?"

Cass wore Bermuda-length red shorts and a crisp white T-shirt with a photo of the *Lady Lobster* printed on the front. "Like my new tee?"

Cass stuck out her chest in an exaggerated fashion and Nell laughed.

"It's lovely."

"Sam took this photo of my boat, and Izzy had some shirts made up. I love it. It'd dress anyone up, is the way I look at it. My *Lady* is irresistible." Cass pulled her hair back as she talked and slipped a bright red scrunchie from her wrist and wrapped it around the thick mass of wavy flyaway hair.

The morning sun behind Cass' head created a halo effect and Nell held back a smile. An angel, Cass had never been. But she won high votes on lots of other personality fronts. "No lobster gear today?"

"The *Lady* is in Pete's hands today. He better take good care of her."

"Pete gave you a day off? That's awfully nice of him."

Cass grinned and her eyes sparkled. "Not so nice. He owes me. I set him up with the gal who works in the stationery store down the street. She's hot, he says."

Nell laughed. She looked down at the newspaper. "So what's new?"

"All kinds of things. Read this." Cass pointed to the right side of page two, where Mary Pisano's "About Town" column always appeared — a chatty piece that complimented citizens doing good deeds, sometimes chastised others, announced events of interest, and afforded Mary a place to get things off her mind.

Nell slipped on her glasses and lifted the paper, reading around the brown rim left from Cass' coffee cup.

NEW DEVELOPMENTS ON THE COVE?

With police working around the clock to solve the Aidan Peabody case and bring peace of mind to our lovely community, cove residents are being ever vigilant in watching out for one another. Our thanks to young Tommy Porter for discovering intruders in the Fishtail Gallery early last evening. All ended well, Tommy reported to this columnist.

But who was responsible for the intrusion into the Peabody home in the middle of the night? One source tells us that a figure was seen departing the cottage well after the Palate had closed for the night. The figure, our source reports, disappeared into the woods behind the house once lights were shined in that direction.

If only those lovely wooden figures of Aidan's could talk.

"So Mary Pisano has turned sleuth," Nell said. She set the paper down and pushed her glasses up into her hair. "This is odd, though — at least if Mary's deep-throat source was telling the truth. Who would have been snooping around Aidan's in the middle of the night? I'm sure it wasn't Willow. She was exhausted last night. I took an extra blanket down to the guesthouse after everyone left, and she was already in bed, nearly asleep. I'm certain she didn't go back to Aidan's place."

Around them, the patio tables began to fill up as the more leisurely Saturday crowd wandered out onto the patio.

Cass leaned toward Nell to keep their conversation private. "Besides, Willow didn't have a key to Aidan's house, only the gallery."

"Although we both know that doesn't necessarily stop Willow from getting in places."

"But who is this source? You can't see Aidan's house unless you're in that little alley beside the gallery or in the garden. Someone would have had to be snooping around himself to see anything suspicious."

"I suppose it could have been Tommy. He might have felt he had to check again."

"No, I don't think so. Tommy told me he

got off at midnight and was meeting someone for a drink at the Gull. I think Tommy has a girlfriend."

"Well, good for Tommy. I was hoping he'd finally give up on Izzy."

Cass laughed. "I guess fifteen years is long enough to hold a crush. Okay, if it wasn't Tommy Porter, who was it?"

The last person Nell had seen snooping around Aidan's was D. J. Delaney. But he snooped in broad daylight and didn't seem to care a bit about who saw him. Unless . . . unless there was something in Aidan's house that would help his cause. And breaking into someone's house was a little different from invading private outdoor space, something better done under cover of darkness if one wanted to avoid jail time.

Nell took another sip of her coffee and looked through the fragrant steam at the steady line of people walking onto the patio, newspapers under one arm, balancing a coffee cup in another hand, ready to begin their Saturday with Coffee's brew and a relaxed moment of time on the patio. She didn't realize she was looking directly into the faces coming through the patio door until one of them spoke to her.

"Good morning to you, too, Nell."

Rebecca Marks walked over to Cass and

207

Nell and paused beside their table. She smiled politely at each of them. A white sundress hung from tiny straps over Rebecca's bronze shoulders. It was simple and elegant, and showcased a perfect tan on a well-toned body. Her hair was pulled back into two long ponytails, which cascaded down her back like platinum question marks.

"I'm sorry, Rebecca. How rude of me to stare. I wasn't really seeing anyone. My thoughts were far away."

"At least as far as Canary Cove, I'd bet," Rebecca said. "That seems to be on people's minds these days."

"I suppose it is," Nell said.

"Would you like to sit? It looks like most of the other tables are filled," Cass offered.

Nell watched Rebecca look around, unsure of the invitation and slightly uncomfortable, not a common look for the self-possessed woman. Rebecca was in her late thirties and possessed one of those fine-boned faces that would always resist aging. She'd look ten years younger than her peers as she approached each new decade. Her striking blond looks made the glamorous artist a well-known figure in Sea Harbor in the couple of years she and Ellen had lived there. Nell suspected half of the teenage boys in Sea Harbor had crushes on

Rebecca.

But in addition to her looks, she had a talent — they all admitted that. Her designer jewelry beads and one-of-a-kind bowls and vases attracted visitors from all over the area.

Cass and Nell watched Rebecca's green eyes survey the patio. She was looking for more interesting tablemates, Nell supposed. Finally, she shrugged and set her coffee cup down, then her large buckled purse, and finally swiveled her slender hips onto the chair.

"The cove must be feeling Aidan's absence," Cass said, attempting conversation.

Rebecca leveled a look at Cass, taking a drink of her coffee as if giving the statement serious thought. "Yes, I suppose that's true. His death leaves an empty gallery on the street — that's not a good thing — and some people will miss him, I suppose. I'm just not one of them. And I'm only telling you that because I am sure you know it already. I wasn't crazy about Aidan. He was meddlesome and took his role as head of the arts council way too seriously. Just ask Billy Sobel. Willow may have done some of us a favor."

"But you didn't always feel that way."

"That was a lifetime ago."

"What makes you so sure Willow Adams killed Aidan?" Nell was gentle in her question, seeking a truthful answer. Rebecca's rumors were harmful to Willow, and perhaps a frank conversation could temper them.

"How am I sure? It's as clear as the nose on your face. It's right out there for all to see. She had every reason to kill him. She hated him — I heard her say so myself just the day before she killed him."

"You were in Aidan's shop that day?"

"Yes. I had to talk to him about something. Willow was saying something to him that he seemed confused about. Shocked, I guess you'd say. And then the two of them went out into the garden. Jane came in right after that looking for Aidan. She heard it, too. Can you believe that he had a daughter and he didn't tell any of us?"

"Maybe he didn't know he had a daughter." Or didn't know how to find her. Nell felt sure now that Aidan would have been a presence in Willow's life, had he been given the chance. The more she learned, the more she suspected it was the grandparents who had made sure that wouldn't happen. She didn't want to drown Willow in suppositions right now, but was hopeful that in the days to come, Willow would somehow discover that her father wasn't the bad person she grew up believing him to be.

Rebecca's brows lifted and her eyes flashed. "Aidan knew everything," she said simply.

A shadow behind Rebecca fell over the table, blocking the morning sun, and Nell looked up into Ellen Marks' narrow, pleasant face. Ellen was older than Rebecca by probably a half dozen years, Nell supposed, and a stark contrast to the striking Rebecca. She wore her usual outfit today, light slacks and a bright blouse. Her brown hair was styled attractively and practically, and she greeted the group with a smile.

Nell had worked with Ellen on a benefit for Father Northcutt's children's center and liked her generous spirit. She was tall and straight, and the only resemblance that Nell could find between the two sisters were their ocean-deep green eyes — sometimes unnerving in their challenging, steady gaze.

"I'm so sorry to disturb you," Ellen said. "I spotted Rebecca as I walked by and had some gallery details to discuss with her."

"You've developed quite a following at the gallery, Ellen. Sometimes it's so busy, I can't get in the door. You're doing a great job."

"That's because of Rebecca," Ellen said modestly. "We have a whole new display of her beads — she's been literally working

211

night and day to get them done. And she's blown some paperweights, too. And lovely glass vases. You'll have to stop in."

"I will," Nell said. "I hear your remodeling is nearly finished. Skylights, a new studio. Lots going on."

A look passed between the two women, and then Ellen answered pleasantly, "Yes, it's beautiful. Rebecca had the eye for it all."

"And Ellen the purse strings," Rebecca said with a short laugh. She slid back her chair and stuffed her paper napkin into the empty mug and stood. "Thanks for the chair and the company. I hope this sordid mess surrounding Aidan's death can be cleared up soon, and we can go back to business as usual. This has been an interminable week."

It sounded to Nell as if Rebecca were assigning them a task — *solve this soon or else.*

As if it were theirs to solve.

"Is there something new?" Ellen asked. "Chief Thompson told me it was all wrapped up."

Rebecca tucked her arm in Ellen's. "It is, El. No worries, dear. I guess they just need to discover a few more details about the Adams girl." Her words trailed behind her as the pair walked out the patio gate and onto Harbor Road.

"So now it's our job?" Cass said as the pair walked off. Her dark brows lifted.

"My thoughts exactly. Perhaps it's because we've befriended Willow. If we don't think she did it, then it's our job to find out who did."

"Rebecca seems pretty convinced that Willow is guilty."

Nell nodded. Rebecca seemed *positive* that Willow had done it. And that was puzzling. Did Rebecca *want* Willow to be found guilty? Overhearing one conversation, especially when Rebecca herself had probably been heard hurling words at Aidan, didn't seem solid enough somehow. Nell wedged a bill beneath the sugar bowl to tip the young teen cleaning the outdoor tables. For everyone's attempts to make this a simple murder, it simply wasn't turning out that way. Not at all.

Nell normally stayed away from the Seaside Knitting Studio on Saturday afternoons. Izzy, Mae, and Mae's twin nieces, Rose and Jillian, had their hands full, especially during the summer months.

But this Saturday, Cass, Nell, and Birdie all showed up to help Izzy with a head hugger class. A group of summer people from Rockport and some friends of Izzy's from

Beverly were joining locals to make Izzy's head hugger project a huge success. Izzy had suggested that it would be a perfect summer project — knitting the caps for children or adults who had lost their hair. Izzy discounted the softest, finest yarn she could find, and by summer's end they'd have enough caps to warm any head needing a soft, gentle caress and protection from winter chills. She'd planned it for the end of the day when the crowds were dwindling and even shop owners could sneak away and join the group.

On her way to the back knitting room, Nell passed the magic room and stepped in for a minute to greet Laura Danvers' baby, Skye. The two-year-old's blond curls bounced as she looked up at Nell and grinned. In her arms she cradled one of Izzy's old dolls. Izzy had filled the room with toys and books and beanbag chairs, a haven for little ones when their mothers needed some minutes alone with needles and yarn and adult friends. Rose and Jillian, or Mae herself, kept careful watch and the room became a favorite hideaway. The magic room had been a stroke of genius — and Sea Harbor mothers agreed. Nell waved at Rose, her supple teenage body folded as easily on the floor as a three-year-old's, and walked down the three steps into the back room.

The chatter of excited, happy women greeted her, some seated at the table, others in small groupings of chairs, and Birdie and Cass camped out on the window seat. Rachel Wooten had joined them, and Nell was happy to see Ellen Marks as well. Even Natalie Sobel was giving up a precious hour to lend to the cause, which was a surprise, since Nell somehow didn't picture Natalie as the knitting type.

Nell gave Izzy a quick peck on the cheek, then settled onto one of Ben's old leather sofas next to Ellen.

"I'm glad you could get away from the shop for this, Ellen."

Ellen leaned in toward Nell and spoke above the chatter circulating the room as Izzy passed out yarn and patterns. "We hired some college art students to help Rebecca show off her beads. It gives me time to help with other things, like the arts council. Besides, I'm much more comfortable with office things, keeping books, that sort of thing — the less colorful jobs, I guess you'd say. Number crunching, my dad called it." She laughed softly.

"Which you're very good at, Jane tells me. Without you, she said, the Canary Cove arts council wouldn't know what to do. Most artists aren't very good at the money side of things."

Ellen laughed. "That's certainly true of Rebecca."

"So you get your talent from your father. Does Rebecca get hers from your mother?"

Ellen was caught off-guard by the question. She thought about it for a moment and then said, "Mother, yes, I suppose that's right."

"Well, she is certainly talented."

Ellen nodded, pride softening her angular face.

Nell looked down at the pile of yarn on Ellen's lap. "I think of knitting as a kind of art form. At least it can be. And you seem to love it as much as I do, Ellen."

Ellen picked up a ball of pink angora yarn, as soft and light as cotton candy, and cupped it in the palm of her hands. "Isn't this amazing? Izzy carries the most wonderful yarn. And this hat project is so wonderful."

Nell smiled at the respect Ellen afforded the luxury yarn. Izzy knew more about fibers than anyone she knew. She purchased it carefully, making sure of the integrity of the fiber, as well as knowing about the goats or sheep or alpacas from which it was harvested and where it was woven. It was nice when that knowledge was acknowledged. "Does Rebecca knit?"

Ellen laughed in a tone that clearly answered Nell's question. "She has many talents, but knitting isn't one of them."

The tinkling of Izzy's silver bell indicated quiet was expected, and a hush fell over the group. Nell watched her niece with pride as she held up Birdie's multicolored cap and told them what a treat was in store for them. "For the newcomers today, you will find that these hats are great fun to knit — but the satisfaction that comes afterward is even better. Some of you who summer here but live elsewhere haven't experienced winter on Cape Ann."

Laughter and empathetic groans greeted the comment.

"So imagine facing it without the comfort and warmth of a head of hair." Izzy talked a little more about knitters all around the country giving their time to supply hats and caps to friends and family, oncology centers, children's hospitals — wherever warm, soft hats were needed to comfort bare heads.

The women took turns touching Birdie's feathery cap and looked at pictures Izzy had downloaded from the Web — hats in vibrant colors and fanciful designs. "I think you've

217

all picked your patterns and I've a boatload of yarn to pick from, and wonderful, experienced friends available." She motioned toward the group near the fireplace and window. "We're here to help you get started, pick up dropped stitches or for those of you vacationing here, simply to suggest good restaurants for dinner. Now let the good times begin." Izzy smiled and stepped down from the small box she used when speaking to a crowded room. She walked over to Nell, a soft cotton skirt swirling about her long tan legs.

"Great crowd, Aunt Nell."

"Great instructor," Nell said back.

"I invited Willow — she's nearly half done with the hat she started Thursday."

"She turned you down?"

Izzy nodded. "Brendan was taking her sailing. I think she's hiding out, frankly."

"Can you blame her?" Cass said, handing the needles back to a first-time knitter whom she had just helped. With Cass' help the older woman had successfully cast on the first row and was proudly showing it to everyone around her.

"People are pretty insensitive sometimes."

Natalie Sobel, sitting nearby, looked up. Her penciled eyebrows lifted inquisitively. "Insensitive how?"

"Well, Mary Pisano's column, for starters. I don't think she meant harm, but she puts in little things that incriminate Willow. Then people repeat them."

"And Willow can't be immune to the talk, certainly," Birdie said. She eyed the first two rows of Harriet Brandley's celery green hat, then helped her loop in a second color.

"Well, I heard from my Billy that she certainly was the perpetrator," Natalie said, the "r" falling away from her words and betraying her Bronx childhood.

"And Bill knows because?" Cass said.

Natalie shrugged. "Billy knows a lotta things." She slipped a folded piece of gum into her mouth and went back to her knitting.

"When do you think the James paintings will be ready to see?" Nell asked, diverting the conversation from potential conflict.

Natalie perked up. "Maybe this week. Monday, maybe. Brendan is helping, working hard. Cleaning the gallery, getting the best lighting. They're glorious, you know. But with all this Aidan Peabody business, Billy was dragging his feet, thinking it didn't seem right to have a festive occasion. But I told Billy that his friend Aidan wouldn't want him to do that. He would want Billy to have a reception so people could see the beautiful paintings and to have much success."

Nell listened politely. Nothing she'd heard in the last couple weeks indicated Aidan was thrilled about the exhibit. She wondered, briefly, if Aidan had known that it would take attention away from the other artists, maybe create an atmosphere counter to the usual laid-back summers on Canary Cove.

"Aidan and Billy argued, sure," Natalie was saying, her needles clicking erratically. "But that's because they were like brothers."

Nell bit back a smile at the brothers analogy.

"Well, if you have something," Ellen said, "be sure to include all of us, Natalie."

Nell noticed the upward tilt of Natalie's chin as Ellen spoke. "Of course," she said stiffly. "Of course. Everyone will know."

Ellen didn't seem to notice Natalie's body language. "We can help, too, if you need anything. Just let us know."

"We are managing just fine, Ellen. There is a lot to do, but we can do it."

Natalie's words were pointed, as if delivering a message to each of them. But one, Nell suspected from the looks on people's faces, no one understood. Natalie folded up her knitting and stuffed it into a designer bag at her side. Nell noticed that the stitches slipped off the needles, but it was clearly not the time to mention dropped stitches. Natalie was leaving.

"Isabel, thank you for doing this wonderful thing with the hats," she said to Izzy. Then she turned to the small window group and nodded, avoiding Ellen Marks and directing her smile to Nell and Birdie. "I will see you ladies at the Sobel Gallery. You will be most welcome. Good-bye."

Natalie's departure would have been speedy and quick, if Purl hadn't taken that opportunity to jump off the window seat and land directly in front of Natalie Sobel's high-heeled sandals.

Nell was up in an instant but not in time to prevent Natalie from tumbling forward toward the archway and steps leading to the rest of the store. With a scream, Natalie dropped her heavy purse and fell to the floor, her tight red skirt hiking up and the contents of her purse spilling across the bottom step and floor below.

"Natalie, I'm sorry," Izzy murmured, bending over and checking Natalie's face.

Cass turned the music up a decibel to defray attention from the embarrassed woman, and Birdie stood between Natalie and group, providing some privacy as they

221

helped her to her feet. "I'm fine, just fine," she insisted as Izzy urged her to sit down.

"Let me help," Nell said, scooping up the contents of Natalie's purse. She picked up several lipsticks, a small wallet, a compact, the knitting needles, loose yarn, car keys, and a hairbrush. A diamond bracelet had landed beneath a chair; several sparkly rings rolled within Nell's grasp. And then her eyes fell on several glass items that had rolled beneath a chair. She looked at them, and then, as quickly as she could, she shoved the four tiny airplane bottles of vodka into Natalie's purse.

The exhibit festivities were starting a little sooner than expected, she thought.

CHAPTER 18

They hadn't planned a women's night out, but after Natalie's embarrassing fall and the completion of the hat class, something was clearly needed. Mae and her nieces had nicely cleaned and closed up the shop — all the toys were on shelves in the magic room, the computer shut down, and the display of plush organic baby alpaca yarn was straightened and piled high on the round table near the checkout desk.

Izzy turned on the outer spotlights and the security system that Willow's arrival had reminded her was needed. She held her keys in her hand.

"Looks like time to call it a day."

"Ben is sailing with friends," Nell said. "Anyone free for dinner? It's either that or we sit down right here and regroup. There are enough rumors and innuendos going around right now to kill a moose."

"If we can do this with food, my brain

cells will work much better. But I'm not cooking," Cass said.

Birdie laughed and patted Cass' hand. "We second that, dear. You're *not* cooking. And I agree, Nell. The police aren't an inch closer, and each day Willow's reputation sinks a little deeper into the swamp."

Izzy walked back from the corner of the room and snapped her cell phone shut. "Sam, it seems, is in the fishing and sailing group. We had tentative plans for tonight, but I've been upstaged by a halibut or cod or something. They are having way too good a time with their smelly fish to come home, so I'm a free woman. How about you, Birdie?"

"My plans for tonight included watching *Ocean's Eleven* and eating a BLT, wild thing that I am."

"Okay, then, where shall we go? A place where we can hear one another is my only criterion."

"And preferably a place with a fine wine list," Birdie said.

"Sam had a table reserved at Ocean's Edge for the two of us. We can talk there — and they have decent wine. Let's see if they can add two chairs to the saved table." Izzy slipped her purse over her shoulder and dialed the restaurant while the group headed for the front door.

They drove together, all four of them, in Izzy's well-used Jetta — the little car she'd bought when she traded in her law-practice BMW two years before. She named the car Greta and loved it dearly, though a hybrid lurked on the edges of her mind.

The Ocean's Edge was a big white restaurant with enough windows to keep Shawn Lanigan, Sea Harbor's top window washer, busy all year long. It clung to the rocky shore right in the middle of the village and was surrounded by grassy lawns that sloped down to the harbor and hosted picnics, fireworks, clambakes, and a gazebo, where local entertainers performed and young lovers met on warm summer nights. Nearby, Pelican Pier, dotted with gulls, fishermen, and strollers, jutted out into the water.

The Edge had good food, a spacious porch that swung around the octagonal-shaped restaurant, and a waitstaff that had grown up in Sea Harbor and came back every summer to carry steamed clams and oysters on the half shell to eager customers.

"Thanks, sweetie," Nell said as Gracie Santos, a childhood friend of Cass', greeted them warmly and led them to a table on the deck. Though the restaurant was always busy on Saturday nights, Gracie found them

225

a table on the porch slightly separated from the others by a large fern and colorful pots of daisies, argeratum, and zinnias. Tiny Christmas lights circled the deck, hanging from pillar to pillar and swaying slightly in the breeze coming in off the ocean.

Gracie wrote down the wine Birdie selected, and Cass added a platter of calamari to the list. Gracie chuckled at her friend's weakness for anything fried. "For you, Cass," she said, "I'll bring the extra large platter."

Once Gracie disappeared, Nell wasted no time. "It's only been a week since Aidan died, but it's been an eternity in Willow's life. She needs to be able to mourn her father — no matter how she feels now."

"She certainly can't do that with the police breathing down her neck." Cass sat back in her chair.

"None of us can mourn him properly," Birdie added. "Aidan was our friend. This awful shadow is hanging over all of us. We need to bring resolution to it all. Walking around the cove is not the pleasurable stroll it used to be."

"Not to mention that someone did murder Aidan. And that someone may very well be walking down Harbor Road every day, right past the Seaside Knitting Studio. Sitting at

226

a table next to us at Coffee's —"

Izzy ran her hands up and down her bare arms. "It gives me the chills."

"So what do we have so far?" Birdie asked. "I think better when I can see thoughts written out on paper." She took a blank tablet from her purse and pushed it in front of Izzy. "The light out here is lovely but not conducive to eighty-year-old eyes."

"Eighty?" Cass lifted one eyebrow.

"Hush, Cass, dear." Birdie paused to sip from the wineglass Gracie held in front of her. "Lovely," she approved and turned back to the group while Gracie filled their glasses.

"To our well-knit friendship," Birdie said, holding her glass in the air.

"To friends," the other women chorused.

The crisp calamari appeared in the next minute, served with a tangy Thai lime dipping sauce. "Try it," Gracie urged. "You'll love it."

And they did, sticking the slivers of fried squid into the cilantro, basil, and mint sauce. Sips of wine soothed the spicy aftertaste, and after ordering dinner, Nell brought the group down to business once again.

She tapped her finger on the table. "We need to step back. We're in the middle of the forest and not seeing the trees," she said.

"I think that there's something going on over at the cove that is flying right by us."

"The key is to find others who might have wanted Aidan dead," said Izzy, looking down at the yellow pad. "D. J. Delaney for sure. Frankly, he bothers me. A lot of people are having trouble with him. Natalie Sobel said the house he built for them is a mess."

"His motive is strong — he's been hungry for that land as long as I've known him and was mad as a hatter when Aidan bought it up right in front of him those years ago. He didn't have the money then to buy it himself, but he never got over it. And never had nice things to say about Aidan because of it. I think he's always resented him."

"Not to mention that the Delaney company is having trouble right now," Cass added. She looked around to see if Gracie was within earshot. Married to D.J.'s son, Joe, Gracie often shared Delaney family gossip with Cass. "Gracie says he's not a bad guy — but when push comes to shove, his company and pocketbook come first. I've heard lots of stories from my fishermen buddies about D.J. trying to turn a piece of land into something that will pad the pocket. And he's not above cutting corners where it suits him. Rachel Wooten has seen a lot of complaints come into the city offices. He's always looking for new places to develop." Cass piled more calamari on her plate and then licked off her fingers.

"And it's often at the expense of a beautiful park or playground or preserve. I think that's why Aidan clung to his land so tightly. It afforded Canary Cove a bit of green space."

"So D.J. has motive. Could he have actually done it?" Izzy doodled around the words on her pad of paper.

"I think that's what makes this so hard for the police," Nell said. "Ben talked to Chief Thompson, and he said anyone could have put the poison in the drink. Canary Cove was crawling with tourists, vacationers, and residents that night. And Aidan's gallery was packed, just as it always is. It was hot, and everyone had a glass or bottle of water or beer or wine in hand. Aidan had been working a couple of hours before we saw him. I suspect that the drug was dropped early in the evening because by the time we saw him, he was feeling terrible — we just didn't know how terrible."

"And then there's Rebecca," Cass said. "I think she knows more than she's saying. There was something off about her today when we talked at Coffee's."

"She seems so absolutely sure that Willow

did it — that's what's odd to me," Nell added. "She doesn't add anything to what we know — that Aidan was Willow's father, and Willow yelled at him that day, but there's a certainty in the way she talks."

"What about Ellen?"

Izzy chewed a piece of calamari thoughtfully. "Ellen comes into the shop often — she's a great knitter. And sometimes we get a chance to talk briefly. She was in a couple weeks ago, right after Aidan and Rebecca broke up, and her reaction to the breakup was odd. I don't think she cared much that Rebecca and Aidan weren't a couple any longer. And she indicated Rebecca didn't care much either. 'She can have anyone she wants,' was her take on Rebecca and men. That's probably true."

"Killing someone for breaking your sister's heart may have been a motive in early historical romances, but it seems a rather unlikely motive now," Birdie said.

They laughed.

"True," Nell said. "I think Ellen, like a lot of the others, thought Aidan was a little too pushy when it came to the council meetings. Jane said that some years, depending on who was leading the committee, the meetings were pretty tame. But somehow Aidan managed to inject a little spice into things. But that was Aidan. If he was going to do the job, he'd do it right, even though I suspect he didn't even like being head of the group. He just figured it was his turn and he was paying his dues."

"I never thought of Aidan as pushy or dictatorial." Birdie looked up and smiled as Gracie appeared again, this time carrying a broiled seafood platter, mounded with stuffed shrimp and oysters, chunks of fresh lobster, and the Edge's special crab cakes. Grilled corn on the cob lined the platter. A fellow server removed the appetizers and set a clean plate in front of each of them.

"Enjoy, ladies," Gracie urged, positioning the platter in the center of the table.

Birdie refilled wineglasses as Gracie disappeared inside. "So what were the complaints about Aidan?"

"Like Nell said, he took the job seriously," Cass said. "We had a drink together one night at the Gull and he told me that everyone had a different agenda. Rebecca and Ellen — and Bill Sobel, too — wanted out-of-town advertising, that sort of thing, which would bring in more tourists. Sherrie Steuben, who owns that new handmade paper shop, couldn't begin to pay for advertising in the *Globe* or *Times*. Aidan understood that and sided with the artists who weren't as interested in reaching the whole world. He thought their dues would be better spent on things like fixing up that old dock so no one would break their neck on it."

"A good idea," Nell said. "Ben and Sam docked there one day to catch a bite at the Palate and nearly fell off the end. It's rocky and very deep out there. Falling through rotted wood wouldn't be a good thing."

Izzy looked up from her scribbling on the pad. "So Rebecca? Does she make the list or not?"

"I suppose," Birdie said. "At least until we have a chance to gather information that says otherwise. Though I still say being dumped is a weak excuse for murder."

"But I think that Rebecca knows more than she's saying."

"I agree. And don't forget Mary Pisano's column — someone was in Aidan's house snooping around last night. I bet it was Rebecca. And she probably had a key since they were an item for a while." Cass picked up a crunchy cob of corn.

"But what would she have wanted from Aidan's house?"

The group had no answer.

"Maybe a talk with Mary Pisano should be on our to-do list," Nell suggested.

They were all silent for a bit, knowing that if the leaps they took were too wide, they could fall into the chasm.

"Rebecca was in the shop the day Willow was there. She said she was there because she needed to talk to Aidan about something. I wonder what that was about."

"I'll ask Ellen," Izzy said. "She comes in the shop a lot."

"Should Billy Sobel be a suspect?" Izzy asked.

Nell had been wondering the same thing. She remembered the look on Billy's face at the funeral. Sad. Distraught. Maybe even a touch of guilt. And Aidan had given him a hard time about his exhibits, apparently, making him jump through hoops. Sometimes it even seemed a little unfair to Nell. And it certainly must have seemed that way to Billy and Natalie.

"The police have talked to him, according to Hank," Birdie said. "Not a lot goes on over there that the Jacksons don't see or hear from the Palate deck. Merry saw the police go into the Sobel Gallery and promptly took herself over there to check out a new Rhodes photograph he'd gotten in."

"And to eavesdrop."

"Well, mostly that, yes."

233

"Billy was upset, Merry said. And extremely nervous. He stumbled over his words, gave silly answers, admitted that he and some others didn't like the way Aidan Peabody was dictating to the artists and dealers in the cove."

"Dictating?" Nell broke in. "That's silly."

"Billy started out calm, Merry said, but the more he talked, the redder his face got and he kept fiddling with those gold chains around his neck. He was perspiring like crazy, she said. Well, she didn't actually say 'like crazy.' Merry is a bit more colorful in her descriptives."

"Well, frankly, if Billy was going to kill anyone, I think it'd be his wife," Cass said lightly.

"Catherine, shame on you," Birdie chastised. "But Natalie can be difficult, can't she? Colorful, to say the least, though I like her. She adds a bit of color to the cove."

"She just signed on with a decorator from Beacon Hill to redo the whole gallery," Izzy said. "She asked me for names. I guess she thought because I lived there once, I'd know all the decorators."

Nell held back a smile as memories of Izzy's Beacon Hill apartment popped into her head. A kitchen table, a bed, and a couple of chairs from the Beacon Hill home she and Ben once lived in — that was about it. But Izzy was not into decorating at that time in her life — she was into keeping up as a fledgling lawyer in a powerful law firm.

"That's interesting," Birdie said. "Billy had a slight cash-flow problem as of late, I thought. I wonder who's paying for the decorator."

"Maybe this exhibit will take care of that. And maybe that's why he was so mad that Aidan was slowing things down."

"Do you suppose Aidan objected to the remodeling plans for Sobel Gallery? The artist committee may need to approve that, especially if it involved outdoor changes. And knowing Natalie, the changes could be . . . well, perhaps a bit showy?" Birdie took a drink of her wine and motioned to a waiter to please bring another bottle.

"Something doesn't seem quite right with Billy, now that we're talking about it," Izzy said, drawing doodles around the "B" of his name. "He's been kind of . . . well, skittish. Sam and I saw him that night Aidan died — we went into his studio because Sam wanted to see if the James paintings were there. Billy kind of barked at us when we asked, like he was fed up with people asking."

Gracie had placed warm sourdough rolls

235

on each of their plates, along with cubes of sweet butter, and was now uncorking the fresh bottle of wine and asking if anyone needed anything else.

"Goodness," Birdie said, "we're closing you down."

"Not quite, Ms. Birdie. I still have a few tables out here and some inside. And the bar is plenty full. Crazy in there tonight. But I saved you all some key lime pie. It's on its way."

Between bites of the Ocean's Edge's sweet pie and sips of lattes, the knitters' to-do list grew more organized. Besides the logical people to talk to, they would keep their eyes and ears open and remain tuned in to their suspicions as they went about their days. And in a town the size of Sea Harbor, that just might be enough to turn some of the murky gray areas into vivid Technicolor.

Or Dolby sound.

The shattering of glass broke into the soft music coming from the porch speakers. It was followed instantly by shouting from the bar and drew the knitters' attention toward the open bar area at the front of the restaurant.

"That's a familiar voice," Nell said.

With that, the four women left their signed credit card receipts, leaving extravagant tips for Gracie, and gathered up purses and sweaters before heading across the porch, up to the open bar area.

A young waiter, his stance uncomfortable and his eyes focused on the sea of broken glass littering the floor, stood beside the tall bar table with a broom in his hand.

Sitting precariously on the stool, his arms spread haphazardly in the spill of scotch across the table, his eyes as red as the blood on his cut hand, sat Billy Sobel.

"Bill, are you all right?" Nell stood close to him on his other side, bending low so he could hear her.

With great effort, Bill lifted his head and turned toward the familiar voice, trying to focus on Nell's face.

The smile that followed was weak and disconcerting. A smile that wasn't a smile at all. A smile that held sadness.

"Nell," he said, his voice barely audible above the music from the bar. He paused for a moment, as if struggling to collect his thoughts. Finally his vision seemed to clear and he looked as steadily as he could at Nell.

"I'm a mess, aren't I?"

His voice was slurred with alcohol and anguish. "Life's a wicked mess right now. I shouldna done it. None of it."

And with that, his heavy head dropped

unceremoniously to the table, his eyelids closed, and Billy Sobel gave in to the comfort of inebriated stupor.

CHAPTER 19

"How much of what a drunk man says can he be held accountable for?" Nell asked, a question that she had reworded a dozen different ways, hoping that one of them would bring an answer. She took the Sunday *New York Times* from the backseat of the car and walked beside Ben across the gravel parking lot to the restaurant.

Though they didn't make it every Sunday, breakfast at the Sweet Petunia was a treat Ben Endicott didn't forgo lightly. Nell's anxiousness over the episode with Billy Sobel didn't come near to being a valid reason to give up Annabelle's egg special of the day.

"We'll talk about it there," Ben had assured her. "After one cup of Annabelle's Colombian brew, we'll be much better equipped to figure it all out."

None of the knitters had slept well, Nell knew. Birdie had called at seven, and Izzy had stopped by on her way to meet Sam for a run not long after.

With the help of several young waiters, they had folded Billy into the backseat of Izzy's Jetta. Cass and Nell had generously agreed to take the other two seats in the back, and as Cass said later, if it hadn't been so sad and so smelly, it would have been quite hilarious. They kept the windows open and drove the short distance to the Sobel home, located in a lovely neighborhood on the north shore just a short distance from Birdie's estate. The front of the house was well lit when they pulled into the circle drive and at the sound of the car, Natalie appeared, a robe wrapped tightly around her waist and her face, without makeup, looking young and vulnerable.

Without words, they pried Billy out of the car, maneuvered him through the front hall, and, following the point of Natalie's red fingernail, into a den at the rear of the recently finished house. There they eased him down onto the cushions of a leather couch. He began snoring immediately.

Only when they headed back toward the front door did Natalie speak. "He's a good man, you know. I've known lots of men. My Billy is the best — he never cheats on me. He never hits me. He treats me like a queen."

Nell looked at Natalie and attempted a smile.

"Billy is under a lot of pressure. He just isn't himself these days."

For a brief moment, Nell was tempted to embrace Natalie Sobel. She hardly knew the woman — Billy had brought her back to Sea Harbor last Thanksgiving, like a prize, some thought. He announced they had gotten married in Atlantic City, and then threw an extravagant party in Sea Harbor to celebrate his much-younger wife. Not too many people had gotten to know Natalie. She helped in Billy's gallery sometimes, but her favorite pastime seemed to be shopping. Nell often saw her browsing in the stores along Main Street in Gloucester, the antique shops in Rockport, or out at the mall, which she seemed to love. But last night, as she stood beneath her porch light, it was clear to Nell that what Natalie loved most was Billy Sobel.

"Looks like Annabelle has quite a crowd today," Ben said, looking through the door into the cheery restaurant.

"Ben, you say that every Sunday."

"And it's always true. It's so nice to be able to be right at least once a week." He smiled a satisfied smile and wrapped an arm around Nell as they walked into the cool interior of the restaurant.

A wave of enticing smells — bacon, eggs, coffee, fresh fruit, and warm maple syrup — met them at the door. And Stella Palazola, Annabelle's teenage daughter, was there to meet them as well.

"I've got a table for you," she announced cheerily. "You're outside today because it's so nice and sunny."

"Well, thanks, Stella. That's mighty nice of you," Ben said.

Nell followed, finding herself basking in the familiarity of it. Stella said the same thing every summer Sunday, too — and Nell suspected she'd say the same thing even if they were having terrible weather and it was pouring rain.

Annabelle's restaurant was located on an unmarked lane that wound up a slight hill on Canary Cove. From the restaurant windows or the deck, one looked over the whole artists' colony, the small lanes and gardens behind the studios, and the ocean beyond. The restaurant was nearly hidden — a fact Annabelle was just fine with. Though other Sea Harbor businesses relied on vacationers and tourists for their summer income, Annabelle did fine by catering to the artists who lived and worked on

Canary Cove and the locals who couldn't go longer than a week without one of her frittatas or eggs Benedict served on a layer of fresh spinach. Though Nell considered herself a good cook, she admitted that her hollandaise sauce paled next to Annabelle's.

As soon as they sat down at a table near the railing, Stella returned with the glass coffeepot and filled their mugs. Steam rose up and fogged her glasses but she didn't seem to notice. "So," she said, leaning over the table, "did she do it?"

Nell looked up from the menu. "Do it?"

"Kill him. Did that Willow girl kill Aidan? Or was it Rebecca? Aidan dropped her like a hot potato, you know. Or a stranger who disliked Aidan? Maybe someone he jilted, someone jealous of him. Or who?"

"Stella, I don't think that's . . ."

Stella went on as if Nell hadn't spoken. "They ate here a lot when they were, you know, together, because she can't cook — Rebecca, that is — and they argued about everything. Well, not Aidan so much, because he didn't like to make a scene, but, like, it didn't stop Rebecca. And then their affair was over." Stella snapped her fingers. "Just like that — *poof.* And then he was dead." Her brows lifted above the upper rim of her glasses.

"It might not be so simple, Stella," Nell began.

Ben had already spread the *Times* out on the table and was deep into the "Week in Review," his weekly protection against Stella's chatter.

But Stella, it seemed, had moved on as well, her gaze no longer focused on Nell, but looking beyond her to a couple sitting several tables down.

"He's here," she said in a hushed tone. "And he's with *her.*"

"Who?"

"My art teacher."

Nell turned slightly in her chair, trying, inconspicuously, to follow Stella's gaze.

Brendan Slattery and Willow Adams sat several tables down, tucked into the corner of the porch.

"Is he not like the coolest?"

"I didn't know you were into art, Stella."

"Everyone is. We're all trying to get into Mr. Slattery's class. He's not married. He used to live in Maine. And he's an insomniac — did you know that? Sometimes he used to doze off in class and kids would take his picture and put them on the Internet. I have one above my bed. He's so like hot."

Nell tried to squeeze into the mind-set of a seventeen-year-old. Brendan was attractive — that was true. He had a runner's body and a shadow of a beard covering his strong chin. She watched him lean in toward Willow, dark, brooding eyes looking intently at his dining partner. She knew Brendan was over thirty — slightly old to capture teenage hearts, she would suppose. But apparently not. Nor did he seem too old to capture a twenty-two-year-old's heart, if that was what was going on with him and Willow. It was hard for Nell to tell. They were spending a lot of time together, which Nell found comforting. Willow needed someone to lean on right now, and though she had the knitters and Ben behind her, it didn't hurt a bit to have a tall nice-looking man beside her as well.

Brendan spotted Nell, then, and waved.

"He waved at me!" Stella said.

Nell looked down at her menu. If a simple wave brought such pleasure to Stella, who was she to rob her of it?

"I think I'll take the special," Nell said, folding the menu and handing it to Stella.

Without acknowledging the order, Stella stuck her pad of paper into the pocket of her short, swishy skirt and walked off. Breakfast would come, but what it would be was anyone's guess. The certainty was that it would be delicious.

"Ah, here you are." Izzy's shadow fell across the table. "Room for two more?"

"Sure thing," Ben said, folding the paper over and pulling out a chair.

Izzy's hair was still damp from a recent shower, and she'd changed from running shorts to a soft cotton skirt and tank top. Her face was flushed and her eyes bright. "Had a great run."

"I have a hard time keeping up with her. Between Willow and Iz, I'm left in the dust." Sam took off his sunglasses.

"You ran with Willow?"

Izzy nodded. "She was heading down to Sandpiper Beach when I left your house, so she joined me. Then we met Sam. I think Willow runs to block out the world. She's really into it. Sometimes Brendan runs with her, she said, but he has trouble sleeping some nights, and last night was one of them."

"So we hear," Nell said, nodding toward Stella. "Stella knows all."

Izzy laughed.

"I think the running is good therapy for Willow."

"No doubt."

Sam agreed. "She tries to be blasé about everything that's going on, but when you catch her unguarded, she looks like the weight of the world is on her shoulders."

Nell nodded toward the table down near the kitchen door. "She's here."

Izzy turned her head. Willow's and Brendan's heads were inclined toward each other, and it looked like they were deep in conversation. "We had invited her to come with us — but she was headed toward Brendan's. I am sure it was Sam's raving restaurant review that convinced her to bring Brendan over here."

"Any news on the murder case, Ben?" Sam asked. He picked up the coffeepot that Stella had left and refilled cups all around.

"I talked to Jerry Thompson again today. The police are perplexed, frankly. He said they are looking into it being someone from out of town — someone from Aidan's past, maybe. But they're still unwilling to eliminate Willow as a prime suspect. Opportunity. Motive. Everything. That inheritance is hard to hide under the rug. And the fact that she showed up two days before Aidan died doesn't look good, either."

"Except she knew nothing about the inheritance." Izzy frowned at Ben as if he were somehow to blame.

"Who else are they looking at? There are certainly others with motive and opportunity — we have a whole list. Take Billy Sobel, for example."

Ben and Sam had both heard the story in detail. "Even through the haze of alcohol, his words were clear," Nell said.

"He said he was sorry he did it," Izzy repeated slowly.

"But can we jump from that 'it' to murder?" Sam asked. "Couldn't he have been sorry for something else? Maybe simply for being drunk and making a scene. It was kind of embarrassing for a reputable art dealer."

"I don't think so, Sam. He was clearly distraught," Nell said. "And there was something not right about Bill at Aidan's funeral, too."

"But why would he kill Aidan?" Izzy cupped her chin on her hands, her elbows on the tabletop.

"Aidan was tough on Billy. Unfairly so, Jane and Ham thought. They tried to talk to him about it, but he always changed the subject. But something was going on. There was something peculiar about that whole exhibit planning."

Nell looked up as Stella arrived at the side of their table, balancing a tray with four plates. Each one was heaped full of cheesy vegetable frittatas stuffed with fresh tomatoes, asparagus, and peppers and topped with a dollop of sour cream with a wavy red line of hot sauce running through it like a river.

Sam sat back and eyed the plates. "Stella, my love, I have died and gone to heaven."

Stella giggled.

Sam took the plates from her tray and passed them around the table.

Ben waited until Stella was once again out of earshot. "I've been thinking about Billy. He came to me not too long ago for advice on a business plan for the Sobel Gallery. Just wanted to know what I thought. He was wanting to increase revenue. The plan wasn't half bad, but it wasn't going to get him close to what he needed this year. I gave him some suggestions — a special exhibit, for one. But if Aidan interfered with his plans, and how he ran his business, there's no telling what Billy might do."

"Or what any of us would do? How do you know until you're there? People have probably killed for far flimsier reasons." Nell added a few drops of cream to her coffee and stirred it thoughtfully. "Billy is a puzzle to me. He told me once that he spends a lot of time in Atlantic City at the casinos — which is where he met Natalie. He also goes to Foxwoods regularly. Although he didn't actually give me an accounting, he indicated

249

that he'd lost big on occasion. But on the other hand, when he does well and has a lot of extra cash, he gives it to others if they need it. Aidan told me he'd helped several artists starting up in Canary Cove, like that little stationery store. And when Merry and Hank started the Artist's Palate, Billy was so excited to have his favorite beer close by that he gave them money to pave the parking lot. Even Lampworks Gallery has benefited from his generosity. I think Billy knew the Marks women before they moved here, although it didn't seem to matter to him if he knew you or not. If you needed help and it was for a good cause, Billy was there if he could be."

"And now he has a new wife, who likes nice things — and that could cause some pressure." Izzy told them about the array of things that had fallen from her purse in the knitting studio.

Sam laughed. "I always wondered what women carried in those things. I'd like to go through yours someday, Iz. It'd hold a small hippo."

"In your dreams, Perry."

Nell wiped her hands on a napkin and pulled out a sleeve of the sweater that Izzy had sent her way. The peridot yarn was therapy for her fingers, soft and comforting.

She found herself pulling it out late at night when she and Ben sat on the deck, and carrying it around with her.

"Natalie came in for some yarn the other day," Izzy was saying beside her, "and she told me she was taking over Billy's books. Apparently she'd discovered his generous gestures and decided maybe she'd be a better captain of the bank account."

Ben shook his head. "I can't imagine that is sitting well with Billy. But knowing him, he'll find a way around it."

"She said they were having house problems. D. J. Delaney built it for them, and they've got a boatload of problems — plumbing, foundation, the whole works. Billy is furious, but also in need of cash because D.J. is calling it in. And Natalie is furious because she's found proof that Billy has stupidly lent out more money than any sane person should ever loan to another human being. Her words, not mine."

The talk of plumbing problems turned the conversation to Sam's new place, and he and Izzy began discussing the things that would need to be done.

Ben quietly opened the paper and slipped his reading glasses out of his pocket while Sam and Izzy bantered over paint colors and throw rugs.

251

Nell leaned back in the comfort of their company, lulled by the conversation that required nothing from her, and let the soft cashmere yarn and rhythm of knitting soothe her spirit. None of the talk about Billy's finances had moved them any closer to what had happened to Aidan, nor what had caused Billy's binge drinking the night before.

She looked over the porch railing, over the treetops and tightly knit neighborhood of Canary Cove. She and Ben usually ended up at the other end of the porch, a table closer to the door. From this vantage point, her view of the galleries and shops and ocean beyond was slightly different. The woods just below the deck were more dense, and the path that meandered through them nearly invisible. Nell followed the path down toward the shops and realized with surprise that on this side of Annabelle's, the woods that separated the hilltop restaurant from the occupied shops was Aidan's land — the lush property fragrant with pine trees, wild roses, and honeysuckle vines. She looked down the side of Annabelle's gray-shingled restaurant, thick with climbing hydrangeas and wisteria, and looked along the well-worn path. Aidan's small home was visible in the distance and, beyond it, slightly to the side, the private garden, bordered by crape myrtle and filled with lush plantings — purple-blue hydrangeas, filmy sea grasses. Looking down on it, she could barely make out the tended flagstone path and the stone bench where she'd last seen Aidan Peabody, but it was as clear in her mind's eye as if she were standing right in the middle of it. She rubbed her bare arms against the sudden chill the thought of that night brought on. Just a week ago, she thought. One short week.

So intent was Nell on the garden that she saw little else until movement at the edge of her eye brought her focus back to the path that led from the gallery to the garden, then wound past Aidan's cottage and up into the hilly woods. Two figures walked slowly away from the cottage, up the small hill.

When Aidan was alive, people often walked there, away from the artists' colony to the upper road and beach on the other side of the cove. Aidan even kept the rutted path tended for folks who liked to take a gentle hike through the wooded area, a gesture once complimented in Mary Pisano's "About Town" column.

"Aidan Peabody deserves a certificate of appreciation for his largesse," Mary had written. "When the mile-long path through the Peabody woods became overgrown and hikers had difficulty traversing the rise, Peabody hacked away roots and vines, added small granite slabs in the roughest spots and marked the beginning of the trail with one of his fanciful wooden sea urchins. A true citizen."

Nell smiled at the memory. They had teased Aidan about it, accused him of running for city council, but it didn't surprise any of his friends, not really. He did what he thought was right for the people of Sea Harbor — and stubbornly stood up for what he deemed wrong or inappropriate. A trait that had earned him dear friends. And enemies.

Nell watched the hikers without much thought and saw them pause in a small clearing, just visible from Nell's vantage point. One of the figures waved an arm in the air as if to make a point, an animated gesture that could have indicated pleasure — or anger. The sun, falling on the tiny open space like a spotlight on a stage, caught the glint of a familiar gold chain. Billy's beefy arm was dark with hair, his head nearly bald. In the patch of sunlight, it was clear that it was the owner of the Sobel Gallery.

And beside him, her hands at her side,

stood the slender figure of Ellen Marks.

"An interesting friendship," Nell murmured, more to herself than aloud, but Izzy heard and followed Nell's gaze beyond the railing and through the woods.

"Well, I'll be," she said. "Are Billy and Ellen friends?"

Nell sat back so Izzy could see better. But Billy and Ellen had begun walking again and soon disappeared in the trees as the path rose up the hill.

Nell nodded. "Rebecca's not crazy about Billy, but I think he finds Ellen levelheaded and a nice person to talk to — and Billy helped them out when they opened their shop, just like he helped a lot of other people."

"I wonder where Natalie is. I can't quite imagine her traipsing through the woods."

Nell laughed, thinking of the many pairs of stiletto heels she had seen Natalie wear around town. "No, she doesn't seem the woodsy type." She looked back toward the woods.

"I'm surprised to see Billy this morning at all, much less hiking up a hill. He must be feeling horrible."

"One would certainly think so. He must have a cast-iron constitution."

"Did you tell Ben about last night?"

Nell nodded. "He plans to talk to Billy later today. There were too many other people in that bar who could misinterpret what he said. Better Billy and Ben talk to the chief before someone else does."

"I'm sure he'll explain it away in two sentences." Izzy leaned back and craned her neck to see if anything more was happening. "Jeez. Aunt Nell, look."

Nell turned on her chair and looked down through the trees at more movement on the trail.

Her hands were wrapped around a walking stick nearly twice as tall as her five-foot frame, but it didn't slow the determined walk. Dressed in long shorts, a red sweater wrapped around her shoulders, and her cap of snow-white hair gleaming in the sunlight, Birdie resolutely and steadily made her way up the path, her eyes glued to the figures a short distance ahead.

"What is she doing?" Izzy said in hushed tones, hoping the Sunday *Times* had enough news to hold Sam's and Ben's interest.

"She was having breakfast with Jane and Ham down at their place earlier today. She must have spotted Billy. Maybe she wanted to make sure he was okay."

"Or wondered why he was walking up behind Aidan's house, is more like it.

Sometimes you're just too nice, Nell."

Ben looked up from the paper. He'd pulled out the sports section and given it to Sam. He looked from Nell to Izzy and back again.

"You two look like you're up to no good."

Izzy and Nell started eating their eggs.

"I mean it, Nell. I can see the wheels turning in your head."

"Ben, you know that the wheels turn slowly in Sea Harbor sometimes. Maybe it's not a bad thing we're turning our own."

"They may turn slowly, but they turn, Nell. Jerry Thompson is on this one."

"Nothing's happening, Uncle Ben. Nothing at all." Izzy ran her fingers through her hair.

"We need to do something. And talking to Billy Sobel is right up there on the list. We need to know what he was talking about last night."

Ben pushed his chair back and stretched his legs. "Here's what I think you need to do. I think you need to cool your heels. And that goes for Cass and Birdie, too. This isn't a game of Clue, Nell. Someone murdered Aidan Peabody. Intentionally."

Sam folded up the paper and set it aside. "So are you thinking Bill Sobel is involved in this?"

Ben scratched his head. "Well, at the least there are some questions that need to be asked."

"He's a nice guy. He's handled some of my photographs for me. Did a great job with the last exhibit. But I guess none of us knows what another guy —"

"Or gal," Izzy dropped in.

"Okay — or gal" — Sam offered Izzy a grin — "will do when pushed too far."

"That's right," Ben said. "And unless a stranger came into town, murdered Aidan, and then disappeared, that someone — that murderer — is probably someone we know."

"And maybe even someone we like," Nell added.

The thought sobered the group and they sat in silence for a minute.

Nell turned away, her gaze drifting over the treetops. The murderer could be an acquaintance, someone she rubbed shoulders with at the market, or had coffee with, or was on a committee with. An awful thought, not easy to digest. Leave it to Ben to sprinkle them with a little bit of realism on a sunny Sunday morning. But she knew exactly what he was doing — building a case for caution. Protecting those he loved. And even when she found it irritating, she loved him dearly for it.

"Take Willow, for example," Ben went on, his voice low and even. "We're so quick to defend her — and count me in there among the best of the defenders. I happen to think the lovely young woman couldn't kill a slug. But it's because we like her, and we somehow feel responsible for her. If we're really being objective — and I'm not saying we should be — but the real facts are that we don't know much about her and what she might have done or not done. We don't know what went on between her and Aidan. And she doesn't talk much to us. Willow is still a mystery."

The shadow that fell over the table wasn't carrying a tray or pot of coffee, and Nell knew instinctively, even before looking up into those familiar dark eyes, whom she'd see standing at the table's edge.

Willow Adams was alone, her dark hair pushed back haphazardly behind her ears, and her black eyes troubled. She seemed even smaller, Nell thought, than the sleeping, tired girl they had found in Izzy's window all those days ago.

"I shouldn't have been listening," Willow said. "I just came over to say hello."

"Willow, you need to understand the context," Nell began.

Willow held up one hand to stop her

explanation. "No, you're right. All of you. I know your words aren't meant to be hurtful. You've been nicer to me than anyone in my whole life. But you don't know much about me — that's true." A wry smile lifted the corners of her mouth. "The truth is, there isn't very much to know. I am what I am. But you need to know this much — and I swear on my mother's grave that it's the truth — I didn't kill my father."

Willow sucked in a lungful of air, as if the last statement had depleted her supply. She rested her palms on the table, and then she continued, her voice strong and in charge. "But you need more from me than that."

"No, Willow. That's enough. We believe you." Nell reached over and put her hand on top of Willow's.

Willow shook her head, her hair moving in slow motion, back and forth across her shoulders. The black in her eyes deepened and looked into Nell's.

"No, it's not enough. What I need to do is help you find the person who killed Aidan Peabody. I owe you that."

Ben had started to rise as soon as Willow approached the table. This time he made it all the way up.

Nell couldn't tell who made the first move, Willow or Ben, but in the next minute his arms were wrapped around Willow tight, and Willow hugged him right back.

A ruckus down the deck drew them apart, and Ben looked over the top of Willow's head to a table a short way away.

D. J. Delaney sat with a huge plate of eggs and bacon in front of him, and directly across the table were two of his foremen, eating oversized portions of Annabelle's Sunday special.

"They wanted double orders," Stella whispered, coming up to their table. "Can you believe anyone could eat that much?"

But it wasn't the food that had the other outdoor diners staring at the table.

It was Natalie Sobel, dressed in a pink lace blouse and standing tall on matching heels. She looked at the construction workers as if she were going to kill them.

"Our house is sinking," she screamed at D.J.

D.J. continued to chew on a bite of English muffin, his fork shoveling into a mound of eggs. His brows lifted and he smiled quizzically at the two men across from him.

"Don't you look away from me, D. J. Delaney," Natalie screamed. "And wipe that smirk off your face. We know what you are. You are a crook. A crook," she yelled.

And then she took a deep breath of air,

calmed herself, and dug into a shiny black purse hanging from a gold chain across her shoulder.

"It's done. We've just finished the paperwork," she said.

"For what?" D.J. asked, finally looking at Natalie.

"For suing the pants off you, you poor excuse for a human being."

And with that, she slapped an envelope right in the middle of his eggs and stomped out of the restaurant, her fine skinny heels tapping across the room.

The front door slammed shut and several cups rattled on a tray.

Stella pushed her glasses up to the bridge of her nose. "Sundays at Annabelle's," she said, half to herself. Then she pushed a pencil behind her ear, shrugged, and walked off to fill some empty water glasses.

262

CHAPTER 20

Izzy walked across the back room of the knitting studio. Outside, the sky was overcast, casting dark shadows across the room.

"Birdie, you can't be doing things like that," she scolded, her flip-flops slapping the floor more soundly than usual. "You're seventy-, eightysomething — you shouldn't be following people up hills, pretending you're Kinsey Millhone or Jessica Fletcher."

"Izzy, my dear, when will you begin to understand that age doesn't dictate actions. What is that saying Hallmark is so fond of — it's not how old you are but how . . . Oh, dear, I never get it right. But what matters isn't how old you are but what you do with those years. And if I chose to live them proving that a sweet young girl is innocent, then I shall jolly well do so." Birdie's voice was unusually caustic.

"Calm down, Ms. Favazza. I'd say you live your years mighty well. Just don't go getting yourself killed in the process." Cass walked across the room with a bottle of water in one hand and a lumpy knitting bag in the other.

Cass had pulled her thick hair back and tied it at the base of her neck with what looked to Nell like a piece of thin rope. Probably something from the *Lady Lobster,* she thought, amused.

The late-Sunday-afternoon gathering was impromptu. It was Nell's idea, stimulated by spotting Birdie in the woods, Izzy's new quota to have a dozen chemo caps a week, and the emotion lacing Willow's voice that morning, yearning for an end to the horrible mess that had put her life on hold.

Knit caps. Regroup. Cocktail hour, the text message read. It still mystified Nell how Izzy sent lightning-fast messages with her thumbs. Her own were limited to single words, and she'd only recently learned to add periods.

"This mess just has me seeing red," Birdie said. "What are we missing here? People are starting to lock their doors in Sea Harbor. We've got to put an end to it."

She sank back into the sofa, her red tennis shoes barely touching the floor.

Nell pulled her sweater from her bag. More head hugger hats were the goal, but she could easily knit up several of those at meetings she had scheduled this week. Willow's sea sweater — as she had begun to think about it — was less portable as it grew. And besides, if truth be known, the intriguing, intricate designs that magically appeared as she worked the cable stitches running from the top of the sweater to the bottom had become something that she couldn't put aside for long. And the texture of the yarn brought comfort to her fingers and her spirit.

"What were you going to do if Billy or Ellen turned around and saw you?" Izzy stopped straightening up the stray scissors, yarn markers, and measuring tapes on the worktable and looked over at Birdie.

"I would have said, 'Good morning. Lovely day, isn't it?' I certainly had as much right to be there as they did. What's the matter with all of you? A person can't take a stroll in Aidan's woods any longer? I think Aidan would have loved me being there. In fact, I felt him right there beside me. And I told him his path needed tending. A body could trip on those ruts."

Birdie was right, Nell thought. Aidan would have loved the image of the tiny white-haired woman with the huge walking stick climbing his hill. Especially if it brought them closer to finding out who killed him. And most especially if it cleared his daughter from suspicion so she could go on with her life.

"So what's the upshot?" Cass sat on the window seat, her legs crossed kindergarten-style, with Purl purring contentedly in the circle formed by her legs. A gusty wind blew in from off the ocean and Cass reached behind her and closed one of the windows. "Why were Ellen Marks and Billy Sobel strolling through the woods together? Did you talk to them?"

Birdie pulled her needles from the bag. Her cap was half finished, a delicious seamless concoction of hand-spun cotton in shades of yellow, blue, and cherry. It was her fifth cap in two weeks.

"Yes," she said, a satisfied look spreading across her lined face.

"Well?" the knitters' voices rose up in the salt-scented air and melded together as one.

Birdie's needles clicked to the beat of Elton John crooning about dancing in the sand. Without a pause, she pulled a ball of brilliant cherry cotton from her bag and slipped a strand around the needle, beginning a new row and a new color to the body of the hat. Though it was best to keep the caps smooth on the inside so they would be

266

soft and comfortable, she'd decided to form tiny knit flowers to sprinkle on the outside.

"When I got to the end of the trail, they were sitting at the top on those lovely wooden benches the women's club donated, the ones tucked off to the side, protected by that stand of arborvitae. They didn't see me at first. Their heads were bent, but I could tell Ellen looked worried about something — Rebecca, maybe? I think she worried about her sister like a mother hen.

"Billy was two sheets to the wind, as you might imagine. He looked like he was struggling to keep up with what Ellen was saying, so she raised her voice, as if that would help him focus. And I heard her tell Billy what a good friend he'd been — and she knew he'd help her out if she needed it."

"Why did she need help? What kind of help?" Cass pulled forward, not wanting to miss the punch line, and Purl jumped to the floor in a graceful leap. The fanciful child's cap Cass had been knitting fell from her lap to the floor, the silky strands of yarn waving in the breeze like a peacock's fan.

"I can't really say."

"Why?" Izzy and Nell chorused.

"Because I don't know. They must have discussed whatever it was while I was still out of earshot. But they both looked upset

— Ellen more worried, and Billy sad." Birdie finished a band of cherry on the hat, then pulled out a lemony yarn, wrapped it around her needle, and worked it into the next row. "They could have been talking about Aidan."

"Why Aidan?"

"Because when I first spotted them, they were standing at the trail head — the spot where that lovely little wooden figure of Aidan's sits, right beside his house. And they were both staring at the house as if Aidan himself was about to walk out the door."

"So Ellen was worried about Rebecca — or something." Nell's words came out slowly, inviting them all to make sense out of them.

"Something like murder?" Izzy pulled out the first assumption playing on each of their minds and laid it out in front of them.

"I can't get my arms around that," Birdie said. "Rebecca is emotional and spontaneous, but murder?"

"She certainly didn't like Aidan. She told us that herself."

"Why *did* they split up?" Cass asked, carrying a trayful of wineglasses to the table. "It happened abruptly, right? Aidan brought her to a Friday supper one week last month

— they seemed reasonably happy."

"Though Rebecca was quiet that night, I remember. And Aidan, too."

"And then the next week Aidan came alone."

"And he brushed off questions about it," Izzy said. "I remember, because I asked him about her. But breakups happen, I guess. Especially with the Rebeccas of this world. Besides, I thought they were an odd couple to start with."

Nell retrieved Birdie's chilled bottle of wine from the refrigerator and walked back into the room. "It didn't seem like a traumatic breakup — you're right. Aidan seemed fine. And Rebecca was out and about, flirtatious as ever. She didn't act like her life had changed much."

Nell was thoughtful for a minute, thinking of the few Friday nights that Aidan had brought Rebecca to dinner. She had the feeling from the beginning it was a relationship Rebecca had manipulated. And Aidan, for lack of other interests at the time, had gone along with it. Rebecca was beautiful. Witty.

She pulled out the cork and poured the pinot into the glasses on the coffee table. Izzy had put out a platter of crisp pita pieces and a round of Brie, some napkins, and small knives. A bowl of freshly picked strawberries made Nell smile with a touch of pride. Izzy had learned about balancing color and taste, sweet and tangy, from her many meals in her aunt's kitchen.

As the others reached for the wine and spread buttery Brie over the pita chips, Nell walked over to the open window and looked out over a fleet of white billowing sails as the boats scurried back into the harbor beneath the gray sky. The wind was strong and the blue sky they'd enjoyed in the morning was gone, the sky heavy with gray clouds burdened with the weight of rain.

She breathed in the earthy, slightly iron scent, mixed with the salty breeze. It wasn't far away. A summer storm.

A sudden flash of lightning lit up the darkening sky, and seconds later, thunder rolled across the water like an oncoming freight train. They needed the rain. And the timing was good, Nell thought. The rain would come tonight, and tomorrow Billy Sobel would have a clean, rain-washed day for the opening of his James exhibit. At least there were bright spots in the midst of the murkiness of murder.

And perhaps the rain would wash away some of the unanswered questions, too, and allow them to make sense of the puzzle pieces that were scattered right there in front of their eyes. Willow's inheritance. Aidan's relationships. Aidan and Billy Sobel . . . D. J. Delaney. And who? Who else could have wanted to end Aidan Peabody's life?

When the bell above the front door chimed, Nell glanced at her watch, then looked over at the archway that led into the front of the store. The others looked, too, knowing Mae had turned off the computer and gone home for the day shortly after they'd arrived. She had waved at them from the doorway, her car keys in hand. "Don't forget to lock up on your way out," she'd reminded them.

Willow Adams appeared in the archway.

But it wasn't the same Willow Adams they had seen just hours before.

Instead of long thick hair held in place with great difficulty, Willow bore a cropped, dark head of hair, wavy and full and short. It moved of its own volition, with thick curls and waves defining it irregularly. Raindrops glistened off the surface of a bright yellow slicker too big for her body, which covered her almost down to her ankles.

Although Nell could see at a glance that Willow had taken a scissors to her own locks — and perhaps without a mirror — the

271

weight and robust body of her hair hid the defects and the results were stunning.

Her face, pale just ten days ago, was tan now from daily runs along the beach and riding Nell's old bike across the cape and back again. She looked healthier, Nell thought, even beneath the burden of her father's murder. A sprinkling of freckles formed a pattern across her cheeks and nose, and the mass of waves that now freely framed her face highlighted enormous dark eyes.

Beneath the open raincoat, Willow wore a gauzy cotton blouse that Nell suspected came from Izzy's own closet. It was white as snow against her sun-touched skin. But it was her eyes that drew Nell's attention. They were lit in a way Nell hadn't seen since that first day, when they'd found a determined young girl with a mission, sitting in Izzy's shop window. Flashing dark eyes.

"Wow," Izzy said. "Willow, it's great!"

"Come, sit, dear," Birdie urged, wanting a closer look but reluctant to disturb the yarn or the kitten sitting on her lap.

"Terrific," said Cass. "I think I'll have you do mine."

Willow allowed a smile, and touched her hair with her hand, then combed her fingers through it. "I got sick of people looking at me. Maybe they won't recognize me now."

Nell held back a reply but her heart ached for the young girl. Willow, for all her efforts, was even more striking with the short haircut. Her enormous eyes were unmistakable. Even if people didn't know who they were looking at, they would look. And Willow would feel their stare and think it was because they thought her guilty of a terrible thing.

But it would probably be because she was strikingly beautiful.

"I went to the police a few hours ago," Willow said, shifting to a business tone and clearly wanting to divert their attention from her self-styled haircut.

"A couple of the younger guys were in there playing darts," she continued, slipping out of the raincoat and hanging it on a hook. She sat down on the couch next to Birdie and kicked off her sandals. "So I asked them if they were going to arrest me. And if they were, I said they should just go ahead and do it. Right then and there. I was tired of waiting for the bomb to drop. One of the guys ran and got the chief from his office like he was afraid of me. Like he thought I'd drop poison in his Diet Coke if he didn't behave."

Willow looked up at Nell. "Ben was in the office with Chief Thompson. I hope he's not in trouble."

They laughed, and Willow laughed, too.

"I think we're okay on that score," Nell said, "though you never know about Ben." He had gone over to talk to him about Billy before someone from the Edge did. The young waiter — and the bartender, standing nearby — had heard what Billy said as clearly as Nell.

Ben was convinced Billy would have a plausible explanation for his drunken words, but it needed to be addressed. And better from him than someone else. Rumors sometimes traveled at the speed of a sailfish in Sea Harbor.

"The chief said he couldn't arrest me because he didn't have enough evidence, but they were still checking things out, he said. He was nice, but that Tommy Porter cowers in the corner when he sees me. I swear he thinks I have an ax in my backpack."

"Chief Thompson is a good guy," Izzy said. "And Tommy has probably fallen in love with you. That's how he shows it sometimes."

"You're right about the chief being nice. I told him if he wasn't going to arrest me, then he needed to give me what was mine, and he didn't bat an eye."

"They had taken some of your things?" Izzy said.

Nell frowned. As far as she knew, the police hadn't been to the guest cottage. And surely they'd have checked with her first.

Willow shook her head. She held up a silver ring. Keys dangled from the circle.

"Aidan's studio?" Nell asked.

"My studio," Willow said. "And my house. There's even a piece of paper to prove it." She forked her fingers through her short hair and looked at the four knitters intently, her enormous eyes still flashing. "So. Should we go?" she asked.

Willow's hope coated her words. Somewhere, somehow, in Aidan's small house or in the depths of his studio and gallery would be the puzzle piece that was missing. Somehow they'd find something that meant nothing to the police, but everything to Willow Adams.

Nell took a deep breath and wondered how much of Willow's zeal was directed at discovering the murderer and clearing her own name, and how much was directed at discovering the father she never knew. A week ago she wanted nothing that belonged to this man who had never acknowledged

275

her existence. Today she was claiming his property.

"I just thought," Willow went on, "that maybe we'd find something there. All of us . . ."

"You shouldn't go over there alone, I agree," Nell said.

"That's what Brendan said — but he's helping over at Billy's and can't get away right now. He wants me to wait until tomorrow so he can go with me. But I thought . . . I mean, you all have been working hard to figure this thing out, and I thought if you weren't busy . . ."

At that instant a crack of thunder shook the small shop and the lights flickered, then went out completely.

Izzy grabbed for a flashlight fastened to the wall and clicked it on. It was a lantern-style light, and she set it on the table. Soft, eerie shadows played against the wall. The lights flickered again, and the hum of the refrigerator greeted the lights' return.

"The lights may be short-lived," Izzy said, looking out the window at the harbor. One strip of lights, over near Canary Cove and the Artist's Palate and pier, had not returned, and the pelt of rain was growing louder against the rocks. She pulled the casement windows closed. "It's still partially dark on the cove."

"This might not be the best time, Willow," Nell said gently. "You may not have lights over there, and the storm will probably intensify. How about if you come home with me shortly and we'll heat up last night's seafood chowder? Tomorrow — in the light of day — we can sort through things together."

The others echoed the sentiment. Exploring Aidan's property on a stormy night was not enticing, even to Cass and Izzy, whose love for adventure sometimes went a tad too far, in Nell's opinion.

Willow sat quiet for a moment, and Nell knew her heart and spirit were already over in the vacant house, wondering if she'd find any trace of herself in the house her father had left her.

Nell was half tempted to give in, when a pounding on the door broke into the conversation. It was the side door, the one that led from the alley directly into the cozy knitting room, and Izzy was up in an instant. She pulled the door open.

Natalie Sobel, her makeup smudged and running down her face in dark rivers, stood alone on the wet steps, her rain-soaked blouse clinging to her shivering body.

277

CHAPTER 21

"Come in out of that rain," Izzy urged, one hand touching Natalie's shoulder and pulling her out of the pelting rain.

They all turned and stared at the rain-drenched woman, standing in a puddle in the middle of Izzy's knitting room.

"It's Billy," Natalie said. She wiped her face with the back of her hand. "I can't find him."

"You can't find him? I don't understand." Nell took Natalie's umbrella and set it by the door. The thought of Billy Sobel being lost was rather incongruous. Even considering his actions the night before.

"I'm sure he's okay," Izzy said. "He's probably at the gallery, getting things ready for the exhibit."

Natalie shook her head so vigorously that drops of rain water flew in all directions. "No," she said strongly, refusing an easy explanation. "Billy came home from the store a few hours ago. We had some drinks. A bottle of wine. He was feeling . . . amorous. And then he got a phone call."

She looked at Nell.

"I think it was your husband. I heard Billy say Ben's name."

"If it was Ben who called, Natalie, there's nothing to worry about. He and Jerry Thompson just had a question for Billy." Nell hoped to heaven she was speaking the truth and not lying to Billy's distraught bride. She agreed with Ben that Billy would have a good explanation, but she knew, too, that her belief in her friends was robust . . . until she had a firm reason to believe otherwise. And although Billy was more of an acquaintance than a friend, she'd known nothing to make her think ill of him.

Izzy, Nell, and Cass nodded, silently sharing Nell's hope that worry wasn't warranted. But Billy's outburst weighed heavily on their minds.

"The police chief wanted to talk to him?" Natalie's brows lifted clear into her hairline.

"They're still trying to figure out the Peabody murder, Natalie. They're questioning everyone who knew Aidan."

"But they've already talked to Billy. Why again?" Natalie twisted the edge of her damp silk blouse until it resembled a narrow string of macramé.

"They still don't know what happened, that's all."

Willow sat quietly on the couch, and it was several minutes before Natalie noticed her. She frowned, then looked at Nell as if Willow weren't in the room. "Is that Aidan Peabody's daughter?"

Nell nodded. "Willow, this is Natalie Sobel."

The two women eyed each other. Natalie looked like she wanted to speak, to suggest that maybe the police should come to Izzy's knitting studio if they wanted information — and should leave her husband alone.

"When did Billy leave the house?" Nell asked, diverting attention.

"Almost immediately after he got the phone call. No, wait. He got one more call. He swore when he saw the number on his cell phone, then looked resigned and took the call."

"Did you hear what he said?"

She shook her head up and down and rain drops flew in all directions. "Yes! He said, something like, 'Okay, okay. Don't cry,' he said. 'Don't cry, I'll come.' I think that's what he said, but he'd been drinking a little — that bottle of wine — so I wasn't sure.

"But then, when he snapped the phone

shut, he swore again, and Billy, he tried not to swear in front of me. And then he kissed me, and said he'd be back soon. He had a couple of errands, he said, but he'd be back for dinner. But he didn't come back. He knew we were having a special dinner together. It's our eight-month anniversary, and I had the Edge cater us a nice lobster dinner. We got the champagne. And he got me this."

Natalie pulled apart the top of her blouse to reveal a diamond necklace. Bright, big, sparkly diamonds that Nell suspected would blind one in the dark.

Natalie beamed through her tears.

"It's beautiful. Billy is a thoughtful man." Nell wondered what their first-year anniversary would bring.

"But he's not so thoughtful right now."

"Billy is so friendly," Izzy said. "He talks to everyone. I bet he's at the Gull, maybe telling people about the beautiful necklace he got for his beautiful bride."

"I went there first," Natalie said, accepting the compliment but dismissing the excuse. "Jake said he'd come in for just a few minutes. Sat alone at the bar and didn't talk to anyone. Just guzzled down a few beers. Guzzle, guzzle, just like that. And then he walked out. No good-bye. Just left."

Nell checked her watch. It was after seven, not too late. Dinnertime. Natalie's worry seemed extreme. She wondered if she was simply a nervous new wife. Because he was a dealer who met with clients, she suspected Billy's work would often serve up irregular hours. But Billy's drinking, and being depressed about something — that, in Nell's opinion, was worth concern. That, and missing an anniversary that clearly was important to his wife. Was it the prospect of talking to Jerry Thompson that upset him? She wanted to slip out of the room and call Ben, but that would be too noticeable and might worry Natalie even more.

"He was upset," Natalie continued. "He was worried. And he wouldn't share it with me. He just shut me out."

Natalie's tears began again and she slumped down on one of the chairs. The eyeliner had disappeared from beneath her sad eyes, and small meandering trails ran though her makeup and down her chin.

"Did you think Billy would be here?" Nell asked.

Natalie shook her head again. "No. But the light was on here. And you are such nice ladies. You've known Billy longer than I have. I just thought maybe . . ."

"Maybe we'd be able to help," Birdie

finished. "I bet you dollars to doughnuts that Billy will be home in a jiffy. He will know you're worrying about him, and he'll come home and want a big plate of pasta with his lobster. You mark my words."

Natalie offered a small smile.

Izzy walked over with a glass of wine and handed it to Natalie. "Would you rather have a cup of tea?"

But Natalie was already drinking down the wine, looking grateful for something to hold on to. "I had not seen this side of Billy before. He was so distracted, all these recent days. And he's not been himself, not so loving, for days now. He gets mad at me because I'm doing his books now — but that should be a help to him, not make him mad. He's distracted and distant. But it must be a stage he is going through. My Billy is a good man." She looked around at each of them, as if begging them to repeat her words.

"Billy loves you. And if he has something on his mind, he'll share it with you when he's comfortable." Nell also hoped that would happen soon after he'd shared it with Jerry Thompson. And she prayed that what Billy Sobel had done was nothing more serious than running a red light on Harbor Road.

"I should go look some more." Natalie forced a smile and looked around the room, avoiding Willow's face. "Maybe he is at the Gull now, drinking beers with the guys. The drinking I can handle, s'long as I know my Billy's safe."

The last comment was spoken plaintively, and Nell knew before Birdie spoke that dinner tonight would be late. Natalie driving around Sea Harbor's rain-slick streets was an accident in the making.

"We can help, Natalie," Birdie said. "We know Sea Harbor better than you do. And, Nell, you have that big tank of Ben's here — we could all pile in and do a little looking. And when we're through, we will probably find Bill Sobel asleep in his own bed."

Natalie stood immediately and Nell could see that it was just what she needed — a little companionship to calm her down. And Birdie might be right — he'd be home before they dropped Natalie off.

While the others were putting away their knitting, stashing the wineglasses and cheese in the galley kitchen, and gathering bags, Nell stepped into another room and called Ben. He answered on the second ring.

Nell suspected the answer before she asked the question. Ben had told the chief about Billy's comment the night before, and then Jerry had called and suggested they get together to chat. Not a big deal. Just to check one more thing off the list.

Billy had said that'd be fine. He'd be there in ten minutes.

And he never showed.

Nell snapped the phone closed, slipped the hood of her rain jacket over her head, and quickly followed the others to the car, tucking away the unanswered questions about Billy Sobel. Maybe, just maybe, he was at his gallery.

But first, a slow drive down Harbor Road, with Izzy, Cass, and Willow jumping out of the SUV and running through the rain into the Edge, the Gull, and several small restaurants. No, no one had seen Billy in the village-shops area. But Archie Brandley was doing some inventory work in his bookstore and thought he had seen Billy on his Harley, weaving down Harbor Road, headed toward Canary Cove.

On the way around the bend to the cove, they noticed utility trucks and two men climbing poles with flashlights attached to their helmets, but streetlights along the main street in the artists' neighborhood were still dark.

Nell pulled up in front of the Sobel Gallery and they all sat there for a minute, peering through the sheets of rain. It was plunged in darkness, just like the shops on either side. Natalie didn't have a key, but if Billy was inside, he was sitting in darkness. Not a likely scenario, and his Harley was nowhere to be seen.

They drove slowly down the road and turned into the Artist's Palate parking lot just in time to see Hank and Merry Jackson getting into their car. Hank shielded his eyes against the glare of their headlights, then recognized the Endicott SUV and ran up to the window, the hood of his rain jacket flapping in the wind.

"Have you seen Billy?" Nell asked, rolling down her window. Rain slid into the car.

Hank nodded. "He drove up on his Harley not long before the lights went out — an hour or so ago. Sat around for a while, tapping his hands on the counter, all alone, checking his watch. Made us nervous. Billy's a friend, and we'd have helped him if we could, but he didn't want to talk. He seemed to have a lot on his mind.

"While I was in the kitchen, he talked Merry into giving him a bottle of bourbon and he took off in the rain. Billy was definitely a little off tonight. Acted like he didn't even know it was raining. Didn't have his helmet on or nothin'." Hank shook his head. "He probably headed on home. Not much else you can do on a night like this."

Merry honked the horn impatiently. Hank waved and started to hurry off. Then he stopped short and called back, just before Nell closed the window, "Merry says she swore there was someone waiting for Billy over near his Harley and that's why he raced off. Said it was someone in a yellow rain slicker. But hell, I don't know how she could see a thing in this downpour. She says I'm blind, that he's probably got another girlfriend already."

For a minute no one said a word. They sat still in the car, hoping Natalie, squeezed into the backseat, hadn't heard Hank's words.

They waited, wondering.

Finally Nell twisted in the seat until she could see Natalie in the shadows. Her face was dark, her brows pulled together.

"Natalie?" Nell said. "What do you think? Want to look further?"

But Natalie had made a decision.

"Please, just go home. The bum. I will not worry about him. I don't care what happens to him. Just take me home so I can watch my favorite Sunday show."

She set her face, hard and determined, hiding any worry behind anger at her husband's thoughtlessness.

Nell turned out of the parking lot, still unsure if Natalie had gotten the gist of Hank's comment, and hoping she hadn't. With the rain beating on the car roof, it was possible her hardened look was simply one of exasperation. Nell hoped so.

With the sound of the wipers lulling them all into silence, Nell headed for the Sobel home for the second time in two days.

Billy's bike wasn't in the drive when they arrived, but Natalie resolutely refused their offer of dinner or company and stomped into the house, closing the door firmly behind her and shutting off the porch light.

"I wonder if they have a doghouse," Cass murmured.

"Billy's going to need one," Birdie said.

"What do you think is her favorite show?"

They all agreed: *Desperate Housewives.*

CHAPTER 22

The phone rang at six a.m., pulling Ben and Nell out of a deep sleep.

Nell had awakened just once during the night, close to dawn. She'd slipped out of bed and silently opened the bedroom French doors, and looked out over the trees toward the ocean. The rain had stopped earlier and the air was redolent with the sweet earthy fragrance of a well-watered lawn.

She breathed in deeply, and her thoughts turned to Billy Sobel. For Natalie's sake — and Billy's, too — she hoped he was sound asleep beside his wife. But he'd been troubled. Something was definitely not right with Billy. Perhaps today they would find some answers, once the police had a chance to talk to him.

She and Ben had talked for a long while the night before — of Billy's lifestyle and the lure of other women. Of his recent peculiar actions and the heavy drinking — at least over the past few nights. And he'd been with Ellen Marks earlier that day — not with his wife. They were good friends. Could it be more than that? If Birdie had heard correctly, Ellen had turned to Billy for help, maybe with Rebecca. But of all the people affected by the week's happenings, Rebecca Marks somehow seemed one of the least affected.

And then Nell's thoughts faded, and the soft sea breeze relaxed her body and diminished the day's concerns. She'd slipped back into bed beside Ben, looping one arm around his solid, comforting body, and drifted off to a blessedly dreamless slumber.

Nell tugged herself from sleep now as Ben reached for the phone, being the one more accustomed to early phone calls. They always made Nell's heart skip a beat, then pound fiercely until Ben assured her things were all right. Early phone calls never bore good news, in Nell's imagination, and on the first ring her thoughts would turn to her sister or to Izzy, to Birdie or other friends or family.

Ben was far more philosophical, knowing he often got calls from fishing friends who had a sudden yen to head out to sea for that choice striper or bluefish, or sailing buddies who woke up to a brisk breeze and needed someone to help raise the jib.

But the tone in his voice this morning told Nell that it wasn't a pleasure trip the caller was suggesting.

He hung up the receiver and swung his legs over the side of the bed. His hands gripped the mattress edge and his head hung low between his shoulders. And then he looked back at Nell, who was patiently waiting for the news she didn't want to hear.

Ben reached across the summer blanket and covered her hand with his own.

"Billy Sobel drowned last night."

Nell sucked in a sudden breath, and when she released it, the sadness slowly seeped into her body.

It was the day that was to have been Billy's special show — the opening of his new exhibit. The day after his eighth-month wedding anniversary.

But Billy Sobel was dead, his body discovered by Finnegan, an old-time Sea Harbor fisherman who was rowing his boat around Canary Cove just as the sun came up. He spotted the body pressed by tide waters and the storm against the rocky banks and outbrush near the old Canary Cove dock, just a short way from the Artist's Palate. What

291

had caught his eye first, Finnegan told the police, was the sun glinting off the shiny chrome of Billy's Harley, parked at the edge of the water.

Billy had drowned off the end of the old dock that jutted out into the water, just down the gentle slope of land from the parking lot. The rickety structure that had been the subject of many heated arguments at monthly Canary Cove art council meetings.

It was rotten, some said.

A waste of money to fix, others thought. Just tear it out.

But they had all continued to use it, to jump off the wobbly end for a dip in the deep, cold water. To sit beneath the small wooden canopy that sheltered bodies from too much sun.

It was the Canary Cove artists' private domain, though not really. But no one else cared about it, and so it was theirs.

It was the pier that Jane, Ham, and Aidan had stretched out on one hot summer night, their legs hanging over the end as they drank Sam Adams and mused about the kind of funerals they'd want to have someday.

And the day had come for Aidan, way too soon.

And now for his neighbor Billy Sobel.

■ ■ ■ ■

Nell called Izzy before the news started spreading on the radio and to the early-morning crowd at Coffee's. The body was discovered too late to make the paper — a blessing, Nell supposed. At least Natalie would have a few hours without the entire town talking about Billy's death.

Izzy suggested a slow run down Sandpiper Beach was in order, and she appeared at Nell's door before she had finished tying her running shoes.

In minutes they had walked the windy path through the Endicotts' wooded land, across the beach road, the short bridge that sometimes spanned tidal streams, and to the smooth beach beyond. They ran in silence for a while, each collecting thoughts, turning them over, musing in private. It was a pattern they'd established early on. They would run in tandem, but each would have her own space, too. And then talk would come when the time was right.

" 'Billy killed Aidan,' is what the police are thinking," Nell offered presently, knowing Izzy's thoughts were hovering close to her own. "And then he might have committed suicide out of regret. He was drunk, Ben said, but they are keeping that from Natalie for now. No need to cause her more grief."

Izzy looked over at Nell, her elbows pumping evenly beside her hips. "The drunk part is believable, since we know he picked up a bottle of bourbon from Hank's place. And before that, he'd had beers at the Gull. But what possible motive would he have for killing Aidan?"

"They seemed to have been arguing about Canary Cove affairs recently. Like the James exhibit."

"That's a mystery in itself. Why would Aidan have cared about the exhibit? You'd think he'd have welcomed it, unless there was a jealousy thing going on. Maybe Aidan didn't like flashing openings, and with Natalie involved, it might have been flashy. But I don't think he had a jealous bone in his body. Do you, Nell? Not about women or art or anything. He seemed totally comfortable in his own skin."

Izzy slipped a scrunchie around her hair as she ran. The ponytail bounced between her shoulder blades to the rhythm set by her body. "That was one of the things I liked so much about him."

"You're right. He wasn't the jealous type. Not at all. I wonder if we're misreading the whole thing. And Billy, too. Maybe something totally unconnected to Aidan was bothering Billy. Something that was causing him to be depressed. And that's what made him drink so much recently. Maybe Ellen knows something." She said the latter half to herself, mentally making a list of things they needed to check off. There were way too many questions still filling the air around Sea Harbor for this to be wrapped up so neatly with the suicide of a nice man.

Izzy ran on and Nell followed, her head high and the breeze riffling through her hair, lifting it from her neck. Running along the packed sandy beach with Izzy was one of the many cherished treats that came with Izzy's move to Sea Harbor. But her niece's firm, trim body provided a definite challenge for Nell when it came to conversation and running, at least at the same time. She glanced over and noticed with a slight sigh that Izzy barely broke a sweat when running with Nell at the required slower pace, and her breathing was even. Her tank top showed a slight darkening between her breasts, but the glistening on her forehead was slight — and her voice was as strong as if she were sitting on a chaise.

Sensing her aunt's labored breathing, Izzy slowed down, then paused at the edge of the water. She dug her toes into the wet sand and leaned over at the waist. Her fists on her hips, she breathed in deeply. They were on the far edge of the Sea Harbor Yacht Club, where the sand was tended and smooth and their footprints joined dozens of other early-morning runners who chose the smooth surface over the rocky shore farther north.

In the distance, the Sea Harbor breakwater jutted out into the sea. Fishermen dotted the thick granite slabs, their lines heavy with bait, and nearby, crayon-colored buoys bounced in the water, marking a whole colony of sunken lobster traps, including Cass'.

Nell shielded her eyes from the sun and looked out over the seamless expanse of sea and sky. She pinched her tank top between two fingers and peeled it free of her damp skin. "This is why we will never need therapists," she murmured.

Izzy smiled. "It beats a couch."

In silent agreement, they turned and began walking in the direction from which they'd come, back toward homes and showers and a Monday that was already turning warm, heralding an indecently perfect summer day. The calm after the storm.

But not so calm. It was a day to comfort Natalie. To deal with another death. To try to make sense of it all. To mourn Billy Sobel.

"It looks like Willow beat us out here today." Nell pointed ahead.

"Aha," Izzy said, shielding her eyes and looking at a short dock that stretched into the water from the front of the yacht club beach. "I think you are right on."

Willow sat on the side of the pier, her legs hanging over the side. She was dressed in running shorts and a ragged tee with the sleeves cut off. Her short dark hair puffed out around a headband, silky waves curling around the band on both sides. Next to her, similarly dressed, was the tall lean body of Brendan Slattery. Willow's body leaned gently against his side. Even from a distance, Nell could see the smile on Willow's face, the tilt of her head. The gentle support of the man sitting next to her. They were deep in conversation.

"That's nice," Izzy murmured. "Sometimes I watch you do that with Ben, just lean into him."

"Willow needs that." Brendan had stuck by Willow from nearly the first day, always unobtrusively, but Nell would see him sometimes through the kitchen window, walking down toward the guesthouse door. Or the two of them walking up from the

297

beach, through the shady path in the Endicott woods. In less than two weeks they'd found friendship. And perhaps more, Nell thought.

And then the same discomforting feeling she'd had when Izzy decided to major in law, or when she dated her first college man who seemed to have been around the block too many times for Nell's comfort level, suddenly seized her. It was that mother bear urge to protect, sometimes without rhyme or reason.

She didn't want Willow hurt. Nell shook off the irrational shiver.

Izzy dragged her toe through the sand as she watched the couple on the dock, a wavy line matching up to a line of small shells and sea glass.

Nell looked down at the crude design formed by Izzy's toe. Lines intersected forming an interesting design. "Patterns in the sand," she murmured. "Just like our lives, crossing over one another. Changing. Altered by the tide's ebb and flow."

Izzy looked down, too. She leaned over, picked up a stick, and drew several more shapes — circles, squares, lines intersecting. "Maybe it's because we're knitters that we see patterns everywhere. Even in the sand."

Nell nodded. *Maybe so, or maybe it's*

because there simply are patterns everywhere — and figuring them out, learning why and how and when lives intersect might help us bring peace to this little town.

Her thoughts moved to the lives that had so dramatically intersected with their own in recent days — Aidan and Willow, Billy, Natalie, Rebecca and Ellen and the other artists who felt the loss of Aidan Peabody. Even D. J. Delaney, trying to walk away with Willow's inheritance and turn it into an inn.

"Nell and Izzy, hi —" Willow waved vigorously, nearly toppling off the dock as she shouted above the sounds of the sea.

It was the kind of wave one used to greet friends. Inch by inch, Willow's defenses had broken down around Izzy and Nell, Cass and Birdie. And Nell suspected the small wedge — if there even was one — was about to disappear completely.

Willow and Brendan had climbed off the dock and were walking toward them, their running shoes in their hands and happy smiles on their faces.

"You two got an early start," Nell said, shielding her eyes against the sun's glare.

"Crack of dawn. Brendan appeared at the cottage door with a promise of coffee at the end of the run. What could I say?"

Their bright spirits made Izzy and Nell

pause, realization sinking into both of them at the same time.

Izzy frowned and bit down on her bottom lip.

"So you don't know," Nell said softly.

The couple looked at her curiously.

Of course they didn't. They'd been out on the beach before most of Sea Harbor was awake, and they would have missed even the early-morning Coffee's crowd, who would have heard from the fishermen, who heard the news from Finnegan.

"Billy Sobel drowned off the Canary Cove dock last night," Nell said. She paused for a moment as her words sunk in, and then continued. "We don't know if it was an accident or suicide. There's talk that he might have been depressed."

Willow's shoes dropped to the sand. "He drowned . . . last night?"

"We don't know exactly when."

"While we were looking for him?"

That thought had come to Izzy and Nell as well. When had Billy died? While they were in the parking lot, just above the dock, looking for him?

"Why would Billy commit suicide?" Brendan asked, his arm going around Willow instinctively. "I saw him yesterday morning in the gallery. He seemed okay — a little strange, maybe, but okay. Natalie had been after him about the books. Since she started keeping them, Billy had to toe the mark a little more."

Willow shook her head back and forth slowly. She pulled off her headband and dropped it to the sand, looking at Nell as if she could change her words. "Not another death."

"Some people think Billy killed your father. And he was despondent because of that, so he killed himself."

Nell didn't say what surely passed through all their minds — that if the police believed this story, Willow would no longer be a suspect, and at last she could go on with her life. They wouldn't say it out loud out of respect for Billy, but the fact that Billy's suicide — if, indeed, it was — would prove to be a good thing for Willow couldn't be too far from their thoughts.

"I sure never imagined Billy a murderer," Brendan said. "He had a temper — everyone around Canary Cove knew that — and he had it in for Aidan this summer. They seemed to disagree on most things going on around the cove. But murder? That's a whole different bag. And suicide? But I guess when you're drinking, you're not thinking straight."

"Maybe it was an accident," Izzy said.

"Is there a note?" Willow asked. "Isn't there supposed to be a note when someone commits suicide? Maybe it was a sad, unfortunate accident. And now that poor woman will be berating herself for being so mad at him last night. How awful for her."

Brendan looked confused. "What woman?"

"His wife. We drove her around in the storm last night," Willow said. "She was looking for her husband."

"Did you see Billy? Where did you look?"

"No, we never saw him," Nell said. "We followed his trail as far as the Artist's Palate, but it was raining so hard that Natalie decided to just go back home and wait for him."

They filled Brendan in on the events of the evening. But none of the discussion led anywhere, accept for the devastating awareness that the five women might have been just a few yards from where Billy Sobel sat on the dock, drinking a bottle of bourbon. And about to die.

CHAPTER 23

"The whole town is talking about it," Mae said. "Imagine, Billy Sobel killing Aidan. He had a temper, sure, but goodness gracious, getting mad enough to kill someone? Now that amazes me. And suicide? Billy Sobel?"

Mae took a credit card from a customer and ran it through her machine, then handed the woman a sack of merino wool and a sock pattern — along with her usual pinch of advice. "Use the kitchener stitch on the toes and you'll be a happy camper," she encouraged the customer.

While Mae was occupied, Nell checked the messages on her cell phone.

Willow would be a few minutes late meeting her and Izzy in Canary Cove.

Ben was heading to Gloucester for a late-afternoon meeting.

And from Birdie, an announcement that Natalie was cremating Billy and burying him in New Jersey. Now what did she think about that?

Mae's glasses had slipped down to the slight bump on her long nose and she pushed them back in place with one finger. "What do you make of it, Nell?"

For a second, Nell had to unscramble her thoughts and messages to figure out what Mae was talking about. *Billy. Murder. Suicide.* When she spoke, she surprised herself at the robust belief behind her words.

"I don't think Billy killed Aidan Peabody. And I don't think Billy committed suicide."

"What are you saying, Nell?" Mae jerked off her glasses and pushed them up into her graying poof of hair. She stared at Nell, ignoring Harriet Brandley's request for a pair of number eight bamboo needles.

"I'm saying that someone else killed Aidan. And that Billy either accidentally fell off the end of that dock or . . ."

She was relieved that Harriet persisted in her pursuit of needles and saved Nell from finishing the sentence. Or . . . or *what,* for heaven's sake? What had she intended to say?

Izzy appeared at her side and nudged her into the back room. "I don't know if I can get away right now. Will you and Willow be okay?"

304

A group of women was sitting around the table with coffee, yarn, and a dozen half-finished chemo hats in front of them and Izzy nodded in their direction.

"I need to help a few of the beginning knitters."

Before going their separate ways early that morning, Willow had reminded Nell and Izzy that she had the keys to Aidan's house.

Standing beside her, Brendan had insisted he would go with her. She shouldn't be facing this by herself.

Nell and Izzy agreed that they would go, too, though Brendan made it clear they'd be fine with just the two of them. But Nell insisted. The flux of emotions that Willow was experiencing would only be intensified when she saw her father's home for the first time. And the more distractions, the better.

"That's fine. Brendan is going to go, too."

"He's been a surprise light in all this. He seems to brighten Willow's days."

Nell nodded. "I don't know what we'll do other than poke around a little. But at least Willow won't be alone. The house is hers now, after all, and she needs to take this first step. And then, in time, discover there what she needs to discover."

Nell met Willow at a small tea shop that had recently opened on Canary Road. It had two tables inside and two out on the street. In the summer months people sipped iced tea at the small tables, and in colder weather, hot chowder would be served up with the tea to hungry artists and art lovers. Small teapots decorated the inside shelves and the tables were old, with small, uneven chairs. It reminded Nell of a dollhouse, and she decided the first time she saw it that it wasn't a place for the Bens and Sams in her life — they would surely break something.

But Polly Farrell, the new owner, brewed amazing tea, and the crumpets were moist and flavorful.

When Nell walked up she saw Willow through the window, standing at the counter ordering fresh raspberry tea for the two of them.

Outside, Rebecca Marks sat at a table by herself. Her elbows were on the tabletop and her head was balanced on her hands, as if the support were needed to hold it in place.

"Hello, Rebecca."

Rebecca looked up, surprised, it seemed to Nell, to hear a voice.

Nell smiled at the attractive woman in the bright turquoise sundress. Handblown beads, strung on a narrow cord, were looped around her neck and caught the fading sunlight. But her eyes, usually bright and lined like those of a model on a magazine cover, were half closed.

"I don't often see you here in Canary Cove at this time of day."

"I'm meeting someone." Nell nodded toward the shop's interior.

From inside the store, Willow spotted Nell through the window and waved that she'd be out in a minute.

"You're meeting her," Rebecca said, following the exchange with tired-looking eyes.

"Willow," Nell said.

"Yes, Aidan's forgotten daughter. It makes one wonder what else he forgot."

"Are you all right, Rebecca?"

"I will be fine. I have the artists' curse."

"Oh?"

"Insomnia. But Ellen swears I do my best work at three a.m., so I guess it works out okay in the long run."

"But it must make the next day quite gruesome."

"Sometimes. Today's not bad. Ellen is helping Jane out at the council, but we have plenty of help in the gallery, and I'm taking it easy. Doc Hamilton helps me out if I must get a full night's sleep. A little bit of Nembutal does wonders when I need it."

Nell nodded.

"I seem to have misplaced the magic pills, though — hence my sleepless night. But no matter. I'll be fine. On to more interesting things. Where are you and Aidan's daughter off to?" Rebecca's tone was flat, clearly making small talk without much interest. "It still baffles my mind that she found him like she did."

"I know you didn't like Aidan, Rebecca," Nell said, not quite sure where the conversation was going, but uncomfortable with Rebecca's tone. She hoped it was caused by the lack of sleep. "But I guess I'm not sure why."

Rebecca took the question and seemed to play with an answer before she spoke again. "I don't like it when people try to control everything. Aidan did that with the arts council. He irritated everyone, always seeming to know the answers to things. Ellen, of course, had to go to the council meetings because she's the only one around here with good business sense — myself included — and she helped with that side of things. I know sometimes Aidan put pressure on her, too, being rigid about reports and insisting that things be done his ways. It didn't bother Ellen much, but that's because she wouldn't let it bother her — that's just how she is. But Aidan irritated others, I know.

And he had a fit when D. J. Delaney suggested an inn on some of that unkempt land Aidan owned. I think D.J. would have outright killed Aidan if he could have."

"But you and Aidan were close not so long ago."

Rebecca laughed, but it wasn't a happy sound. She shrugged. "Aidan was too — I don't know — too cerebral for me I guess. He wasn't that much fun, not really. And he had secrets. Take this daughter for example . . ."

"Whom he might not have known about."

Rebecca's perfectly plucked eyebrows lifted over her tired eyes. "Oh, he knew about her. At least he suspected there might be a child, whatever sex it might be. He told me as much. I think he even tried to find her once."

"Are you sure?"

Rebecca blew off the question. "It doesn't matter. It was a long time ago. He got drunk one night and talked a little about it. I was only half listening but I knew some girl had said he got her pregnant. That much I know I heard.

"And my relationship with Aidan was complicated, if that's what you're interested in, just like he was complicated. But he couldn't deal with it. So it ended. And once it was over I realized he hadn't been a good choice from the beginning."

Good choice? An odd word to use, Nell thought, unless one was picking out fresh tuna from Hennessey's seafood stand.

She was relieved when Willow walked through the door, carefully balancing full cups of iced tea.

Willow handed Nell a tall cup.

Rebecca had gone back to reading a magazine, seemingly uninterested in further conversation, and didn't look up when Nell and Willow greeted each other. They'd only gone a few feet when Nell realized there was a topic that she and Rebecca hadn't addressed.

"Rebecca," she said, turning around and raising her voice above the whirr of a scooter racing by. "I'm so sorry about Billy Sobel. Another sad loss for Canary Cove."

Rebecca looked up. "I suppose Ellen is the one who needs your condolences on that front. She and Billy have known each other a long time. She's quite upset. Me? I thought Billy was a poor excuse for an art dealer and should have stuck to gambling. He didn't know fine art from a hole in the ground, in my opinion." And with that, she lowered her head and continued to turn the pages of her magazine.

"Interesting lady," Willow murmured under her breath.

Nell attempted a smile and an excuse. "Well, you know artists."

Willow looked down the street at the Fishtail Gallery. A carved wooden fish with an enormous tail hung from two iron chains above the locked door. It creaked slightly in the breeze.

"I wish I did," she said softly.

Nell put her arm around Willow and felt a slight quiver pass through her body. "You'll get to know him, Willow. And I suspect you'll be enriched by what you learn."

Later, Nell would tell Ben about the conversation and confess that she had no idea why she had said those words. But as soon as she had, she believed them with a ferocity that defied contradiction.

"Is Brendan coming?" Nell asked as they crossed the road.

"He'll meet us. He was going to sneak out early — he's helping Jane and Ham today, then has to check in on Natalie. He kind of feels he needs to keep an eye on her."

Of course. Brendan might have gotten to know Natalie better than any of them, working in the shop and helping Billy with paintings and paperwork. And it was a good thing there'd be a strong young man for her to lean on.

Although gallery doors were open and people milled about in the cool interiors of the shops, Nell sensed the melancholy just below the surface. Canary Cove was sad. Tourists wouldn't notice, but the artists and shop owners felt the burden of loss. It was palpable. Billy's death and the awful circumstances surrounding it were beginning to penetrate the neighborhood.

Aidan's shop was dark, the door locked, no lights peeking through the imaginative creatures in the display window. Nell and Willow walked past the shop and turned into the narrow lane beside it, walking back toward the garden and house beyond. Aidan's small Jeep was pulled off the alley, hugging the side of the studio. A flagstone pathway connected the studio and shop to the garden, and beyond that, another pathway connected the garden to Aidan's home.

Beside the home and on up the hill grew the thick stand of pines and oak trees that just a day before Billy and Ellen Marks — with Birdie close behind — had strolled through.

Willow checked a large round watch on her wrist. "Brendan should be here. . . ."

Nell and Willow looked down toward the Brewsters' studio. There was traffic in and out the front door, but no sign of Brendan. Willow pulled out her cell and pressed in a number.

Nell took that moment to walk the pathway into the small garden, still lovely in spite of a lack of pruning and pinching. The recent rain had deepened the color of the burgundy knockout roses, and the white rose of Sharon blooms were brilliant against the deep mossy green of the small magnolias. A lone Japanese maple spread its branches over the stone bench where Aidan Peabody had taken his last breath.

"Brendan's not coming," Willow said, following Nell into the garden. "He's over at the Sobel Gallery, trying to put things in order, I guess."

Willow slipped her phone into the pocket of her cropped slacks and shrugged. "He wanted us to wait until he could come. Brendan thinks we can't quite manage this by ourselves, silly man. I've been without a man in my life forever. And I manage just fine."

Aidan's home had been a vacation home before he bought the land years before. He'd immediately winterized and updated it, added skylights and fresh paint, and Nell loved the cozy, clean spaces he'd created.

She'd been there a half dozen times, most often for pre- or post-exhibit gatherings when he'd open his doors and the guests would flow from home to garden to studio.

But today there was no music playing, no laughter and flow of food. No handsome Aidan Peabody greeting friends at the door.

Nell watched his daughter unlock the door to his home and, with a firm step, enter.

Nell followed just behind, taking her lead from Willow.

Willow paused on the hardwood floor and looked around. From this vantage point, you could see through the whole house — into a small neat bedroom on the east side of the house, a den just to the left, and the entire back of the house was the living and cooking area — wide-open with windows that opened up to the woods behind.

The house was simple and clean, with friends' paintings hanging on the white walls; the kitchen shelves were open and filled with pottery plates, cups, pots, and pans. Nell recognized some of Jane's pots, and a watercolor of Ham's hanging above a small fireplace. And on a wall of shelves — with one standing boldly out in the open — were Aidan Peabody's wooden creations, forbidding anyone to get very far into the room without smiling.

"I guess he couldn't be all bad," Willow said softly, walking up to a red-lipped sea nymph posing near the back windows.

Nell held her thoughts to herself. *No, he wasn't all bad, Willow. Maybe he wasn't bad at all.* And Nell hoped against hope that exploring his life through his home and his friends would teach her who her father truly was.

"I think I'll just wander," Willow said, and Nell agreed that that was a good plan. "There's no hurry, dear," she said. "We have tomorrow and the next day and more after that."

In truth, she had no idea what Willow's plans would be. There'd been no official report on Aidan's murder, only a day's worth of suppositions and assumptions pointing the finger at Billy Sobel. It made people more comfortable, Nell supposed. It was a neat package that they could get their arms around. Both deaths were accounted for. Life could go on.

But what about Natalie Sobel's life? Nell wondered, walking into the small den. What did she have left? Memories of Billy ruined by rumors. A gallery full of artists' work that she probably cared little about. The James paintings, of course, would at least provide her with a financial cushion. But she suspected that what really mattered to Natalie Sobel was Billy. Her Billy was gone.

One wall in Aidan's den was filled from floor to ceiling with books, and near the front windows was an old library desk. The one flat drawer was askew, a remnant of the police search, Nell supposed, although Tommy Porter prided himself on making sure nothing had been left a mess after a search. Nell walked behind the desk, where a small wooden filing cabinet stood unobtrusively, its two drawers also open a crack. Inside, papers were tossed around, files shoved back into place hastily, not what she would have imagined Aidan's desk to look like.

She remembered the mention in Mary Pisano's column of seeing someone around Aidan's house. Billy? Would he have had reason to come in here? And what would he have been looking for? She renewed her intention to talk to Mary Pisano about that night — she could probably shed some light on it. She seemed to have a firm grasp on the goings on around Canary Cove.

A tall carved cabinet in the shape of a fisherman stood guard near an easy chair, and Nell could almost picture Aidan Peabody, his feet up on the leather footstool, reading through the many books on his shelf.

She scanned the titles, impressed with the breadth of subjects — from the history of watercolor to deep-sea fishing and sailing. He had books on Sea Harbor and the granite quarries. Books on American crafts, on framing art, and on notable artists. There were several books on his desk and she picked up the top one. She'd seen the same book in Archie's bookstore window — a book on New England artists — but when she had gone to buy one, Archie was sold out. *People are more interested in James,* Archie explained, *now that we have paintings right here.*

Nell opened the book and looked for familiar names, pleased to see a section on Ham's watercolors and Jane's amazing pottery. Sam Perry was mentioned in a section on photography, his arresting photos of the working fishermen of Gloucester filling several pages. The biggest section was on Robert James, the reclusive artist from Maine, his lovely watercolors of ocean scenes and Maine sunsets now a collector's boon. Aidan had been reading it, she could tell. They had the same habit of making notes in the columns, underlining things of particular interest, and taking a yellow marker to special sections.

Messing up the book, Ben would say.

Nell smiled and set the book on the corner of the desk, along with several others that she knew would interest Ben. They were Willow's now, but she was sure she wouldn't mind Nell and Ben borrowing them for a short while. She'd read the section on James and at least be more informed for the exhibit, if indeed there would still be one.

"His house is nice," Willow said, wandering into the den from the family area. "It's not what I expected." She sat down in the leather chair delicately, as if it might protest if she were too rough. "I look around and I want to know what he thought while he lived in this house. Did he think of me? What did he know of me? Why didn't he ever come back to find me?" Willow leaned her head back against the cushions and scanned the wall of books.

"Your dad was a scholar," Nell said. "Did you know that? He knew more about art than anyone in Sea Harbor."

Willow nodded. "My mom never went to college."

"You mentioned that. But she lived in Madison when your dad was a student?"

"I always used to think she was the student — she told me as much. I guess she wanted me to think she was a coed, not a small-town runaway. And it worked — from the time I was little, I knew I would go there, too. But if you do the math, my mom was only seventeen when I was born. So sixteen when she got pregnant. Unless she was supersmart, she wasn't a college student."

"What do you think happened?"

"My grandparents wouldn't talk about it much. But at Grams' funeral, her friend told me that it broke Grams' heart when my mom ran away. And they couldn't find her for almost a year. Then someone saw her in a restaurant in Madison, where she had gotten a job, and called my grandparents.

"They got in the car and that's where they found her — a pregnant waitress in a run-down fast-food place."

"Did anyone try to contact your father?"

"The story always fell apart then. He was already gone, my mom said. Or leaving that day. And she'd cry, every time I asked, so I stopped asking. Grams would only say that he was no good. No decent man would get a young girl pregnant. He would burn in hell, she said. And if he came anywhere near them, they'd have the sheriff arrest him for rape."

"Did he know about you?"

Willow shifted in the chair that held her

father's shape and smell and looked over at Nell. "I don't know. I'm hoping he'll tell me."

CHAPTER 24

It was dark when Nell and Willow got back home, and Nell still had to take food over to Natalie's. Since no funeral service was planned, she was receiving guests at her house, Birdie had told Nell — and Birdie's suspicion was that if there was going to be any food or drink to greet the guests, they were going to have to bring it.

Willow had headed immediately for the guest cottage, claiming tiredness and the need to be alone, but Nell knew from numerous phone calls to her cell phone that Brendan was concerned about her, and would probably be showing up in the drive any minute.

"I wasn't sure if she had a family doctor," Ben said when he and Nell discussed their plans for the evening. "Natalie hasn't been here that long — so I sent Doc Hamilton over."

Nell kissed him. "Leave it to you to think

of that. She must be in shock."

"What are the books?" Ben asked, nodding toward the stack on the kitchen island. He pulled out a box of foil and tore off a piece for the platter he'd picked up from Ned's Groceria in Gloucester.

Nell eyed the array of parmigiano-reggiano, aged Gouda, chunks of fresh sausage, and imported mustards, and made a mental note to replenish her supply of cheese before next Friday's supper. Ned's was one of those stores she couldn't drive past without stopping in to taste whatever new cheese was featured on the tasting tray. And though she went in for a taste, she always went home with a sack filled with sausage and cheese and fresh bread or crackers.

From all appearances, Ben had picked up her habits.

"The books?" Ben handed Nell her purse.

"Oh, yes, the books. I took those from Aidan's library. They looked interesting — and there's one on James' life and paintings that I should probably read. I was never that crazy about his work, but maybe I just need to be more educated."

Ben slipped on his glasses and surveyed the other titles, pulling out a coffee-table book of the world's finest sailboats. "Good job, Nell — this is one I've been wanting to look at." He held the cheese in one arm and shoved open the door to the garage for Nell to pass through.

They drove to the Sobel house in silence, each alone with their memories of the colorful art dealer. Billy was well liked, in spite of his sometimes colorful outbursts. And most agreed that since marrying Natalie, he had calmed down some. Natalie certainly seemed to be in love with him, in spite of the age difference. They were an odd couple, many thought. The Tony Soprano look-alike and the Atlantic City showgirl, or so the rumors went. But Nell suspected there was a bond there that they both cherished. And Natalie's grief would be enormous.

"Izzy and Sam are here," Ben said, pointing to the Jeep parked at the curb. There were only two other cars parked in front of the Sobels' home, and Nell was relieved. They would have a chance to get the food arranged before the house filled with people.

Sam appeared at the door and nodded toward the living room, where Ellen and Rebecca Marks sat on either side of Natalie, each one holding a hand and taking turns murmuring their condolences.

Nell followed Sam into the well-equipped Sobel kitchen.

Birdie, Izzy, and Cass were already at work, opening cupboards in their search for napkins and plates, glasses and pitchers. Sam and Izzy had brought wine and bags of ice that Sam set in the sink while Izzy searched for ice containers and baskets for the rolls.

"You make a good kitchen crew." Rebecca leaned against the doorframe, a glass of wine in her hand.

"Thanks," Nell answered. "We're a well-oiled machine."

"Do you do funerals often?" She picked an olive off the relish tray and popped it into her mouth.

"Whenever necessary," Cass said. "Better watch your step. Ellen may be hiring us next."

Rebecca smiled and took another olive.

The sound of new voices in the front room drifted back to the kitchen, and it was evident that more visitors were filing through the front door. Nell was pleased. Natalie didn't know that many people, but Billy had known everyone, and it was important for Natalie that people come.

She saw Harriet and Archie Brandley, and Harry Garozzo and his sweet wife, Margaret. Harry stuck his head in the kitchen and held up a sack with five loaves of Italian bread sticking out the top.

"I knew where to find my ladies," he said, and walked over to kiss Nell on the cheek. "Sad day. Poor Billy."

"No more death, I say. Enough already." It was Hank Jackson, looking as if he were somehow responsible for Billy's drowning. He set a case of beer down on the counter, then rummaged around for an opener and snapped the tops off several bottles. He picked one up, took a long swig, and then looked around the kitchen sadly. "We saw him that night, Merry and me. We talked to him in the rain. We shoulda made him stay inside until it stopped."

"Hank, we were there, too, remember? Sometimes things are going to happen no matter what we do." Nell rested a hand on the restaurant owner's arm. She had entertained the same thought several times that day. If they had gotten out of the car, would they have seen Billy's bike? Would they have spotted a sad, hunched-over body down on the dock?

Ben had been quick to jump in and squash the thoughts. *Of course not. The rain was coming down in sheets. There was no electricity. How could anyone have seen anything? And who in their right mind would have thought of looking down the path to the dock*

325

on such a miserable night?

Survivor's remorse, Nell knew, was alive and strong. But given time, the reality of situations usually became clear.

"My sweet darlings," Natalie Sobel said, walking into the kitchen and embracing Nell and Birdie, then Cass and Izzy, in giant, perfume-scented hugs.

Her makeup stayed in place tonight, though the tears still came in small trickles, wandering down her cheeks. Nell could see that Natalie had worked hard to put her face on and to pull herself together for guests. It was also clear — bless Ben Endicott — that she was under Doc Hamilton's care and medication. There were times not to feel things. And tonight was one of them.

The evening passed in a blur for Nell. They had planned to set up the food they'd brought, to offer their condolences, and to leave early, but it was clear there was no one in charge, no relatives of Natalie's. No one to make sure that Natalie was all right and the food got served, the paper plates thrown away, and the ice refreshed.

Birdie looked at Nell and Ben, and in turn, they looked at Sam, Izzy, and Cass. Sam shrugged and dug into the bag to fill a bucket with fresh ice. "I'd say we're here for the long haul," he said. "Cold drink, anyone?"

A while later, as the crowd began to thin, Nell found herself alone in the den with Ellen Marks. "I'm so sorry about Billy, Ellen," she said. "I know you were good friends."

Ellen's tears were fresh, and she pulled a tissue from the box on the desk and nodded. "Billy was good to us when we opened Lampworks — he helped me figure things out, helped me . . . helped me handle Rebecca — you know how she can be sometimes — and personal things. I could confide in Billy. We understood each other. We were alike in some ways."

Nell nodded, although she didn't quite understood what Ellen was getting at. "Birdie mentioned she saw you and Billy walking in Aidan's woods yesterday. She could see that you were a comfort to each other."

"A comfort?"

"About Aidan, she thought."

Ellen was silent.

Nell continued. "I know Billy was angry with Aidan. Do you know why?"

Ellen took a breath as if she were about to say something, then thought better of it.

"Aidan and Billy were having troubles, it seemed," Nell prompted.

"Aidan sometimes interfered too much. At least Billy thought so. He could be that way, I guess."

"You've been on the arts council for a while now. So you've seen those two go at each other. What was the problem there?"

"I guess they did have problems with each other. Sometimes. Billy had a temper."

"Do you think he could have killed Aidan?"

Ellen looked down. For a long time she didn't say anything. She clasped her hands tight. When she looked up again, her eyes were sad. "I don't know. I don't think so. But I just don't know. What I do know is that Billy was troubled when I saw him yesterday. He should have been happy about things: Natalie, the exhibit. But he was distracted. Upset. Like he regretted something he'd done. He wasn't himself — that much I know."

The ringing of the doorbell disrupted the conversation, and Nell excused herself and headed to the hallway.

Ben was already at the door when Nell got there.

Jerry Thompson stood on the step, a relieved look on his face at the sight of Ben.

"Come on in, Jerry," Ben said, holding open the screen door. "Mighty nice of you to come. I know Natalie will appreciate it."

"Do you have a minute to talk, Ben?" the chief asked. "Before I see Mrs. Sobel, I mean?" He nodded a greeting to Nell.

"Sure thing. How about the den?"

Jerry and Ben retreated to the den, and Nell walked into the kitchen and picked up a dish towel. Birdie handed her a washed platter. "What's the chief doing here?" she whispered.

"Maybe he's just paying a condolence call," Izzy said. "He's a pretty nice guy — and he knew Billy."

"Sure he knew him. Billy was a suspect in a homicide." Cass spoke up from her post at the dishwasher.

"Jerry was brought up right," Birdie said. "I knew his mother well. He would come to pay his respects."

"Maybe," Nell said.

But it came as no surprise to her when Ben emerged from the den a short while later and asked where Natalie was. In the next minute he was leading her, one arm around her shoulders, into Billy's den. He closed the door behind her softly, the way one did in a hospital or library, and returned to the kitchen.

Birdie turned off the water in the sink. Sam put down the garbage bag, and Cass,

329

Izzy, and Nell stood still, looking at Ben intently.

Speak, their silence said.

"The police think . . . ," Ben began. "They think Billy had help drowning."

"But how . . . ?" Nell began.

"Billy couldn't swim. That was one factor. And he could have fallen off the end of the dock, just as we thought. But Jerry doesn't think it was unintentional. And it looks like he tried to save himself, tried to grab on to one of the metal bars that the kids used to use as steps to hoist themselves back onto the dock when they'd been swimming."

Nell remembered the steps. When Izzy was a teenager and vacationed each summer with Ben and Nell, she and her friends would often go down to the artists' dock, as they called it, to swim. It had a vague, slightly dangerous appeal, Nell supposed, though she much preferred they swim at the beach. She remembered going down with Ben one rainy day when she knew the kids wouldn't be there, just to check it out, to be sure it was safe. Back then the dock was healthier — the wood sturdy and the metal rungs held firmly in place and formed a ladder to get out of the water below. The small roofed area was solid, too, and provided a place to get out of the sun.

"And then?" Nell asked.

But before Ben answered, she knew what the answer would be.

Merry had seen someone with Billy. She had told them as much — she was sure there was someone else standing in the parking lot with Billy Sobel.

"Jerry said it looked like he grabbed that pipe and held on firmly. With both hands, Jerry said."

"But . . . ," Birdie prompted.

"But his hands were badly bruised. Stepped on. Until he finally let go."

CHAPTER 25

"They always look to the wife first," Archie Brandley said, handing Nell her sack of books.

Archie read nearly every mystery novel that came through his bookstore, and offering advice on how to solve crimes needed little encouragement.

Nell nodded. "They need to look at everyone, yes. But Natalie Sobel was in my car that night, Archie. We were out in a bad storm looking for her husband. And she has five of us to back her up."

"But you weren't with her all night, right?" Archie looked at Nell intently through dark-rimmed glasses.

"No, but she was in no condition to go out again on her own, believe me."

"But she *could* have. So she's still on the list."

"And what possible reason would she have?"

Archie coughed suggestively into his hand, peering at Nell over the cup of his hand. His brows lifted high and created a wrinkled forehead full of possibilities.

Nell knew Archie was simply playing devil's advocate. He didn't know Natalie well, and it was almost easier to think of her as the murderer, rather than suggesting that a longtime Sea Harbor resident had done this terrible crime. But Natalie gave no impression that she was leaving the house that night. And they'd seen the television screen flash on before they were out of the driveway. Natalie seemed to have been settling in to weather the storm — whatever that storm would bring.

"So what'll happen with the exhibit, do you suppose?"

"It probably won't happen. I can't see Natalie wanting to go through all of that." It was too bad, but she certainly understood. The paintings would probably be turned over to Sotheby's or some other auction house and someone would buy them up, one by one, and they'd disappear into home galleries.

Nell picked up her sack and walked out into the bright afternoon sunlight. Natalie had had to be sedated the night before. Doc Hamilton had come back, and a neighbor had volunteered to spend the night.

But the early edition of the *Sea Harbor Gazette* wasn't cutting anyone any slack. One murder, one possible murder, two weeks apart was enough to raise flags all over Cape Ann. People were scared.

The police, the paper reported, were under enormous pressure to put it all to rest.

And pressure, to Nell, was worrisome. She and Ben had sat for an hour that morning, cold coffee sitting on the small deck table between them, pondering this latest, awful event. The pressure could lead to mistakes. To mistaken arrests.

"They're thinking the two murders must be connected," Ben said.

"Which leaves Willow in the clear, hopefully. She was with me all that Sunday evening. And that little thing couldn't kill a Billy Sobel if her life depended on it."

"I agree that Willow didn't do it. But that little thing has the strength of an ox. Don't sell her short. I think she must have been pulling calves in Wisconsin before she landed here."

Nell laughed and didn't disagree. The waiflike image Willow had projected that first night was long gone. Her body might be small, but she could swim in the ocean

334

against tough waves, and the running — whether it was done for therapy or exercise — certainly kept her trim.

A buzz from her cell phone caused Nell to step back from the curb, just in time to avoid the flurry of sand and stones spun up from the wheels of Merry Jackson's new Miata. Merry whizzed by, waving gaily at Nell. She picked up speed just beyond Izzy's shop, hugging the curve like a race driver.

Not for the first time did Nell utter her gratitude that Merry had married Hank Jackson. Hank had sense, and with his help his young wife might actually live beyond her thirty-fifth birthday.

Nell might have forgotten the phone, except another beep caused her to pull it from the pocket of her jeans and look down. A text message from Cass. She frowned. She'd still prefer voices.

Lottsa lobsters, the note read. And Cass had used all the correct letters. *Laudable,* Nell thought. She'd get this texting down if it killed her.

She pressed Cass' number, wondering as she often did, how many cell phones Cass had gone through — and how many littered the bottom of the sea, scattered among her traps. A great many, Nell suspected. In his latest quest for techie gadgets, Ben went through many phones, also. And each castoff was sent Cass' way and accepted with profound gratitude.

Cass answered on the first ring, her voice loud over the sound of wind blowing across the water. She had more lobsters than she needed today — could Nell believe it? — and she'd promised Sam she'd give him a bunch for that clambake he kept talking about. She'd barter for the clams, too. Could Nell call everyone and spread the word?

Nell felt slightly guilty. There was such turmoil right now — but being together might be the best thing in the world. And the lobsters wouldn't wait for the weekend — that was certain. Who knew? By week's end there might be only pregnant lobsters down on the bottom of the lobster floor, and Cass would have to toss them all back.

It was a surprise that everyone was free — Jane and Ham, Izzy and Birdie. Willow and Brendan. But Nell suspected the need to be together and talk — and the chance to see Sam's new home — would cancel other plans in a heartbeat, even if people had other plans.

A call to Ben assured Nell he'd get there early to dig the hole and start the fire.

Nell checked her watch. This plan put a rush on other things she needed to get done today. Not the least of which was to check on Natalie and make a quick visit to Canary Cove.

Natalie was not alone when Nell arrived. She sat in the middle of the living room, her eyes glassy and an untouched sandwich in front of her.

"I just wanted to check on you, to be sure you're all right, Natalie."

Natalie excused herself from the busy group of women — members of the Altar Guild sent over by Father Northcutt, Nell suspected. She followed Natalie into the kitchen.

"My Billy may have been murdered." Natalie sat on a wrought-iron stool and pulled a Kleenex box from the center of the island. "I could have murdered him plenty of times — sure — but only in my mind. I loved him. Who did this to me?"

"That's what we need to find out." Nell pulled out the other stool and sat on it, her sandals resting on the bar.

"He couldn't swim. My Billy lived on the ocean — and he couldn't swim a single stroke. I signed him up for lessons at the Y over in Gloucester, and you know what he did?" A hollow laugh escaped Natalie's red

337

lips. "Well, he didn't go swimming is all I'll say."

Natalie's pencil-thin eyebrows lifted, and Nell could see that the memory brought tears close to the surface.

Sometimes, Natalie said, if Billy could explain the time away, he'd travel down to Foxwoods. And when Natalie questioned why the short drive to Gloucester took him away for a whole day, Billy changed plans and put together a fine poker group that met in the back of a mechanic's shop in Gloucester once a week, during swimming lesson time. It was his own little version of *Guys and Dolls,* Natalie said with a sad smile.

Nell smiled, too. And it was just as likely that the money he won at his "swimming lessons" was lent to someone who needed it more than he did. Billy did things like that.

"The feud between Billy and Aidan Peabody is such a mystery to all of us — do you know what it was all about?"

Natalie waved her hand in the air as if the question was old and used up. "That was business stuff, nothing to worry about. That's what Billy told me when I would ask him."

"He hadn't always disliked Aidan, had he?"

"Billy disliked people who got in his way. And he was worried the last few months about business. So he was more irritable, and Aiden sometimes made it harder to do business."

"I think there might be a connection in their deaths. To have two Canary Cove people, both important members of the art community, die within two weeks of each other — that's just a coincidence I can't buy."

Natalie sighed. "Look at that Willow person closely — I know she's your friend. But we know she had a reason to kill Aidan. And she was hanging around Billy's shop, too."

"Oh?"

"Billy told me that himself. At first, before Aidan died, she was asking a lot of questions about the Fishtail Gallery. And then after Aidan died, I don't know, but she'd come in while I was there, just looking around. She never bought anything."

Brendan, Nell thought. That was probably why she was in Billy's shop.

"Was Billy's business okay?"

"Billy was sometimes too generous. You know what I mean? He gave money to every Tom, Dick, and Harry. So I insisted that I take over all money. All bank accounts. I

339

brought a little money to the marriage, too, you know, and I didn't want Billy giving that away. Besides, we had expenses, the house, other things. And I am very good at keeping dollars straight. I have a gift for that."

"Will you sell the gallery?"

"I'm not making those kinds of decisions today. But, Nell, you know and I know that I don't know about art. Money, yes. Art, not so much."

"Well, whatever you decide, Ben and I will help, Natalie. You won't have to do it alone."

Natalie reached out and patted Nell's hand. "You're a good lady. I know you will help. The Brewsters have promised, and even the Marks gals. And that sweet Brendan — Billy liked him so much."

Nell wasn't surprised at the list of offers Natalie had already received. Of course they'd all help. Ben would do any paperwork, and they were all up to packing boxes and arranging shipments and cleaning. And there'd be more people, too, once the need was there.

"I know you have people who want to see you, so I will be off." Nell scribbled her phone number on a pad of paper and slid it across the island. "You'll call me with the slightest need."

■ ■ ■ ■

Without clear intent, Nell followed the curve in Harbor Road that Merry Jackson had made earlier that day, and drove around the bend of ocean into Canary Cove.

Canary Road was busy with people, eating ice-cream cones or carrying bottles of water, their sunglasses reflecting the blue sky. Some carried bulky bags with names of a gallery printed along the outside.

It was a typical summer day.

And not typical at all.

Nell pulled into the Artist's Palate parking lot and saw Merry standing just outside the restaurant, chatting with a group of young friends. She waved until Merry saw her, then excused herself and walked over to Nell's car.

"Like my new wheels, Nell?"

"It's a beautiful car, Merry."

"I got it up to eighty along the old highway."

Nell cringed.

"So what brings you over here in the middle of the afternoon? Would you like a beer?"

"No, thanks. I was thinking of what you said the other night when we came by looking for Billy."

"Jeez, that's awful about Billy. Who would want to kill him? Natalie didn't like it here much, I don't think. She never quite got in the groove of Canary Cove. But there'd be an easier way to leave than killing her husband."

"I would think."

"Ellen is upset. She was here earlier today. She was going to walk down to the dock. She had a flower to throw in the water. I didn't want her to go alone, so I walked along with her. It was still pretty muddy down there from the rain. We couldn't see any footsteps, though we couldn't really get on the dock. They still had it ribboned off. I guess they'll finally fix it now. Ellen and Billy were real buddies, even though Rebecca didn't like him much."

"Billy was helpful to them."

Merry nodded agreement. "He would do things like that. He was a good guy when he liked someone."

"What I really wanted to ask you about was Sunday night when we came looking for Billy."

"In the middle of that downpour. I remember. I was anxious to get home to see if we had electricity."

"Hank mentioned that when you saw Billy

that night, you didn't think he was alone."

"Right, when he was leaving. Hank thought I was crazy but that's because he doesn't see nearly as well as I do. I swear he needs glasses. He's forty, for Pete's sake."

"He probably does," Nell said. "It's a good thing he has you."

Merry nodded. Her long, shiny hair fell over her shoulders, and she brushed it back with one hand. "Billy was alone when he came in. And upset, like he had to do something awful — you know what I mean? I tried to get him to talk to me because he looked so darn upset. But you know Billy. He doesn't want anyone to think he's needy. So he clammed up totally. I could see his reflection in the bar window, looking out toward the parking lot every few minutes, like he was expecting someone. Drumming his fingers on the bar. Checking his watch. And he was cursing the rain something awful.

"So I told him to relax, the rain would stop. No need to build an ark. He wouldn't even laugh, just kept sitting there, the only one in the whole restaurant. Then the lights went out, and Hank came in and said Billy had to leave, that we were heading home. Without saying a word, he took the whole bottle of bourbon he'd been nursing, walked out the door and across the parking lot to where he'd left his Harley."

"But the parking lot was dark?"

"Dark as sin. But there was still a string of lights on across the harbor, and a couple of cars going by. And I could see him moving toward his bike. I moved over to the window, and I swear there was someone standing there beside the bike, waiting for him."

"Do you have any idea who it was?"

She shook her head. "I wish I did. Hank doesn't believe me. 'Who'd be out in that crappy weather?' he said. 'Well, Billy was,' I told him."

Nell smiled in spite of the serious topic. Merry was unpredictable, but there was something innately sweet about her.

"Hank was a little worried about Billy leaving with that full bottle of liquor — though by then it was only half full, so when we got ready to leave, he took his humongous flashlight and looked around the lot, but he was gone. The bike was gone. The lot was empty. But I'd swear on my wedding ring that when he left, he wasn't alone."

CHAPTER 26

Nell wanted to stop in to see Rebecca and Ellen, but that would have to wait until tomorrow. The least she could do for the clambake was pick up dessert — and she was already late.

The Marks women had already left the Sobel house the night before, before Chief Thompson came in with more disturbing news. But they would know about it. Nell was certain that by now the entire town was aware that Billy Sobel's death might well be a murder — the second in as many weeks.

She slowed down as she passed the hand-blown glass studio. Rebecca's lamp-blown beads were hanging in the window from clear fish line, stunning pieces of glass in many shapes and colors floating in the air. They were magical.

Rebecca was standing not far inside the window, talking to a customer. She looked lovely, as always, her silky hair floating around her shoulders, her back straight, her shoulders tan and lovely.

But her appearance hid an ambiguity that Nell found discomforting. She never walked away from a conversation with Rebecca Marks feeling as if she knew her any better. And her comments about Aidan and their relationship in recent days had been equally perplexing.

When Nell shared them with Ben, he had agreed. It reminded him, he said, of a girl he hung out with in high school. They had a standing agreement that if neither had a date for the annual prom, they'd go with each other. It was convenient, he had said.

But there were no adult proms in Sea Harbor — and Aidan Peabody never had trouble getting a date. He didn't need the convenience of Rebecca Marks.

And Rebecca seemed to hold Billy Sobel at a distance, too, almost as if she were afraid of him. She was certainly an intriguing mix — showy self-confidence but mixed in with fear. Uncomfortable, at the least.

A few weeks ago, such encounters and conversations would probably have passed by Nell without a second thought. But with her friend Aidan dead and buried, with Billy's body in some coroner's cold, impersonal room — and with a murderer still free —

even odd conversations took on ominous overtones.

Nell turned her attention back to the winding Canary Road, gradually picking up speed. She drove around the graceful bend of land bordering the ocean. It was one of her favorite spots in Sea Harbor, with the sea grass growing wild and free along the narrow road and the sounds of horns in the distance, rolling in like fog from incoming fishing vessels. She smiled, in spite of her troubled mood, and headed toward Harbor Road, Harry Garozzo's deli, and comfort food. A key lime pie would be just the thing to top off an evening on the beach.

Ben had gone hours earlier to Sam's new beach house, driving out with Birdie and an SUV full of food: rolls, cheeses, potatoes, and cobs of fresh corn from the market. Cass and Izzy had met them there with bulging plastic sacks of cherry stone clams and a cooler filled with lobsters, which had been swimming in the ocean just hours before.

By the time Nell arrived, the bulk of the work was done. Sam had dug the hole earlier in the day and lined it with large rocks collected from above the tide line. When Ben arrived, they all walked the beach — Ben and Sam, Birdie, Cass, and Izzy — filling tubs full of rockweed. When the rocks were hot enough to spit a drop of water back at them, they all scooped up handfuls of the wet seaweed and coated the pit thickly.

The sizzling smell of the fire and familiar popping of the seaweed greeted Nell as she pulled her car off the beach road and into the gravel drive of Sam's new home.

In the short week he'd had the keys, Sam had somehow managed to make the place his own — at least partially so. Through the windows on either side of the open door, Nell could see clear through to the other side of the house — and far beyond, to the endless expanse of the sea.

"Isn't it nice?" Izzy appeared from inside the small cedar-shingled house, opened the door, and relieved Nell of one of her sacks. "It's nearly picture-perfect. A little lacking in furniture, but that'll come, Sam says."

"It's lovely," Nell said. She followed Izzy inside.

The builder had clearly loved nature — nothing distracted from the view outside the windows. One end of the living area was anchored by a simple fireplace with a cherry mantel and soapstone surround, and built-in bookcases and cabinets, all a shiny white,

348

made up for Sam's lack of furniture. The single cushy sofa, coffee table, butcher block kitchen island — and a couple of tall stools — were all he needed, at least for now.

"And he has a mattress," Izzy called out from the behind the refrigerator door. "The rest is on order."

Voices outside drew Nell's attention to the group gathering around the fire. Several dogs from up the beach ran by, chasing a Frisbee. The owner waved as he walked by.

Ham and Jane had shown up, and helped fill the pit with mounds of potatoes, corn on the cob, and the scrubbed clams and fresh lobster. As soon as Cass, Jane, and Willow covered the feast with more wet seaweed, the men grabbed corners of the tarpaulin and covered the steamy feast, then fastened it firmly with a round of rocks.

"Beer, bring on the beer," Ham intoned, and he and Ben went up to drag the cooler from the back of Sam's Jeep.

Izzy went over and looped an arm around Sam's waist. He wore torn madras shorts and a T-shirt, damp and sticky with sand and seaweed. "Good job, Perry. Jeez, I could get to like this place."

"More than that little apartment above the shop?" He rubbed one large hand along her back.

A salty breeze came in off the water, carrying with it the sweet smell of summer. Izzy smiled into Sam's day-old beard.

Nell watched the two of them, standing together, their bare feet buried in the sand. An image she would share with her sister when she called her over the weekend, reporting in on what a gift it was to have Caroline's daughter, Izzy, so present in her life. And now Sam, too — a childhood friend of Izzy's brothers from summers on their Kansas ranch. The older friend who teased Izzy crazy back then, and who found her again a half country away, and didn't drive her crazy anymore. At least not in the same way. It made Caroline chuckle when Nell filled her in, as sisters do. And it filled Nell with a warmth she wouldn't have anticipated.

She looked beyond Izzy and Sam, to Cass and Birdie up on the deck, stretched out on the Adirondack chairs, watching daylight fade over the ocean. Ham and Jane had walked down the beach, their footsteps weaving with the edge of the tide, bending over now and then to pick up a shell or piece of smooth sea glass that would find its way into a piece of Jane's pottery.

"Wicked nice?" Ben said, coming up behind Nell and wrapping a light sweater around her shoulders.

She nodded against his chest. It was, indeed. The respite they all needed from the fogginess of their days.

"But the world is still out there with all its warts and unsolved problems, is what my Nell is thinking."

She moved her head again. "But that doesn't mean this isn't a lovely moment. It's these moments that get us through the rest."

"I talked to Jerry before coming out here," Ben said.

Sam and Izzy, hearing the police chief's name, stepped closer to hear what Ben would say.

"They've been looking into Billy Sobel more closely than we knew, it seems, looking for a connection between him and Aidan. The rifts those two had were more than rumors, apparently. But they couldn't nail down a logical reason, at least not one that would lead to murder. There were disagreements, maybe personality problems. Billy had a temper, and they haven't ruled him out completely as Aidan's murderer. But it just doesn't quite add up, Jerry said. There are certainly those who *want* Billy to be the culprit, and Jerry is aware of the comfort in that kind of closure. Billy is dead, too. So no mess, no bother, to put an awful, practical spin on it. But they're going to talk to Natalie, see where it goes."

"Which just might send her over the edge," Izzy said. "She's not the most stable woman in the world, especially now. This is an awful time for her."

"She'll be okay, Iz. She's a tough lady," Ben said.

"But if Billy killed Aidan, then how do they account for *his* death?"

"If, in fact, someone did make sure that he didn't get back up out of the ocean, they don't think it was a local, Jerry said. The police have already done lots of prying into Billy's New Jersey ties, even before he was killed. It seems Billy's longtime business associates weren't always the most upstanding citizens. He owed money, too — to a couple of tough guys. Everyone knew he gambled. They're looking into it on that end now, and have pretty much dismissed his murder as having a local connection. Fact of the matter is, people here liked Billy. He was a good guy."

"Natalie said he got two phone calls that night. One was from you, Ben, and the other must have been from the person he was meeting down at the dock. It had to have been someone he knew."

"I agree. That's a wrinkle."

"I don't understand how they can tie this up so quickly. It just happened." Nell took the beer that Sam offered her.

"As I said, they'd been prying into his life before he was ever killed. Maybe that's why Billy was so jittery those past few days, afraid something would be discovered."

"So they don't think there's any connection between the two deaths?"

Ben forked his fingers through his hair. "That's the thinking."

That, Nell thought to herself, was a fly-by-night assumption. Some people might be able to paint the conclusion they wanted and go on with their lives. But she knew for a fact that most people were not that way. And especially her family and friends so closely touched by these murders. Comfort and closure would take a lot more than suppositions. It would take knowing without a doubt who killed Aidan Peabody and Billy Sobel. And knowing that the person who did it was safely and permanently behind bars.

But there wasn't any sense in ruining a lovely clambake with her thoughts. They could wait. They would have to wait. But tomorrow was another day, and even without easy access to the black tablet in her purse that held her week's schedule, Nell knew what the next day would bring.

"Have you met any of your neighbors, Sam?" she asked aloud, determined not to ruin the evening. She looked up and down the beach at the lovely beach homes, each one different and inviting in its own way. This stretch of the Sea Harbor coast was mostly residential, with small lanes leading to clusters of houses nearly hidden in stands of trees on the roadside, and wide-open to the sea on the other.

"Harriet and Archie Brandley's daughter lives a few houses down, on a little lane that runs back from the sea." Izzy pointed to a gabled house across the road with a fenced-in area filled with children's play equipment.

"Brendan lives right over there," Willow piped up. "Just beyond that white fence and stand of pines." His house was nearly invisible, but just a short walk from Sam's.

"He's a good chap," Sam said. "He brought me a bottle of scotch and a case of beer when I moved in, then helped me make a dent in at least a few of the bottles."

"Where is he, by the way?" Nell asked.

"Brendan'll be here," Jane said, carrying over a plate of bruschetta, each piece coated with creamy goat cheese and sprinkled with toasted pine nuts. The group helped themselves without hesitation. "He was our Clark Kent this afternoon. The police were at the Sobel Gallery, and when Natalie showed up, they suggested she leave until they were finished with their investigation. She became irate and essentially staged her own sit-in, poor thing, berating them and yelling at them to leave. She said it was her gallery, her things. It was pretty emotional. Brendan offered to take her to the Palate for something to eat and then take her home. He'd been helping Billy in the gallery a lot, and I think he understands her a little better than we do. We owe him big. And I think poor Tommy Porter will see that he gets a certificate of valor from the Sea Harbor PD."

"But he was determined not to miss the clambake. He promised he'd be over before the lobsters were cracked," Ham added. "He just wanted to be sure Natalie was okay."

Nell listened, feeling a pinch of guilt. She had meant to check in on Natalie again that afternoon, maybe bring her along to the clambake, but time had gotten away from her. She vowed to stop in tomorrow — and tucked away a silent thank-you to Brendan for his kindness.

"Sam Perry, your kitchen is useless," Cass

355

yelled from the deck, using her cupped hands as a megaphone. "No butter. How're we gonna eat our corn? And lobsters without lemon butter? Where are you from, man?"

Sam laughed and yelled back. "My kitchen is worse than useless. I wouldn't even have salt and pepper if Izzy here hadn't done a little care package thing for me."

"No biggie," Willow said. "I know Brendan has plenty of everything — he's quite a cook. I'll just run down —"

"Can you get in?" Izzy asked.

Willow gave an impish grin. "That's not exactly a problem for me."

The group laughed, but Willow quickly confessed that she had a key. She'd given up breaking into places, she said, at least for a while.

"I'll walk with you," Nell said. "I'd love to see the inside of Brendan's place. These houses are so lovely."

Together they walked down the beach, their bare feet kicking up sand and their heads held back to catch the evening breeze.

"Brendan's place is different from Sam's — a little more rustic. I think it's the hiker in him."

Willow motioned for Nell to follow her up the steps and into a screened-in porch running along the side of the brown-shingled house. Inside, the dwelling was clean and cozy, with a large stone fireplace along one wall, rough and rustic. A galley kitchen was off to the side and the dining table showed signs of Brendan's teaching and his own hobby — a stack of art books and cups filled with pens and colored pencils.

Nell absently perused the titles of the books. Some textbooks, some on painting, and a familiar book on New England artists — the same one Archie Brandley had run out of.

People wanted to learn more about the reclusive artist so they could view the found paintings with knowledge and knowing some tidbits about his life, Archie had said.

Nell remembered that she had her own copy, confiscated from Aidan's den, and made a note to look at it soon and then pass it back to Willow. Brendan, apparently, was one of the lucky ones who had gotten one before Archie ran out.

"Here it is," Willow said, pulling a box of butter from the refrigerator. "What else?"

"Maybe some Tabasco sauce."

Willow opened a cupboard and took out a slender red bottle. A row of medicine and vitamins was lined up on the shelf beneath.

"It looks like Brendan is into vitamins,"

Nell observed.

"He's kind of a health nut. Calcium, vitamins B, K, X — whatever. I don't take much of anything myself. I don't like medicine. Except one night when I was really upset and couldn't sleep. Brendan lent me one of his sleeping pills — he has trouble sometimes. I was out like a light."

"What was it?"

"That one." Willow pointed to a small bottle.

Nell slipped on her glasses and looked at it. "This would definitely put you out," she agreed. "My brother-in-law had a terrible bout of insomnia in college and had to take Nembutal a couple times."

"Yeah. Brendan is so healthy — but that sleeping problem is the pits. He loves to hike — and worries sometimes that he'll be camping up on a mountaintop and won't be able to sleep all night, and then he'll have to climb down without being alert. He's a very careful guy."

Nell walked through the living area. "This is a lived-in place. It's comfortable. It looks like Brendan." She pointed to a GIS-rendered topographic map tacked to the wall. "The White Mountains — one of my favorite spots. Is that where Brendan hikes?"

"I think he hikes wherever there's a rise in

the ground. He runs over in Ravenswood Park sometimes, just for the view. But yes, he talks a lot about the White Mountains. He knows every trail, I think. He has a stack of pictures somewhere."

Willow looked around, then picked up a stack of photographs from the bookcase and handed them to Nell.

Nell slipped on her glasses and looked through the photos. "What memories these bring back. Ben and I camped our way through graduate school. We'd go up to the Whites every chance we got." She held one picture up to the natural light. Brendan was sitting on top of a mountain with peaks of smaller mountains in the background. "Amazing," she murmured.

"Is any of it familiar?"

Nell nodded, smiling. "I think this is Mount Lafayette. We've hiked to the top several times, though the trails can be tricky. It's a beautiful part of the country." Nell put the photos back and spotted more signs of Brendan's hobby — hiking gear was stashed in the front hall: a backpack and boots and a rain jacket. On the wall was another topographical map of all the New England peaks. His running shoes were nearby, and a bike was visible through the back door.

"I think he is at home here — he likes Sea Harbor — though he misses the mountains. I don't think he'll stay here forever. He's like me: a wanderer."

"Does he have any of his own paintings here?"

"He's funny about his paintings. He told me he's very good. But then he changes the subject. I think he'd like to be known for being a great painter — but I told him that'll be kind of hard if he doesn't let anyone see them."

Nell smiled. "Maybe he's modest."

"Maybe. I found one in his den — he never finished it, though." Willow led Nell across the hallway into a small room with a television set, a desk, and more bookshelves. Willow pulled out a painting from beside the desk.

Nell looked at it admiringly. It was a lovely watercolor of a sunrise over the ocean, the play of color on water nearly blinding to the eye. The view was an unusual one, from high above, as if he had been sitting on a hill or mountain — Cadillac Mountain, maybe. A harbor and sailboats were visible before one's eyes fell to the spectacular sunrise — but it was only roughed in and part of the scene was missing. "He's a talented young man."

"Not that young." But Willow clearly agreed.

"Will he finish this?"

Willow shrugged. "Maybe not. Brendan is pretty religious about his paintings being one hundred percent plein air. And to finish this, I guess he'd have to climb that same mountain again, find the same view."

"I guess that's one of the disadvantages of restricting yourself that way."

Willow nodded and slipped the painting back down next to the desk.

The slamming of a door brought them back into the hallway, where Brendan stood with a surprised look on his face.

"Company?" he asked, frowning. "I didn't see a car."

"I hope you don't mind, Brendan," Nell began. "We're raiding your refrigerator. We walked down from Sam's. His food supply is pitiful."

"No — of course I don't mind. I'm pretty well stocked. That's one thing I do well — eat."

"And I see you do well on other fronts as well. Willow showed me one of your paintings. It's lovely, Brendan."

Brendan looked at Willow. "Painting?"

"You know. That half-finished one."

"Oh. That's not worth seeing. You

shouldn't be showing anyone that, Willow."
He walked toward the door. "Anything else
we need from here?"

"I think we're set," Willow said.

"Good. I'm starving."

Nell and Willow followed Brendan down
the steps to the beach. "Is Natalie doing all
right?" Nell asked his back.

"She's in shock. She gave the police a hard
time today — I guess you heard — but, hey,
it's understandable. She just lost a husband.
She's trying to figure out what she should
do."

"What we need to do is figure out who
committed these murders and put it all to
rest."

"It sounds like the police have a grip on
it. It's still hard for me to believe that Billy
would kill Aidan Peabody. But I guess it
makes sense."

"It doesn't make sense to me," Nell said.

Willow was silent.

Nell could tell that it was still hard for her
to be in the middle of conversations about
her father.

They walked down the steps to the beach
and headed back toward Sam's. The two
dogs were still chasing Frisbees up and
down the beach, their owners enjoying the
cool breezes, and youngsters appeared on

the beach with their parents, one last chance to skim a stone along the darkening seas before night called them to their beds.

In the distance, steam from the pit rose above the tarp and a soft breeze carried the smells down the beach.

"Natalie isn't trying to make decisions about her life at this difficult time, is she?" Nell asked.

"Well, you know she never liked it here much."

"But she seemed to be fitting in better in recent weeks."

"She says she has a lot of friends back home in New Jersey — and the gallery was Billy's thing, not hers. She doesn't even like art. She already has people interested in the James paintings, she said, and once those are off her hands, she could pretty much do anything she wanted to do. Billy was considering that, I think, when he died: just letting someone take them off his hands."

"And not have an exhibit here?" That was a surprise. Canary Cove had been counting on the exhibit to bring new crowds to the art neighborhood. She wondered what else Billy had planned that he hadn't shared with the rest of them. He had certainly been concerned about something the week before his death.

"Billy was hard to read. An interesting guy and I liked working in his gallery with him, but he wasn't very, well, stable — at least from what I could see."

"Recently, at least," Nell agreed. "He's always been a little tough, maybe, but a kind man underneath it all. It was only recently that his behavior became erratic."

Willow was quiet between them, her arms swinging beside her as they walked. She looked up at Brendan. "I didn't know Billy at all, but I know for sure something was on his mind," she said.

"He said something to you?" Brendan asked.

She nodded. "He was talking more to himself, I think. But I was there in the gallery, waiting for you. He was tapping his fingers on the glass counter like beating a drum, looking frustrated. He mumbled something like 'Enough already.' And then he looked up and saw me. He looked startled at first, and then he told me, just out of the blue, that he needed to go to confession, and he wondered if I knew when Father Northcutt's boxes — that's what he called them — were open."

Brendan stopped and picked up a stone. He skimmed it into the water. "Maybe he knew that whoever he owed money to wanted to call it in?"

"I don't think so," Nell said. "I simply don't buy that theory, that someone from his past had come to Sea Harbor and killed him. For starters, there weren't many people around that night. A strange car — a stranger — would have been noticed. And we think Billy was waiting for someone. Merry Jackson said he was looking at his watch, looking out the window."

"Did Merry see him with someone?" Brendan asked.

"Yes, she did. It was raining so hard she didn't recognize the person, but she swears she saw someone. We also know he got a phone call from someone earlier that night.

"And even the place where he was killed — that's an old dock that only people from around here know about. I think someone from Sea Harbor killed Billy — and Aidan. And we need to find out who did it sooner rather than later."

"Time to uncover our feast," Pete yelled from down the beach, and Nell's sentence was torn off and carried on the breeze.

"We need Brendan's strong arms to help pull off this tarp," Ben added.

The flurry of food, friends, and chilled glasses of white wine and beer pushed the talk of Billy Sobel into the background.

And as they sat together on the steps and on the Adirondack chairs in front of Sam's new house, savoring bowls of juicy clams and lobster swimming in butter, disturbing thoughts were tucked away and replaced by a few hours of family, friends, and the treasures of a clambake.

But the conversation with Brendan and Willow stayed with Nell into the night. She needed to talk to Birdie, Izzy, and Cass.

Sometimes thoughts that became tangled in her head were just like a half-finished sweater pulled out from the bottom of an old knitting bag, the strands tangled, seeming not to fit together. A sweater started a year before, then forgotten for one reason or another.

But once you pulled it out again and stretched it out on the table, examining each stitch, picking up any that were dropped — the pattern would become clear. Sometimes.

The pattern of happenings in Sea Harbor was certainly a messy one right now, in desperate need of straightening.

The unanswered questions were becoming suffocating.

For starters, Nell thought — sitting in the protective warmth of friends and wiping the juice of fresh corn on the cob from her chin — why was Billy Sobel, a self-proclaimed nonchurchgoer seeking Father Northcutt's services?

And perhaps that was the next straggly piece of yarn that a Thursday night gathering would help straighten out.

CHAPTER 27

Nell knew as soon as she and Ben finished their morning coffee and Ben drove off to a business meeting in Boston that if she didn't move quickly, she'd be stripped of the resolutions she'd made the night before.

She'd already received three phone calls and one request to attend an impromptu meeting of the Sea Harbor Historical Society.

What she needed to do before she did anything else was stop in to see Natalie Sobel. And that wouldn't happen if she didn't leave the house soon and stop answering her phone.

But Birdie had beat her to it.

"Nell, dear," Birdie said, "I'm meeting Natalie at the tea shop in Gloucester — she gets her hair done near there. You'll join us."

Nell smiled into the phone. Birdie had tried to pull her aside the night before at

Sam's, but the evening had passed way too quickly and there was little chance to talk privately. And then they had all gone their separate ways, Birdie riding with Pete and Cass, and Nell following Ben home, his car filled with a trunkload of coolers, a few tarps, and some long metal pokers they'd used for the clambake.

But they were of the same mind — and she knew Izzy and Cass, too, were wanting to regroup, to spread their thoughts out in neat rows on the knitting room table. And to try their best to put the pieces of the pattern together.

The Pleasant Street Tea Shop was one of Nell's favorite places to sit and compose herself, to think things through, and to almost always find a friend to chat with.

And she hadn't had a slice of their cinnamon bread in days.

Nell arrived a few minutes before Birdie and Natalie, and spotted Cass' mother, Mary Halloran, pushing her chair back from a table in the front of the shop. Father Northcutt sat opposite her, eyeing the remnant of a flaky scone as he got ready to leave.

"Nell," Mary called out, her white head bobbing as she waved.

Nell walked over to the table and greeted

them. Seeing Father Northcutt reminded her of the conversation she'd had with Willow about Billy's interest in confession.

"Father Larry," she said cautiously, understanding the priestly seal of secrecy, "did Natalie and Billy Sobel join Our Lady of Safe Seas? I don't remember seeing Billy at church."

"Ah, poor Billy, God rest his soul," the priest said with a brief bow of his head. After an appropriate pause, he looked up again. "Natalie Sobel is becoming a devout member. She comes to the seven o'clock on Sundays, Nell, which is why you never saw her there. Too early for you." He winked. "And this past Lent, Natalie was there every morning. She's a good woman, in my humble opinion. Now why are you askin', my dear?"

"I just wondered about Billy."

"Billy, bless him, not so much. Natalie was working on him, though. And he came by the day he died, if you can believe it. Wanted to learn about confession, he told me, but I was off to a parish council meeting, so he said he'd come back." The good-sized priest pushed back his chair and left some bills beside the teacup.

With promises to get together soon, Mary and Father Larry walked out the door and across Pleasant Street to Mary's car. Mary Halloran was probably promising to join one more church committee that needed her drive and energy, Nell thought. She was an Irish dynamo, and Nell honestly didn't think Our Lady of Safe Seas could survive without her.

Nell watched them through the window for a minute, but her thoughts went almost immediately back to Billy Sobel. He was upset that day — that whole week if Brendan read him right. He was troubled. Because someone was threatening him? Because someone wanted something from him?

"A penny for your thoughts," Birdie said, coming up beside her.

"Birdie," Nell said, startled for a moment, "you could be a cat burglar."

"Certainly an option. But I already have far more money than I need, so it wouldn't be a sensible choice. Now why are you standing here daydreaming?"

"I have a head stuffed full of puzzles, I guess." Nell shifted the large bag hanging from her shoulder and hugged Natalie, who came in on Birdie's heels. She motioned toward two empty couches along the side of the shop. "Shall we?"

It was quiet and almost empty in the tea

shop now — but it wouldn't be the case when the lunch crowd drifted in. This was a good time to have come, and their tea order and a plate of cinnamon bread appeared almost instantly.

Nell settled into the couch across from Birdie and Natalie.

Natalie's eyes were still slightly swollen from crying, but her makeup was perfect. She wore a pink silk blouse and white slacks, pressed and fluid. The diamond necklace that Billy had given her for their eight-month anniversary circled her neck — and her hair was perfect, cut and styled and teased into place. The color was deeper than usual, and Nell noticed several highlights that ran from her hairline to the tips.

Most of us, Nell supposed, felt better when we looked better. Perhaps that was Natalie's beauty-day motivation.

Billy's cousin had come to be with her, Natalie was telling Birdie. He was close to Billy, even in recent days. Not always such a good influence on each other, in Natalie's opinion, but he was family. "My days are filled right now — lawyers and phone calls. That sweet Brendan Slattery is a godsend."

"Is there any more information on the circumstances surrounding Billy's death?"

"Just what you know. What the papers say. Someone from Jersey." Her hands flew in the air and the light bounced off her diamond rings. "But no one in Jersey would kill Billy. It makes no sense to me. I don't think it even makes sense to the police. So Billy gambled a little? Had some business dealings with people the police like to pick on? That doesn't mean one of them killed him. They liked Billy. And you know what else makes no sense? Why Billy would talk to anyone on that dilapidated old dock."

"I suppose it was out of the way — private. A lot of places had closed because of the storm and those that were open, like the Gull, wouldn't have been very private."

"And it had that little overhang where they could talk out of the rain," Birdie added practically. She picked up a strand of pink yarn and began a new row.

"If private is what Billy was looking for," Natalie said, a trifle too loud, "he has a beautiful den at home that I decorated myself just for himself." Natalie twisted a white lace handkerchief that she'd pulled from her bag.

"I suppose Billy took his cell phone with him," Nell said, more to herself than out loud. The second phone caller would certainly be of interest.

"It's swimming with the cod," Natalie said.

"Do you have any ideas, Natalie? I suppose the police have asked you all this."

Natalie shook her head slowly. "At first I tried to think of someone. I thought and thought. But I've decided it musta been an accident. I think maybe he just drank too much. And then he fell off the end of that rotted old dock. No one would ever hurt him."

"Yes," Birdie assured her.

Nell understood why Natalie had come around to the accident thesis. It made sense in a way — Billy was drunk. And he couldn't swim. And an accident — as tragic as it was — was easier to live with than murder.

But an accident didn't explain Billy's bruised hands, which had been perfectly normal an hour before. Ben had wondered if he had fallen on his motorcycle; maybe doing so had crushed a hand. But the police said Billy's Harley was in pristine condition. An accident also didn't explain the fact that someone was most probably with him — and could have rescued him if he'd accidentally fallen off the end of the old dock.

"Did anything unusual happen last week?"

"Billy was upset, sure. First the problems with the exhibit, getting the paintings

374

cleaned and ready. And Aidan's murder. Billy and Aidan didn't see things eye to eye, but he didn't want Aidan Peabody dead, no matter what anyone says. Billy didn't hurt people. And he was a little mad at me, too, I must confess." Natalie lowered her head, regret showing on her face.

"How so, dear?" Birdie reached over and patted her knee.

Natalie looked up and flapped her hand in the air. "Because I insisted that I be in charge of the bank accounts. But Billy wasn't doing a good job, and someone needed to step in and put her foot down. Besides, I had ways of getting him to not be so mad." She smiled coyly.

Nell listened, her mind going in different directions — from Aidan to Billy, from arguments, as best she could tell, that couldn't hold the weight of murder. She took a bite out of the cinnamon bread and realized suddenly that breakfast had been only coffee, not nearly enough to hold her through the morning. She smiled at the sweet girl behind the counter and suggested they might like a plate of scones as well.

"What about Rebecca?" Birdie asked, twisting on the couch to look into Natalie's face. Her almost-finished sock lay on her lap.

The mention of Rebecca brought a smile to Natalie Sobel's sad face. "Rebecca? She's one for the books, isn't she? She's a pretty woman — I will grant you that — but she doesn't know how to dress. Do you think? Billy knew Rebecca's uncle from Jersey — a rich old codger. He's on his deathbed, Billy said. And Rebecca, fair-haired child that she is, is set to inherit a boatload of money if he ever dies. That's what matters to Rebecca, if you ask me. Money. She was crazy to be spending old man Early's money before he even died — signing on with D.J. for a fancy house. But she likes nice things, Rebecca does."

Nell held back a smile. Those were the exact same things Natalie had done — but the similarities seemed to have escaped her. She wondered, briefly, if Natalie knew that before she entered Billy's life, he had helped the very woman she was chastising. Without Billy's help a couple years ago, the Lampworks Gallery might still be a glint in Rebecca's or Ellen's eye.

"Those things cost money, you know," Natalie went on, sealing her opinion of Rebecca.

"Maybe they can do those things because the gallery is doing well," Birdie suggested, her voice low. She hoped Natalie would follow her example. Natalie was being far noisier than the three little boys playing with trucks at the end of the long room.

"Ellen hadn't ever mentioned an uncle to me," Nell said. Not that she would have, but a pending inheritance was something that might have found its way into conversation. "I didn't know they were going to inherit money."

Natalie shook her head. "Not Ellen. Rebecca. The uncle is an old rich guy, almost dead, Billy said. Very, very set in his ways. Not such a nice man, I gather, but he has more money than Fort Knox. But then, sometimes money comes with strings, and that's the worst kind. Billy always used to say that."

"So the uncle was —"

"Is. The old man isn't dead yet. And Billy told me just last week that the uncle had been sitting up, talking. You just never know, do you? Healthy people fall over dead. Dying people sit up and talk. But should Mr. Early pass, Rebecca will be sitting pretty. Billy's cousin Jackie will know more. Jackie knows everyone. You'll meet him."

"So only Rebecca will inherit his money?"

Nell thought the look Natalie gave her and Birdie held a clear message: It was taking these two bright women way too long to

377

understand the situation.

"Yes, Rebecca will get his money. That's why they moved up here, to stay out of the way, you know."

But Nell didn't know. And she suspected Natalie didn't know either. Clearly, she was speaking from the medication Doc Hamilton had provided for these stressful days.

"So when did all this happen? This rich uncle . . . ?" Birdie asked.

"When did it happen? He was her uncle always, I suppose." Natalie frowned.

"No, I mean, Billy's involvement, knowing about this inheritance, all of that."

"Billy found out about it by accident. He's known Rebecca since she and Ellen opened their shop. But the name had changed, you know. Ellen was the one who told him about the inheritance, not Rebecca. And then Billy put it together, that August Early was Rebecca's uncle." Natalie held out the palm of each hand as she said the names: "Rebecca Early. August Early.

"Ellen and Billy were friends. And when Rebecca started spending money she didn't have — like that house they were building north of town last year? Well, D.J. — the crook — started demanding payment. Things were tough."

"Well, your Billy did have a big heart —

we all know that." Birdie smoothed out her sock with her fingertips.

"Way too big sometimes, in my humble opinion."

"Do you think so, Natalie? I imagine that Billy got pleasure from helping others out."

"But not so much pleasure when we needed the money ourselves. Do you know how much money he gave away? How much do you think? Guess."

Nell wasn't sure that was any of her business, but Natalie continued. "Thousands and thousands and thousands. I found the sheet listing the amounts, the dates."

"And to people you didn't know?"

Natalie shrugged. "Who knows if I knew them? Billy wouldn't tell me names — he said that would invade their privacy. Their confidentiality. I said, 'what are you now, a priest?'

"He would only tell me why they needed it, for this or that — all great reasons, in Billy's mind. I insisted he write it all down: the dates, the amounts, and what it was for. And when I got the list, we sat down and we had a very serious talk. Every single one of those people was going to pay Billy back — and soon. I demanded he do that. And if he didn't do as I asked, I told him, I would leave him. Right then and there. No

379

discussion."

Natalie's voice cracked slightly, but she continued, finishing her thought. "So Billy did it — for me, because he loved me. He swore on his mother's grave that he had contacted every single person — and they were all paying him back. The money was already in the bank — he showed me the statements. People weren't liking the pressure — it wasn't Billy's way to be so strong with them — but it had to be done. Billy wasn't Santa Claus, after all. And we had our own bills to pay."

"So everyone paid him back?"

"Everyone but one. A big one, I am very sad to say."

Nell took a sip of her tea. Billy must have hated pressuring people to pay him back. But Natalie had a point. A loan was a loan, after all. She wondered if any of those debts were paid by his old gambling buddies. It would fit into the police's hypothesis that it might have been someone from out of town who paid a visit that night.

The waitress slid a plate of scones onto the table along with a stack of napkins and three plates. Nell mouthed her thanks and immediately slipped a scone onto her plate.

"So now you have the distasteful task of collecting the last one." Nell broke off a corner of the scone with her fork.

Natalie's face fell. "No. My dear Billy didn't want to leave that task to me." But the comment wasn't one said out of gratefulness. "There won't be any more collecting. And the $250,000 that hasn't come in — yes, you heard me, $250,000 — will never grace our bank account."

"What do you mean? You're Billy's beneficiary. That includes what people owe him."

Natalie's head moved back and forth again. Slowly. Dramatically. One manicured finger lifted in the air and wagged slightly. "No. But that's what you would think, wouldn't you? That a man's wife would be able to get what is due to her?"

"Well, yes." Nell wouldn't have worded it quite like that, but that was the gist of it.

"You're wrong. And this is why you're wrong. Billy Sobel wrote it into his will that all debts were excused upon his death. Every single solitary one. He showed it to me the day he wrote his new will — right after our wedding. He said it with pleasure, like I would be proud of his generosity. I saw it in black-and-white with my own two eyes. Now what do you think of that?"

381

CHAPTER 28

It was a whole day before Birdie and Nell had a chance to talk about what they thought of *that.*

But when Nell had a chance to talk it over with Ben, she shared it with him in detail. And his first thoughts were close to her own: Someone somewhere owed Billy Sobel a boatload of money.

And once Billy was dead, they owed him nothing.

"And if that isn't a motive for murder, what is?" Ben was intrigued, but said the words slowly, thinking through the suppositions as he talked.

"It doesn't connect Aidan's and Billy's deaths, though, at least as far as I can figure out." And for reasons she couldn't articulate, she felt there had to be a connection.

Ben walked over to the stove where Nell was stirring flour into wine and butter for her own special version of clam chowder. It was a special request from Cass. Before Cass became a Thursday night regular, she thought all soup came in a small square package or a can that you added water to, and Nell's chowder continued to delight her, like a child with a new toy.

Ben rubbed her neck lightly with his thumb and finger and leaned into the steamy smell of garlic and butter, a hearty splash of white wine, and a hint of fresh tarragon.

Nell poured a quart of half and half into the mixture and continued to stir.

"It's not me, is it? It's all about the chowder."

Ben nuzzled her neck. "Absolutely."

Nell managed to press an elbow into his chest.

She put the wooden spoon on a dish and stepped to the side.

Ben stepped around her, his eyes on the aromatic steaming pot. He picked up the spoon and dipped it into the liquid. "Money is one of the primary motives for murder." He tasted the thick soup. "Amazing. I may take up knitting."

"You'll get some. You always do. Well, what do we do with this information?"

"First, we probably should consider the source: a distraught widow speaking out of her grief."

"But you agree it's a motive for murder."

"Sure. And so are a lot of things. Could there have been other debts? Maybe tied to a casino? Not one, but maybe several? So do we suspect all of those people? Or just the ones we know . . . and that's *if* we know them. These folks could all be wearing visors, smoking cigars, and gambling their life away at some casino."

Nell thought about that for a minute. "I don't know, Ben. I don't want to think anybody did this — even the ones I don't know about."

"Here's another consideration. It's less than a week since Billy died. Maybe we need to keep our ears open and let things be for a few days. See what develops. This is serious stuff, and we can't accuse everyone we come up with who might have a motive. And in the end, there's always the possibility that Billy smashed that hand another way, like Natalie said. Maybe he slipped on something. It's rocky as hell down there. It all could have been an awful accident."

"Of course," Nell said.

But Nell knew that they couldn't let it drop, not even for a few days. But there was something missing from the whole picture. And she couldn't quite put her finger on it.

Not to mention the fact that if her suspicions were right and this was a homespun crime, they might all be in danger. Waiting for something to happen simply wasn't an option, especially considering what that something just might be.

As so often happened, the knitters were all thinking on the same wavelength, and when Izzy's e-mail went out that afternoon insisting that they all be on time, Nell wasn't surprised. Her e-mail read:

We have two critically important things to do:

1. Finish four more caps.
2. Figure out why our friends died — before we end up with a third funeral shaking up our lives. Willow needs closure. We need our summer back.

Nell thought the mention of a third funeral was a little dramatic, but perhaps these times called for drama.

And it surely put a more definite face on the fear that she herself was beginning to feel.

Nell was pleased that Willow wanted to come, too. She had been spending more time in the guesthouse working on her fiber pieces, she told Nell. It kept her sane. But she needed an outlet. She needed friends.

Friends, Nell thought. That was nice. Seven sharp, Nell told her.

She put the soup in the refrigerator, all ready to heat up and simmer the clams and tomatoes at the last minute, a bunch of fresh tarragon to sprinkle on top. Ben had become addicted to Ned's Groceria, he told her, and stopped by on the way back from Boston with a sack filled with imported cheeses, olives, and tiny pickles. A loaf of herb bread. That would hold them for the evening. Certainly plenty of food for thought.

But between now and seven o'clock sharp, Nell had things to do. *Homework,* was the way she thought about it.

Rebecca was standing near a display of her lampwork beads when Nell walked in. She looked up and smiled, though her smile, as always, was slightly reserved. "Hi, Nell. May I help you?"

Nell walked over and fingered one of the beads hanging from a black cord — a large glass round with shards of purple, green, and bright gold shooting through it. "This looks like a tiny lotus paperweight. I don't know how you get such amazing detail."

Rebecca picked up a second bead and

held it at eye level, dangling it from the cord. "This is my current favorite. It's a little like looking through a kaleidoscope, don't you think?"

Nell turned it with her fingers. Blue and purple and green waves swirled from the inside out in a graceful pattern. "Amazing. I could look at these all day."

"So you came to look?"

"No, I came to talk."

"To Ellen? She'll be back in town tomorrow."

"Actually it's you I wanted to talk to."

Rebecca's face showed little emotion. Not surprise nor curiosity. "Well, then, shall we sit?"

Rebecca and Ellen had remodeled their shop to look more like an elegant living room, filled with beautiful art, than a shop or gallery. She motioned to two chairs near the side window, separated by a small table. "I can spare a minute."

Nell had planned the visit to slip in the door just before closing. She suspected, as was the case, there would be few customers to vie for attention.

Nell set her bag on the floor and crossed her legs, leaning forward slightly. "Rebecca, I think there are things you aren't telling us — things that might help us find out who

387

killed Aidan . . . and Billy."

"I think we know that. Billy killed Aidan."

Nell frowned, wondering at her unfortunate choice of words, but Rebecca quickly went on.

"Billy was fed up with Aidan. He was making it hard for him to run his business. And we all know that Billy Sobel could be a hothead when he wanted to be."

"Yes, I heard that, too. It's flimsy, unless there is more to that story than we know."

"Ellen thinks there may be. She said Billy was distraught the day he died. Brendan may have some ideas, too. He was privy to both places — Aidan's and Billy's. And Billy seemed to trust him, though he seemed a little milquetoast to me. Followed Billy around too much."

Nell wasn't interested in Rebecca's opinion of everyone who worked in Canary Cove, but she had to admit she hadn't thought about talking to Brendan. And Rebecca was right — he'd somehow been taken into the Sobels' confidence. She made a mental note to talk with him — and to thank him. He'd been a wonderful help to Natalie.

"And what about Billy?" Nell asked.

"Probably some crime-world character. Billy had a colorful past."

"I can't quite get my arms around a stranger coming to Sea Harbor on a terrible, stormy night and killing him. Besides, Archie Brandley tells me that a gun would have been far more typical and efficient if that were the case. Archie has studied more crimes in novels than the Sea Harbor police have solved."

"So if not a mobster or 'unsavory business associate,' as the Sea Harbor newspaper calls him, then who? And why?"

"You weren't terribly fond of Billy, I hear."

"Me? You think I killed Billy Sobel? That's the silliest thing I ever heard." Rebecca's laugh echoed in the empty shop.

Nell was beginning to think it was, too, but she felt certain that Rebecca was holding back with some information.

"Besides," Rebecca went on, "if you must know — though I personally think you should let the police do their work and leave this alone — Billy Sobel saved our hides. If it weren't for him, Ellen and I might be in jail right now."

"In jail?"

"Well, debtors' prison or some such silly thing. I was never crazy about Billy because he nosed around in my business and I hate that. He didn't respect people's privacy. He didn't. And just for the record, Aidan

389

Peabody wasn't much better."

"How did Billy help you?"

"We overspent a little on fixing up the shop and remodeling our house. D. J. Delaney would have sent vicious dogs after us, but Billy felt sorry for us, probably because he and Ellen were old friends, and he helped us out. It was a while ago, before he married that intolerable woman."

"So you owe Natalie money now?"

"We paid that debt back the first year we were here. Ellen is a stickler for that. She didn't want to take advantage of the fact that Billy was a friend of hers."

Rebecca began shifting in the chair as if she'd been sitting too long or had more important things to do than chat.

Nell decided to beat her to the punch. She looked at her watch. "I need to get ready for my knitting group," she said. "And I have the feeling I may have kept you too long."

"Well, yes," Rebecca answered. "But I'm glad you came by. It was good we could clear these things up." She stood and held the door open, her back straight and her guarded smile in place. Then, before Nell had a chance to step away from the door, she heard the click of the lock and watched Rebecca walk back into the interior of the glass studio.

Nell looked down at the Sobel Gallery. She wondered if Brendan was still there. Natalie had mentioned that he had pretty much taken over things for her. She walked briskly to the front door of the gallery and peered inside. There was a light on in the back room, where Billy had fixed up a small office and workroom for his framing equipment. She could hear footsteps, and knocked loudly on the door.

She waited, then knocked again. Nell stood there for a minute longer, then checked her watch and turned to walk away.

She glanced back, more out of habit than anything else, and saw a long shadow fall across the back doorway. She frowned, but before she could take a step back toward the shop, the shadow disappeared. All was quiet within the shop.

CHAPTER 29

The sky was darkening when Nell walked into the near-empty knitting studio.

Mae was on the phone with a customer and immediately hung up when she saw Nell. "Lordy, you're going to throw out your back," she scolded, taking the large tureen out of Nell's arms.

"Thanks, Mae. Busy day?"

"You can't imagine. Wicked busy. And it's only Thursday. Izzy had another hat class — she must have a trunk load by now. We get the craziest people in here for that. It's kind of touching. Birdie brought a carload over from that retirement home where she teaches tap dancing. Some vacationers stopped in. And some of my nieces' friends came, too. Oh, and Natalie Sobel, can you believe it? She wanted to think of someone besides herself, she said, and sat right down in the middle of the teenagers. She sat next to Mary Pisano who had her notepad out the whole time, hoping to gather tidbits for her column, would be my guess. And I would guess Natalie gave her a few."

Nell smiled at the thought of Natalie Sobel sitting in the middle of a group of teenagers with tiny Mary Pisano at her elbow, probably recording every word that came out of Natalie's mouth. And many of the comments would likely make it into her "About Town" column. And Natalie, Nell suspected, would have enjoyed every bit of it. People handled their grief in different ways.

Izzy was busy picking out a Nora Jones CD and Willow and Birdie sat on the window seat, admiring Willow's smooth edge on a pale blue cashmere hat.

"Ah, soup's on," Izzy said when Nell and Mae walked down the steps. "I smelled you coming." She took the tureen from Mae and set it down on a large hot pad on the table.

"Mae, take some of this before you lock up and leave tonight," Nell said. "I always bring enough for an army."

"Where's Catherine?" Birdie spoke up from the couch.

At the sound of her name, Cass came in from the front of the store. "Sorry I'm late. I got your stern e-mail, Iz, but I wanted to pick up this cobbler from Harry's before he closed up."

"Perfect," Izzy said. "Here's tonight's agenda. Eat and talk. Wash hands. Knit and talk."

"You're getting awfully bossy, Ms. Chambers." Cass put her cobbler down on the table.

Izzy didn't smile back. Instead, she picked up a white sack sitting on a chair and slipped out a large piece of drawing paper. "Here's why."

She unfolded the large sheet of paper and set it down on the table. "This somehow made it into my store. It actually has Nell's name on the top."

Beneath Nell's name, were the words, printed in neat, exact letters:

Choose one:

1. MIND YOUR OWN BUSINESS.
2. KNIT ONE, PURL TWO, KILL THREE?

"Izzy!" Nell's hand flew to her mouth. "How? Where did you find this?" A slice of fear as wide as the ocean cut through her.

"It was in one of our own bags — of which there are a million others. It's plain and white with little handles. It was sitting on the floor near the computer. There were a jillion people in here today, and identical sacks like this were coming and going. So it didn't stand out in any way. We almost threw it away because it was slightly torn on the edge."

"I wonder if whoever did it knew we'd all be here tonight."

"Maybe. And that's half the town."

"But it had to be someone who came in the store," Cass said. "That narrows it a little."

"Not necessarily. It could have been left outside and the mailman brought it in. Or someone handed it to someone coming in. It could even have hung on the doorknob and someone brought it in," Birdie said.

"Birdie's right. When we're busy, we don't know who's coming or going."

"But it tells us one thing, and that's that the murderer is still out there. The police can say what they want to say, but our intuition is right." Nell started dipping the ladle into the tureen and filling the bowls that Izzy had set out. She would be much better if her hands were kept busy. The sight of the threat was searing and awful.

Willow sat still as a statue on the couch, her face pale. "This is awful. If I hadn't come here . . . ," she began.

"Then there'd only be four of us trying to figure this mess out." Cass filled a platter with the cheese and bread. "Don't talk nonsense, Willow. You didn't do this."

"I think we will spill this amazing chowder if we don't gather around the table," Birdie said, trying to lighten the mood. "And maybe it will help us think better, kind of like being in school. This is a whole new development, Isabel, and a frightening one." She turned and looked at Willow. "And Cass is absolutely right. Regrets and self-recriminations are not helpful. Save your energy for better things. Now come eat."

They all agreed to Birdie's directive, and while Izzy gathered up the knitting sundries and set them on the bookcase, the others pulled out chairs, grabbed napkins and spoons, and settled in.

"I say we start with a hypothesis until we have facts that invalidate it," Nell said.

The others nodded, content to be silent and savor the creamy deliciousness of Nell's clam chowder.

"And what's the hypothesis?" Cass managed between spoonfuls.

"That the same person killed Aidan and Billy would be one," Nell said.

"Fair enough," Birdie spoke for the others.

"I know our hearts have gone out to Natalie Sobel, but I don't think we can discount her. She didn't like Aidan one bit because he was making it difficult for Billy to have his exhibit. She wanted the money those paintings would bring. Money is quite important to Natalie."

"But Billy? I think Natalie really loved him," Willow said. "She wouldn't kill him, I don't think."

"Maybe she did. Maybe she didn't. I agree with you emotionally, but for the sake of exploring all possibilities, consider that Natalie has moved on pretty quickly, even taking a knitting class today, according to Mae. She's been to the beauty parlor, is making plans — she even got highlights in her hair. And she's anxious to get the studio cleaned out. She's ready to move on. All that, and Billy has only been dead four days. She told me herself that Billy didn't always agree with her on how she wanted to spend money. With Billy gone, the money is hers. And the spending of it is hers, too."

"That's logical," Izzy said. She picked up a cracker and a slice of smoky Spanish cheese. "But the fact that Natalie was with us the night Billy died gives her an alibi."

"At least a 'maybe' alibi, anyway," Birdie said. "I can't imagine that distraught woman going out again after we left her that night."

They sat in silence, nibbling on bread and savoring the chowder, trying to put the puzzle pieces together in their minds.

Nell put her spoon down and sat back in the chair. "I still think D. J. Delaney has strong motives. He wanted Aidan's property and wasn't going to get it from him — that was clear. Someone inheriting it — whoever that might have been — was a much better bet."

"Especially if the heir could be convicted of the murder and sent off to prison for the rest of her life." It was Willow, speaking softly but clearly.

The thought of someone framing Willow for the murder hadn't occurred to Nell, but she thought about it now. And if not D. J. Delaney, whoever committed the crime might want to do the exact same thing.

"Billy had filed a suit against D.J. for the faulty construction on his house — not to mention that Billy and Natalie badmouthed him to anyone who came within listening distance, certainly not a good thing for business." Cass helped herself to another piece of the warm herb bread and smeared softened honey butter over the surface. "Pete says Billy expounded regularly in the Gull about D.J. — and Jake had to stop more than one fight over it."

"Natalie let him have it at Annabelle's in front of the whole world. I'm sure D. J. hated Billy. He probably thought that without Billy around, Natalie wouldn't go through with the lawsuit — and in the best of all worlds, would leave town." Izzy poured herself a glass of water.

"Ellen and Rebecca?" Nell proposed. She repeated the talk she had had with Rebecca.

"Billy told me he loaned them money to get started, but that was a while ago — when they first opened the shop," Birdie said.

"Besides, they've paid it back. And if Natalie has her story straight, Rebecca and Ellen will soon be getting a sizable inheritance." She repeated the story of the dying uncle that Natalie told them the night before.

"It's a small world — that's for sure," Cass said. "You never know who will know your family secrets."

"I have this feeling that there's something right there in front of us, something we're not seeing." Nell felt like she was surrounded by annoying gnats. And she couldn't swat them away — little tidbits of disjointed facts that didn't add up to murder. Artists feuding, Billy's gambling days, unhappy construction workers, and an exhibit of paintings that might never happen.

Izzy began cleaning away the bowls, while the others cleaned up the crumbs and washed their hands, moving from table to more comfortable seating and knitting bags.

"Nell is absolutely right. We're missing something important here. It's being lost in this clutter of facts, things we've repeated dozens of times over the past days." Birdie pulled out her knitting. She'd finished her socks and had begun a bright red zippered hoodie for her housekeeper, Ella. Izzy had ordered the perfect yarn for it, a blend of soft wool and angora, guaranteed to help keep Ella's arthritis at bay during harsh winter days.

"What we're missing is the link. Something that would give one person the same strong reason to kill both Aidan and Billy. Aidan was killed because of X. And Billy knew about it. So whoever else knew of X, or wanted X, or didn't want anyone else to know about X — *that* is our murderer."

"I can't think in Xs, Birdie. You're giving me a headache." Cass wrinkled her forehead in mock protest.

"I don't think the money Billy lent the Markses is a motive, especially since we know it was paid back. And even if it hadn't

400

been, it would have been excused." Nell repeated the odd provision to Billy's will.

"What a sweet man. My Sonny did the same thing. Maybe it's some kind of custom."

"Billy lent money to plenty of people. But Natalie says there's only one big loan that wasn't paid back before he died. And now it will never be."

They all fell silent, their needles matching the rhythm of their thoughts.

Nell lifted Willow's sweater from her bag. She had enough worked to appreciate the diamond and zigzag patterns that would adorn the soft cardigan. Once again, Izzy had picked the perfect yarn for the perfect design.

Across from her, Willow reached out and ran one finger over the intricate design. "I won't ever take this sweater off." The smile that reached Nell was completely without reserve. Warm and gracious and familiar.

Birdie had completed the cast-on row for Ella's sweater and begun the knit-one-purl-one ribbing. "Sometimes it's right in front of you. And that's why you can't see it. It's like a dropped stitch. As long as the knitting is bunched up on your lap, you'll never see it."

"When I was talking to Aidan that night,

the night he died, he brought up Billy's name. . . ." Nell paused to pull up the memory. It seemed so long ago now. "It was in reference to the James exhibit, I think, though I couldn't understand him very well. He was sluggish and difficult to understand. But there's a connection there that we're missing, I think."

Izzy nodded in agreement. "Me, too. We always gloss over it because the edges are too rough."

"We know Aidan had a problem with Billy showing them — but I feel we've been over that a dozen times."

"And then Aidan died. And Billy was going to show the paintings, but then he died."

Again, their fingers worked rapidly, looping yarn, knitting and purling.

Cass stood and walked over to the window. She looked out at the harbor lights. "Who else cared about that exhibit?" she asked.

"I guess we all cared, in a way. It would have been nice for the artist community."

"And Aidan was all about what was good for the community. So . . ."

So why not this exhibit? Their thoughts played with the puzzle, mentally shuffling pieces around in the warm night. Nell had been puzzled by it for days. She knew Aidan well. And this was not like him. When she'd talked it over with Jane and Ham, they were equally perplexed.

"Brendan cared about the exhibit," Willow offered. "He was helping Billy every chance he got."

"Rebecca said the same thing. She reminded me that Brendan was in both shops for weeks now — helping Aidan when he was busy and spending lots of time in the Sobel gallery. He's worked in Jane and Ham's gallery, too."

"He's a quiet fellow," Birdie said. "Smart, but quiet. Maybe that's why we haven't thought to ask him. But sometimes still waters run deep. Brendan just may have heard something he doesn't even know is important."

Nell made a mental note to talk with him. Birdie was right. Overhearing scattered conversations, little bits here and there, might help them join some of these strands together.

The pounding on the front door scattered their thoughts.

Izzy got up and hurried into the front of the shop.

Nell followed close behind.

"You're just like a mama bear," Izzy whispered over her shoulder. "Do you think

403

there's evil out there waiting to pounce on me?"

"Yes," Nell answered simply.

Mae had closed and locked the front door, but the store lights were still on.

Izzy pulled up the shade on the door window and peered into the lined eyes of Natalie Sobel.

Izzy opened the door.

Natalie Sobel stood on the step, a puzzled look on her face. Her hair was slightly mussed, and her cheeks and nose were flushed.

Oh, dear, Nell thought. *Déjà vu all over again.*

"Why was your door locked?" Natalie scolded. "I left my yarn here. I need it to finish my hat."

"Natalie, we're closed. That's why the door was locked."

Natalie spotted Nell and stepped past Izzy. "I saw your car, Nell. I knew you wouldn't mind."

Before finishing her sentence, Natalie was moving through the store, her heels echoing in the empty rooms. The smell of liquor followed Natalie, though she seemed steady enough on her feet.

Nell and Izzy looked at each other behind Natalie's back and shrugged in defeat.

Natalie paused in the archway to the knitting room and smiled at the rest of the group. "I certainly hope I'm not disturbing you ladies," she said. "I forgot some things, and I need to keep busy. Keeping busy . . . well, it's important now."

"Of course, Natalie," Birdie said.

Natalie looked around the room, then spotted the white paper sack sitting on the bookcase.

"That's your bag?" Nell said sharply, following her across the room.

Natalie pulled it open. "Yes, it's mine, but it's empty."

"What was in it?"

"My yarn. My bright blue yarn." She frowned. "Where is it? I paid for it, Izzy. Mae will tell you."

Izzy looked around the room and spotted another identical sack, exactly like the one Natalie held. She pulled it open and saw several skeins of yarn. "Here it is."

Natalie looked relieved. "I couldn't finish my hat without it."

"How are you doing, Natalie?" Birdie asked. She set the beginnings of the hoodie on her lap and pushed her glasses into her hair.

"I'm better, thank you. The police are finally finished messing up my gallery. Now

405

I can get in and sort through things. Make sense out of it all. Brendan, bless him, is helping me. And Billy's cousin Jackie will come tomorrow, too, though I'll have to keep an eye on him."

Nell frowned. "Why is that?"

"I'm afraid he'll sneak off and find someplace to gamble. They seem to smell it — him and Billy both. It's in their blood." Natalie sat herself down on an empty chair, her sack of yarn and purse on the floor beside her.

"I know you have a lot on your mind, Natalie, but I've a favor to ask."

"Of course. If I can do something for you, I will certainly do it. You've been kind to me. All of you have."

"Do you think I could come by the gallery to see the James paintings before you crate them up? This may be my only chance to see them unless they show up in a museum somewhere — and I'm intrigued."

"Of course you can. Others have asked to see them as well. The Brewsters. My neighbor. Such a good idea, Nell. Does tomorrow sound good? Maybe noon?" She looked at the others. "You're all welcome. Billy would surely like you to see them. They're beautiful. Such amazing scenery. He was a true artist."

Natalie spoke proudly, as if she were personally responsible for the dead painter's talent. Then she spotted the half-empty wineglasses on the table and looked suggestively at Izzy.

Izzy got up, poured her a glass, and set it on the coffee table in front of her.

"Why, Izzy, dear. Thank you." Natalie picked up the glass and winked at her hostess. "This is a lovely idea, Nell. A viewing. A cocktail party."

A party? Nell thought. And wondered briefly if Billy Sobel was turning over in his grave. She suspected he just might be. "I think there might be others, too. Ellen mentioned wanting to see the paintings."

"Of course. The Marks girls. They appreciate fine art. And speaking of Rebecca . . ." Natalie shifted in her chair and looked over at Nell. "Billy's cousin arrived today. He says that Rebecca's Uncle August has rallied. He's not on death's door anymore, though probably not too far away. Now isn't that one for the books?"

"Rebecca and Ellen's uncle in New Jersey," Nell explained to the others. "The one who had been ill."

"No," Natalie corrected. "He's Rebecca's uncle, not Ellen's. The old man just isn't very nice, Billy said. He would cut Rebecca

407

out of the will in a split second if he knew about her and Ellen."

Cass looked up. "Back up, Natalie. If he's Rebecca's uncle, then he's Ellen's uncle. I'm confused."

Natalie looked puzzled for a minute. And then the confused look disappeared and a look of amusement filled her face.

"You think Ellen and Rebecca Marks are sisters? No, no. Rebecca was Rebecca Early before she was Marks. Ellen and Rebecca went off to Connecticut two years ago and got married."

CHAPTER 30

Ben was still up when Nell got home. "Somehow I figured you might need to talk, my love," he said, and Nell followed him out to the deck.

At first they sat in silence, Nell collecting her thoughts, sorting through the maze of stray facts, some that fit together, many that didn't.

"We were determined to straighten things out," she began, welcoming the cup of tea that Ben handed her. "To sort through the past two weeks and see what's missing. Among the five of us, we thought we'd see holes and irregularities — things that didn't line up quite right. Inconsistencies. And now there's this development, this gambling debt."

Ben sat with his feet up, drinking a brandy and taking in Nell's news of the night about Rebecca and Ellen. "I suppose when Billy told Natalie all this, he expected she would keep his confidence," he mused. "Not to mention Ellen's confidence."

"But she's no longer bound by that," Nell said. "Or at least in her mind, she isn't. And I suppose now that the uncle isn't dead, it doesn't matter anyway — all their secrets were aimed at making sure they got the inheritance."

"But it's still an issue of privacy," Ben said. "If Ellen and Rebecca moved here for privacy for whatever reason, that's what they should get. We all want that, and Natalie shouldn't be disturbing that."

Nell agreed. "The inheritance is sizable, Natalie said. And the old man would pull it if he knew about Ellen and Rebecca. They established a legal relationship in Connecticut a couple years ago. But before they had told anyone, they found out about the uncle's will. Even back then, he was 'scheduled to die any day,' as Natalie put it. And they'd be the benefactors. Or at least Rebecca would."

"But only if she stayed in her uncle's good graces. I guess that's why they moved up here, out of the line of fire."

Nell nodded. "Ellen confided in Billy, which bothered Rebecca terribly. And her relationship with Aidan was all for show. Except when Aidan figured it out, he felt used. I can't say I blame him. It's the deception that would bother him. Aidan was nothing if not honest, and he expected other people to act the same way."

"So Rebecca disliked the fact that Aidan knew."

"Apparently. She isn't the most trusting person. And she hated that he and Billy knew things that could affect her life. It was a power issue. They had power over her. And she was desperately afraid that it would get back to her uncle."

"It's unfortunate," Ben said. "I wonder how Ellen feels about all this — about putting her life on hold until someone died. It doesn't seem like her kind of thing."

Nell agreed. Ellen was pleasant — and she loved to knit, certainly in her favor. This must have been difficult for her, all this pretending. "Confiding in Billy may have brought comfort to Ellen. That's probably why she did it. At the least, she had someone to talk to. Billy had been good to Ellen and Rebecca."

Nell told Ben about dropping Natalie off, and the small notebook that held the moneys owed to the couple. "All debts owed were forgiven upon his death. What an interesting man."

"A generous gesture," Ben agreed. "But

that information in the wrong hands could get a person killed. Did people know about it?"

"He didn't hide it. I called Jane on the way home and she said Billy joked about it sometimes at the council meetings. But they were all friends. No one thought twice about it. Besides, until Natalie came along, Billy never pressured anyone to pay him back, apparently."

The breeze off the ocean was cool, and the smell of the mint in her tea wafted up. She held it beneath her chin, the steam rising up and clearing her breathing.

Clearing her thinking was another matter.

Natalie had seemed in need of company as much as in need of her yarn, and she was reluctant to go home. She talked on at some length about her life with Billy: how they had met, how he convinced her life with him would be a frolicking ride filled with glamour and success.

Nell had listened closely, thinking maybe something would slip out that would fit into the disjointed puzzle they'd laid out on the table earlier. No one wanted to talk about the murders in front of Natalie, so instead they concentrated on their knitting and even Cass finished a whole hat as they nodded and smiled at appropriate places.

Finally, unable to keep her eyes open, Birdie suggested calling it a day.

Cass agreed — she and Pete had an early morning checking her traps, and all of them could use a good night's sleep.

Birdie allowed no discussion from anyone, including Natalie, and they'd cleaned off the table, helped Nell and Izzy lock all the windows, and did, indeed, call it a day.

Willow had her bike — with the new headlight Ben had insisted on installing. Nell suggested she drive Natalie home. She didn't know her level of tolerance, but two glasses of wine had gone down rather quickly.

Nell had pulled the car into the Sobel driveway and idled the engine while Natalie collected her bags. She turned on the seat and looked over at her passenger.

"Natalie, I have a question about something you said yesterday at the tea shop. You mentioned that you didn't know the names of the people who owed Billy money. Billy kept that private, but he told you the reasons for the loans, right?"

Natalie nodded. "He thought that would convince me that we didn't need to demand payment. But the reasons don't matter, do they? A loan is a loan is a loan."

"Do you remember the reason for the loan

413

that wasn't repaid before Billy died?"

Natalie pulled her brows together in the shadowy car, trying to remember. Then she leaned over and opened her large black bag. She rummaged around in it for a minute, then pulled out a small notebook with a rubber band around it.

"I took notes when Billy and I talked about business matters. It helped me remember the important things."

Like who owed you money, Nell thought.

Natalie clicked on the car's overhead light, wet her finger, and paged through the notebook. "Yes, here it is as clear as day. It was to repay a gambling debt. One big whopping gambling debt."

She looked at Nell gravely. "Gambling," she said, one thin brow arching. "It's the worst kind of debt. Sometimes people get killed over things like that."

Nell looked over at Ben now. His eyes were closed, but she knew he was still awake. She had told him nearly everything they'd discussed — except for the crude threat that had been left in Izzy's shop.

Crude, she thought. That was what it was. It had frightened her at the time, mostly because it had landed in Izzy's shop. Had it appeared in her own mailbox, it would not have carried the same weight of worry. But now, sitting beside Ben on her deck, the note itself was less frightening. It wasn't the work of a trained hit man or organized crime — that was evident. But it brought certainty to her conviction that no matter what the newspaper or the neighbors or the police were saying, nothing was wrapped up.

Aidan's and Billy's murderer was walking around Sea Harbor.

And that was frightening, indeed.

Nell awoke early on Friday and reached across the bed, her eyes still half closed. It was empty.

She pulled herself awake and looked around. The windows were wide-open, and the morning breeze filled the gauzy curtains like sails on a ship. Birds chirped and the horns of fishing boats heading out to the open sea were faint in the background.

The more immediate noises were the whirr of the coffee bean grinder and voices. Several voices.

Nell slipped out of bed and into a hoody and light sweatpants.

Izzy and Willow sat on stools at the kitchen island in running shorts, their hair damp and scrunchies wrapped around their wrists like bracelets.

Ben poured each of them a cup of strong coffee.

"What's up?" Nell asked. "Is Ben's coffee so good that you got up at dawn for it?"

"Just couldn't sleep, is all," Izzy said. "Willow and I hit the beach at the same time, so we ran together."

"You've had trouble sleeping for a few days, Izzy," Nell said, concerned.

"Just too many things going on."

Willow dug into the pocket of her sweatpants and tugged out a small envelope. She set it on the island. "Here, Iz. Magic Nembutal. Sleep like a baby. At least that's what Brendan says."

Nell frowned. "That's not aspirin, you know. Be smart about medicine, Willow."

Willow assured her that she would. "I'm overly cautious about things like this."

Izzy smiled. "Me, too. I think I'll try yoga."

"So what do you make of the Rebecca and Ellen story?" Izzy finally asked.

Nell took the cup of coffee that Ben offered her. "I think it was a kind of mystery that was out there — and it led us down the wrong path. We sensed the secrets, so we tried to figure them out. There were disconnects, so we automatically connected it to the murders of Aidan and Billy."

"Nellie, I think you're right," Ben said. "It's interesting. Here's what I make of it. I think all of Rebecca's worries, all of Ellen's cover-ups, all the differing messages we've gotten by attending that story line, if you will, have simply pulled attention away from what was really going on in Canary Cove.

"Rebecca didn't like Billy and Aidan, and that's that. She probably doesn't like me, either. Apparently she's not crazy about Natalie Sobel. Some people don't like other people. But Rebecca's not going to kill me over it, nor Natalie, just like she didn't kill Aidan and Billy. I'd stake my life on it."

Hearing Ben speak so frankly and clearly brought such relief to Nell that she broke out in a huge smile, leaned over, and kissed him on the cheek.

"What's that for?" Ben asked.

"Just for doing that thing you do. Sorting through things so clearly. I think you'd be a great knitter, Ben. You can certainly get rid of straggly ends."

Izzy agreed. "It's huge, Uncle Ben. Like finishing that first cleansing edit of a law school paper."

"Come on, you two, this is going to go to my head."

"But the hard part is ahead of us," Nell said. "So who's left? D.J. is still out there with motive and opportunity."

They all nodded.

Ben shook his head. "He's almost too obvious. Jerry told me D.J. is clean when it comes to following the law. Just barely, but he manages to walk the line. Not even a parking ticket. He knows the law well enough to stay just this side of it. I don't think he fits the profile. He's talked people out of property for years and probably has had a fair number of lawsuits brought against him, but he's never murdered anyone for land. So why now?" Ben paused and took a drink of coffee, thinking through what he'd just said.

Then he went on. "But I'd be the first to admit that that isn't proof. It's a gut feeling with a few facts tossed in. And you're probably right to keep him on the list. Jerry Thompson is probably doing the same. Profiles don't always prove true."

"My instincts are with Ben's," Nell said to Willow and Izzy. "I think we need to look at the original problem between Aidan and Billy. That's where we've messed up. We stumble over it every time we talk about this. So what are we missing?"

"We know that Aidan wouldn't have objected to something that would have helped Billy succeed. He was all about helping the other artists and gallery owners. So their little feud — if that's what it was — didn't make sense. So we need to focus on that, and try to make it *make* sense."

"Well, on that topic, Brendan says the paintings are amazing," Willow said. "He says it's the best work James has ever done."

"These paintings have been hovering over these murders somehow, and none of us has seen them. Odd, isn't it? I'm looking forward to stopping by today. Is everyone going?"

"I'd like to see them," Willow said immediately. "Definitely. Brendan showed me a glimpse of one. It's really kind of a mess over there, so don't expect a grand showing. A lot of the work has fallen on Brendan. It's making him cranky, but it'll soon be over."

"I imagine he's a big help to her. And he knows a lot about the paintings, being an art teacher and an artist himself."

Willow nodded. "Brendan talks about the paintings a lot. He will be a good docent to have. And speaking of paintings," she said, looking over the island at Nell, "Brendan and I stopped by Aidan's — he wanted to look something up in that book on New England artists that Aidan had. I told him you borrowed it, and he was kind of anxious

419

to borrow it back."

"Of course," Nell said, and made a mental note to pass the book along after she'd had a chance to read the chapter on the James paintings. "I'll look at it this morning and bring it to the gallery. Will that work?"

"That's good enough for me. I won't see him before then, anyway."

"What was the painting like?" Izzy asked.

Nell was wondering the same thing. She'd seen a dozen photographs of paintings James had done and some in a small museum in New Hampshire. But the lost paintings had an aura of mystery about them.

"It was spectacular, though I must admit, my judgment was colored by Brendan standing at my shoulder, telling me how fantastic it was. I brushed him away. I like to make up my own mind about art.

"But it was very cool. The scene was a valley with a stream flowing through it, and a haze — like clouds — hovering over the ridge. It was so dramatic. And at first I wasn't sure why. But then I realized the artist had painted it from above, looking down on the ridge from an even higher point, and I don't think I've seen a lot of watercolors like that. At least not by plein air artists."

"Sounds like something that will be worth seeing. You could be an art critic, Willow,"

Ben said. "Fine job. So . . . are we set then for the 'showing'? I'd like to take a look, too. Willow has piqued my interest."

"I'm in." Izzy's hand shot up. "It'd be a shame to let them slip through our hands and not at least get a look at them. We'll probably be reading about them in the *New York Times* when some art dealer pays a zillion dollars for them. And we'll be able to say we were there when they were just little paintings in a crate."

Ben laughed. "My sentiments exactly."

"Maybe seeing the paintings will help us all get our thinking straight. Seeing the paintings is important. It's what this is all about after all — or might be, anyway."

"Okay, so it's a date?"

They all signed on, with promises to call around to see who else might want to see the impromptu exhibit, and while Ben cleaned up the coffee cups and Izzy and Willow went off to shower, Nell called Natalie to tell her she just might have a crowd.

But the word "crowd" set Natalie in high gear. Her voice lifted in sheer joy. Of course. She'd have her reception after all.

Six thirty. The Sobel residence.

"It will be small and intimate," she told Nell. "Just our friends.

"And, dear Nell," Natalie had added

before hanging up, her mind already on to the flowers she'd need to order, "would you be so kind as to bring wine and hors d'œuvres?"

CHAPTER 31

Nell wasn't sure how it happened. It just did. And Natalie wouldn't take no for an answer.

But one by one everyone tried to tell Nell why it was a horrible idea. Seeing the paintings was great. But a festive affair — not so great.

Jane and Ham couldn't believe that Nell would cancel Friday night dinner — this Friday of all Fridays, when they needed her cooking, their good friends, and Ben's martinis, almost more than life itself.

Izzy was about to rebel. "Not another evening over there," she moaned. "Haven't we paid our dues?"

Sam was more circumspect. "Hey, the lady's lonely. It'll be one hour out of our lives."

"Sometimes I hate you, Sam Perry," Izzy had retorted. "This is no time for good sense and compassion."

But Nell would take *no* from none of them. They would all go. It was important that they be there. But at that exact moment — if they had asked her why — her answer would have been ill formed. A feeling. A deep, strong feeling that she couldn't shake.

Even Willow expressed some regret over the evening's plans. She showed up on the deck, after coming up from the guesthouse, and plopped dejectedly on a chair while Nell finished a phone call. "What is it?" she asked, snapping the phone closed.

"Brendan is furious."

"Why?" And then Nell thought better of the question. Of course he'd be furious. Someone had to move those paintings. And move them with great care. And that someone, of course, would be Brendan. "I wonder if Natalie considered how much work this would be for Brendan."

"I don't think so. And Brendan sees no reason for it. A quick pass through at the gallery would be plenty for everyone."

"If truth be known, he's probably right."

"I'm going over there now. I told him I'd bring him coffee and one of Harry's cannolis."

"A perfect mood-altering treat."

"I hope so. Natalie is working him too

hard. He'll be glad when this is all over. He's been a little tense these past couple days."

After Willow left, Nell finally made her way upstairs to the shower. Her thoughts were heavy as she stepped into the bracing pelt of warm water. She lifted her face to the spray and welcomed the cleansing wash. She needed to jar herself, to shake the uncomfortable feeling that she wasn't seeing something that was right smack in front of her nose, begging her to look at it.

It was a niggling thought — something that was stuck in the back of her mind. That pesky fly that wouldn't give up.

Ben had shared a similar feeling with her before he went off to help Sam work on the dock in front of his new home. "But I feel we're close, Nell," he'd said. "I'm going to call Jerry when I get to Sam's and see what's new on his end." He promised he'd pick up some cheese and be home early.

Nell had barely dried her hair and slipped into cotton slacks and a loose scooped-neck top when Birdie appeared in the kitchen, a frown as deep as a Cape Ann quarry creasing her forehead.

She set an empty cup of Dunkin Donuts coffee on the counter, then pulled herself up on a stool.

"Did you ride your bike holding that coffee?" Nell asked.

"No. Cup holders. Just like on baby strollers. My bike may be old but its accoutrements are up-to-date. Nevertheless, I spilled most of it."

"Does that frown say you're not pleased about Natalie's art gathering, as she is calling it?"

"No, I want to go see the paintings, so I'll go. The frown is frustration. This whole thing is frustrating, but seeing those darn paintings may be the best thing to do. They may stand up and tell us who did it. It's one of the few stones we haven't turned over."

"My thoughts exactly." They'd talked about the paintings for weeks — the source of the animosity between Aidan and Billy. And not one of them — except Willow — had even glimpsed them. Nell hoped they would speak to them, even if what they said wasn't what she and the others would want to hear.

Birdie shook her head as if she could clear it all away. She took a drink of her now-cold coffee and set it down again. "So maybe tonight will be worth it. Maybe when we see the paintings, something will connect."

Nell nodded. She glanced at the clock. It wasn't even nine, but she felt like she'd put in a whole day.

"Birdie, are you up for some coffee? Ben's is hours old and I am in need of a good strong cup."

The crowd at Coffee's had thinned as people left for jobs. Nell and Birdie had their choice of tables outside, and they picked one right beneath a small red maple. Mary Pisano sat nearby, her ever-present pad and paper on the table in front of her. She waved at Birdie and Nell and urged them to join her.

Nell and Birdie both found Mary delightful. Her husband had been a working fisherman for nearly twenty-five years, and Mary filled her many hours of alone time by recording just about everything that went on in Sea Harbor.

"I'm just sitting here watching the world go by," she said cheerfully, her dyed-brown curls bobbing as she talked. Large round sunglasses shielded her eyes from the glare.

"And writing it all down to put into that column of yours," Birdie said, pulling out a chair. "Just be sure you say I looked youthful and spirited as always."

"And you certainly do, Birdie. Now both

of you sit and tell me what is up that I don't already know about."

Nell laughed. "That would be a short list. As a matter of fact, I need to ask you something."

Mary leaned forward, interested and her fine brows lifted.

"That column you wrote after Aidan died . . ."

"The night someone broke into his house. Yes, I remember. The same night Tommy found Willow Adams and Brendan Slattery rummaging through Aidan's gallery."

"Willow's gallery," Birdie corrected.

"Yes, I suppose. That will take some getting used to."

"Mary, who saw someone that night?" Nell asked. "How did you know about it?"

Mary looked around to see if anyone was listening; then she looked back at Nell. "Nell, you know I can't reveal my sources."

"Of course not. I just thought that, well, it's over now, so maybe it wouldn't matter."

Mary's cheeks turned pink. "Well, it was me. Ed was gone that whole week, and I thought that things were about to pop in Canary Cove, so I strolled on over there."

"It was late."

"I keep my mace and whistle at hand. I'm nobody's fool."

"Of course not."

"And what did you see?" Birdie prompted.

"I saw a beam of light in Aidan's house — the room right in the front of the house, just inside the front door. And then the light went out and someone slipped out the door — I was in the garden, so I was close enough to hear the door click and lock shut."

"So it wasn't a break-in."

Mary shook her head. "I don't think so. The person was medium tall, and headed up through the woods, along that path that Aidan tended. Then disappeared. I thought it had to have been Willow — except then I saw her the next day. She's a little thing. And the person I saw was much taller."

"You don't know who it was?"

"No. There were no lights on around Aidan's house or the woods. Pitch-black. I had a flashlight, but I didn't want to turn it on. That might have gotten me in serious trouble. I don't even know for sure if it was a man or a woman. Just that the person wasn't hefty, was of medium build. And moved quickly, clearly not wanting to be seen. Whoever it was must have had a key. And apparently nothing seemed to be missing."

Nell thought about the open drawers and

the messy papers. Someone had been looking for something. And Mary's description didn't sound like Billy Sobel at all.

"What are you writing about today?" Nell asked. They'd asked enough questions. Any more and Mary might be writing about Birdie and Nell playing sleuth.

"Today I'm writing about the summer program for children at the art academy over on Canary Cove. I decided that they could use some positive press."

"A wonderful idea."

"I spoke with that charming Sam Perry, and he let me sit in on his photography class. It was wonderful. The kids love it. Sam says I should put a plea in my column for donations, too, to keep the academy going. And I shall do exactly that."

Mary pushed back her chair and stood up. "And now, dear ladies, I am off to my computer. I've some serious writing to do." She gave them each a quick hug, and disappeared through the gate and down the street, her bag swinging from her shoulder.

Birdie frowned. "That's odd."

Nell was having the same thoughts. "You mean about the funding for the academy — I thought so. Jane mentioned it to me in passing. I'm sure that Tony Framingham designated a large chunk of money to that

430

foundation when his mother died. How could they be short?"

"Not to mention last summer's huge benefit. Maybe there's been a mistake in the numbers."

"That must be it," Nell agreed, and tucked the troubling thought in the back of her head. The work of the arts foundation was too important not to take this seriously — as soon as there was a minute, she'd talk to Jane about this more.

By the time they got back to Nell's, it was almost noon. And Izzy and Cass were walking in the front door at 22 Sandswept Lane.

"We decided to spend our lunch break here," Izzy said. "If you're insisting we go to Natalie's tonight, you can appease us with leftovers."

Cass headed for the refrigerator.

In minutes the island was cluttered with a cheese tray and thick slices of bread. Izzy pointed to some sliced turkey and Cass found a bottle of homemade mayonnaise.

"Be careful not to get mayonnaise on that book," Nell cautioned, pointing to the New England art book.

And I need to remember to take that book to Brendan, Nell thought.

"Well, how odd," Nell said out loud,

answering her own thought.

"What? The book?" Izzy speared a thin piece of white cheddar to top off the turkey.

Nell frowned. "No. But Brendan wanted me to bring him this book — it's Aidan's copy. What's odd is that I saw a copy in Brendan's house the night of the clambake — so why is he so anxious to see this one?"

Izzy took the book from Nell's hands and flipped through it. "Maybe here's why," she said, and pointed to a random page. "Aidan wrote in his book. Sometimes that's where you get the really good information. And Aidan was such an art scholar that he probably had interesting things to say."

Of course, that was it — Izzy was right. Nell remembered now. That was part of what had drawn her attention to the book in the first place: wanting to read what Aidan thought of Robert James. She guessed it made sense that Brendan would be interested in what he had to say as well.

Nell took the book back and leafed through a few pages. She frowned, then read a little more. Aidan had added his own touch to the book, underlining and using a bright yellow Magic Marker to highlight sections.

"Something we should know?" Birdie asked.

"I'm not sure. There's an interesting section on Robert James' life — and I suspect Aidan makes it even more interesting." She set the book next to her purse, where she couldn't forget it, and vowed to read more of what Aidan thought of Robert James. Perhaps the argument was as simple as Aidan thinking the man wasn't really the master he was held up to be and Billy thought otherwise.

"What's this, Nell?" Birdie held up the envelope Willow had left on the counter. A small pill cap had rolled out onto the surface.

Izzy picked it up. "Sleeping pill," she said.

"Nembutal?" Birdie asked.

Nell nodded. There seemed to be a lot of insomnia going around lately, she thought.

"Are you planning on making a Mickey Finn?" Birdie joked. "This was big in Al Capone's time. Archie and I were talking about it the other day. You mix a little of this and a little chloral hydrate in a drink, and you've got your man."

"A Mickey Finn . . ."

Birdie and Nell thought of it at the same moment. *The Sea Harbor Gazette* had used the drink to get some mileage in a headline: *The Art of a Mickey Finn,* the reporter had written.

And the article was about Aidan's murder — and the poison of choice.

Izzy wiped the mayo from the corners of her mouth and washed her hands in the sink. "What are you thinking, Nell?"

"I'm not sure. It's probably nothing. But you know, no matter how we feel about going to Natalie's tonight, it may bring us a giant step closer to getting our summer back. And here's why."

Izzy had to get back to the shop, and Cass had to meet her brother on lobster business, but both left the Endicott home with the hope that Nell was right and that the clouds over their little village were shifting. They didn't have all the pieces in place — but the ones that were out on the table fit together so neatly it was frightening. They had headed in the wrong direction all along, but picked up some interesting information on the way.

"Birdie, I need a favor. Could you hunt through that stack of albums and find some of hiking trips Ben and I took thirty-five years ago?

Birdie laughed. But when she looked into her friend's face and saw the expression in Nell's eyes, she headed to the bookcase, where the Endicotts stored dozens of albums detailing lives well lived. And she knew exactly what hiking trip was on Nell's mind.

Nell gave Birdie some details while she worked, and when Ben came home, Birdie and Nell filled him in. Ben listened attentively, then left Birdie to her work digging through picture albums while he left to check into some other records that might make interesting viewing. Benefit funds were public record. And Rachel Wooten could point him to the right file in minutes.

In the meantime, Nell sat at the island, her glasses on and Aidan Peabody's annotated version of Robert James' life in front of her.

James was a fascinating artist, Nell soon discovered. Many critics agreed that he was a master of plein air art — and he lived up to it precisely, never using photographs for his work, but painting in the air, as it were. Painting what he saw.

A section highlighted by Aidan's yellow Magic Marker revealed to Nell that Robert James was a recluse. He lived in Maine in a Gothic-style house set back off the road. During his lifetime, he had given few interviews, preferring to live a life of relative obscurity and letting his beautiful paintings tell people who he was and how he saw life.

435

And then, finally, down in a corner of the page, in Aidan's own writing, was one of the reasons that Robert James was a recluse.

It certainly explained some things.

But did it add up to murder?

CHAPTER 32

Willow was pulling into Nell's driveway on the old bike just as Nell walked out the front door.

"Willow, you're just the person I was hoping to see. I've a favor to ask."

Willow was fine with Nell's request, as Nell knew she would be. And her plea to go along was not unexpected.

"I'm still not comfortable going into Aidan's house alone," Willow said, as they drove toward Canary. "But even so . . . Well, I want to be there, to spend time there."

"You'll feel more comfortable once we get this all solved, Willow. And hopefully that will be soon."

"What are we looking for?"

"I'm not absolutely sure. Just suspicions. It's a case of 'I'll know it when I see it.' I think that someone was looking for something in your father's house. And if we can find it, it might tell us a thing or two about

Aidan's death."

Willow unlocked the front door and the two of them walked into the familiar hall-way.

"It's a little bit like coming home," Willow whispered. "That's silly, isn't it?"

Nell gave her a quick hug. "It's not even the slightest bit silly."

Nell didn't think the time was right yet, but one of these days she'd try to explain to Willow that having her here right now cushioned the loss of their friend Aidan in unspoken ways. It didn't lessen their sad-ness, but it filled in some of the hollow spots in a lovely way.

"I am thinking the den might be a good starting spot for me. Maybe while I scrounge around, you could water some of those thirsty-looking plants."

Nell suspected that wandering around alone — but having someone nearby — was the best way for Willow to acclimate herself to the house her father had lived in. To smell its smells, listen to its silent voices.

She opened the desk drawers again, then rummaged through the wooden filing cabi-net. The papers in both were largely incon-sequential — old furniture orders, a clean-ing bill, a repair bill for a washing machine, to-do lists. "Surely you can do better than this, Aidan," she whispered.

After exhausting the folders, Nell sat back in the desk chair and looked over at the fisherman statue standing guard. "Please give me a hint, sir," she said aloud, looking up into the carved, craggy features of his charming face.

Later she told Ben that she was sure he spoke to her. Right then and there.

Or maybe it was the memory of the will that the police had found in one of Aidan's statues. Or the many times she'd watch admirers in the gallery open up the figures that Aidan carved, exclaiming with delight over the bookshelves behind a mermaid's fins or the secret drawers that magically appeared when one tugged on a fisherman's belt buckle.

This fisherman was special, Nell told Ben. It was the backs of his waders that opened wide, leaving enough room for a nice neat file drawer. Flat, unobtrusive. Hidden.

They decided Aidan wasn't even trying to hide it — many of the papers were ordinary things: mortgage papers, car licensing records. It was probably Aidan's everyday filing cabinet — safely ensconced behind a fisherman's tush.

It only took Nell five minutes to find the reports she suspected she might find. And even at a glance, she knew the numbers would tell her an interesting story. An alarming story.

They made one more stop on the way back home, and Willow kept the car idling while Nell ran in to the small building that housed the Canary Cove arts association building. "Here, Esther," she said to the volunteer at the desk. "Just thought I'd make a donation to the summer arts academy."

"Well, bless you, Nell," the volunteer replied. "We need these, you know. These aren't the easiest of times."

"When is the next council meeting?" Nell looked beyond the desk to the office in the back.

"I think Jane told me she wants one in a couple of weeks." Esther looked down at a large daily calendar on the desktop. Nell leaned over and looked as well, then looked through the open door of the single office in the back that Aidan had once spent time in.

Esther followed her glance. "Nope, no one is here today. Jane was in yesterday, but that's it. Lots of tourists, though. I'm almost out of brochures and maps."

"And that's a good thing for business," Nell said, and waved good-bye. In minutes, she and Willow were back in the driveway at 22 Sandswept Lane.

Ben and Birdie were waiting.

CHAPTER 33

Nell dressed nervously. Behind her, Ben rubbed her neck and told her it would be okay. She nodded, running her hands down the sides of a summery sleeveless dress. Yes, it would be okay.

But how could they have been so misled?

Cass and Izzy had come by earlier to help sort through it all. And everyone admitted they'd been toying with the same loose ends. Once they had it all out on the table, they poked fun at themselves. It seemed so clear. Every one of the facts sat in front of them. But they were so numerous that they crisscrossed over one another — like the lines in the sand when the tide goes out. A huge labyrinth that was finally beginning to make sense.

They'd taken the wrong fork in the road early on — and they had found something they weren't even looking for.

If they were right, Birdie said solemnly,

one path led to deception.

The other to murder.

Nell had suggested canceling the whole evening. She'd make up an excuse to Natalie. The puzzle wasn't knit up as tightly as it needed to be. At least not all of it.

But Ben convinced her otherwise. There were gaps to fill in, sure. But the evening's events might help do that very thing. Besides, Ben said, he wanted to see the paintings. In fact, they should all want to see them.

As they talked, Nell agreed. So far, some of their suppositions — and those of Birdie, Cass, and Izzy — were simply that. Thoughts. Guesses. Not much more. But Ben agreed to call Natalie ahead of time. If she wanted to call the gathering off, then they would help her do that.

But Natalie Sobel, as Ben and Nell suspected, would rather clean dirty ovens than call off a party. No matter what.

Nell asked Willow to ride to the Sobel house with them. They needed to talk to her about a couple of things, they said.

Willow agreed. Brendan would be helping Natalie anyway, she said — and frankly, he was a little cranky, having to lug everything around all day and manage Natalie's many moods.

"I can see his point," Nell said quietly.

In addition to the knitters, Natalie had extended the invitation to the artists in Canary Road who had expressed interest and neighbors and some friends. She'd even invited Jerry Thompson.

"I think she's sweet on him," Birdie said, chuckling. She was feeling a trifle stiff from pouring through the Endicott photo albums for two hours, but had neatly stacked up the ones they needed, priding herself on a job well done.

Ben had made another run to Ned's Groceria in Gloucester and come home with a magnificent bread-and-cheese tray that needed no more than toothpicks and small knives to service it. He packed it carefully in the back of the car along with the wine Natalie had requested, and they headed down Sandswept Lane and into the night.

And on the way, they had talked to Willow about the James paintings, telling her what they knew. The book from Aidan's — from her dad's — had helped them understand the paintings better. And Robert James, as well. In fact, Aidan's scribbles in the book had helped them understand, at last, why he and Billy Sobel were at odds with each other.

Izzy and Sam had picked up Cass and Birdie and pulled up just behind Ben's SUV.

Natalie greeted them with a nervous hug and apologies for the cracked front step. "D. J. Delaney is going to be the death of me. The toilet's broken. The awning fell off. My poor house is going to fall into the ocean. The step is crooked. Can't you see that it's crooked?" She pointed down to the concrete, then erased her frustration with a wide red hospitable smile. "Now come in, come in," she urged.

Ellen and Rebecca arrived shortly afterward, and Jerry Thompson not long after that. When Natalie spotted Jerry, she hugged him so tightly, Nell thought he might choke. The police chief had done a good job of gaining Natalie's confidence, Nell thought, and she wondered if others noticed the blush that crawled up the chief's neck.

Ben had reached Jerry that afternoon, but they'd only had a minute to talk. They'd talk later, they both agreed.

Natalie had done a lovely job of fixing up the house, and soft guitar music played in the background. Candles were lit on low tables and an embroidered cloth covered the dining table, where they placed the cheese platters and wine. In spite of everything, Natalie Sobel was determined to have her party, and Nell gave her enormous credit for that. In the same circumstances — having just lost a husband and about to lose more — she wasn't so sure she could hold up.

"Come, come," Natalie commanded. "You must meet Billy's cousin." Natalie ushered them into the kitchen, where a replica of Billy Sobel stood at the sink, drinking a scotch and soda and entertaining Doc Hamilton, who lived next door to Natalie, with great gestures and a booming laugh.

When Natalie called out his name, Jackie Sobel came at them with open arms as if greeting long-lost relatives, kissing Willow and Nell on both cheeks. As Nell pulled away, she noticed that the smiling Jackie had tears in his eyes.

"I loved my Billy boy, you know?" he said gruffly, and wiped the moisture away.

Ben and Sam walked up and joined the group, engaging Jackie in childhood tales of life with Billy. "And then he married that gorgeous woman over there and turned over a new leaf," Jackie said, nodding toward the doorway, where Natalie stood beside Jerry Thompson. Jackie winked. "Well, not completely, okay? I won't lie to you. Billy still hit the tables with me now and then. Won some. Lost some. We were a formidable pair, Billy and me."

Just then Ellen walked into the kitchen, looking for a glass of water, and Jackie's attention shifted. His face lit up.

"Ellen, baby," he called out to Billy's friend, and stepped over to properly greet her. Kisses on both cheeks led to a bear hug, and it made Nell think of the many times she'd seen Billy do the same thing when he'd see a friend in the gallery or on the street. They had the same mannerisms, these cousins.

And then she frowned as she watched Ellen and Jackie engage in conversation — Ellen more subdued, but Jackie happy to see someone he knew.

Of course, she thought with a start. She shivered in the warm house, then walked out of the kitchen to find Ben.

He was in the living room, pouring wine for Ham and Jane. Standing next to Jane, Rebecca Marks looked weary. Not just bored, as Rebecca sometimes looked, but like she'd rather be anywhere but standing in Natalie Sobel's living room. And she looked tired, as well. Nell wondered if she had had another bout of insomnia. She was all out of the Nembutal prescription, she'd said.

Nell pulled Ben aside and spoke softly to

him, then went to make sure that Willow was doing all right and to touch base with Birdie, Cass, and Izzy.

Willow was in the kitchen with Izzy and Cass, filling pitchers of water. Brendan was nowhere to be seen. Jackie Sobel stood with Birdie near Jackie's case of beer.

"It's good that you came, Jackie," Nell said. "I know it meant a lot to Natalie. And to us, too. We were Billy's friends."

A mixture of beer and emotion had left Jackie vulnerable, and his eyes grew moist.

"He did right by people," Jackie said. "They don't make 'em like Billy anymore."

"You're right, Jackie. Without Billy's help, some of the artists in this town would never have gotten the start they needed."

Jackie nodded and took a swig of beer. He wiped his mouth with the back of his hand. "I know that to be true, I do. You know, people think he gambled too much. Natalie thought that, I know. And maybe he did. But I know for a fact that he also tried to help people get off gambling if he thought they were doing too much of it. Billy wasn't an addict. And he wouldn't let anyone else be, either."

"And my guess is, if someone had a gambling debt, Billy would understand — and he'd try to help them."

"Sure. Did it many times. He was the best."

Natalie waved at Jackie then, and he excused himself to be introduced to her neighbors.

Nell looked around to make sure the food trays were filled. Natalie's intimate gathering had grown to something more sizable, but people were not staying too long, Nell noticed. Just long enough to view the paintings and taste some of the exotic cheeses that Ben had bought that day. That and a nightcap, then home.

Natalie had put the paintings in Billy's spacious den, and Nell helped her usher people in that direction.

Brendan stood just inside the den's wide double doors, looking slightly uncomfortable as guests drifted in and out, drinks in hand. Archie Brandley walked in carrying a copy of his book on New England painters, ready to look up facts for anyone interested.

It reminded Nell that she had never dropped her copy off with Brendan as he'd asked. Aidan's copy. She wondered if he was thinking the same thing as his eyes met hers, then quickly flitted away.

She walked into the kitchen and spotted Ben. He looked at her, his brows lifting and the understanding of more than thirty years

449

of marriage speaking to her without words. *It's time to see the paintings,* his look said. Nell nodded, and he walked across the room, touched her lightly in the small of her back and followed her into the den.

Most of the guests had already viewed the paintings and were back at the dining room table, where fresh cheese platters and open bottles of wine awaited them. Others had already headed on home.

Brendan greeted Nell cordially, but there was a new distance between them. An unease. When Ben walked in behind her with Birdie, Cass, and Izzy completing the group, Brendan's stance was clearly uncomfortable.

They stood quietly in front of the paintings. They were lined up — five scenes done by the plein air artist, one next to the other: brilliant scenes of mountains and cloud covers and unusual views of ravines, all captured in colors that came alive in light and shadow beneath the artist's masterful brushstrokes.

Ellen and Rebecca joined them, admiring the paintings that had been given such attention. Billy Sobel's paintings.

Standing behind them, Brendan tried to detail the kinds of strokes that James perfected and the way he created light out of color. Nell had read similar reviews in the book she'd scoured just hours before.

"The color is richer and the strokes more defined in these paintings," Brendan said, his voice gaining strength as he talked. "These paintings will take their place alongside the masterpieces."

Nell looked at them with great familiarity and rubbed the goose bumps that rose up along her arms. She'd been there, seen that view, and Brendan was right: The scene had been captured beautifully.

Jackie Sobel stood near the door, unsure of the art discussed, but clearly interested in their value.

"They are beautiful," Nell murmured. She turned around and looked at him. "These are lovely. Truly the work of a talented artist."

Jane and Ham murmured their agreement. "There's no question about that," Jane said.

"But Robert James couldn't possibly have painted them, could he?"

Brendan stared at Nell as if he were seeing her for the first time.

"Of course he could have. James was a master of plein air art. These paintings are worth a fortune."

For a moment the silence in the room was

deafening to Nell. It echoed wildly. Then Brendan spoke again, more softly this time, a kinder tone to his voice. "These may have been his final paintings before he died, which makes them even more valuable."

"Apparently Aidan Peabody had met Robert James — did you know that?"

"He was a recluse — everyone in Maine knew that."

"That's right. And he usually only gave phone interviews. But as any of Aidan's friends know, Aidan could talk anyone into anything."

Soft laughter relieved the tension slightly.

"And he convinced Robert James to let him come up to meet him and talk with him."

"He wrote an article about James after that," Brendan said. "I remember reading it when I was in school."

Nell noticed the slight sheen of perspiration on Brendan's forehead, but she marveled at his tenacity. "But it's what Aidan didn't write in the article that's of interest here. He didn't write that Robert James suffered from a form of congenital paraplegia," Nell said. "James didn't want people to know that he could only get around on forearm crutches."

"That's interesting, Nell, but it doesn't

really relate to —"

"But it does relate to these paintings, Brendan. Because James was the consummate plein air artist, just as I believe you are. Because of his inability to climb or walk up inclines, all his scenes had to be painted at sea level. Robert James could never have climbed Old Bridal Path Trail, which is what you'd have to do to paint these scenes."

"You may not believe us capable of it, Brendan," Ben said, "but Nell and I hiked up to that very spot on our honeymoon. It's fantastic. Birdie found some photos of it today that we brought along, just in case. But you know that, because you had to climb up there to paint these." Ben shoved his hands in his pockets and looked again at the paintings.

Nell thought back to the maps in his home, the photos she looked at. The marked trail.

"That's nuts. You're all crazy," Brendan began. But when he looked around at the circle of people standing in front of the paintings, his voice faltered.

And then he took a new stance and spoke more boldly. "These are amazing paintings. Billy Sobel thought they were James' work. And anyone else he showed them to thought the same. Until Aidan Peabody with his frig-

453

gin' intellectual elitism told him otherwise. Aidan thought he knew everything. These are five brilliant works of art. Brilliant. No one knew the difference."

The sound in Brendan's voice was almost childlike, pleading for people to recognize what a fine artist he was. And then he stopped, suddenly. The group turned to look at him, and he realized where he was leading people. He stared back, then took a few steps toward the door.

Beyond the den, music played and scattered cocktail chatter grew dim.

But in Billy Sobel's carefully decorated den, all was quiet.

It took one minute for Brendan to collect himself. He lashed out, his voice slicing through the silence. "No. Now you *are* crazy. It's not what you're thinking. I didn't kill Peabody. Or Billy. You're crazy as fools if you think that." He backed up to the den door opening as if to flee, leaving his paintings behind in a rush to freedom and away from accusing eyes. "No way did I kill those two guys."

"No," Nell said softly. "You didn't kill them, Brendan. We know that, though for a long time, we were on a path that said you might have."

Jane and Ham walked into the room, then,

454

and Nell noticed Jerry Thompson was with them. It was late, and in the distance, she could hear Natalie saying good-bye to departing guests.

Ellen had gotten up from the couch and whispered to Rebecca that it was getting late. They should be leaving soon, too.

Nell looked over at her sadly.

"Ellen, we found the papers in Aidan's house. The ones you couldn't find that night that you entered his house and searched for them. You must have taken a spare key Aidan gave Rebecca and then forgot to get back from her. But you looked in all the wrong places. Aidan had an unconventional filing system, you see . . ."

Ellen's brows pulled together. "Papers?" she managed to say.

Rebecca looked up at Ellen, her mouth open, but no words came out.

"The art council reports that indicated you'd been slowly depleting the foundation's money. The reports Aidan confronted you with the day before you killed him. It only took minutes to confirm what we all thought — that last summer's fund-raising gala and other generous gifts to the foundation had made it flush. There was enough money there to run the arts academy for several years. And it's nearly gone."

455

"No, it's not. You're wrong. Ellen, please . . . tell them they're wrong." It was Rebecca's choked voice, barely recognizable.

"It'll be all right, Rebecca," Ellen said softly. "Don't worry."

"Worry? Ellen, you stole from our friends? From the foundation that you cared about? That we both cared about?" Rebecca stood up and pressed her back against the wall, staring at the woman a foot away who had built a house for her, managed her career, her gallery, her life.

"Cared about? Rebecca, it was you I cared about, not a foundation or a job or a gallery. It was all about you." Ellen's tone was steady, but when she looked at Rebecca, her eyes were filled with such raw, naked emotion that Nell was forced to look away.

Ellen had done it all out of love. Every single bit of it. The foundation embezzlement to pay for the things Rebecca wanted — the house, the studio. The gambling to put money back into the foundation. A vicious, awful circle. And then murder, to release her from her final debt — to her friend, Billy Sobel.

"The money . . . it wouldn't have mattered . . . ," Rebecca began, but her voice failed her and she stopped.

"Of course it mattered, Rebecca," Ellen said sadly. "You matter. You are the only thing in my whole life that ever mattered. But it was your money I lost, Rebecca — what you brought to our relationship. I knew you'd never forgive me if you knew what I'd done. And then one terrible thing led to another, and I was so desperately afraid I'd lose you."

Rebecca slumped back down on the chair.

"Aidan knew everything," Nell said. "He read the financial reports, knew the figures were skewed. And he knew that Ellen was the only person who had access to it."

Ellen's voice dropped to a whisper. "I knew if you found out, Rebecca, you'd leave. So I went to Billy. And dear Billy — he understood. He'd bail me out. We'd fix the books, make it better. We'd paid Billy back once, we'd do it again. And our life would be good again."

Nell knew that beneath the surface was the other thing that Ellen was counting on. If she could stall until Rebecca's uncle died, there'd be more than enough money to make everything right. To cover her crimes. Aidan was gone. She had control over the books. No one would ever have to know.

Ellen could barely pull her eyes away from Rebecca. It was as if once she did, the connection would snap forever, and her life would crumble to the floor.

When she finally looked away, her voice switched to an eerie monotone, as if someone else had taken over for her, and she had simply disappeared.

Nell hoped that Doc Hamilton hadn't left yet. He'd be needed to refill Rebecca's Nembutal prescription — it had run out, she suspected, because Ellen had used it to make the Mickey Finn that she'd slipped into Aidan's drink. And Ellen might need something as well.

Rebecca's makeup was completely gone now, and sitting in the dark shadows of the room, she looked as vulnerable and defenseless as a sixteen-year-old. She covered her face with her hands, her grief swallowing her up.

Nell had to restrain herself from wrapping her up and taking her home.

Natalie had slipped into the back of the room as Ellen was talking. A look of total disbelief filled her face as she stared at the woman who had killed her husband. The outstanding debt, the $250,000. It was Billy's gift to his friend Ellen. The gambling debt.

Ellen spotted her. "It's you who is to blame for this, Natalie," she said calmly.

458

"Billy would never have made me pay him back. But you insisted. I begged him that night. I sat in the rain next to him and begged him to honor our friendship, to forgive the debt so I could make the foundation books balance before Jane got her hands on them.

"But he couldn't, he said. Not without losing his wife. He would if he could, but his hands were tied — he couldn't bear the thought of you leaving him. And then he finished off the bottle, and when he tried to stand, he slipped on the wet dock and tumbled off the end. I couldn't pull him back, of course. He grabbed the rung, but I couldn't do anything to help him. He was so much heavier than I am."

So you stepped on his hands, and let him drown in the churning sea.

The words echoed silently in the sadness of the room.

An awful, eerie silence was broken only by the agonizing cry that escaped Natalie Sobel's lips. In the next second, she fell into a dead faint, saved from the hard wooden floor by Chief Jerry Thompson's strong arms.

CHAPTER 34

Many of the Canary Cove neighbors and artists pitched in to give the Peabody house and Fishtail Gallery a thorough cleaning, opening windows, scrubbing floors and kitchen cupboards.

But it was Nell, Cass, Izzy, and Birdie who stayed with Willow, going through bookcases and drawers, making beds with fresh-smelling cotton sheets, and filling her house with flowers from Aidan's garden.

They talked as they worked, putting the last weeks of summer into their proper place.

Rebecca had decided to stay on in Sea Harbor, hiring a new manager for the shop and moving on with her life. She was brave, everyone said.

But when Izzy and Nell stopped in her gallery the day before, Rebecca had taken them into the private office, shut the door, and broken down in tears. All the secrets, living a pretend life, was painful for her, she said. Distasteful. But Ellen had insisted, knowing they risked losing the inheritance if they acted otherwise.

"Ellen was so afraid of losing you," Nell said. That was what this was all about. "Losing the one person in her life who held her together."

Rebecca's sadness was profound. "I didn't care about the money. I honestly didn't. I only cared about Ellen. And I hated pretending to be something I wasn't. I think that's why I was so nasty to everyone," she said. Her eyes, if not her words, asked them for forgiveness.

"I think Rebecca will be fine," Birdie said. "But it will take a long time for everyone to heal."

"She's using her uncle's money to replenish the foundation," Nell said. "It's a start. And a generous gesture. You're right, Birdie. Rebecca will be fine, though Ellen's crimes will be difficult for her to forget or forgive. This is certainly a start."

"I feel sorry for Brendan," Izzy said. "He was so obsessed with his own talent, so angry that people didn't recognize it, that it ate him up."

"I wonder if he would have eventually let it slip, just to let people know that he was as good as Robert James — at least in his mind. And he'd proven it by his deception, by others accepting his work as that of the master."

"It may have come to that," Nell said. "He wanted recognition so badly that he might have admitted his guilt on his own."

"What will happen to him?" Willow asked.

Nell could see that she still carried a fondness for the art teacher. But Willow was resilient. "As far as being prosecuted, probably nothing will happen. He didn't forge James' signature yet. And didn't receive any money for the paintings, though that was clearly his and Billy's plan. Natalie discovered papers that offered half of the sale to Brendan, something that would have been mighty difficult to explain to her when the time came."

"But he's lost his job. Sea Harbor High has canceled his contract," Birdie said. "It's understandable, but a shame. Brendan was a talented artist and, if Stella Palazola speaks the truth, a fine teacher."

"He'll go back to Maine, maybe. I don't think he would ever have been happy in New York." Willow emptied a pail of water into the kitchen sink. "And then, hopefully, he'll grow up."

Birdie led the way into Aidan's den and

switched on a light. It was that magical time of evening when light played off the trees and filtered in through the curtains, casting shadows on the braided rug on the floor. Through the open windows the sweet smell of roses drifted in from Aidan's garden.

They sat together on the floor, even Birdie crouching down beside Izzy, her short legs sticking straight out in front of her. A circle of unlikely friends.

Willow leafed through the stack of letters retrieved from a secret cubbyhole in the back of Aidan's mermaid. Since they'd found them earlier that day, they hadn't left Willow's hands.

No one had found the stash, not in the police's search of the house or the deep cleaning that Jane and Birdie gave to every inch of the family room. No one noticed the small latch in the mermaid's elaborate fins that opened up to a hollowed-out space, not until Willow herself ran her hands over the finely crafted wood and felt the tiny protrusion. A little brass knob, nearly invisible in the carved fold of wood.

Nell wasn't sure why Aidan had hidden the letters — though he was a private person and she supposed it was in character. Or maybe it was an effort to keep them safe under the mermaid's watchful eye.

They had sat with Willow as she opened every single letter. Each one addressed to a post office box in Madison, Wisconsin, and returned, unopened. Occupant unknown. Aidan had made a deal with the post office to keep sending them back if they went unclaimed, even after the grace period ran out. It was a connection, he thought, and he paid the charge willingly.

Nell supposed he hoped that one day a letter would come back. And he'd go looking again. Or maybe get a call.

Each letter detailed a father's search for a child. Although Aidan never knew with certainty that there was a child, his letters expressed a yearning and a connection. He felt the child's presence, he had written in one of the letters.

And he thought of her always, another said.

It wasn't clear why the baby became a she, but Aidan seemed to know. Or maybe it was wishful thinking. His little mermaid. In one letter he talked about a small mermaid he carved and kept on his desk to remind him of this little girl growing up. Somewhere. It was the little mermaid Ben had suggested buying. The one Aidan stalwartly refused to sell.

The letters were sporadic — more frequent in the beginning, but always at least once a year.

Willow stood and walked over to the desk. She slipped them into the drawer.

"You came here to meet your father," Nell said. She pushed herself up off the floor and slipped onto a cushioned chair.

Willow looked over at Nell and nodded. She smiled slowly.

At least it was a beginning, Nell thought. And a strong one. The letters told her so many things, and Aidan's home and art and studio would tell her more. Each day.

"Are you ready for your exhibit, young lady?" Birdie asked. "All the ladies from my tap-dancing class are coming."

"We should have them do a number," Willow teased.

"I've got Natalie Sobel going over there with me. She used to be a dancer, you know."

"Birdie, no," Izzy said, stifling a laugh.

"They love her. I must say it's not the kind of tap we're accustomed to, but it's good to be open to new things. We now have some men joining the group."

"So . . ." Cass paused dramatically. She stood and looked about the room.

They all looked up. "So?"

Cass' gaze settled in on Willow, and the

knitters knew what was coming. They could always count on Cass to pull out the questions lurking in their heads.

"So . . ." Willow looked confused.

"So, are you going home? Or are you staying? Let's get it all out there."

They all turned to look at Willow.

She forked her fingers through her short dark hair — a habit she'd developed since giving herself a new hairstyle. "So . . ." And then she laughed.

It was a joyful laugh. Light and airy, just like the last week had been. Perfect Sea Harbor summer days.

Willow stopped laughing and looked around the room.

"Jeez, you guys," she said. "I am home."

CHAPTER 35

It was a perfect summer night. The sky was as black as the bottom of the sea, and stars were scattered everywhere — as if a giant hand had flung them from above in a wild, joyful gesture. And the fireworks that exploded in the midsummer sky were not a surprise this night, but a promise made on the Art at Night posters. And a promise kept.

Art at Night, [the posters read]
A celebration of Canary Cove art.
A celebration of summer.
Fireworks, food, drink, and music.
And featuring the fiber art of
Willow Adams.

"I knew you were hibernating this past week," Izzy said, "but I had no idea that you'd managed to put together so many lovely pieces."

"Only four," Willow said. "But I love

467

them. I started them the day I came. But they've been in my head forever."

They stood in the outer room of the Brewster Gallery, where Jane had set up a reception table filled with flowers from Aidan's garden. Willow's artwork hung in the inner room, a clean white room with perfect lighting.

Jane and Ham had insisted that Willow's first show be in their gallery, against a solid white wall with perfect lighting.

"Nell and Birdie are in charge of food," Jane dictated, "Izzy the flowers. And Cass can be the cheerleader and put posters down on the dock."

The Brewsters had wanted Willow's opening to be on its own day, a special, grand affair — but Willow was stubborn. She wanted it to be a part of the Art at Night festivities instead.

"But having your own opening would place all the attention on your art," Jane had argued. "You wouldn't have to share the stage."

Nell suspected that was part of Willow's strategy. She'd had enough time in the spotlight in the past month to last a lifetime. She was ready to get off the stage and be normal again.

Her explanation to Jane was simple. "The

first time I met some of you was at Art at Night," she said. "And I know Aid . . . I know my dad loved that event. He had notes all over his office, most on how to showcase everyone else in this neighborhood except himself."

And so all had agreed, but only if the flyers that were tacked to bulletin boards in Coffee's, over at the city offices outside Rachel Wooten's office, in Archie's bookstore and Harry's deli — and a huge poster in the window of the Seaside Knitting Studio — mentioned Willow's exhibit at the Brewster Gallery.

"Shall we go in before others come?" Jane asked, her hands motioning toward the exhibit room.

They filed into the room — Ben and Sam, Birdie and Cass and Izzy. Nell followed Jane and Willow.

Ham was in the back of the room, adjusting the angle of the lights from a small panel in the wall.

"Jane, it's perfect," Nell said in a hushed voice.

And then she stood back with the others, a single line, looking up at a wall of amazing texture.

As the narrow beams of light focused on each individual work, Nell caught her breath, and for the first time the full impact of Willow's creations sunk in.

"Patterns in the Sand," Willow called the series.

Four pieces, each one different. Each one born of sea and sand and the colors of nature blended together. Willow had used cashmere and sea silk, fine wool and tangled pieces of Izzy's organic cotton. Strands of boucle yarn that were left over from Cass' socks.

The first piece in the collection used shades of tan, smooth and chunky yarn tangled to simulate the rolling dunes of sand after a storm. She had created shadows and texture, twisting and smoothing strands of yarn into wavy shapes, then binding them together invisibly. And in the next two, sea glass and yarn that looked like clam shells and flat green seaweed appeared in the sand.

In the final piece, a strip of sea appeared at the top of the oblong creation, rippling waves of every color of blue, the yarn twisted and fashioned until the waves seemed to come right out of the wall and Nell could almost smell the ocean. Some strands of the sweater Nell had nearly finished for Willow appeared in the water.

Below the robust sea was a span of patterned sand, smooth and wavy to resemble the ripples in the sand left by the receding tide — a pattern as complex as life itself — hills and valley, rivers and small rolls of land intersecting one another, then narrowing into single streams.

Nell stepped back, alone, and feasted on Willow's art. There was no question in her mind.

She knew before Ben Endicott uttered a single word whose home would welcome the final piece in the series.

And she knew exactly where she'd put it. Along the clean white wall in the family room, guarded by a carved wooden statue of a fisherman, his eyes gazing out to sea and an enigmatic smile lifting the corners of his mouth.

THE INSIDE-OUT KNIT CHEMO CAP
KNIT HEAD HUGGER

DESIGNED BY JOYCE FORKER,
used with permission.

Materials:
#8 and #10 (US) knitting needles
One skein soft yarn of your choice (please see note below)

Pattern:
Cast on 80 stitches on size #8 (US) needles
K1, P1 (garter stitch) for 1 3/4 inches.
Change to size #10 knitting needles.

1st Row: Purl

2nd Row: Knit 1, Purl 1 across.

Repeat rows 1 and 2 until cap measures 6 inches from beginning.

Top Shaping:
K2, K2 tog. Repeat from ** across.
Purl 2nd row and all even-numbered rows.

3rd Row: *K1, K2 tog*. Repeat from ** across.

5th Row: Repeat 1st row.

7th Row: Repeat 3rd row.

9th Row: K2 tog across.

11th Row: K2 tog across. Purl across.

Break off yarn, leaving an eighteen-inch tail. Draw yarn through remaining stitches and pull up tight. Fasten off on wrong side of cap. Sew seam smoothly and evenly, leaving no bumps.

For tips on yarn choices and other patterns, please see

www.headhuggers.org
www.ChemoCaps.com

and other online sites found by using such key words as *chemo hats* or *head huggers*.

Babies, children, and adults who have lost their hair are very vulnerable to cold — and you can make a difference, as so many knitters already have. My thanks to Sue Thompson for her help in introducing me to this wonderful effort.

ABOUT THE AUTHOR

Sally Goldenbaum is a sometime philosophy teacher, a knitter, an editor, and the author of more than two dozen novels. Sally became more serious about knitting with the birth of her first grandchild and the creation of the Seaside Knitters mystery series. Her new fictional knitting friends are teaching her the intricacies of women's friendships, the mysteries of small-town living, and the very best way to pick up dropped stitches on a lacy knit shawl.